Simon Scarrow is the *Sunday Times* bestselling author of the *Eagles of the Empire* novels, including THE BLOOD OF ROME and DAY OF THE CAESARS. He has co-written two previous novels with T. J. Andrews, ARENA and INVADER, both *Sunday Times* bestsellers, as well as many other novels. Simon has always been fascinated by history, and he shared his passion for the subject as a teacher before he became a full-time writer. He lives in Norfolk.

T. J. Andrews was born near Barking Abbey and grew up in Essex, not far from the Ancient Roman garrison at Colchester. After several years in publishing he became a full-time writer. He lives in St Albans.

To find out more about Simon Scarrow and his novels, visit www. scarrow.co.uk and www.catoandmacro.com.

Praise for Simon Scarrow

'A new book in Simon Scarrow's series about the Roman army is always a joy' *The Times*

'Blood, gore, political intrigue . . . A historical fiction thriller that'll have you reaching for your gladius' *Daily Sport*

'Gripping . . . ferocious and compelling' *Daily Express*

'I really don't need this kind of competition . . . It's a great read' Bernard Cornwell

'Scarrow's [novels] rank with the best' *Independent*

'A satisfying bloodthirsty, bawdy romp . . . perfect for Bernard Cornwell addicts who will relish its historical detail and fast-paced action' *Good Book Guide*

'A fast-moving and exceptionally well-paced historical thriller' *BBC History Magazine*

'Blends together the historical facts and characters to create a book that simply cannot be put down . . . Highly recommended' *Historical Novels Review*

SIMON SCARROW
AND T. J. ANDREWS
PIRATA

HEADLINE

First published in Great Britain in 2019 by
HEADLINE PUBLISHING GROUP

First published in paperback in Great Britain in 2019 by
HEADLINE PUBLISHING GROUP

2

Cataloguing in Publication Data is available from the British Library

ISBN 978 1 4722 1372 3

Typeset in Bembo by Avon DataSet Ltd, Bidford-on-Avon, Warwickshire

Printed and bound in Great Britain by Clays Ltd, Elcograf S.p.A.

MIX
Paper from
responsible sources
FSC® C104740

Map illustration by Tim Peters

Headline's policy is to use papers that are natural, renewable and recyclable
products and made from wood grown in well-managed forests and other
controlled sources. The logging and manufacturing processes are expected
to conform to the environmental regulations of the country of origin.

HEADLINE PUBLISHING GROUP
An Hachette UK Company
Carmelite House
50 Victoria Embankment
London EC4Y 0DZ

www.headline.co.uk
www.hachette.co.uk

CONTENTS

THE EASTERN MEDITERRANEAN AND EUXINE SEA, AD25

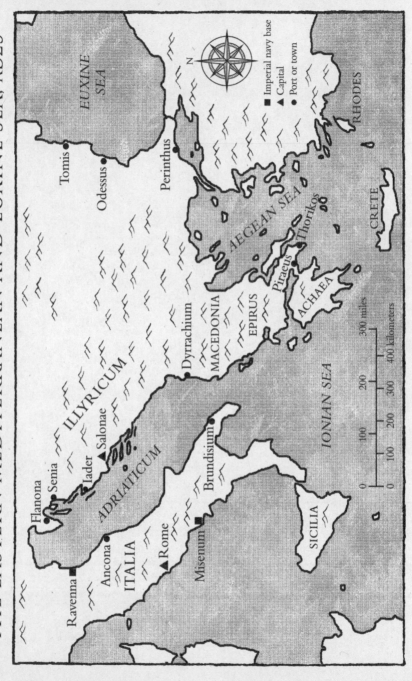

CAST LIST

Telemachus: A young Greek orphan
Nereus: Telemachus's elder brother, a slave
Nestor: A feared pirate chief
Agrius: Captain of pirate ship *Pegasus*
Caius Munnius Canis: Prefect of the Ravenna fleet

Selene
Clemestes: Captain of the ship
Leitus: First mate
Geras: A sailor
Syleus: A sailor
Dimethus: Ship's steersman

Poseidon's Trident
Bulla: Captain of the ship
Hector: First mate
Castor: Quartermaster
Sciron: Expert in torture
Longarus: Ship's lookout, one of the youngest members of the crew
Virbius: Senior hand
Bassus: Thracian fighter
Proculus: Ship's carpenter
Lasthenes: Syrian pirate
Calkas: Ship's steersman

CHAPTER ONE

Piraeus, early AD *25*

A sharp gust of wind and rain blasted the Greek captain as he staggered down the dimly lit street. It was a foul evening in early spring, and the streets of the port were deserted. Clemestes hurried along, occasionally glancing over his shoulder at the three heavy-set figures a short distance behind him. The seasoned captain of the merchantman *Selene* had recently returned from a successful voyage to Salamis, landing a cargo of garum and salted fish. Although the journey had provided him with only a small profit, barely enough to cover the expenses of his crew and ship, Clemestes had fared better than most of his fellow seamen. Times were hard for the merchant captains of Piraeus, after two years of poor harvests and pirate attacks that had caused a drop in trade passing through the port. Several had been forced out of business, and many of those who survived were forced to borrow substantial sums from the merchants to cover their losses. Clemestes had decided to celebrate a rare successful trip with a skinful of mulsum at one of the local taverns, and as dusk settled over the port and the light faded, he'd left the Jolly Sailor to return to the warmth of the small cabin aboard his ship. A short while later, he had spotted the men following him.

The rain continued to fall steadily, pattering against the shingle roof tiles of the surrounding buildings as Clemestes passed through the gloomy back streets of the warehouse district. At this late hour the storehouses were usually busy with teams of stevedores unloading the goods from newly arrived merchantmen, much of it bound for Athens, but the streets in this part of the town were eerily quiet now. The threat of attack from the bands of pirates who were known to prey on the main trade routes had unnerved the local merchants and shipowners, with many of them reluctant to risk transporting their goods across the Empire, and Piraeus had suffered badly as a result, plunged into a period of economic turmoil from which she showed no signs of recovering.

Clemestes glanced over his shoulder again as he continued down the street. The three men were keeping pace with him, brown tunics hanging from their burly physiques. They had remained a steady distance behind him, following his every move and never quite disappearing from view. At first he'd dismissed the notion that they were following him. But then he had caught a glimpse of their faces in the glow of an open doorway, and recognised them from the crowd at the tavern. They had been sitting at a trestle table in a darkened corner, drinking and watching the other patrons with interest. An overly keen interest, Clemestes now reflected anxiously. There was no doubt in his mind. These men were footpads. They had seen him leaving the tavern and intended to rob him.

He swallowed hard and faced forward, pulling his cloak tight across his front as he increased his pace, cursing himself for not noticing the footpads earlier. If he had spotted his pursuers as soon as he'd left the tavern, he could have easily sought safety in another of the many cheap watering holes and wine shops that did a brisk trade along the main agora. Instead, he had been too busy congratulating himself on the success of his voyage, and had only become aware of the footpads once he had veered off the main thoroughfare, making his way through the shady winding alleys of the warehouse district. Now there was nowhere for him to hide, nowhere to seek shelter and wait for the footpads to abandon their chase. No one to save him once they sprang their attack.

He shivered beneath his cloak and looked behind him once more. The footpads were now twenty paces back, moving swiftly in spite of their bulky frames. Clemestes himself walked with a pronounced limp that slowed him down, the result of an old injury he'd sustained during his years as a ship's mate, and with a rising sense of dread, he realised that his pursuers would soon catch up with him.

Shaking off the drunken fog behind his eyes, he decided that his best hope was to cut through the maze of storehouses and try to lose the footpads before returning to *Selene*. He had grown up in Piraeus, running errands for the warehouse managers as a young boy before joining the crew of a small fishing vessel, and he knew the streets in this quarter of the port better than most. Better than the men following him, he hoped. With luck, he might be able to shake them off, and then he would be free to make his way back to the safety of his vessel and crew.

He darted down a side street and made a series of quick turns, heading in the direction of the large commercial emporium situated next to the quayside. A fetid stench of human waste hung in the air as he hurried onward. His heart was beating faster now, and he prayed to the gods to protect him from his pursuers. He passed a smaller abandoned warehouse, another painful reminder of how Piraeus had fallen on hard times due to the depredations of the pirates. Although there had always been a few crews terrorising the sea lanes, picking off unsuspecting merchantmen from time to time, the situation had worsened in recent years as the pirates, emboldened by their initial successes, had undertaken frequent and more daring raids across the eastern Mediterranean and beyond. The situation was now so bad that Clemestes had already decided to retire from the business as soon as he'd paid off his debts. In a year or two he planned to sell off *Selene* and settle down on one of the islands in the Aegean. He'd marry a local girl, buy a plot of land, tend his crop, and spend his evenings drinking in one of the local inns, swapping sailing tales with the other old sea dogs. If he managed to live that long.

His heart fell as he saw that two of his pursuers were still behind him and drawing closer. He turned and limped on. In the distance he heard peals of laughter, and knew he was close to the quayside. Once he reached the packed quay, the men following would be forced to give up the chase. Although the trade at Piraeus had suffered recently, the port was still bustling with merchants and sailors and wine shop trade even at such a late hour. Surely the footpads wouldn't dare spring an attack in such a busy part of town.

He ducked into an alley to his right, a cramped space between two dilapidated buildings, twice almost slipping as he tried to avoid the trickle of piss and shit that flowed through the streets in this part of town. In the gloom he could see only a few paces in front of him and he had to watch his step carefully as he picked his way through the heaps of stinking rubbish that had been dumped on either side of the alley. A short distance ahead an oil lamp hung from an iron bracket to illuminate the entrance to one of the warehouses adjacent to the emporium, and he felt his heart lift as he realised he had almost reached the quayside. As he pushed on, he felt his foot brush against something hard and bony. He blundered forward, only recovering his balance at the last instant.

'Oi! Watch it!' a voice hissed.

Clemestes stopped and glanced back. In the shadows he could just make out a scrawny youth, a threadbare blanket wrapped around his huddled frame. In the darkness of the alley he had failed to spot the homeless figure and had stumbled over his outstretched legs. The youth looked up at him and scowled.

The urgent sound of footsteps pounding towards him snapped the captain's attention from the wretched boy and he staggered on. He was less than ten paces from the corner, and for a brief moment, he thought he might escape his pursuers. Then he glimpsed a burly shape sweeping into view at the end of the alleyway. The figure stepped forward from the shadows, and Clemestes stopped in his tracks as he recognised the man's shaven head and heavily scarred face. The third footpad, he realised with an icy knot of fear. He must have sprinted ahead of his comrades down one of the streets running parallel to the alley, cutting off the only escape route to the quayside while his two companions kept a steady distance behind their target. Clemestes felt his heart sink. The robbers' plan had worked perfectly. He was trapped.

He spun around as the two other footpads appeared at the entrance to the alley and moved quickly towards him. He glanced frantically about, searching for another way out. But there was none. A cold tingle of terror ran down his spine as the three assailants closed on him. He opened his mouth to cry for help, but one of the robbers sprang forward in a flash and slammed a fist into his stomach. The sea captain gasped as the air was driven from his lungs and he doubled over, clutching his midriff. The same footpad swung a boot at him and sent him crashing to the ground. A jarring pain erupted inside his skull as the other two men set upon him, delivering a flurry of punches and kicks to his body. Clemestes raised his arms in a futile bid to shield his head, but the blows continued to rain down upon him. A boot swung against his exposed flank. Something cracked, and he felt a sharp pain flare inside his chest.

'Get his purse!'

The blows ceased as two of the robbers stepped back. Clemestes reached a hand to his bruised chest, groaning. He tasted blood in his mouth as one of the men, who boasted a broken nose and several gaps in his teeth, dropped to one knee beside him. The footpad reached under his cloak and grabbed the money purse tied to his belt, snatching it free and tossing it to his companion, a squat, bearded man with small dark eyes. The second man peered inside the purse and frowned. Then he looked down at Clemestes, his eyes narrowing to mere slits.

'Where's the rest of it?' he demanded.

Clemestes winced. 'I don't know what you're talking about.'

'Bollocks! I wasn't born yesterday, old man. We heard about the cargo you landed. A mate of ours keeps an eye on all the goods coming in. He reckons you got a decent price for yours. More than the measly few coins in here anyway.' The bearded robber tapped the half-empty purse, then gestured to his comrade with the missing teeth. 'Now tell me where you're keeping the rest of the loot, or Cadmus here will cut your fucking balls off.'

A menacing grin crept on to Cadmus's scarred lips as he drew his dagger. Clemestes swung his gaze back to the bearded robber and shook his head quickly.

'Please! That's all I have!'

'Bastard's lying,' Cadmus snarled. 'I can tell.'

'It's the truth, I swear,' Clemestes protested.

The thief stared down at him for a moment, then turned to the man wielding the blade.

'Cut an eye out, Cadmus. That'll loosen his tongue.'

Cadmus moved towards the captain, the dagger tip glinting in the dim light. Clemestes lay helpless on the rain-slicked flagstones, gripped by the realisation that he was going to die in this squalid alley, and not at the hands of some terrible sea monster or violent storm as he had often feared. His muscles tensed with fear as the blade drew close to his face, and he offered up a silent prayer to the gods.

As he did so, he caught a glimpse of movement behind the footpad. A lithe dark shadow lunged forward from one of the doorways further down the alley and charged at the bearded man, slamming shoulder-first into his back. The robber let out an explosive grunt as he fell forward, crashing into a pile of rubble and rotting wood to one side of the alley.

At the sound of his comrade's pained cry, Cadmus turned away from the captain towards the onrushing figure. Clemestes caught sight of the attacker's face and recognised him as the homeless youth he'd tripped over. He looked on in astonishment as the skinny figure hurdled the fallen robber and advanced on Cadmus.

'Bastard!' Cadmus hissed.

He thrust his dagger at the youth, aiming for his throat. But the young man was faster than the heavily built footpad and deftly evaded the blow. Cadmus grunted in frustration as he stabbed at thin air. He roared and lunged again, slashing wildly and forcing the youth to jerk back out of range, then leaped at his retreating opponent, driving the blade down at his stomach. In one swift motion the youth parried the thrust with a quick sweep of his forearm before he stepped towards his opponent, throwing a punch at the latter's head. There was the dull crack of bone against bone and Cadmus's head snapped back, the dagger tumbling from his grip and clattering to the ground.

'Watch out!' Clemestes cried.

The youth spun around as the robber shook his groggy head clear and scrambled to his feet, launching himself at the interloper. The younger man dived forward and grabbed the fallen dagger before whirling around to face the robber. He dropped into a crouch as the footpad threw a ragged punch at him, neatly ducking the blow. Then he sprang up on the balls of his feet and stabbed out with the dagger, driving the sharpened tip at his assailant's stomach. The footpad grunted as the blade sank deep. His mouth went slack and he wavered on the spot as his eyes lowered to the handle protruding from his guts. A glistening patch spread out from the wound and stained his tunic.

The youth wrenched the blade free as the robber slumped in a writhing heap, and turned to face Cadmus, who had scraped himself off the ground. By now the third man had also rushed forward, and he stood alongside his comrade, the pair eyeing their young opponent warily.

'Come on, then!' the youth yelled. 'Which one of you bastards wants it next?'

Both robbers hesitated. Their eyes shifted back and forth between their wounded companion and the young killer standing over him, clutching the dagger in his bloodstained hand. There was a crazed look in his eyes and his lean muscles were taut, like a wild animal about to pounce. For a moment no one dared to move. Then voices broke the silence, approaching from the direction of the main quay. Cadmus glowered at the youth, then nodded at his companion, and the two footpads turned and sprinted down the alley, heading back through the warehouse district, away from the sound. Relief swept through Clemestes as he watched them disappear from sight.

The youth tucked the blade into his belt and hurried over to him.

'Are you all right?' he asked.

Clemestes forced a smile. 'I'll be fine. Just a little shaken up. I thought those bastards were going to kill me.'

'That lot are nasty pieces of work all right. But they won't be causing you any more trouble.' The youngster cocked his head at the dying footpad. 'One of 'em, at least.'

'No.' Clemestes frowned at the body. 'I suppose not.'

He tried standing up, but the effort was too great and he slumped back down, trembling with pain and shock.

'Here. Let me help.' The youth offered his hand. Clemestes grasped it and rose unsteadily to his feet, grimacing. Every fibre in his body hurt and he struggled to catch his breath.

'Thank you.' He tilted his head at the starved–looking figure standing in front of him. 'What's your name?'

'Telemachus. And you?'

9

'Clemestes, captain of *Selene*.' He bowed his head. 'I'm in your debt, young Telemachus. You saved my life.'

Telemachus shrugged. 'I just happened to be nearby, that's all. Anyone would've done the same.'

'I sincerely doubt that.'

The captain fell silent for a moment as he considered the youth. He was dressed in tattered rags and looked to be no older than fifteen or sixteen. His cheeks and chin were laced with knotted white scar tissue. Another one of the desperate abandoned children of Piraeus, Clemestes thought. The progeny of a visiting sailor who'd enjoyed a quick fling with one of the local women, dumped in the street at birth and left to fend for himself. The port was crawling with them. And yet there was something about Telemachus that intrigued him. This poor, miserable wretch had bested three hardened criminals, and Clemestes sensed a fiery resilience in him.

'Where are you headed?' Telemachus asked. 'I'll give you a hand.'

'My ship,' the captain croaked. He waved a hand in the direction of the harbour and winced. 'Shit . . . They've given me a thorough working-over.'

Telemachus nodded. 'We'd best get moving, in case they return.'

He slipped an arm around Clemestes' back, and the two of them set off down the alley towards the harbour, as the dying man let out a deep groan behind them.

CHAPTER TWO

The rain faded to a drizzle and then died away and the faint moonlight broke through a gap in the dark clouds as Telemachus helped the captain towards the harbour. The young Greek could make out the masts and rigging of the dozens of ships moored alongside it. The sight was an instantly familiar one to him, just as much a part of harbour life as the sounds of the drunken sailors singing and swapping lewd jokes as they returned to their ships for the night. Only a few men braved the chilly, windswept streets leading down from the wharf, fighting one another or playing games of dice. To one side of the quay, pairs of guards patrolled the largest of the vast timbered warehouses. The harbour itself faced out towards a pair of stone moles. Further out, dark waves crashed against the breakwater, bursting in huge white sprays that glittered in the pale light.

Clemestes stopped in front of a large cargo ship moored at the far end of the quay.

'Here she is,' he announced grandly. '*Selene*. Not the fastest ship, by any means. But she's as sturdy as they come.'

Telemachus gazed up at the merchantman. In the faint light of the moon he could see that she had a wide beam and a blunt prow with a high curved sternpost depicting a relief of the Greek goddess Selene driving her moon chariot. A large steering paddle hung from the stern, and a narrow gangway led down from the foredeck to the quay. Without her cargo, she sat high in the water. She was bigger than many of the other vessels anchored in the harbour and cut an impressive sight, he thought.

Clemestes nodded at his rescuer and smiled apologetically. 'I'm afraid I can't offer you much in the way of a reward. But perhaps you'd care to come aboard and have a bite to eat and something to drink? It's the least I can do.'

Telemachus pursed his lips while he weighed up the captain's proposal. He had been living on the streets for long enough to treat kind offers from strangers with the utmost caution. But it had been two days since his last meal, and he felt his stomach growling painfully with hunger. Besides, he reasoned, the captain seemed friendly enough. He nodded.

'Thank you.'

'Good.' Clemestes managed a pained smile. 'This way.'

Telemachus helped the captain up the boarding plank leading to the foredeck. A handful of men lay asleep in the bows, wrapped up in bundles on the deck or lying under tent shelters to protect themselves from the foul weather. Clemestes stopped at the nearest man and nudged him. The man snored heavily and rolled over. The captain shook him more roughly, and this time the man stirred, muttering under his breath, then rose quickly to his feet, a look of concern appearing in his heavily glazed eyes as he noticed the bruises on Clemestes' face.

'Sweet Zeus!' he slurred. Telemachus caught the scent of cheap wine on his breath. 'What in Hades happened to you?'

'I'm fine, Syleus,' Clemestes responded. 'Really. Just got into a bit of a scrap, that's all. Would have been a lot worse if it wasn't for this fellow,' he added, tipping his head at Telemachus.

Syleus arched an eyebrow at the youth. 'Is that so?'

'Wake my cabin boy, will you?' the captain said. 'I'm going down to my quarters.'

'Aye, Captain.'

Telemachus watched as Syleus turned and wove across the deck towards a huddle of figures sheltering beneath a tent erected in the bows of the ship. He shouted at one of the shapes, kicking him awake. A cabin boy a few years younger than Telemachus promptly rose to his feet and hurried towards the aft hatch near the stern, descending the stairs leading down into the captain's quarters. Telemachus and Clemestes followed a short distance behind, moving slowly along the sun-bleached planking. Once they arrived at the hatch opening, Clemestes went ahead, the younger man following him down the stairs into a small cabin built at an angle into the stern of the vessel. The space was cramped and Telemachus had to duck under the low lintel before entering the captain's quarters. The cabin boy finished lighting an oil lamp on the small desk built around the sternpost, dimly illuminating the interior of the cabin.

'Fetch us some food and drink from the ship's stores, Nessus,' Clemestes ordered.

'Yes, master.'

The boy turned and left. Telemachus squinted in the gloom, glancing around at the cabin. There was a narrow cot to one side of the desk, with a sturdy-looking strongbox on the floor next to it. A distinct odour of worn rope and tar

13

lingered in the air. Clemestes eased himself down onto the cot, then gestured to the stool in front of the desk.

'Please. Have a seat.'

Telemachus sat on the stool and tried to hide his discomfort at the slow rocking of the moored vessel.

'First time aboard a ship?' Clemestes asked.

Telemachus nodded queasily. 'I've seen plenty of 'em. Lived in the port all my life, more or less. But I've never set foot on one before.'

'You live on the streets, I presume?'

'Yes.' Telemachus lowered his head in shame. 'Most of my life.'

'What about your family?'

'My parents are dead,' the youth responded flatly.

'But surely you must have some family who could take you in? An aunt or uncle, perhaps? Or a brother? There has to be someone.'

Telemachus shrugged off the question and looked away. A few moments later, the cabin boy returned bearing a platter of cheese, and some scraps of dried beef and bread. He set it down on the desk, then headed up the steps to fetch a pair of Samian-ware cups and a jug filled with potent-smelling wine. Telemachus licked his lips as he greedily eyed the food in front of him. Once Nessus had departed, Clemestes poured watered-down wine into the two cups and passed one to his young guest. Telemachus promptly began shovelling food into his mouth, pausing only to slurp thirstily from his cup. Wine dribbled down his chin as he set the cup down and tore into a strip of dried meat. Clemestes smiled sadly.

'It must be hard,' he said. 'Living on the streets, I mean.'

'You get used to it,' Telemachus replied between mouthfuls

of food. 'Most of the time I just scavenge around the warehouses. The merchants are always throwing stuff out. It's mostly rotten, but you get used to the taste.' He popped a piece of cheese into his mouth and belched. 'Winter's the worst. Nothing but cold and wet.'

'What about your parents? What happened to them?'

'That's my business,' Telemachus replied tetchily. He set down the strip of beef he was holding and looked up at the captain. 'Anyway, what do you care? It's none of your concern.'

'No. It isn't. But you saved me from those thugs. That took courage, which is something of a rare commodity these days. I'd like to know more about the brave young man who rescued me.'

Telemachus shook his head. 'I'm no hero.'

'Nevertheless, most people wouldn't have lifted a finger to help someone in trouble. Indeed, I can think of a fair few who would have turned and walked in the other direction. I'm curious to know what a fellow like you is doing living on the streets.'

Telemachus fell silent for a moment as he looked down at his half-finished meal.

'I never knew my mother,' he began quietly. 'She died during childbirth.'

'I'm sorry.'

'Sorry? It's not your fault. You didn't kill her.'

'No. But still. It's hard, growing up without a mother.'

Telemachus merely shrugged. 'After she died, our father was left to raise the two of us by himself. Me and my older brother, Nereus. We lived in a small place down by the docks at Munichia. It wasn't much, but we made do. Our father worked on the ships. He was a captain, like yourself.'

15

'Here? In Piraeus?'

The youth nodded. 'He owned a merchant ship. A small one. Not as big as this. He tried his best, but it was always a struggle in our household. He was never any good with money, and he'd spend it as soon as he got it. Mostly on gambling and drink. He'd come home from a trip out to sea, take one look at us and then head straight out to get drunk at a nearby tavern. Sometimes he'd be gone for weeks on end. I hardly ever saw him. Nereus was the one who really took care of me. He'd take a few coins out of our father's purse when he had passed out, to make sure we had enough money for food and clothes while he was away. My big brother did more for me growing up than our father ever did.'

He went quiet for a moment and picked at his food. Clemestes watched him in silence. After several moments, Telemachus set down a chunk of bread, looked up at the captain and went on.

'One day we went down to the quayside to see my father's ship come in, like we always did on the days he was due to return. We waited and waited, but there was no sign of her. Eventually it grew dark and we started to worry. Then another ship came in and one of our father's friends spotted us waiting by the quay and came over to us. As soon as I saw the look on his face, I knew that something was wrong. He told us that my father's ship had been caught in a storm off the coast of Delos. The winds had blown her against some rocks near the headland and she'd broken up. By the time another ship came to her rescue, there were only a few survivors left, clinging on to bits of wood and debris.' Telemachus hesitated. 'Father wasn't among them. He'd been lost to the sea.'

'How old were you?'

'Six.' Telemachus counted inside his head. 'That was ten years ago.' He smiled sadly at the captain. 'I can hardly remember what my father looked like now.'

'What happened to you and your brother?'

'My father left behind a lot of debts. After he died, we found out that he'd been borrowing money to fund his gambling habit. Turned out he owed a large sum to one of the port's moneylenders. The man wanted his money back, but there was no way we could afford to pay him. Then one day he arrived with a pair of bodyguards to seize what little property we had and sell me and Nereus into slavery. They grabbed my brother and would've taken me as well, but Nereus fought them off for long enough to allow me to escape into the streets. I managed to give them the slip, but I had nowhere else to go. I've been living rough ever since.'

'That must have been hard. Having to leave your brother like that.'

'I had no choice. If it wasn't for Nereus's quick thinking, we both would've ended up in chains.'

'Where is he now?' Clemestes asked.

'At a forge over in Thorikos,' Telemachus replied, rage simmering in his voice. 'I heard the news from a friend of mine who has a job in one of the workshops. They purchase all their tools from this Roman metalworker based over there, Decimus Rufius Burrus. Anyway, my friend paid a visit to the forge and saw Nereus there. Burrus has got him doing all the dangerous jobs: working the bellows and cleaning out the furnace. That bastard Roman treats his slaves like shit and works 'em to the bone. One of the other slaves died in an accident last month. If my brother is forced to work there much longer, I fear the same thing will happen to him.'

Telemachus clamped his eyes shut for a moment, struggling to control his anger. When he opened them again, he noticed the captain staring at him in quiet reflection. At length Clemestes cleared his throat and leaned forward. 'What if there was a way of purchasing your brother's freedom?'

Telemachus snorted at the idea and shook his head. 'I could never raise that kind of money. The most I earn is a few asses here and there, helping passengers off the ships with their baggage. But it's slim pickings. It'd take me ten lifetimes to save up enough to free him.'

'Perhaps,' Clemestes mused, stroking his chin. 'Then again, perhaps not.'

Telemachus's brow furrowed. 'What do you mean?'

'I could do with a fellow such as yourself in my crew. Someone who has their wits about them and isn't afraid of honest work.'

Telemachus stared at the captain in stunned silence. 'You're offering me a job?'

Clemestes shrugged. 'You need money, and I need someone to help out on my ship.'

A doubtful look registered on Telemachus's face. 'But I don't know the first thing about being a sailor.'

The captain dismissed his concern with a wave of his hand. 'You're young. You'll learn quickly enough. I'll have one of the mates show you the ropes. Besides, you can't do worse than some of the current crew.'

'What sort of work would I be doing?'

'You'd be a ship's boy. You'd be on half-pay to begin with, at least until you prove your worth. Your duties would involve learning about the sails and ropes, taking the watch, and skivvying.' The captain leaned forward and stared at him levelly. 'I won't lie to you. Working on a ship isn't easy. It can be unpleasant and dangerous. But trust me, there's nothing that compares to life at sea. You'll have a chance to see places and make something of your life.' He sat back and shrugged again. 'It's got to be better than living on the streets, surely?'

Telemachus narrowed his eyes. 'I don't understand. Why do you want to help me?'

'You saved my life. I owe you. And you've not had an easy life from the sound of it. I'd like to help you.'

'I don't need your charity. Or your pity.'

'I'm not offering either. Far from it. I happen to think you have the qualities to become an excellent sailor. You're tough and fearless. A little hot-headed, perhaps, but that's to be expected, given what you've just told me. And who knows? If you save your earnings, you'll eventually have enough money to free your brother from that gods-forsaken forge.'

Telemachus stared down at his food, deep in thought. 'When would I start?'

'At once. You'll report to the first mate tomorrow morning. We'll be getting under way as soon as we've loaded up our next cargo and the weather has cleared.' The captain paused as he regarded Telemachus's tattered garments. 'You'll need some fresh clothes from the slop chest as well, I suppose. It'll come out of the pay for your first voyage. Can't have you working on my ship in rags now, can we?' He clapped his hands abruptly. 'Well? What do you say?'

Telemachus paused. An hour ago he had been shivering in the cold and wet, dreaming of one day escaping his pitiful circumstances. Now he was sitting in the warmth of the captain's cabin, with a full belly and the offer of a job with decent pay. He could scarcely believe his sudden change in fortune. And yet he hesitated to accept the generous offer. Life on the streets of Piraeus was miserable, but from the stories he'd heard around the port, working on a ship was a dangerous business. Many vessels were lost to the sea, especially over the winter seasons. Was he prepared to join the crew and risk suffering the same fate as his father? But then he thought of Nereus being worked to death at the forge, and made his decision. He looked up at the captain.

'All right. I accept.'

'Good.' Clemestes stood upright and managed a warm smile. He grasped the hand of the newest member of his crew and shook it firmly.

'Welcome to your new life on *Selene*, Telemachus,' he said with a twinkle in his eye. 'You won't regret it.'

CHAPTER THREE

The sky remained overcast and an icy drizzle pattered across the harbour the following morning as the crew of *Selene* made the final preparations for their voyage. There was a bustle of activity as the sailors cleared the decks and opened up the cargo hatch, while Clemestes dispatched his cabin boy to the local market to purchase supplies of dried biscuit, water and bread for the coming voyage. As the sun shone feebly behind the bank of gloomy clouds, a long line of dock workers arrived from the direction of the warehouses carrying the large amphorae destined for *Selene*'s cargo hold.

After leaving the captain's quarters, Telemachus had been escorted up to the deck by one of the crewmen. Geras was a muscular, cocky sailor, and although he was not much older than the youth, his face was heavily weathered from years spent at sea. He'd shown Telemachus to a space on the crowded aft deck where he could sleep for the night before beginning his duties the next day. After waking from his restless slumber, Telemachus had been handed a faded tunic from the ship's slop chest. Then Geras had introduced him to the first mate. Leitus was a grizzled sailor with coarse greying hair, prominent crow's feet at the corners of his blue eyes, and a serrated scar running across the width of his neck. He stood amidships watching over the crew as they hefted the large clay jars across the deck and down into the hold. Geras hurried away as Leitus cast a withering look at the dishevelled figure standing in front of him.

'So you're the one who fought off those robbers, are you?' the first mate said in a hoarse voice. 'How old are you, lad?'

'Sixteen.'

Leitus creased his windswept features into a frown and snorted. 'Sixteen, he says! You don't look it. I've taken shits that have got more muscle on 'em. How did a lanky streak of piss like you manage to drive off those toughs who attacked the captain?'

'I'm stronger than I look,' Telemachus replied between gritted teeth.

That prompted a hearty chuckle from the first mate. 'That's not saying much. Don't worry, lad. A month hauling ropes on this tub and you'll soon fill out. How much experience have you got at sea?'

'None.'

Leitus looked aghast. 'You've never even been on a fishing boat?'

Telemachus shook his head and looked down at his bare feet. 'This is my first time on a ship.'

'Gods below! Can you swim?'

'No,' Telemachus replied despondently.

A look of palpable disgust formed on the first mate's face. 'So you can't swim and you've never been at sea before. And you claim to be born and bred in Piraeus! Is there anything you *can* do, lad?'

The younger man stared at him. 'I know how to handle myself in a fight.'

'That won't do you much good here,' Leitus chuckled. 'The only killing you'll be doing is down in the cargo hold. Plenty of rats aboard. Place is crawling with the buggers.'

'I'm not afraid of a few rats,' Telemachus answered tetchily. 'I grew up on the streets. It'd take a lot more than that to scare me.'

The first mate arched a bushy eyebrow. 'Brave words. But wait till you get out to sea. There'll be plenty to be afraid of then. There are pirates to watch out for, storms . . . even sea monsters.'

'Sea monsters?'

'Aye.' Leitus wagged a finger. 'A tough attitude might have served you well on the streets, but the sea's a different beast. She can be a real bitch if the mood takes her, and you'd do well to respect her. That's the first lesson any sailor must learn. Am I clear?'

Telemachus nodded uncertainly. 'Yes.'

Leitus's expression darkened. 'That's "aye" to you, lad. You're not a landlubber any more. Now, as a ship's boy you'll be expected to muck in wherever you're needed. I'll teach you the basics. It'll be hard work, but if you follow orders and do your duties, you'll soon be able to shake out a reef and put a tack in with the best of 'em. Understood?'

'Yes . . . I mean, aye.'

'Better.' Leitus turned and grabbed a wooden bucket sealed with pitch and half filled with water and thrust it at Telemachus. 'Here. Your first task. Scrubbing the decks. Captain likes 'em spotless before we get under way.'

'Scrubbing?' Telemachus asked, struggling to hide his disappointment.

Leitus glared at the youth. 'Got a problem with that, have we?'

'No.' Telemachus swallowed and glanced out at the harbour. 'Where are we going, exactly?'

'Moesia. On the eastern coast of the Euxine Sea. Heard of it?'

Telemachus shook his head.

Leitus chortled. 'You're in for a shock. The locals there are savages. Make the bloody Germans look cultured. We'll be landing at a place called Tomis, north of the Thracian coast. Compared to that shithole, Piraeus is a paradise.'

'Why are we heading there, if it's so grim?'

'Mendean wine.' The first mate waved at the amphorae being loaded onto the ship's deck. 'It's all the rage over there. The locals will pay a small fortune for the stuff. The captain should make a tidy profit on his share of the goods.'

'How long will it take us to get there?'

'Depends. The general rule of thumb is, if the journey's fast one way, it'll be slower than a one-legged dog in the other direction. The winds aren't favourable this time of year, so we'll have to beat our way across the Euxine Sea. But there's usually a following breeze on the way back. I'd say about a month for the round trip. Assuming we don't run into any pirates.'

Telemachus looked up at him and swallowed. 'Are we likely to run into them?'

Leitus shrugged. 'There's always a chance, lad. Especially around the Euxine. The seas to the east are crawling with the bastards.' He pointed to his neck. 'How'd you think I got this scar?'

'Pirates did that to you? How?'

'I was working on another ship, the *Andromeda*. This was several years ago now. We were on the way back from Perinthus with a cargo of rice and a few passengers. Two pirate ships jumped us as we were making our way down the Thracian coast. We tried to outrun them at first, but our coward of a captain surrendered as soon as they loosed a few arrows at us. Some of us wanted to fight, but the captain overruled us. The fool thought the pirates would go easy on us if we let them board the ship and handed over the loot.'

'What happened?'

'They executed the captain and killed anyone who tried to resist. Once they had taken everything they wanted, their captain rounded up the passengers and crew and told us he couldn't allow any survivors, in case we identified the pirates to the Roman navy. That's when the executions began. Those bastards murdered the passengers one by one. The elderly, women, children . . . butchered the lot of them.'

Telemachus shivered. 'How did you manage to survive?'

'We were spotted by an imperial warship transporting dignitaries up the coast. As soon as the pirates caught sight of it, they transferred the loot to their ship and fled.' Leitus fell silent for a moment. 'Only four of us survived the attack. One of the others had both his eyes gouged out. Poor bugger. Trust me, lad. The pirates are scum, plain and simple. You really don't want to run into any of 'em. Now get to work on that deck. There's a lot to do before we leave.'

Telemachus passed the rest of the day on hands and knees, working a coarse block of sandstone over the planking to scrub it clean. Once he had finished scouring the decks, Leitus ordered him to empty the bilges in the dark, rat-infested recesses the other side of the hold. It was back-breaking work, and as the day wore on, he felt his spirits sink at the prospect of months of carrying out similar gruelling duties. But then he recalled his brother's desperate plight. Unless he could raise enough money to buy his freedom, Nereus would be condemned to spend the rest of his life working at the forge under his cruel Roman master. He continued his duties with a renewed vigour, determined to do all he could to save his brother.

In the late afternoon, the rain died away and a light breeze gusted through the harbour as the sun sank into the rolling grey mass of the sea. As the light faded, the crew redoubled their efforts, eager to finish their duties and head out for refreshments in Piraeus one last time before they set sail. Once he'd finished his cleaning chores, Telemachus headed for the aft cargo hatch to bring up food from the stores to the bows, where the sailors would be taking their evening meal. He couldn't remember working so hard in his entire life. His muscles felt stiff and sore, his hands were covered in painful blisters and his belly ached with hunger. A wave of tiredness swept over him and he craved nothing more than a few hours of precious sleep.

A rank odour of tar and fish lingered in the air as he descended into the hold and headed for the space reserved for the ship's provisions. Hundreds of amphorae were arranged below deck, stacked vertically and packed tightly with sand. He spotted Syleus and another sailor kneeling in front of one of the stacks as they finished loading up the last of the amphorae. Syleus worked a frayed rope into a knot while the second man held the clay containers in place. After a moment, he stood up, wiping the sweat from his brow as he nodded at his handiwork.

'There. That should do it, I reckon,' he said.

The second man pursed his lips and looked doubtfully at the worn, slackened cord. 'Didn't the captain say we should secure the cargo with at least three ropes? Just to make sure it's held in place, like?'

Syleus waved a hand. 'Bastard's secure enough, if you ask me. Why bother when we could be getting pissed instead? This could be our last chance to get drunk for days.'

'What if the captain finds out we ain't done it how he asked?'

'He won't. That old goat never bothers inspecting the hold. Trust me, it'll be fine.'

'I don't know . . .'

Syleus patted his companion on the back. 'You worry too much, Androcles. That's your problem.' He grinned. 'Come on. I'm thirsty. First round's on me.'

There was a pause, and then a rat scurried along the deck, startling Telemachus. Syleus and Androcles spun around and the former narrowed his eyes as he caught sight of the ship's boy.

'What the fuck are you looking at?' he hissed.

'Nothing,' Telemachus replied warily.

'That's right.' Syleus spat on the floor and moved closer to the boy. His breath reeked of onions, and his eyes glinted with malice. 'Nothing to see here. You understand, lad?'

Telemachus stared at the burly sailor but said nothing. The scars on the man's knuckles hinted at the many fights he had been involved in, and there was no point in antagonising him. In the close confines of the hold, without the element of surprise, he knew he stood little chance against the two sailors. He gave a terse nod of his head and Syleus grinned as he took a step back.

'Good,' he rasped. 'Now piss off out of my sight.'

Telemachus hurried further down the hold as Syleus and Androcles brushed past him and climbed the stairs leading to the hatch opening, laughing and joking. He paused to watch them disappear from view, a leaden feeling in his heart. Syleus had taken an instant dislike to him. It was obvious that the man had a cruel streak and was the type who enjoyed bullying those he considered beneath him. Telemachus would have to watch his step from now on. He sighed heavily. He had been aboard *Selene* for less than a day and he was already making enemies.

On the second morning, the skies cleared and a brisk land breeze whipped up over the sea. Once the last of the provisions had been loaded on board, the crew gathered to watch the captain make an offering in front of the small stone altar on the foredeck, sending a prayer to Poseidon to grant *Selene* safe passage. Then Clemestes gave the signal for the ship to cast off, and the crew sprang into action. A pair of deckhands hauled in the boarding plank, while two more sailors unfastened the mooring cables from the posts lining the quay. Leitus barked an order at Telemachus, and he rushed over to help several crewmen struggling with a long wooden shaft. It was surprisingly heavy, and Telemachus grunted, straining under the weight of it as the crew thrust the ship's bows out towards the harbour waters. Once they were a safe distance from the quayside, Clemestes yelled for the men to run the oars out. At his command, a dozen of the strongest-looking sailors grabbed the giant sweep oars stored on the deck and began to ease *Selene* towards the narrow gap between the moles. As soon as they were through, the captain turned to the crew.

'Ship oars! Raise the mainsail!' he shouted, cupping his hands to his mouth to make himself heard above the rising wind. 'Put a reef in her!'

At once the sailors stowed the oars and several men climbed the rigging and spread out across the yardarm. Leitus called an order and the crewmen unfurled the square sail, the linen canvas rippling in the wind as it spread out. On deck, the rest of the crew hauled the sheets in, fastening them to the belaying pins along the side rails. Then the men atop the yard began lashing the ties to the first reefing line before making their way back down the rigging. It was an impressive feat and Telemachus looked on with admiration at the sailors descending the ratlines as *Selene* surged forward under her heavily reefed mainsail, her bow cutting through the water.

'Dimethus!' Clemestes shouted at the steersman, a burly Nubian sailor standing behind the mast. 'Put her on a port tack. Heading, four fingers!'

The Nubian braced his legs on the rooftop of the cabin and leaned into the tiller with his muscular forearms, adjusting the merchantman's course until it was sailing as close to windward as the captain dared. Telemachus gripped tightly onto the wooden stern rail, his head swimming, the sea hissing around him as *Selene* rose and fell on the swell. A cold sweat began to trickle down his face and a wave of nausea gripped him. He tried to focus on the horizon as a reference point to steady himself, but after a few moments, he pitched his head forward and leaned over the side, emptying his guts into the foaming white spray. He spat out the dregs of vomit, then wiped his mouth and turned back to the deck, holding onto the rail for dear life.

'Seasick already?' Leitus said, grinning broadly.

'Fuck the gods,' Telemachus groaned. 'My head . . .'

The first mate roared with laughter. 'If you think this is bad, wait until we reach the Euxine. It can get pretty rough around there. Then you'll really know what it's like to be seasick.'

Telemachus clutched his stomach, already dreading the prospect of spending several days at sea. 'It gets worse than this?'

'A lot worse.' Leitus slapped him heartily on the back. 'Don't look so glum. You'll get used to it soon enough. Besides, where we're headed, rough seas are going to be the least of your worries. What with all those pirates operating in the seas around Moesia.'

'Won't the navy protect us?'

'Not a hope in Hades. The Euxine is the absolute arse end of the Empire. The Romans couldn't give a toss about policing the area, so they leave it up to the locals to deal with the problem. But they haven't got the money or the fleets to effectively patrol the waters, so the pirates have the run of the place. If we meet any of those bastards along the way, gods help us.'

Telemachus went to reply, but *Selene* lurched, prompting another wave of nausea, and he leaned over the rail again, retching violently. As the wave of seasickness passed, he lifted his eyes and gazed back at the port, the salty wind whipping his hair and stinging his cheeks. He temporarily forgot about the queasiness in his guts and the pounding inside his head as a curious mix of dread and excitement swirled inside his chest.

He was leaving home for the first time, on a ship full of
strangers bound for one of the furthest-flung corners of the
Empire. It was an opportunity to follow in his father's footsteps
and pursue a life of adventure at sea. An opportunity he was
determined to grasp. He took a final glance back at the port.
Then he turned and looked ahead as *Selene* moved into the
open waters beyond.

CHAPTER FOUR

The first days aboard *Selene* passed unhappily for Telemachus. Apart from the endless list of duties Leitus had compiled for him, the new ship's boy had to contend with the constant bouts of seasickness and the taunts of some of the older members of the crew every time he vomited. Each day he toiled above and below deck, emptying out the stinking bilges, scrubbing down the decks and preparing meals. Leitus had a sharp eye and insisted on personally inspecting his efforts after he had completed each task. The first mate never failed to find fault with his work, making some critical remark and compounding the younger man's misery. Soon the nervous excitement of his first days at sea gave way to a profound melancholy and loneliness, and he bitterly cursed himself for agreeing to accept the captain's offer to join the crew.

Each day after he had finished his duties he reported to Leitus, and the first mate instructed him in the basics of seafaring. The lessons were a welcome break from the endless routine, as he learned how to tie a variety of knots and how to unfurl and reef the sails. He practised climbing the rigging and using the lead line to measure the depth of the sea in shallower waters, and in the afternoons Leitus showed him how to manoeuvre the vessel using the tiller and explained the workings of the sails and running gear. Telemachus initially struggled, finding it difficult to concentrate while his stomach continued to churn. But after the first few days, the seasickness started to wear off, and he grew in confidence, demonstrating an enthusiasm and hunger to learn from his mistakes that impressed even the grudging first mate.

At the end of each day, the crew of *Selene* sought anchorage in the safety of a nearby bay or cove. Once the vessel had anchored, the men made their way ashore on the small boat stowed amidships. A fire was lit on the beach and the sailors enjoyed a cooked meal before retiring to the ship for the night. As the last rays of sunlight glimmered on the horizon, Telemachus dragged his weary body over to a clear space on the aft deck and lay down beneath the star-pricked sky while the rest of the crew snored around him. He had never felt so tired in his life. Or so alone. Only Geras made an effort to talk to him during those first few lonely days at sea. The sailor looked across at Telemachus as the latter slumped down on his makeshift bed of coiled ropes at the end of a hard shift, his muscles aching with exhaustion.

'Tough day?' he asked.

Telemachus looked across at him and grunted.

'No shame in admitting it,' Geras went on. 'Some just can't take to the sea, no matter how hard they try. This life isn't for everyone, you know.'

'I'll not quit,' Telemachus responded angrily. 'I'd rather die than fail.'

Geras raised an eyebrow, surprised by the strength of feeling in the younger man's voice. 'What made you want to take a berth on this ship anyway? No offence, but you don't exactly look like the seafaring type.'

'My brother, Nereus. He's a slave. I swore I'd save enough money to buy his freedom.'

'So you decided to try your luck on the ships?'

Telemachus shrugged. 'Seemed like the best way.'

Geras puffed out his cheeks. 'You'd have been better off joining a gladiator school. Or a gang of thieves. Even if you make it as a sailor, it'll be years before you can raise that kind of money.'

'I've got to try something. I have to free my brother.'

'Fair enough.' Geras yawned. 'Me, I'll be spending my pay on tarts and drink. And there's plenty of both in Moesia. The locals there might be vicious, but the women know a trick or two. You might want to do yourself a favour and pay 'em a visit. They'll cheer you up.'

Telemachus smiled half-heartedly. 'Thanks. But I'll need to save every sestertius I can earn. Even if it takes me years, I've got to start somewhere.'

'Suit yourself, lad. But you'll change your tune soon enough once you see how fickle the sea can be.'

'What's that supposed to mean?'

'It's not worth looking too far ahead, is all. Not when the sea can claim any of us at any moment. Being a sailor is better than being a landlubber, but this line of work is riskier than most and every lad on the crew knows someone who's been lost at sea. If you ask me, you're better off forgetting about that brother of yours and enjoying yourself while you still can.'

Telemachus shook his head. 'I can't. Nereus is the only family I have, and I owe him my life.'

On the eighth day, *Selene* passed through the narrow straits between Thrace and Bithynia and entered the Euxine Sea, where a dark band of cloud thickened along the eastern horizon. As he went about his duties, Telemachus detected a tension in the air among the sailors. Even Clemestes looked anxious. The captain was standing on the foredeck, constantly checking the horizon as they sailed north-west along the coast towards Odessus, looking out for any sign of the pirates that were known to prey on merchant vessels. Leitus stood next to him, watching the azure eastern horizon.

'Are we in danger?' Telemachus asked him.

Leitus shrugged. 'No more than any other ship. The waters around these parts are treacherous. The pirates will be hugging the coastline, same as us.'

Telemachus tried not to look alarmed. 'Shouldn't we be sailing further away from the shore, then?'

'Not in these rough waters. It's too dangerous. We've got to stay close to the coastline in case we run into trouble from the elements. This weather isn't looking too promising at the moment.'

'So if we sail too far from the coast we'll get caught in a storm, but if we sail closer then there's a decent chance we'll run into any nearby pirates?'

Leitus smiled faintly. 'Now you're learning, lad. There's never a dull moment at sea.'

'That's one way of putting it.'

Telemachus looked back out to the rim of the sea, feeling more unnerved than ever. Sleeping rough in the slums of Piraeus had been a miserable existence, but the only threats had come from the occasional beggar arguing over scraps of food, and the abuse hurled at him by some of the city's more foul-mouthed inhabitants. Now he was facing danger at every turn.

In the late afternoon, the wind began to strengthen before veering around wildly, and the mood among the sailors worsened as they watched a shelf of dark cloud bounding towards the ship. From the corner of his eye Telemachus noticed Leitus staring out anxiously across the waters, his jaw tensed.

'What is it?' he asked.

The first mate narrowed his eyes at the clouds. 'Looks like a storm. A big one. It's moving fast. It'll be on us soon enough.'

Telemachus followed the sailor's line of sight. The horizon had disappeared behind a dark grey curtain several miles wide, smothering the sun as the howling wind and rain bore down on them. Towards the stern, Clemestes stood on the aft deck, his face tight with concentration as he fixed his gaze on the fast-moving storm and gave the order to steer away from the land.

Telemachus turned back to Leitus and pointed towards the coastline, no more than a mile away. 'Why aren't we heading for the shore?'

Leitus shook his head. 'We need some sea room if we're to avoid the wind driving us onto the rocks.' He spat on the deck and stared at the filthy haze sweeping towards them. 'Looks like we'll have to tough this one out.'

Less than an hour later, the storm struck with terrifying ferocity. The raging wind swept over the merchantman, followed by a torrent of freezing rain. Icy drops slashed down across the deck, spraying the crew and drenching their tunics. Telemachus clutched the side rail in desperation, rain stinging his skin as the vessel lurched and rolled. All around him the sailors held on grimly, shielding themselves from the deluge as the waves crashed around them. Looking up, he could see that the wind was steadily driving the ship towards the coastline. The shore seemed perilously close now, and even though he had spent little more than a week at sea, he immediately understood the danger.

'All hands!' Clemestes bellowed, his voice barely audible above the moaning of the wind in the rigging. 'Furl the sails! Drop anchor!'

Leitus barked at the sailors. Several of them climbed the rigging then shuffled along the yardarm, moving into position with difficulty in the driving wind and rain. At the same time, a handful of men rushed towards the bows to take in the foresail. Telemachus took his place with the rest of the sailors as they prepared to drop the anchor. At that moment, *Selene* rolled on her side and a piercing scream split the air. Telemachus clung frantically to the rail and looked up. Androcles had lost his footing and now hung from the yardarm, his arms wrapped around the spar and his legs dangling in space. The next sailor in line began inching towards him, but then the ship pitched forward heavily again and Androcles lost his grip and fell screaming into the watery abyss. The stricken sailor's cries were cut off abruptly as he was lost to the sea, sinking beneath the grey waves. Several of the crewmen watched the spot where he'd fallen for any sign of their comrade, but there was none.

'Telemachus!' Leitus shouted. He pointed towards the rigging. 'Get up there and lend a hand! Now!'

Fear gripped the ship's boy for a fleeting moment as he gazed up at the yardarm. The thought of climbing up the rigging in such treacherous conditions terrified him. But he grasped the urgency of the situation and thrust aside his fear as he started up the ratlines, determined not to let his fellow crewmen down. The wind shrieked all around him, tugging at his tunic as he swung out and edged along the yardarm, forcing himself not to glance down. The other sailors spread out further along the spar, with the man furthest from the mast taking Androcles' place. Once every man was in position, Clemestes called out the order and the crew furled the sail, working as fast as they could to gather the wildly flapping folds and tie them to the main spar. The rain beat down mercilessly and Telemachus fastened the leather ties as Leitus had taught him. A moment later, the men on the aft deck dropped the stern anchor into the sea, paying out the cable until the flukes caught on the seabed, and the motion of the ship slowly began to steady. Telemachus climbed down the rigging with the other sailors, gasping for breath as he dropped to the rain-swept deck.

Leitus gave him a grudging nod. 'Good work, lad. We'll make a sailor of you yet.'

'What now?' Telemachus shouted.

'We wait for the storm to blow itself out.'

'How long will that take?'

'A while yet,' Leitus said. 'Hours, I'd say. We've not been through the worst of it.'

Telemachus grimaced at the prospect, but there was no time to rest. With the ship rocking at anchor, Clemestes shouted for the crew to begin bailing her out. The vessel tugged at the anchor cable, causing her to shudder and making it hard for the men to keep their footing as they scrambled across the deck. They took it in turns to bail out the water that had rapidly filled the bilges, while the rest of the crew secured the ship, lashing a tarpaulin over the entrance to the hold. As soon as they had finished their duties, they huddled in the shelter of the bow rail, shivering in their dripping wet tunics, a few of the men muttering prayers to the gods. Others stared longingly towards the shore, wishing they were in the comfort of a sheltered port or cove.

As darkness closed in around them, the storm showed no signs of abating. All night long the winds and rain battered *Selene* and her crew. There was no hope of sleep, with the sailors having to work throughout the night in shifts to bail water out of the bilges. The hours passed slowly for Telemachus, his terror deepening with every lurch of the ship, her rigging and timbers groaning under the strain of the storm. The night seemed to last for ever, and each passing moment brought a fresh torment to the ship's boy, fearing that the vessel might founder, or the anchor cable might part under the strain, causing *Selene* and her crew to be dashed to pieces on the rocky coast of Thrace. But the cable held firm.

The storm finally receded the next morning, the wind fading to a gentle breeze as the sun struggled up from the horizon. Soon the rain died away and the sun broke through a gap in the clouds, shading the distant mountains a brilliant gold. The unrelenting fury of the previous night was replaced by the repetitive soft slap of the oily waves against the ship's hull and the dripping of water from the rigging. The cold, tired and hungry sailors dragged themselves to their feet as Clemestes ordered a thorough inspection of the vessel. Any signs of damage were noted on a wax slate by the first mate so that the repairs could be carried out once they reached the port at Tomis.

'Telemachus!' Clemestes called out. 'Bring some food up

for the lads. Can't have them setting sail on an empty stomach. Not after the night we've had.'

'Aye, Captain!'

Nodding briskly, Telemachus hurried over to the aft hatch and untied the ropes fastened around the cleats. As he climbed down the stairs, he noticed something glistening in the cargo hold. Then his eyes adjusted to the gloom, and he froze.

Hundreds of clay shards lay scattered across the hold, amid a sloshing gruel of sand and wine. Strands of rope lay among the broken pieces, and as Telemachus glanced around, he realised with dismay that most of the amphorae had broken loose and shattered, spilling their precious contents across the hold. Only a handful remained intact.

'Hurry up, lad!' Leitus growled as he descended into the hold. 'What's taking you so—'

He stopped short as he caught sight of the carnage.

'Shit,' he muttered, wearing a panicked look on his face. 'Wait here.'

He turned and hurried back up the stairs, calling out to the captain. A moment later he returned with Clemestes. Several of the crew swiftly followed, curious to see what all the fuss was about. Clemestes stood numbly on the spot as he surveyed the damage to the valuable cargo. His face crumpled into an expression of bitter frustration and despair.

'What in the name of the gods happened?' he growled.

'Must have come loose during the storm, Captain,' Geras responded.

'But . . . how?' Leitus cut in. He shook his head. 'Those amphorae were supposed to be tied down tighter than a Vestal Virgin's arse. They shouldn't have broken free. Not even in a storm.'

Syleus, standing among the throng of sailors, shifted uneasily. 'It's them ropes. Buggers must have been badly worn.'

Telemachus went to speak, but caught Syleus glowering at him and quickly changed his mind, clamping his mouth shut again.

'It doesn't matter. The cargo's lost.' Clemestes stared despondently at the shattered amphorae. 'This is going to ruin me. I had to borrow money from the merchant just to pay for my half of the shipment. Now it's all gone.'

The merchantman arrived at Tomis five days later, gliding towards the small jetty. After throwing the broken amphorae overboard, the crew had been tasked with salvaging those few containers still intact and securing them to the racks. A sullen mood hung over the men as they shipped the oars and tossed the ends of the mooring lines to the workers standing on the edge of the quay. Normally they would have greeted their arrival at a new port with enthusiasm, eager to spend their hard-earned pay sampling the dubious entertainments on offer in the town. But the death of Androcles, together with the loss of most of the cargo, had crushed their spirit. Telemachus had briefly considered informing the captain of Syleus's failure to properly secure the wine, but shortly after the incident the sailor had taken him to one side and threatened to cut his throat if he spoke a word of what he had witnessed back in Piraeus. So the ship's boy had kept quiet.

As *Selene* edged closer to the jetty, the shoremen heaved on the mooring ropes and secured them to the posts along the wharf, pulling the merchantman side-on. Then Leitus shouted for the gangway to be lowered and a pair of sailors slid the boarding plank down the starboard side of the vessel and onto the quayside. Once the ship had been secured, Clemestes gave permission for most of the crew to go ashore and drown their sorrows in the nearby taverns. Telemachus longed to join his fellow sailors, but Clemestes made him stay behind to assist the stevedores unloading the few surviving amphorae.

As dusk settled over Tomis, a portly figure with several gold rings on his fingers marched purposefully up the gangway and strode towards Clemestes on the aft deck.

'Captain!' the man called out, panting from the effort of climbing aboard the ship. He paused to catch his breath. 'Where's the rest of my wine?' he continued, waving at the unloaded amphorae. 'There's not but a quarter of the shipment here.'

Clemestes turned to greet the man. 'Herakleidus.' He coughed and made a pained face. 'I'm afraid we ran into some difficulties along the way.'

'Eh? What difficulties?' Herakleidus snapped irritably.

Clemestes lowered his head and took a deep breath before explaining the situation to the merchant, describing the events of the storm and the subsequent damage to the cargo. Herakleidus listened in stony silence, his face devoid of expression.

'Well, Captain,' he said after Clemestes had finished speaking. 'That is certainly a most, ah, unfortunate turn of events.' He feigned a smile. 'If it is indeed true.'

Clemestes frowned. 'What's that supposed to mean?'

'You must admit, it's a highly convenient tale. How do I know that you haven't merely landed the balance of the cargo at some other port and pocketed the profits for yourself?'

The captain looked stunned. 'You're accusing me of lying?'

'You wouldn't be the first captain who'd tried to cheat me. You can't expect me to believe this cock-and-bull story about broken amphorae, surely?'

'It's the truth, I swear on all the gods! Ask any of my men, they'll tell you the same.'

'I don't doubt it,' the merchant responded tonelessly. 'Nevertheless, even if what you say is true, you cannot expect me to pay for a cargo that you have failed to deliver. Our arrangement was for two hundred amphorae of prime Mendean wine. You understand my predicament, I'm sure.'

The captain pursed his lips but said nothing.

'There's also the question of how you intend to repay your share,' Herakleidus added.

'Repay?' Clemestes repeated, frowning. 'What do you mean?'

The merchant nodded at the amphorae. 'Almost the entire shipment has been lost . . . if your tale is to be believed. That includes your half-share. A share that you paid for with money I loaned you. On an extremely generous rate of interest, I might add. A loan that you must repay, regardless of what may have happened to the wine.'

The captain's frown deepened. 'Where am I supposed to get that kind of money?'

'That isn't my problem,' the merchant responded. 'But if you cannot settle your debt with me, then you leave me no choice. I'll be forced to take my case to the magistrate and ask him to seize your ship.' A thin smile formed at the corners of his mouth. 'Pullus is a good friend of mine. I'm sure he'll sympathise with my position.'

'You can't do this!' Clemestes retorted, shaking his head in anger. 'You can't take my ship! She's all I've got. Please, there has to be some other way.'

He stared pleadingly at the merchant. Herakleidus's expression betrayed no hint of pity. Then he smiled thinly, eyes narrowing as he stroked his chin. 'Perhaps there is one way you might be able to settle your debt to me.'

'How?' Clemestes asked, desperation creeping into his voice.

'I overheard some gossip the other week at a dinner party. Some of the other merchants were discussing the latest news from Illyricum. Tell me, Captain. Have you done much trade that way?'

'I've landed at Salonae a few times. It's not far up the Illyrian coast. But I've not done that route for a few years now. Tight bastards, the Illyrians. Bloody difficult to negotiate with, and they never pay on time. Why?'

'Apparently there's been an uprising in the region. One of the defeated chieftains from the Daesitiates tribe returned from exile and started stirring things up with the locals. Fellow by the name of Bato.'

'So I heard. A few of the captains at Piraeus were talking about it. Didn't the Romans put down the revolt?'

Herakleidus nodded. 'Tiberius dispatched a column from the Fifth Macedonica to restore order. They crushed the rebels, put the leaders to death and sold the rest into slavery. But the rebellion has put a huge strain on the local grain supply. Food is scarce and the population is going hungry.' There was a gleam in his eyes as he added, 'A shipment of grain would fetch an extremely high price right now. Enough to clear your debts, and earn us both a profit.'

Clemestes eyed the merchant suspiciously. 'If it's such a

lucrative opportunity, why aren't the other merchants sending their goods to Salonae?'

'They are. Or rather, they've been attempting to. But most of the shipments haven't been getting through. It appears that some of the pirates have heard about the increase in shipping activity and have moved their base of operation to the Adriaticum.'

Clemestes nodded thoughtfully. 'Makes sense. They're always on the lookout for new routes to prey on.'

'Precisely. Now that word about the piracy threat is spreading, many shipowners are refusing outright to sail to Salonae. Or charging outrageous fees. I've been asking around for someone to transport my supplies, without any luck.' Herakleidus paused before continuing, 'Of course, all this panic is driving up the price of grain even further. Anyone who does manage to reach Salonae stands to make a killing.'

'I see,' Clemestes replied tersely. 'My men take all the risk, and you take all the money.'

'If you want to put it that way, yes. But I'm offering you an opportunity to claw back your losses, Captain. And perhaps earn a modest profit on top, once your debt to me has been taken into account.' The merchant shrugged. 'Others in my profession might not be so reasonable.'

Clemestes considered the offer. 'And if I refuse?'

'Then I shall have no choice but to speak to the magistrate and demand that your ship be seized in lieu of payment.'

Clemestes' shoulders sagged. 'In that case, I suppose *I* have no choice but to accept.'

'Captain, don't!' Telemachus cried, springing to his feet.

Clemestes and the merchant simultaneously turned towards the ship's boy, who had been listening to the conversation with a growing sense of unease. He could scarcely believe that Clemestes would accept such a perilous offer. Now he could no longer contain his anxiety.

'It's too dangerous,' he continued as the two men stared at him in silence. 'What happens if we get caught by the pirates? Let this merchant try his luck with the next vessel he can lay his grubby hands on. It's not a good deal, Captain.'

'Quiet!' Clemestes stared at him coldly. 'You're a ship's boy. I'm not paying you to offer your opinions.'

'But Captain—'

'That's enough!' Clemestes snapped. 'If I want your advice, I'll bloody well ask for it. Now get back to work and keep your fucking thoughts to yourself.'

The harshness of the captain's tone took Telemachus by surprise. He nodded and turned away, making his way forward. From the corner of his eye he saw Clemestes straighten his back and nod briskly at the merchant.

'You have yourself a deal, Herakleidus. Tell your men to begin loading the grain as soon as possible. I'll set sail for Salonae at dawn.'

CHAPTER FIVE

A stiff northerly breeze blew across the deck of *Selene* as Telemachus gazed to starboard. In the distance he could see the faint outline of the Illyrian coast, a scattering of barren islands and coves broken by a series of jagged mountains. Grey clouds hung low in the sky, and he could hear the rush of the sea against the waterline as the ship bored its way up along the eastern coast of the Adriaticum. Nearly a month had passed since the merchantman had left Tomis with her load of grain in the hold, and the journey back east had been smooth and untroubled. But after passing the tall cliffs at Dyrrachium, the sky had become overcast and the mood among the sailors changed. Some of the crew stared anxiously out across the sea, as if fearing that a pirate ship might attack them at any moment. Even Leitus seemed uneasy, looking towards the horizon with the same concerned expression as the other sailors.

'How long until we reach Salonae?' Telemachus asked him.

'Day after tomorrow, by my reckoning,' Leitus replied. 'We're making good speed even with a full hold. We just have to hope this wind holds. And pray we don't run into pirates.'

'Tell you what, lads, I can't wait to get there,' Syleus said, rubbing his hands in anticipation as he glanced round at his companions. 'Once we've landed, it's wine and cunny all round.'

'As long as we don't encounter any trouble on the way,' Leitus responded gruffly.

Syleus gestured towards the horizon. 'Look around you. There's no sign of any danger. This stretch of sea is emptier than a banker's heart.'

'For the moment. But the bastards are out there all right. Captain Nestor and his lot have been terrorising these waters for years.'

'Nestor?' Telemachus repeated, frowning.

'The leader of one of the pirate gangs operating along this coast,' Leitus explained. 'He used to run with a gang of brigands around Larissa before he decided he could make more money raiding at sea. His men are the cruellest bastards this side of Piraeus. Mark my words, you don't want to be captured by his mob.'

'We'll be fine,' Syleus replied dismissively. 'No one has seen or heard from Nestor for months now. Trust me, a few days from now we'll be celebrating in Salonae.'

'I pray you're right. For all our sakes.'

Syleus turned and strode back across the deck to finish his duties, swapping jokes with the other sailors. Despite the obvious threat lying in wait for them in the Adriaticum, they went about their tasks with a carefree attitude. Telemachus secretly envied them, wishing he could dismiss the pirate threat as easily as some of the other men did. Only Leitus and the more experienced sailors seemed to share his concerns about the possibility of an attack.

'What will we do if the pirates find us?' he asked, turning back to the first mate.

Leitus shrugged. 'We'd struggle to outrun them. We're weighed down. Even those tossers driving for the blue team at the Circus Maximus could beat this ship in a straight race, and everyone knows only the most useless charioteers race for the Blues.'

Telemachus looked away and gazed out across the water, a knot of unease tightening in his stomach. There was a heavy swell in the sea and the merchantman rose on each wave before slumping down into the trough, her prow cutting rapidly through the water. To the east, the coastline slowly faded from view as they headed further north, until the mountains disappeared and all he could see was the unending rim of the horizon.

'Deck there!' Geras bellowed down from the masthead. 'Sail sighted, Captain!'

Clemestes emerged from his quarters and strode over to the mast, craning his neck up. Geras had one arm wrapped around the masthead to secure himself as he thrust out his other arm. The captain lowered his gaze and squinted in the direction the lookout was pointing. Telemachus chased his line of sight, searching for any sign of the sail. But he could see nothing except the rolling surface of the sea and the gathering clouds.

Clemestes cupped his hands to his mouth and shouted up, 'How many, Geras?'

'One sail, Captain. Two miles out.'

'What's their heading?'

There was a brief pause before Geras made his report. 'Closing on us. Looks like they're coming from the coast.'

'Pirates?' Telemachus wondered.

Clemestes' forehead creased into a frown. 'Perhaps. Or it could simply be another merchant ship.'

Leitus raised an eyebrow. 'In these parts? We've hardly passed any other vessels over the last few days. Most ships are avoiding this route, just like that merchant said. It's bound to be pirates. They must have been hiding in one of the inlets, waiting for prey. We should turn about.'

Clemestes pursed his lips. His face was a picture of indecision as he gazed out at the sea. 'No,' he said after a pause. 'It's too far away to be certain. We'll hold this course for now. The sooner we reach the port, the better. Especially with this weather looking like it might worsen. We can't afford to get caught in another storm.'

'If she's a merchant ship, why is she heading straight for us? We know there are pirates lurking in these waters, Captain. We should turn and get away from them now, while we still can.'

Clemestes rounded on the first mate and glared at him. 'This is my ship! I'm the captain. And I will not change our course unless there's a bloody good reason for it. Understood?'

'Aye, Captain,' Leitus replied through clenched teeth.

'Good.' Clemestes stiffened, then shouted up at the lookout, 'Keep an eye on them, Geras. Call down the moment you see anything else.'

'Aye, Captain.'

Clemestes turned away and looked out beyond the swell of his ship, his jaw clenched and his facial muscles twitching with nervousness. Telemachus leaned against the side rail as he searched for any sign of the approaching ship. For a while he could see nothing. An hour later, he glimpsed the tiny shape of a sail, faintly visible on the horizon as *Selene* pitched up on the crest of a wave. Then the merchantman plunged down again and the triangle disappeared from view.

A moment later, Geras called down from the masthead, 'I can see her hull now, Captain! She's smaller than us. She's flying a pennant from her mast.'

'What colour?' Clemestes shouted up.

Geras hesitated before replying, the anxiety in his voice apparent to all on deck. 'Black, Captain.'

'Black?' Clemestes repeated in alarm. The colour drained from his face. 'Shit . . .'

'Pirates,' Leitus muttered. He thumped a fist against his thigh. 'I fucking knew it!'

Clemestes automatically turned away from his men to hide his reaction, balling his hands into tight fists as he muttered curses under his breath. The moment passed and he managed to compose himself.

'What are your orders, Captain?' Leitus asked.

'We'll have to turn away and try to outrun them,' Clemestes said. He shouted to the helmsman, 'Dimethus! Bring her about!'

The Nubian heaved the tiller to the port side, swinging the merchantman's bows so that she was pointing away from the pirate ship. At the same time Leitus bellowed orders at the crew to shake out the reefs. Telemachus and several others raced into position in front of the rigging, while the rest of the sailors scrambled aloft and spread out precariously along the yardarm. With a shout from the first mate the men bent down and worked the reefing knots loose, easing out the mainsail as far as she would go. There was a thunderous crack and the sheets flickered like snakes under the rippling wind as the men on deck began hauling them in and securing them to cleats.

Selene heeled under the wind and then plunged forward, climbing one wave after another. They seemed to be moving at a swift pace, but when Telemachus looked over his shoulder he was shocked to see that the pirate ship had closed on them dramatically. Her sail was now in clear view as the vessel clawed its way through the water directly aft of the merchantman. He turned to the first mate, his heart beating furiously.

'Will they catch us?'

'Aye.' There was a fatalism to Leitus's voice as he went on. '*Selene*'s a tough old bird, but she's built for size, not speed. The pirates favour lighter craft and we can't take out any more reefs. They'll overhaul us soon enough.'

Telemachus felt a sickening dread in the pit of his stomach. 'What are we going to do then?'

The first mate shrugged. 'Keep holding our course and pray that the weather turns. We can handle rough weather better than a smaller vessel.'

'And if that doesn't work?'

'Then they'll try to board us, and we'll have to grab whatever weapons we can and fight for our lives.' Leitus smiled grimly. 'We'll not go down without a struggle.'

Telemachus drew strength from the first mate's bravado, but he silently cursed Clemestes' hesitancy and wondered why the captain had not turned and run at the first sight of the enemy sail. At least then the merchantman might have stood a decent chance of escaping. Now they were at the mercy of the elements and the determination of the pirates to hunt down their prey.

For the next hour, the sailors remained crowded along

the stern, leaning over the rail as they craned their necks at the fast-closing pirate ship. Clemestes paced up and down the deck, pausing to glance up at the mainsail, taut under the strong easterly wind. But the pirates continued to draw closer and Telemachus knew it was only a matter of time before they overhauled the merchantman.

Clemestes turned to the first mate. 'Break out the weapons, Leitus. Distribute them among the strongest. The rest of the crew will have to use whatever comes to hand.'

'Aye,' Leitus replied grimly. 'All hands!' he shouted. 'Prepare to repel boarders!'

A flurry of activity broke out across the deck. The men moved with a quiet desperation as they made preparations to defend against the pirate attack. At the first mate's command, two of the sailors hurried down into the hold. They returned several moments later carrying a small wooden chest filled with a handful of short swords and daggers, many of them in poor condition. The sailors began handing out weapons to the burliest men among the crew, while others grabbed spare belaying pins from the pin rails, boathooks and whatever other makeshift weapons they could find. Telemachus looked back with growing dread at the enemy ship, its sail close-hauled as the pirates drew ever closer to the merchantman.

'Get a bloody move on, lad!' Leitus shouted at him. 'Grab a fucking weapon!'

Telemachus searched desperately around the deck and seized one of the leftover belaying pins before he raced to join the cluster of sailors gathering around the mast as they prepared for battle. Some of the less experienced men were visibly trembling, and he feared they would not be able to withstand the pirates' fury for long once they boarded the ship. Unless they could outrun their foe, the men of *Selene* were doomed. He was struck by the grim realisation that he would die today, aboard this ship. It was immediately followed by a surge of grief at the thought of his brother. He had vowed to do whatever it took to save Nereus. Now he had failed, and frustration and despair swelled up inside his chest.

A cry went up from the masthead.

'Sail ho!' Geras shouted, pointing to the west. 'Off the port bow, Captain!'

CHAPTER SIX

Clemestes looked towards the horizon and squinted. All eyes on the deck followed the captain's line of sight. After a moment, he shook his head and glanced up at the lookout.

'What can you see?'

'Eight sails, Captain. No, nine . . . ten! Ten sails!' Geras yelled, stretching his arm out over the bows of the merchantman. 'Four or five miles off. I can see them more clearly now. They're warships, Captain!'

'Thank the gods!' Syleus turned to his fellow sailors. 'It must be the Romans. We're saved!'

'Silence there!' Clemestes snapped. He turned back to the lookout. 'What's their heading?'

'They're crossing our bows, Captain. Heading north. Looks like six warships and four smaller craft.'

'Must be a Roman squadron on patrol,' Clemestes mused as he gazed out beyond *Selene*'s bows. 'Perhaps they've been sent to deal with the pirates.'

As Telemachus listened, he felt an overwhelming sense of relief wash over him. 'That's it, then? We're safe now?'

Leitus frowned as he glanced ahead, then aft, his mind

calculating the respective distances of the pirates, *Selene* and the warships and the strength of the wind. Then he shook his head wearily. 'Afraid not, lad. Them warships won't reach us in time. The pirates are too close.'

Telemachus glanced back at their pursuer. 'Can't we go any faster?'

'No chance. Unless the pirates lose their nerve when they sight the warships, they're going to overhaul us.'

Telemachus turned away, his relief swiftly replaced by an intense stab of helplessness. On the streets of Piraeus he'd been forced to rely on his own wits to stay alive. But at sea he was at the mercy of elements far beyond his control, and there was nothing he could do except look on despairingly as the pirates closed in.

A short while later, Geras called down and pointed towards the Roman warships. 'Captain! The squadron's changing course! Heading straight for us!'

Clemestes looked beyond the bows again. Telemachus strained his eyes in the same direction and saw the sails of the warships turning downwind as the fleet manoeuvred towards the drama unfolding to the west. The Romans were racing to reach the merchantman ahead of the pirates, their bronze-sheathed rams cutting gracefully through the sea. The larger ships were running their spidery oars out in a bid to increase their speed, but they were still three miles away. The pirate ship had closed to less than half a mile now.

'Why aren't the pirates turning and running away?' Telemachus wondered aloud. 'Surely they can see the warships ahead of us?'

'Aye,' Leitus replied. 'But the squadron's still some distance off. The pirates will have plenty of time to board *Selene*, kill us, strip the ship bare and make good their escape before the Romans arrive.'

'Telemachus!' the captain shouted above the commotion on the deck. 'Take the tiller. Keep us pointed at those warships. We'll try and hold the pirates off for as long as we can. That might buy us enough time for the Romans to rescue us.'

It was a forlorn hope, and Telemachus sensed the desperation in the captain's voice. He hurried aft and grabbed the tiller from Dimethus. The Nubian nodded at him before moving forward to join the rest of the crew. One of the sailors handed him a pike and the two men took up their positions around the mast with the other sailors as they prepared to face the enemy.

Telemachus tensed his arm muscles and centred the tiller on the Roman warships, recalling the lessons Leitus had taught him over the past several weeks. The merchantman was going as fast as she could, the rigging humming under the strain of the wind. But it was not enough. As the chase continued, he glanced over his shoulder and saw that the pirate ship was so close he could make out the men crowding her foredeck. They cut a terrifying sight, their mouths gaping in a wild war cry. Many of them wore armour over their brightly coloured tunics and brandished axes or short swords, their points glinting dully in the pallid light. He looked ahead again and felt a cold fear clamp around his neck. Leitus was right. The distance between the merchantman and the warships was simply too great, and even Telemachus's untrained eye could see that the pirates would overhaul them long before the squadron could come to their rescue.

As he steered towards the warships, he saw that the pirate ship had changed course slightly, aiming to attack *Selene* on her starboard side. Less than a hundred paces now separated the pirates from their prey. On the other ship's foredeck the men were taunting the imperilled sailors, stabbing their sword points at the sky and beating their chests in anticipation of the imminent assault. Beside the boarders, a separate party reached for their grappling hooks, ready to throw them across at the merchantman once she was within reach. When Telemachus looked over again, the pirates had almost drawn alongside the merchantman, the two vessels lifting as the waves passed under their keels before dipping down into the troughs.

'This is it, lads!' Leitus bellowed defiantly. 'Kill as many of the bastards as you can. Don't show 'em any mercy!'

The enemies' shouts carried across the water as they shaped to throw their grappling hooks. In the next moment, the pirate ship rose on a heavy swell that lifted the bow and dropped it with a sudden violent swoop. The crest passed beneath the keel and the surging water brought the ship's bows swinging in towards the merchantman at a close angle. As Telemachus glimpsed the movement from the corner of his eye, he realised exactly what he had to do to ensure that he and his comrades had a chance of surviving. Reacting instantly, he put the tiller over so that the bow of the heavier merchant-man began to pivot to starboard, towards the side of the smaller pirate vessel. On the foredeck of the other ship a few of the pirates shouted a warning and braced themselves as they realised what was happening. A loud splintering crash split the air as the merchantman's blunt bow smashed into the beam of the pirate vessel. The enemy ship recoiled, the mast shuddering as the shock of the impact snapped the sheets. In the same moment, dozens of pirates were knocked off their feet and tumbled across the deck, crashing into one another. One man had been standing on the foredeck, and he screamed as he lost his balance and fell over the side rail into the sea.

On the next swell, *Selene* rebounded from the pirate ship and the latter came up into the wind, her loosened sail flapping madly as she lost all momentum. Before the pirates could scramble to their feet and reach for their grappling hooks, Telemachus leaned into the tiller again. Slowly the merchant-man began pulling away as a fresh gust of wind filled her mainsail, the momentum carrying her on towards the Roman squadron, leaving the damaged pirate ship in her wake. He looked back and saw that a handful of the pirates had managed to pick themselves up and now stood on the foredeck, hurling javelins and shooting arrows at the fleeing merchantman. But the missiles fell short of their intended target and splashed into her wake. Soon *Selene* had pulled far clear of the pirates, the sailors cheering in triumph and shouting wildly at their unexpected escape.

Clemestes looked over at Telemachus, grinning with delight. 'Good thinking, lad! That'll teach those bastards.'

'We're not in the clear yet.' Leitus watched the pirates with a wary expression.

'Look there!' one of the other sailors cried, pointing beyond the merchantman's bows.

All eyes turned towards the Roman warships. As Telemachus looked on, the squadron divided into two. Half a dozen of the biremes and a trio of the smaller liburnians moved on a course to pass by the merchantman, making for the stricken pirate vessel. The largest warship, flying a broad purple pennant, held course towards *Selene*. Realising that the merchantman had bested them, the pirates scrambled to fix the ropes. Telemachus saw several tiny figures hurriedly set to work, securing new sheets to the sail as it fluttered wildly. Once the ropes had been hauled in, the ship's bows began to swing over, bringing her before the wind. The sail immediately tautened, and with the wind behind them, the pirates were soon able to beat a hasty retreat towards the open sea.

'They're running.' Clemestes let out an audible sigh of relief. 'It's over. We're saved. Thank the gods.'

The remaining Roman ship stayed on her course directly towards the merchantman. Telemachus strained his eyes at her. This ship was larger than the rest of the squadron, with three banks of oars either side and a catapult mounted on a tower constructed atop the forecastle.

'That's a trireme,' Leitus explained as he noticed the curious look on the youth's face. 'A "three", as they call 'em in the service. Used to be the workhorse of the imperial navy.'

Clemestes wrinkled his features into a deep frown. 'I wonder what they want with us.'

'Looks like we're about to find out, Captain.'

As the ship drew closer, she shipped oars and hauled her wind, and Clemestes gave the order for the crew to heave to. After a pause, a skiff was lowered over the side of the warship, and Telemachus spied two figures sitting in the stern, their helmets and armour glinting as the sun broke through the clearing sky. The skiff bobbed up and down on the waves as a pair of oarsmen propelled it across the gap between the two vessels before slowly drawing up along the starboard side of the merchantman. Clemestes shouted an order and a rope was hastily lowered. Then the two uniformed figures climbed up the side of *Selene* and hauled themselves onto the deck, leaving the oarsmen in the skiff.

The taller Roman straightened up, his breastplate gleaming

beneath his long red cloak as he searched the faces of the sailors lining the deck. 'Where's your captain?' he demanded in Latin.

Clemestes strode briskly over and stretched out a hand. 'Welcome aboard! Captain Clemestes of *Selene* at your service. And you are . . . ?'

'Tribune Caius Munnius Canis.' The man glanced at the captain's hand but did not shake it. 'Prefect of the Ravenna fleet. This is Quintus Attius Musca, my senior navarch,' he added, tipping his head at the lean, weathered-looking officer at his side. The man was carrying a haversack, Telemachus noticed.

'A pleasure,' Clemestes said, discreetly withdrawing his hand.

'That was, ah, nicely played back there,' Canis remarked. 'Unusual, but highly effective. You should consider yourself fortunate, Captain. Not many ships in these parts have managed to give those damned pirates the slip.'

'We wouldn't have been in trouble to begin with if we'd turned about sooner,' Leitus grumbled in a low voice as he stood beside Telemachus.

Neither the captain nor the Roman officers appeared to overhear the first mate. Canis cast an eye at the cargo hold before he continued in his officious tone, 'Where were you headed when they attacked?'

'Salonae,' Clemestes replied. 'We've a full hold of grain. Hoping to fetch a decent price when we land.'

The prefect smiled. 'You'll do a lot more than that, I imagine. Hardly any ships have managed to get through in the past few weeks, what with the pirates roaming freely up and down the coast. We've been running extra patrols on both sides of the sea, but it hasn't deterred them in the slightest, I'm afraid. You were lucky you ran into us when you did.'

'Yes.' Clemestes smiled weakly. 'Thank you.'

'How long were they following you?'

The captain thought for a moment. 'Four hours or so. Not much longer than that. We spotted them soon after we raised anchor and set sail this morning. Came out of bloody nowhere.'

'I see.' Canis narrowed his eyes. 'I'll need you to point out to Musca the location of your last anchorage. That may give us some indication of where the pirates' base of operations is. It's about time we moved in and crushed the scum. They've been getting too bold by half lately. There's barely any shipping venturing out in these waters, thanks to those bastard pirates.'

Clemestes looked surprised. 'I didn't realise the situation was so serious.'

'Oh yes,' Canis responded bitterly. 'That's why my ships are having to patrol this far out from Ravenna. It was bad enough when the pirates started attacking the trade routes, but now they've taken to raiding the smaller ports up and down the Illyrian coast as well. Even some of our own patrols have come under attack. That's how we learned about them.'

'What happened?' Clemestes asked.

'A month ago I received word that a number of merchant ships had failed to arrive at Salonae since the beginning of the sailing season. Naturally I assumed that they had foundered at sea. Just to be certain, I ordered a small detachment to patrol the far shore and keep an eye on things. One bireme and a liburnian. The pirates jumped them and boarded the bireme, killing most of the crew. The liburnian managed to escape and returned to Ravenna with the news. Since then we've been trying to stamp out the pirate threat. The merchants and council leaders in Salonae are upset about the damage to their businesses, of course. But I simply don't have enough ships to cover the entire sea.'

'I thought the Ravenna fleet was at full strength.'

Canis chuckled. 'So did I, before my appointment to the prefecture. It's an ageing fleet. Most of the ships were captured at Actium and taken into the imperial navy by Augustus. Needless to say, quite a few of them haven't been to sea for years, and the ones that are seaworthy are in need of constant repair. As it stands, we can just about keep a couple of squadrons afloat. We've enough ships to keep our side of the sea protected, but not much more than that.'

Leitus coughed into his fist. He glanced at Clemestes, then spoke up. 'Begging your pardon, Prefect, but how are we supposed to continue trading if the routes ain't safe any more?'

A flicker of irritation crossed Canis's smooth face. He stared levelly at the first mate before replying in an icy-cold tone, 'Rest assured, these pirate scum will be dealt with in due course. It's merely a question of when. As soon as we have located their base, we'll deliver a fatal blow to their operations. None of them shall be spared. Every pirate who dares to hunt in these waters will be wiped out, one way or another. You have my word.'

There was a cool look of determination in the prefect's eyes as he spoke. Clemestes waved a hand at the fleeing pirate ship and the pursuing Roman warships. 'What about that lot? Are we safe?'

Telemachus glanced aft. The smaller, faster pirate ship had a good lead over the biremes and liburnians as she fled downwind.

Canis stared at the ships before addressing the captain. 'Oh, I should think so. We'll hunt them down eventually. In the meantime, I suggest you take shelter for the night somewhere along the coast. You're safe to carry on to Salonae once we've caught the pirates.'

'And how long until you clear the sea of these animals?' Clemestes asked. 'Months? I've got a business to run, mouths to feed. You can't expect us to worry about getting captured every time we leave port, sir.'

The prefect smiled thinly. 'You needn't be concerned. Those miscreants won't get very far. Our ships might not be as fast as theirs, but they're more than up to the task.'

'And if they outrun you?'

'They won't. No doubt they'll make for one of the islands along the coast. Then we'll have them trapped. With luck, we'll even take one or two prisoners and find out more about their base.'

He nodded at Musca, and the Roman navarch took a goatskin map and a stylus set from his haversack. Canis turned back to Clemestes and gestured at the map.

'Now, Captain. If you'd just like to show us your last anchorage point . . .'

A while later, Canis and Musca climbed back down the side of the vessel into the skiff and returned to the trireme. Shortly after that, the warship set sail and headed off in the same direction as the rest of the squadron. In the distance, the triangular sail of the pirate ship hovered close to the shimmering horizon as it drew ahead of the Romans. Telemachus stood beside Leitus, watching the far-off pursuit with a mixture of relief and foreboding as *Selene* got under way once more.

'Reckon they'll catch up with them?' he asked.

'Who knows? One thing's for sure, I don't fancy our chances if we run into that lot again. The gods might not favour us a second time.'

Clemestes waved a hand dismissively. 'Don't worry, Leitus. You heard the prefect. We're safe enough for now. Those pirates won't be causing us any more problems.'

Leitus looked anxiously at the departing warship, then glanced away. 'I hope you're right, Captain. For all our sakes . . .'

CHAPTER SEVEN

Late that afternoon, *Selene* steered towards the Illyrian coast, and as the last rays of the sun glowed on the horizon, Clemestes gave orders for the crew to make landfall. The helmsman skilfully guided the cargo ship into a bay with a shingled shore set between two narrow rocky headlands. Beyond the shore the scrubland rose on a steep incline towards a sprawl of stunted trees. Further inland, Telemachus could see a dense forest stretching out towards a series of distant mountains rising out of the land like giant fists. Tall cliffs stood either side of the shore, sheltering the beach from the open sea. The bay seemed peaceful enough, he decided, and he relaxed a little as the merchantman steered in.

When the ship was a short distance from the shore, the crew furled the sails and dropped anchor, the cable rasping as it paid out through the aft hawse. Clemestes had decided to celebrate their close escape from the pirates with an extra amphora of wine from the ship's stores, and the men hurried to finish their duties, eager to get ashore and help themselves to a drink.

With the vessel secured, the sailors lowered the boat down the side of the merchantman and loaded it up with food for the evening meal. A cooking fire was lit a short way up the beach, and leather tankards were filled with wine and distributed among the crew. Soon the mouth-watering aroma of roasting meat filled the night air as the men sat around the flickering flames. Some sipped their drinks in silence. Others tried to lighten the mood, telling stories of the distant lands they had visited or arguing over the respective merits of the brothels in Alexandria and Gades. Telemachus sat quietly and gazed out at the encroaching blackness beyond the dark hulk of *Selene*.

'Drink up, boy!' Geras grinned. He handed Telemachus a cup filled to the brim with wine. 'Here. This'll put hairs on your back. And a few other places too.'

Telemachus took the cup and pressed it to his lips. He ignored the potent smell and took a tentative sip of the wine. The foul-tasting concoction burned the back of his throat, and he leaned forward, coughing and retching.

'Gods! What is that stuff?'

'Cretan wine.' Geras grinned. 'Captain knows a merchant who gets him a good deal on it. Cheap as they come, but it's got a kick to it. Better than that watered–down Gallic crap they serve in the taverns anyway. Cheers.' He raised his own cup in a toast, took a long gulp of wine and belched in satisfaction.

'Do you think the pirates are still out there?' Telemachus asked, looking out towards the darkness.

'Fuck knows.' Geras shrugged. 'Probably.'

'You're not worried about running into them again?'

'There's always danger at sea. If we spent all day worrying about what might happen out on the water, we'd never leave port.' Geras waved a hand at the other sailors. 'Why d'you think we live from day to day? Only the gods know what might happen tomorrow, so we may as well enjoy today.'

'I suppose.'

Geras slapped him on the back and laughed. 'Cheer up. You're the hero of the hour. There's not many who could've done what you did. That took quick thinking, that. You saved us all.'

Telemachus shook his head. 'I did it to save my brother.'

Geras looked at him closely. 'You must really care about him.'

Telemachus lowered his gaze to the burning embers and nodded. 'Nereus is the only reason I'm here. He's all the family I had left after my parents died. I'd do anything to get him back, to see his face again.' He looked up. 'What about you? Why did you become a sailor?'

'Can't remember. I've been at sea since I was ten. My old man was always trying to convince me to follow in his footsteps and join the imperial service, but I wasn't having any of it. Too much like hard work. All that yes–sir–no–sir bollocks. All I wanted to do was travel, get roaring drunk and enjoy the company of a few reasonably priced tarts. When he found out I'd decided to join a merchant crew, the old bastard gave me the beating of my life. I'll never forget it.'

'I'm sorry.'

'Sod him. This is my family now. This lot. Becoming a sailor was the best decision I ever made.'

Telemachus smiled warmly. 'I'm beginning to see the attraction. Although I can't say the same for this wine.'

Geras leaned in close before he replied. 'You showed some bloody good seamanship today, lad. As a matter of fact, I reckon you're finally taking to the vocation.' He necked the dregs of his wine and flashed a broad smile. 'Perhaps you'll make a sailor after all.'

After their evening meal, the crew returned to the ship in a contented mood. Their inebriated laughs and shouts echoed across the bay as they bedded down for the night, their bellies full of wine and food. A crescent moon shone in the cloudless sky, reflecting on the surface of the water like a thousand dull sword points. As *Selene* rocked gently in the calm waters, Telemachus lay down on the deck and stared up at the distant glittering stars, feeling the warm embrace of the wine and the cool breeze carrying in from the sea. The other sailors soon drifted off to sleep, and the bay was silent except for their loud snoring, the creak of the rigging and the soft slap of the water against the rocks.

Despite the stress and exhaustion of the day, however, Telemachus found it impossible to sleep. For the first time since accepting a berth on *Selene* he truly felt part of the crew, and he sensed something of the deep bond that existed between these men. Maybe Geras was right. Perhaps he did have a promising future as a sailor.

As the hours passed, his thoughts turned towards his brother. He wondered how many voyages it would take until he'd earned enough money to buy Nereus's freedom from his Roman master. At the end of the meal Clemestes had taken him to one side and promised to increase his pay to that of a regular sailor once they landed at Salonae, as a reward for saving the ship from the clutches of the pirates. The news had filled Telemachus with joy. On a full sailor's pay he would be able to save much more than on his meagre half-wage. Perhaps once Nereus was free, the two of them could serve together on *Selene*. If they worked hard and saved every spare sestertius, one day they might have enough money to buy a merchant ship of their own, just like their father had done. They could sail to the distant shores of the Empire and make their fortune . . .

His idle thoughts were interrupted by a faint splashing sound, just audible above the crew's drunken snores and the breeze whispering across the deck. He sat upright and pricked his ears. When he heard the sound once more, he crept over to Geras and shook him awake. Geras stirred into consciousness and focused his bleary eyes on Telemachus as the latter kneeled beside him.

'What is it? What's going on?'

'Did you hear that?' Telemachus said softly.

'Hear what?'

'Listen!'

Geras stilled his breath and strained his ears. After a few moments he rubbed his eyes and moved over to the side rail, squinting into the darkness. Telemachus joined him, struggling to make out details in the wan moonlight.

'Look!' he whispered. 'Over there!'

He pointed out towards the black mass of the cove nearest to the bay. Geras looked in the same direction. As they watched, the shadowy outline of a vessel emerged from the gloom and crept ghostlike under oars towards the anchored merchantman. Her mast had been unstepped to make her less visible against the starlit sky, but as she moved closer, Telemachus recognised her sleek outline from the previous day, and the blood chilled in his veins. The pirate ship was less than a quarter of a mile from *Selene*, he realised.

'Shit!' Geras hissed. 'The pirates! They've found us!'

Around the deck, the other sleeping bundles slowly began

to stir. Leitus sprang to his feet and immediately rushed over to the rail next to Telemachus and Geras. Clemestes followed them, looking sleepy and confused.

'What? What is it?' he demanded irritably. Then he started with shock as he caught sight of the approaching ship. He froze, staring in surprise and horror. 'No,' he gasped, shaking his head. 'It can't be!'

'Bastards have given the Romans the slip.' Leitus gritted his teeth. 'They must have hidden in the cove next to us and seen us approach. Now they've got us trapped.'

By now the other sailors had roused, and alarm quickly spread at the sight of the oncoming enemy vessel. Now that the element of surprise had been lost, there was no need for stealth, and the oarsmen rapidly increased their rhythm, the oars sweeping forward then back again as the pirate ship closed on *Selene*. Telemachus could see the shadowy figures crowded on the foredeck, the growls of their commander clearly audible above the rush of the sea. There was no chance of eluding them this time, he realised despairingly. They would have to stand and fight.

'Prepare the men,' Clemestes said to Leitus. '*Now!*'

Leitus turned and bellowed an order. The crew rushed across the deck, grabbing whatever weapons were to hand as they prepared to face the attackers. Amid the confusion, the first mate snatched up a boathook and thrust it at Telemachus.

'Looks like you'll get to do some fighting after all, lad.'

Telemachus grasped the wooden shaft and hurried over with Geras to the port side to join the rest of the men as they prepared to confront the attackers. He sensed their fear and desperation. Some of the sailors looked terrified at the prospect of facing the better-armed pirates, their crude weapons shaking in their grip. Others glanced anxiously around, as if debating whether to try and swim to safety and flee inland. The odds were stacked against *Selene*'s crew, and Telemachus could feel his heart beating rapidly inside his chest at the prospect of imminent battle. He clasped his hand tightly around the boathook and snapped his gaze back to the pirate ship, tensing his muscles.

On the aft deck of the other vessel the commander barked an order. The oars stopped dead in the water at the last possible moment. Then the ship swung round and there was a dull thud as her bows struck against the port side of the merchantman. At once, the men on the foredeck launched their grappling hooks, hurling the iron spikes through the air. The barbs lodged in the timbers, and the pirates dragged on the ropes, pulling them tight and drawing the ships together. Then one of the attackers bellowed a savage battle cry as the first wave of boarders clambered up onto the rails and leaped across the gap, landing on the deck before they turned to face the sailors.

'*Get them!*' Leitus roared.

CHAPTER EIGHT

The sailors hurled themselves at the enemy. Two of the crewmen were swiftly cut down as the men met in a manic frenzy of swinging clubs, hacking axes and slashes from daggers and swords. Telemachus charged at a broad-chested man wielding a curved dagger. The pirate brought his right arm back and slashed at his opponent in a wide arc. Telemachus jerked nimbly backwards, evading the blow as the glinting blade swept narrowly in front of him. The pirate's momentum carried him forward a step, and in one rapid motion Telemachus sprang forward and thrust up with the boathook. The man's eyes bulged as the iron spike and hook punched through the flesh underneath his chin with a soft crunch. He spasmed and gasped before Telemachus wrenched the hook free, tearing apart flesh and tendon and muscle. The pirate fell away, blood spurting out of the dark gash in his throat.

The ship's boy turned and searched for his next opponent. All around him the sailors were locked in a brutal struggle for their lives against the pirates, and above the sound of axe blows and sword clashes he heard Clemestes shouting encouragement to his men. To one side Dimethus roared savagely as he slammed a belaying pin into a pirate's face with a dull crack.

But the fight was desperately one-sided and the sailors began to fall back from the side rail, retreating towards the mainmast as the sheer weight of enemy numbers began to tell. Already several of the crew lay slain on the deck amid dark puddles of blood, and Telemachus knew they could not hold out for much longer against the savage assault. Amid the melee he spotted Syleus dropping his weapon and throwing his hands in the air in surrender. But the pirates' blood was up and two of them swiftly cut him down. Syleus's agonised screams rang out across the ship as he disappeared beneath a flurry of sword thrusts.

'Look out, lad!' Leitus cried.

Telemachus saw a flash of steel in the periphery of his vision and spun quickly to his right. A fat, dark-skinned pirate wearing a leather cuirass thrust his short sword at him, driving the point at his throat. Telemachus instinctively ducked before the blow could connect and stabbed out with the boathook, gashing the man in his thigh, tearing flesh. The pirate hissed in pain as he clamped a hand to the wound, then launched a clumsy thrust at Telemachus. The latter easily avoided the blow before he stabbed out again. This time his aim was deadly accurate and his opponent doubled over as the hook buried itself in his groin. Telemachus twisted the weapon and the pirate gasped in pain as the hook lacerated his vitals, then keeled over, the shaft still buried in his bloodstained crotch. Telemachus tried to wrench it free, but the hook had firmly embedded itself in the man's bowels.

He turned as he heard a scream to his side and saw one of the sailors lying stricken on the deck, blood gushing out of the severed stump of his arm. A huge pirate towered over him wielding a broadaxe. He swung the weapon back over his head and brought it crashing down on the sailor's face in an explosion of blood, gristle and bone.

'Over here, you bastard!' Telemachus shouted, enraged. 'Come on!'

The pirate yanked his weapon free before turning to face his young opponent. He was immediately joined by another pirate gripping a curved blade. The two men closed in, sensing an easy kill. Telemachus reached down and grabbed the short sword from beside the man he had just cut down, then whirled to meet the two pirates as they stepped towards him. By now the deck planking was smeared with blood and viscera, and the axeman almost slipped as he lunged at Telemachus, swinging his weapon in a vicious upward arc. Telemachus dropped low and the axe whooshed past his head, missing by inches, juddering as it struck the mast with a splintering crack. As the axeman struggled to prise the weapon free, Telemachus sprang up and stepped closer to his opponent, slamming the pommel of the sword against the side of the axeman's skull. The pirate grunted as he went tumbling across the deck, crashing head-first into the side of the boat stowed there.

In the same breath Telemachus glimpsed a flicker of movement at his side and turned too late to face the second pirate. The man slashed at him before he could retreat, and the ship's boy gasped in pain as the tip of the sword grazed his shoulder. The pirate's lips parted in a pitiless smile as he saw the warm blood trickling out of Telemachus's flesh wound, and he moved in for the kill, thrusting again. As Telemachus stumbled backwards, he slipped on the bloodied planking, the sword falling from his grip as he crashed to the deck. The force of the impact drove the wind from his lungs, momentarily stunning him. He shook his head clear and reached for his weapon, but the swordsman moved swiftly to kick it away before he could grasp it. Telemachus looked up and froze. The tip of the pirate's sword glinted wickedly under the bright moonlight as he shaped to plunge it down at his opponent.

'No you fucking don't!' a voice shouted.

The pirate glanced to his left as Geras charged at him with a manic roar, wielding a pike in a two-handed grip. The swordsman wheeled away from Telemachus and parried the blow, deflecting the iron tip away from his flank before stabbing out wildly. Telemachus snatched up his own sword and swung it in front of him in a chopping motion, slamming the edge against the pirate's ankle. The pirate howled as the sword cut through tendon, shattering his ankle bone, and he dropped to one knee before Geras kicked him in the back, knocking him to the deck. He tried to get up, but the sailor fell on him before he could recover, driving the pike tip into the back of his skull.

Geras tore the pike free, then turned away from the bloodied heap and held out a hand to Telemachus. His face and arms were spattered with blood and his features were screwed into a wild, desperate expression. Telemachus opened his mouth to thank him.

'Save it for later!' Geras shouted. 'We're not finished yet.'

As Telemachus stood up, Clemestes bellowed at his men to fall back, and the sailors steadily retreated towards the stern as the pirates continued to pour over the ship's side. Glancing around, Telemachus saw that only a handful of the crew remained standing. The rest lay slumped on the deck, along with at least a dozen pirates. A few had tried to make a run for the side to jump into the sea, but they were cut down by the enemy.

Telemachus stood shoulder to shoulder with the other sailors as the pirates encircled them. The men of *Selene* had offered a resolute defence of their ship, but now the outcome had been decided. All was lost. There was nothing else to do except kill as many of the pirates as possible before they were overrun. He drew in a deep breath as he prepared to go down fighting.

As the pirates edged closer, a voice called out from behind the front ranks. At the command, the pirates pulled back from the tight knot of sailors, keeping their weapons raised as they warily eyed the defenders. A moment later, a space opened up between them and a dark-haired figure stepped forward wearing a pair of leather breeches and a black cuirass decorated with intricate silver and gold swirls. He gripped a heavy falcata with a bronze hook-shaped handle in his right hand.

All eyes turned to the man as he picked his way past the corpses on the deck. He stopped a few paces away and looked over the handful of sailors crowding the stern of *Selene*. An eerie quiet descended, the sounds of the fighting replaced by the pained cries of wounded and dying men and the erratic breathing of the survivors.

'My name is Bulla,' the man said. 'Who is your captain?'

There was a beat before the reply came.

'I am. I'm the captain,' Clemestes said, stepping forward and raising a trembling hand.

Bulla looked at him. A slight smile formed on his lips. 'Your men have fought well, Captain. But it's over now. Tell your crew to surrender.'

Clemestes hesitated briefly, then bowed his head and released the pike from his grip. He turned to his men. 'Lay down your weapons, boys.'

There was a long pause, followed by a dull clatter as the rest of the crew reluctantly followed their captain's example and threw down their weapons one by one, until only Telemachus was left. He held on to his sword for a moment longer before releasing it. Bulla turned back to Clemestes and grunted.

'I've never seen a merchant crew fight so hard. These are good tough men you've got here, Captain. Fine effort. I think I'll take the survivors for my ship.'

Clemestes shook his head and tried to hide his fear. 'My men are sailors, not thieves. We're of no use to you.'

'I disagree.' Bulla nodded at the throng of pirates surrounding the crew. 'All my men were sailors at one point or another. They simply changed sides when I made them a better offer. Your men will be no different.'

'What if we won't join you?'

The pirate captain shrugged. 'Then you can die here, and rot at the bottom of the sea. The choice is yours.'

Clemestes took a step forward and pointed towards the aft hatch. 'Listen, I'll make you an offer. Take our cargo. It's yours . . . all of it. Even the money in my strongbox. Just let me and my men go. I beg you.'

'Why would I do that?' Bulla asked, rubbing his stubbly jaw.

'You've got what you wanted. It's the cargo you're after. You don't need to rob me of my crew as well.'

'No.' Bulla shook his head. 'You're wrong. I lost some good men tonight. More than a few. I need to replace them.'

'My crew won't join your ranks,' Clemestes replied, stiffening his neck muscles. 'It would be easier if you just let us go.'

'Is that so?' The pirate captain arched a slender eyebrow and smiled. 'We'll see about that.'

There was a sudden glittering movement as he punched his arm out and swung his falcata. The curved edge arced through the air and cut through Clemestes' neck in one clean blow, the merchant captain's head toppling to the deck. His body remained upright for an instant before collapsing, to gasps of shock from the crew. Telemachus looked on in horror as blood spurted out of the ragged stump of Clemestes' neck and pooled around his headless corpse.

Bulla stared down at the dead captain for a moment with contempt. Then he turned to address the other sailors.

'Now listen,' he began. 'Your captain was a fool. But my offer still stands to the rest of you. Join my crew, swear an oath to our cause and you will be spared. Those of you who demonstrate your loyalty will be rewarded with a share of any loot we retrieve. Refuse, and you will suffer the same fate as your captain. Those are the terms. I suggest you choose more carefully than he did.' He stood back and eyed the sailors, waiting for their response.

Silence fluttered across the moonlit deck as the crew wrestled with his offer. One or two simply stared at their dead captain in terror, while others eyed the pirates warily. After a few moments, Dimethus stepped forward and bowed his head to Bulla. The others soon followed, one after the other. Telemachus wavered for a moment, torn between his fear of the pirates and the prospect of a grim death if he refused their captain's offer. His survival instinct finally won, and he joined the rest of the crew. Bulla smiled at them in satisfaction and sheathed his falcata with a rasping hiss as he beckoned to one of the other pirates.

'Hector!'

A fat, scarred veteran with matted dark hair approached. 'Aye, Captain?'

'Take these men aboard the ship and swear them in.' Bulla swept an arm across the line of sailors. 'Any of them complain . . . cut out their tongues.'

Hector grinned at the surviving crew. His gaze came to rest on Telemachus, and there was a cruel look in his eyes that chilled the young sailor's blood.

'What about this lanky streak of piss, Captain?' he growled. He gestured to the slain axeman. 'Bastard killed Pastus.'

'Is that so?' Bulla studied the ship's boy closely. He looked at the boy's blood-splattered tunic, then down at the broken bodies strewn about his feet, and raised an eyebrow. 'You killed one of my best men, I see.' He thought for a beat before turning back to Hector. 'Very well. Take him down with the others.'

The scarred pirate pursed his lips. 'The men won't be happy about that, Captain. Pastus was popular with the rest of the crew. They'll want to see this piece of shit gutted.'

'Too bad. We need all the men we can get right now. Especially ones who can handle themselves in a fight.'

'As you wish, Captain,' Hector replied, struggling to mask his disappointment. 'What about the ship?'

Bulla considered. 'Strip her bare then cut her adrift. She'll serve as a nice warning to others. Anyone who cooperates with the Romans will be shown no mercy.'

Hector nodded, then turned away, shouting at the rest of the pirate crew, 'Well? What the fuck are you lot waiting for? You heard the captain. Grab the loot and load it onto the ship!'

The pirates set to work immediately. Several of the men threw open the cargo hold, while two others made for the captain's private quarters below deck. The rest were detailed to search the bodies of the dead, removing rings and any other items of value. Sacks of grain and rice and supplies from the ship's stores were carried out of the hold. There was a splintering crack as one of the pirates smashed open Clemestes' strongbox, followed by a cheer of delight when he discovered the small stash of silver coins inside. Meanwhile, Hector shoved the new recruits aboard the pirate ship, his sword raised and ready to strike down anyone who tried to make a run for it.

When the last of the cargo had been transferred, the order was given for the pirates to return to their vessel, and the grappling hooks were retrieved as the men clambered over the side rail and abandoned *Selene* to her dead.

As the first hint of dawn fringed the horizon, the pirate vessel cleared the bay, her decks heaving with the spoils of the attack and a dozen recruits. Telemachus stood on the foredeck with the rest of the crew, looking on with despair as *Selene* slowly disappeared into the distance. He allowed himself a moment's anger at the abrupt end to his short-lived career as a ship's boy, then forced his thoughts to turn to the immediate future. He had always been able to quickly adapt to whatever circumstances he found himself in, a skill he had honed during the many years he'd spent living on the streets of Piraeus. His quick wits had saved him before. He would need those instincts more than ever if he was to survive the dangerous new situation he found himself in.

'What'll happen to us now?' he asked Geras.

The sailor shrugged sullenly. 'I'd imagine they'll do what

pirate crews always do with sailors they capture. They'll make us swear an oath of loyalty, press us into their ranks and put us to work on board this ship. Unless they're running low on money. Then they might sell some of us into slavery to raise a few sestertii. Either way, we're in for a rough ride.'

Telemachus swallowed. 'I see.'

'So much for hoping for a quiet life at sea.' Geras cursed under his breath and shook his head. 'I should've listened to my old man and joined the imperial navy. At least I wouldn't be surrounded by these madmen.'

'Could be worse,' Telemachus responded.

'Oh? How's that, lad?'

'We're still alive. There's that, at least.'

Geras grunted and looked away.

Telemachus forced himself to think clearly in spite of the growing dread in his chest. Despite their dire circumstances, they had been spared the grisly fate of some of those crews unfortunate enough to be captured by the pirates. According to Bulla, they would have the opportunity to earn a place among his men, and perhaps share in the lucrative profits to be had from looting merchant shipping. Perhaps all was not lost. Then he looked up at Leitus and saw the first mate shaking his head sadly at the distant merchantman.

'We might be alive, lad,' he said. 'But I'm afraid that's where our luck ends. We're well and truly fucked now.'

'How so?'

Leitus tipped his head at *Selene*. 'The Roman navy will stumble upon her soon enough. And when they do, they're going to be even more determined to hunt down the men responsible.'

'Then there's still a chance we'll be rescued?'

The first mate watched the merchantman for a moment longer. Then he turned back to Telemachus, his eyes filled with apprehension.

'Don't you understand, boy? The prefect will send his ships to hunt down and crush Bulla and his men . . . including us. When the Romans attack, we're going to be caught right in the fucking middle of it.'

CHAPTER NINE

Dusk gathered around the pirate ship as she glided slowly towards the beach. On the aft deck of *Poseidon's Trident*, Captain Bulla stared at the shoreline and the distant mountains beyond. After sailing north until the evening, the captain had decided to seek a safe anchorage in the mass of islands and inlets lining the Illyrian coastline. It was getting dark, and with the ship carrying a full hold and riding low in the water, he didn't want to sail on through the night and risk running aground on any shoals.

He turned to Hector. The first mate had a rare talent when it came to killing and striking fear into other men. That was why Bulla had selected him as his second in command, in spite of the man's limited seafaring abilities. They had sailed together on *Poseidon's Trident* for the past five years, commanding a crew of some of the most bloodthirsty, violent pirates to be found in the Empire.

'Have the men prepare to beach.'

'Aye, Captain,' Hector responded gruffly. He tipped his head at the bedraggled group of captive sailors huddled nearby. Many of them bore fresh scars from the bitter skirmish that had been fought the previous night. 'What about these miserable scum?'

Bulla considered for a moment. 'We'll initiate them as soon as we've landed. The ship's undermanned. It's about time we pressed them into the ranks.'

Geras watched the first mate move away and shook his head bitterly.

'Bastard pirates. We would've landed at Salonae by now if we hadn't run into this lot. We could have been getting blind drunk and sampling the local talent. Instead we're stuck on this tub.'

Leitus gave his companion a hard look. 'Bloody typical. We're being pressed into service by the most notorious cut-throats on the Adriaticum, and all you're worried about is missing out on a few tarts.'

Geras shrugged. 'Just saying.'

Telemachus glanced around the bay. 'Where do you think we are, Leitus?'

The older sailor stared at the mountains and rubbed his greying stubble. 'We passed Ragusa a while back. This must be one of the islands near Corcyra Nigra. Looks like we'll be setting anchors for the night. Their base must be further to the north somewhere, I imagine.'

'Maybe the navy will find us before we get there,' Geras suggested.

'In these islands?' Leitus snorted. 'I doubt it, lad. Even if they do stumble upon us, the Romans won't treat us any differently from the other pirates.'

The youth furrowed his brow. 'But we *are* different. Aren't we? We're not pirates. Their captain forced us to surrender and join his crew.'

'Forced or not, as far as Rome's concerned, we're all the

same. Besides, why would they believe our story? Every captured pirate from here to Miletus claims they were taken against their will.'

'Leitus is right,' Geras cut in. 'As soon as we accepted the captain's offer, we became enemies of Rome. Fairly or not, we're all marked men now. Either way, we're fucked.'

Telemachus swallowed hard. 'Should we try to escape?'

'Not unless you want your head to be parted from your shoulders. You make a run for it, this lot will cut you down before you can get far. We're bloody miles from the nearest port.'

'What are we going to do, then?'

'Keep your head down,' Leitus said carefully. 'Don't make any enemies, and for the gods' sakes, try not to get killed.'

The sailors fell into gloomy silence as *Poseidon's Trident* approached the beach. Hector shouted a command and all spare hands moved towards the aft deck to help lift the ship's bows on approach. While several of the other prisoners muttered prayers to the gods or talked in low whispers about the possibility of escape, Telemachus watched the pirates cautiously. Although he feared these men, his initial dread had gradually subsided as his restless mind turned to thoughts of survival. The sailors aboard *Selene* had often swapped tales of atrocities committed by the pirates, but they had also mentioned the riches such crews had plundered. If that was true, he might yet make his fortune, as a pirate instead of a ship's boy. And if he was going to be a condemned man, he might as well die rich . . .

A jarring shudder shook him out of his thoughts as the bows ground to a halt on the shingle. Bulla shouted for the men to ship oars, and a sturdy gangway was lowered down the starboard side of the prow. The pirates swiftly disembarked, bringing ashore amphorae filled with wine to celebrate their successful raid. Several cooking fires were lit on the shore, and soon the faint aroma of roasting pork wafted across the decks. Telemachus felt his belly growl painfully with hunger. It had been almost a day since any of the sailors had eaten anything, and the thought of a cooked meal provided fresh torment for the captives.

Once the decks had been cleared and the hatches covered, Hector strode briskly over and kicked the nearest sailor. 'Get up, you worthless shits!'

Telemachus climbed slowly to his feet with the other men. His muscles were stiff and sore from the long hours he'd spent on the deck, and the shallow flesh wound on his left shoulder throbbed with painful intensity. But his physical discomfort was nothing compared to the anxiety tightening in his guts.

'What's happening?' he asked.

Hector stared at him, his face glowering with hatred. 'Time for you to be sworn in, boy. You and the rest of your happy little band.' His lips parted in a sinister grin. 'Hurry along. Captain's got a surprise for you.'

'Surprise?' an overweight sailor with thinning hair repeated. 'What do you mean?'

The pirate's grin widened. 'Now that would be telling, wouldn't it?' Then his expression hardened. 'Get a fucking move on. All of you. The captain's waiting for you on the beach.'

He turned and led the sailors towards the gangway. Telemachus, Leitus and Geras fell into step behind the others as they shuffled along the weathered planking. The portly sailor ahead of them kept glancing around nervously, his eyes wide with fear.

'This can't be happening,' he whimpered. 'It can't be. I have to get back to my family.'

'Quiet, Nearchus!' Leitus hissed sharply. 'Want to get us all in trouble?'

Nearchus fell silent and faced forward, his shoulders slumped as the sailors descended the plank and made their way up the pebbled beach. The flames from the fires licked at the darkening sky, illuminating the faces of the pirates. They were arranged in a loose throng around their captain, holding leather cups brimming with wine and cheering wildly. Bulla stood next to an iron brazier, his arms folded across his broad chest, beneath which hung his belted sword. Next to him stood a squat, heavy-set Syrian with a thickly matted beard, stoking an iron shaft in the embers of a fire. The orange glow of the flames reflected in his menacing black eyes.

'Shit,' Geras whispered. 'This doesn't look good.'

'No,' Telemachus replied as he looked around at the surrounding bay. It was fringed by a line of cliffs. There was no way off the beach, and he instantly dismissed the idea of trying to escape. Leitus saw the look on his face and leaned in close, dropping his voice to a low whisper.

'Whatever happens, lad, don't show any fear. Don't give these bastards the satisfaction.'

The excited shouts of the pirates grew louder as Hector led the sailors forward until they were only a few paces from Bulla. The captain raised an arm and signalled for them to stop, and a hushed silence descended over the beach. Then he stepped forward and cleared his throat.

'Men of *Selene*,' he began. 'Today is the best day of your

pathetic lives so far. Today you are no longer the lowest scum of the shipping trade, earning a pittance while some greedy Athenian merchant gorges himself on the profits. No. That life is over. Today you will join the ranks of a new crew. From this day on, each of you will serve on a ship whose name strikes fear into the hearts of men the length and breadth of the Adriaticum . . . *Poseidon's Trident!*'

A full-throated roar went up from the gathered pirates. Telemachus glanced at the other prisoners. Some stared wide-eyed at their captors. Several appeared resigned to their fate, watching the captain with sullen expressions of defeat. Nearchus's hands were trembling with fear, Telemachus noticed. He swung his gaze back to Bulla as the pirates fell silent once again and their captain went on.

'Some of you will have heard stories about our way of life. About why we turned to robbery on the sea lanes of the Empire. For those of you who haven't, you should know this. Many of us served on merchant ships once. We know what it's like to suffer the rancid food and the daily humiliations, earning barely enough to make ends meet. To be at the mercy of an incompetent captain, working for a Roman or Greek shipowner who couldn't give a fuck about you. Now's your chance to escape all of that. Follow the rules and I promise you will be richly rewarded. But if anyone dares betray us, they will be dealt with severely. Those who steal from the ship's treasury or keep loot for themselves will be put to death. The same goes for anyone who tries to escape or incite mutiny. When you join our ranks, you will be part of a brotherhood. We share hardship and danger, and all the rewards that come with it.' He grinned. 'And if we live long enough to retire from the sea life, we'll be richer than Croesus. You'll have all the coin and wine you could ever want.'

'And cunny!' one of the pirates shouted, prompting a chorus of laughter.

Telemachus looked at his comrades in surprise. To an orphan who had known nothing but grinding poverty, even piracy held out promise. He listened keenly as the captain continued.

'To guarantee your loyalty, each of you will be branded with the mark of the trident. Once you have been marked, everyone will know who you are . . . what you have become. As you know, those Roman dogs across the water show no mercy to those who engage in our profession. The new prefect, Canis, has announced that from now on, any man caught engaging in acts of piracy will be crucified for his crimes. Try to leave us, and you will end up nailed to a cross. Accept your branding, serve this ship well and fight like a bloody hero, and I promise you will be richer than you ever dreamed of. Refuse the mark, and I'll cut out your tongue and sell you on to the slave dealers at the first port of call.'

Telemachus felt an icy chill slither down his spine. Around him some of the sailors glanced at each other in terror as they realised what was about to happen. Then Bulla turned to a pair of burly pirates standing to one side of the crew.

'Bring the first man forward!'

CHAPTER TEN

Fear spread through the captives as the two pirates approached them. Some of the sailors near Telemachus lowered their eyes, while others shuffled backwards in the hope that someone else would be selected before them, delaying their own suffering. The pirates reached out and grabbed Nearchus, clamping their hairy hands around his arms. The terrified sailor pleaded with his captors, begging them to spare him as they marched him towards the captain.

'Please!' he cried. 'Don't do this! I won't run, I swear!'

The pirates ignored his desperate entreaties and shoved him to his knees in front of Bulla, as murmurs of excitement rippled through the cheering crowd. The pirate chief glanced down at Nearchus, regarding him for a moment with a look of cold contempt. Then he turned to the Syrian standing next to the brazier and nodded.

'Mark him, Lasthenes.'

At once Lasthenes yanked the branding iron out of the brazier flames and moved towards Nearchus. The latter began shaking uncontrollably at the sight of the glowing red tip, his despairing pleas barely audible above the colourful taunts the pirates were hurling at him. As Lasthenes drew closer, the sailor tried jerking his head away from the branding iron, drawing more cheers and abuse.

'No,' he moaned. 'Please . . .'

'Shut up!' Bulla rasped. 'Hold him.'

One of the pirates clasped his hand around the sailor's wrist, holding his forearm still. Lasthenes held the iron tantalisingly close to the skin for a moment, a cruel smirk playing on his lips. Then he pressed the trident-shaped head firmly against Nearchus's forearm, drawing a demented scream of pain. The sailor's cries were swiftly drowned out by the drunken roars of the crowd as smoke drifted up from the end of the branding iron, accompanied by a seething hiss as the heated metal burned flesh. The branding lasted three or four agonising moments before Lasthenes withdrew the iron and stepped back and Nearchus slumped forward on the shingle, shaking and sobbing. On Bulla's command, the two pirates hauled him to his feet and dragged him away, the sailor weeping in pain. Bulla shook his head, then turned to Hector.

'Next man forward!'

'Aye, Captain.'

The first mate grabbed hold of Telemachus and pulled him away from his comrades, shoving him forward. 'You heard the captain! Move yourself!'

Telemachus staggered across the sand, his stomach muscles clenching with fear. Several loud boos rang out as the two pirates grasped his arms and forced him towards the brazier. Lasthenes held a cloth around the handled end of the branding iron and kept the head in the flames for a few moments, until it glowed white with heat. Then he removed it and moved towards Telemachus. The latter tensed his muscles and took a deep breath, steeling himself for the imminent pain. He could feel the scalding heat coming off the end of the iron, prickling his skin and singeing the hairs on his arm. All around him, the pirates shouted, urging the Syrian on.

'Mark him!' one yelled. 'Burn the skinny bastard!'

'Make him squeal!' another bellowed.

Lasthenes flashed a wicked grin. 'This is going to hurt, boy.'

A searing pain exploded inside Telemachus's body as Lasthenes pressed the brand against his forearm. Every fibre screamed as he clamped his jaw tightly shut, fighting the agony. The stench of burning flesh filled his nostrils, and an intense wave of nausea stirred in his guts, rising into his throat. He forced himself not to scream, determined to hide his suffering from the pirates. For one terrible moment, he feared he might pass out from the pain, then Lasthenes drew back his arm and Telemachus dropped to his knees, gasping for breath. Bulla stepped forward and looked curiously at the young Greek.

'I don't think I've ever seen that before,' he said. 'The recruits always cry like babies when they're branded.'

'We should burn him again,' Hector suggested. 'On the arse, this time. We'll have him screaming soon enough, Captain.'

Bulla shook his head. 'No. He's got guts, this one. He's taken enough. For now, at least.' He narrowed his eyes at the recruit. 'What's your name, boy?'

'Telemachus,' the latter groaned.

'That's "Captain" to you.' A flicker of recognition crossed the pirate's features. 'You're that ship's boy, aren't you? The one who killed Pastus.'

Telemachus stared back defiantly. 'That's me . . . Captain.'

'Pastus was a good swordsman. One of the best on my ship. And yet somehow you managed to cut him down. Where did a skinny wretch like you learn to fight like that, I wonder?'

'I didn't learn anywhere. I taught myself, in the slums around Piraeus. That's where I grew up. You have to know how to defend yourself.'

'A street orphan, eh?' Bulla considered the younger man for a moment. 'I suggest you have something to eat and get that wound cleaned. We set sail again tomorrow, and you're no use to me if you're too weak to climb the ratlines.'

'Aye . . . Captain.'

The two pirates who had been holding Telemachus lifted him to his feet and marched him over to a nearby cooking fire. Nearchus sat close by, tears streaming down his cheeks as he stared disconsolately into the flames. The pirates threw Telemachus to the ground before they headed back over to their captain, muttering among themselves. A few moments later, another pirate limped over. He was tall and thin, with a shaven head and a heavily wrinkled brow. The brand of the trident was clearly visible on the inside of his forearm. He handed Telemachus a chipped clay cup filled with wine.

'Here,' he said. 'Drink this.'

Telemachus sniffed the contents suspiciously. 'What is it?'

'Wine. We stole a load of it from a supply ship a few weeks ago. Cheap, and it tastes like rat piss, but it's potent. Helps with the pain.'

'Thanks.' Telemachus lifted the cup to his lips and took a long gulp. The wine burned the back of his throat and settled into his belly, but it did little to numb the agony in his arm.

'Name's Castor. I'm the ship's quartermaster.' The pirate

cocked his head in the direction of the other men. 'Looks like you made quite an impression on the captain.'

'If you say so.'

Castor nodded. 'Don't let that lot get to you. They're always hard on the new recruits. Especially the ones they've captured from other vessels.' He frowned. 'How did you end up on a merchant ship anyway? You don't exactly look like the seafaring type.'

'Some footpads attacked our captain in the streets in Piraeus. I happened to be nearby when it happened.' Telemachus lowered his head. 'I fought 'em off, and the captain gave me a berth on his ship as a reward.'

The quartermaster chuckled. 'Some reward! Life on a cargo ship is about as shit as it gets in these parts. You would have been better off staying on the streets, lad.'

'I didn't have a choice,' Telemachus replied moodily.

'What's that supposed to mean?'

Telemachus hesitated. His skull throbbed painfully. 'I joined to help my brother. He's a slave, at a forge over in Thorikos. I thought that if I could save enough money, I could buy his freedom.'

'Well, one thing's for sure. You'll earn more coin on our crew than you would've done on a merchant ship. I know that better than most. I used to be a sailor myself.'

Telemachus looked up. 'You were pressed into the ranks?'

Castor shook his head. 'I sailed with Bulla in the years before we were pirates. We worked on a merchant tub trading out of Delos. Five years ago, this was. Our old captain was a right nasty piece of work. Thought he could treat us like shit, just because he was a bloody Roman. So a few of us killed him and the weasel of a first mate and took command of the ship, with Bulla as our commander. We've been looting the seas ever since.'

'You never thought about leaving his crew?'

'Why would I? I've got a good life here. Better than I had on a merchant ship, anyway. I get regular meals, a share of the loot and the freedom of the seas. And some of the lads aren't so bad once you get to know 'em.'

'I'll take your word for it,' Telemachus said, glancing over at the pirates as they cheered the next sailor being branded. He looked back at Castor. 'Where are we sailing tomorrow?'

'We'll head back up the coast, look for more prey to snap up. Once our supplies run low, we'll head back to our lair, Peiratispolis. The City of Pirates. Heard of it?'

Telemachus shook his head.

'You won't have,' Castor continued. 'It's not marked on any map, and the Romans don't know about it either. More of a small fishing port than a city, actually.'

'How far away is it?'

'Two days' sailing from here, with a favourable wind. It was a thriving port until a few years ago, when a big storm struck the coast and destroyed much of the settlement. A few locals stayed on to rebuild their homes but most of 'em soon drifted away, so we decided to move in and use it as our base, along with several other pirate ships operating in these waters. You'll see it soon enough for yourself.' Castor paused. 'If you manage to survive that long.'

Telemachus sat up with a jolt. 'What's that supposed to mean?'

The pirate glanced around to make sure no one overheard him. Across the beach, a hideous scream split the air as the next captured sailor was branded. The crew cheered again, roaring with drunken laughter.

'Let's just say that some of this lot aren't exactly thrilled about you being pressed into the ranks,' Castor said. 'Including Hector. Word is that he's out to get you.'

'Why? I've not done anything to him.'

'Pastus was popular with a lot of the crew. Him and Hector were good friends. He'll want revenge.'

'For cutting down a man who tried to kill me?'

'That's just the way it is, lad.'

'I'm not afraid of anyone,' Telemachus answered boldly.

'You should be,' Castor warned. 'I'm serious. Hector's a mean bastard. Most of the other lads are terrified of him, and they're some of the hardest men I've met.' He stared at Telemachus with a grim expression. 'Trust me. From now on, you're going to have to watch your back.'

CHAPTER ELEVEN

As the days passed, the skies cleared and warm spring sunshine beat down on the deck. After the cold, wet misery of the winter months, the men took the opportunity to work bare-chested, while the new recruits were put to work scrubbing the deck and repairing the spare sails that the pirates' lives might depend on one day. While a few of the older sailors from *Selene* mourned families and homes they would never see again, many of the recruits swiftly resigned themselves to their fate and soon adapted to their new life.

Telemachus quickly discovered that he had much to learn. In addition to their duties on deck, each evening, when the ship was beached, Lasthenes instructed them in how to fight with falcatas, shields and heavy axes. Telemachus proved to be a fast learner, and he had soon mastered the basic techniques of swordsmanship. It was back-breaking work, but he threw himself fully into each task, determined to prove his worth. The fates had handed him this rare chance to make his fortune, and he vowed not to let it slip away.

But Hector was never far from his thoughts. The first mate had demonstrated a savage cruelty towards the new recruits as soon as they had set sail, beating any man whose work did not meet with his approval. He had marked out Telemachus for special treatment and seemed to devote every shred of effort towards making his life miserable, never missing an opportunity to curse him, or make a sinister threat as they passed each other on the deck. The cramped confines of the ship made it impossible for Telemachus to avoid him completely, despite his best efforts to keep a safe distance, and whenever he looked up, he would see Hector staring at him with a hostile expression from across the deck.

Two weeks passed without the pirates finding any more prizes to loot, and as they passed Colentum, Bulla grudgingly gave the order for *Trident*'s crew to abandon their search and return to their base. After finishing his watch, Telemachus took a modest meal of vinegared water and dried beef on the foredeck. Castor stood nearby, leaning on the rail as he gazed out towards the churning sea.

'How long until we reach Peiratispolis?' asked the youth.

Castor narrowed his eyes at the horizon. 'Should be there well before dark. This old bird's faster than your average merchantman. But with a full hold, she'll be running much slower than that. We'll make land before dusk, at any rate.'

'What happens once we get there?'

'We'll revictual the ship while the captain negotiates a price with our merchant for the cargo. He buys whatever we have, no questions asked. The younger lads will run ashore and get blind drunk in the watering holes, of course. A few of the older lads will spend time with their families.' Castor paused. 'But I doubt we'll be staying long.'

'Why's that?'

The pirate pursed his lips. 'The lads were hoping for a more valuable haul than a load of grain. This lot will fetch a reasonable price with the merchant, but it's hardly going to cover the crew in silver, and the captain's under pressure to find a good prize.'

'I didn't realise things were so bad,' Telemachus said.

'They're not. Not yet, anyway. But we ain't the only pirates operating in these waters. Far from it. Competition is fierce. As you can see, fewer merchant ships are making the trip because they're afraid of being attacked.' Castor smiled ruefully. 'We've been too efficient at our trade for our own good, it seems.'

Telemachus nodded. They had passed hardly any sails since *Selene* was taken, a sure sign that the pirate activity had disrupted the shipping in the area.

'How many crews hunt in these waters?' he asked.

'More than a few,' Castor replied. 'Some of us operate out of the same bases, but we mostly keep to ourselves when at sea.'

'You don't sail together?'

Castor laughed drily. 'Not a bloody chance. There used to be a brotherhood among the Illyrian pirate gangs, but these days it's every pirate for himself. You won't find many of these lads begging to work with the other crews. Especially ones like Captain Nestor and his mob.'

'Nestor?' Telemachus asked. 'He's around here?'

Castor looked at him. 'You've heard of him?'

'Once or twice,' Telemachus said quietly, recalling the stories of the feared pirate captain he'd heard aboard *Selene*. 'Are we likely to run into him?'

'I doubt it. His lot operate further to the north of here. We'll be fine as long as we stick to our own stretch of the sea.'

'What's the captain going to do?' Telemachus asked,

changing the subject. 'If we can't find any ships to plunder?'

'Bulla will deliver. He always does. But it's been a while since we came across a good prize. If he's not careful, some of the crew might turn against him.'

'But he's the captain. They can't just knock him on the head, surely?'

'This isn't the imperial navy, lad. Look around you.' Castor gestured to the other pirates. 'These men come from all over. Thrace, Hispania, Egypt, Lycia. The only thing they've got in common is that they're looking for the easy life. No one's going to take orders from another man unless he can make them rich. If he can't, they'll just get rid of him and choose someone else to lead 'em.'

'So what's the plan? Keep prowling the waters until we find a good ship to plunder? We'll find something eventually, won't we?'

'It's not as easy as that. The captain's got to balance the needs of the crew against the risk of attacking a vessel. The smaller ships tend to surrender as soon as they see the black pennant, but they're usually carrying low-value cargoes. The biggest prizes are the merchantmen running the trade route out of Caesarea. They carry spices, silk, frankincense. Merchants pay a fortune for that stuff. But a lot of their crews have taken to employing retired marines and gladiators as a precaution. Some of the lads have suggested taking hostages or raiding settlements instead, but the captain's opposed to the idea.'

'Why?' Telemachus wondered aloud. 'If it's getting harder to make a living from the sea lanes, surely it makes sense to find new targets?'

'Think about it, lad.' Castor tapped the side of his head.

'Right now, we're just a minor irritant to Rome. The emperor might make plenty of noise about stamping us out, but everyone knows the imperial fleet is in a shit state and they don't have enough vessels or men to patrol the seas effectively. If we start kidnapping high-born Romans and looting villages, they'll be forced to take action. As long as we stick to raids on merchant ships, Rome won't take much notice of us.'

'I wouldn't be so sure,' Telemachus replied warily. 'I've met the new prefect. He came aboard *Selene*. He seems determined to wipe out every pirate he comes across.'

Castor laughed, dismissing the youngster's concerns with a wave of his hand. 'Those navy prefects are all the bloody same. Met one or two myself back in my days sailing merchant ships. They come into the job looking to make a name for themselves. A year or two from now, he'll move on to a more lucrative posting and forget about us. Besides,' he added, 'even if the Romans wanted to, they'd never find us. Not among all these islands. They could search for years without locating our base.'

Telemachus stared out at the horizon, wishing he could share the quartermaster's confidence. He recalled the fiery glare in Canis's eyes as he vowed to hunt down the pirates terrorising the sea lanes. The prefect of the Ravenna fleet would not stop until Bulla and every other pirate in the Adriaticum had been put to death.

Later that day, Bulla tasked Telemachus with emptying the bilges. The pirates did not bother to bail out the bilge water as frequently as their merchant counterparts, and an overwhelming stench wafted up from the grating in the hold as the recruit bent to his task, hauling up large wooden buckets filled with dank brown water, which he emptied over the stern rail. It was grim work, and as he climbed down the ladder in the late afternoon, he felt his arms and legs aching with exhaustion. He had barely had a moment to rest since joining the pirate crew, and he craved nothing more than to improvise a bed from the spare sails and coiled copes lying around the mainmast and close his eyes for a while.

He lowered the bucket into the bilges, pulled it up and stood up from the grating. As he turned around, he saw a trio of figures blocking his path between the sacks of grain on either side. Hector stood in front of the other two pirates, his mouth stretched into a menacing grin and his dark eyes glowing with cruel intent. A dagger glinted in his right hand. He moved towards Telemachus, his grin widening.

'Going somewhere, boy?'

Telemachus stood his ground. 'Let me pass.'

'Or what?' Hector smiled in amusement at the other two pirates. 'You'll gut me like you gutted our friend Pastus? I don't think so. Besides, we haven't given you a proper welcome yet.'

Telemachus glanced at the heavily built pirates either side of Hector, then slanted his gaze back to the first mate. 'What are you talking about?'

'This,' Hector said, brandishing the dagger. The tip gleamed wickedly in the stinking gloom of the hold. 'You killed Pastus. Now we're going to give you something to remember him by. A second mark to match the one on your forearm. That way, every man on this ship will know that you've killed a comrade.'

Telemachus felt a cold dread clamp around his throat. He took half a step back, heart pounding as he glanced around the hold, looking for a weapon or another way out. But he was completely alone. The other recruits had finished their duties and were up on deck. He could hear the thud of their feet as they moved along the well-worn planking above his head, and the muted tones of their voices.

Hector stepped forward. 'Nowhere for you to hide now,' he hissed.

He shifted his weight, thrusting the dagger at Telemachus, who read the move and jerked to the right, stepping just out of the path of the attack. Before Hector could adjust his balance, Telemachus kicked out at him, striking the pirate in the groin. Hector gasped in pain as he folded at the waist, cupping his free hand to his bruised balls. The dagger dropped from his grip and clattered onto the bilge grating.

'Grab him!' he growled at the other pirates. 'Fucking get him!'

The pirate to the right charged at the youth, his features tight with anger. Telemachus dropped low as the man swung at him, ducking the blow, then sprang up, catching the pirate in the midriff. The man gasped and doubled up. The third pirate launched himself forward, dropping his shoulder and catching the young recruit with a sharp blow to the side of the head, knocking him backwards. Telemachus briefly saw white, recovering his vision just in time to see the other pirate throw another punch. As he jerked aside to evade the blow his foot knocked against the bucket of bilge water next to the grating, and he tripped and fell, landing on his back, the filthy dark water tipping out and spilling over him.

He tried to get to his feet, but one of the pirates swung a boot at his side, kicking him in the ribs and winding him badly. Telemachus looked up and saw all three of the men towering over him. The first mate broke out into a triumphant grin as he realised his opponent was cornered. He snatched up the dagger from the floor whilst the other two men dropped down beside Telemachus, pinning him to the deck.

'Got you now,' Hector snarled. 'You'll be screaming this time, I'll make bloody sure of it.'

The dagger tip drew close. At that moment, the sound of pounding boots echoed through the hold as someone approached from aft. The two pirates holding Telemachus down immediately jumped to their feet and all three men spun around to face the approaching figure. Telemachus looked up and saw Bulla standing in the light of the open hatch.

'What's going on down here?' the captain demanded, frowning.

Hector straightened up. 'Nothing, Captain. Just an accident, that's all. Lad slipped when he was emptying out the bilges. Me and the lads were just telling him he should be less clumsy.'

Bulla looked towards Telemachus. 'Is that so?'

Telemachus hesitated. From the corner of his eye he could see Hector giving him a hard stare. He knew that if he told the truth, he would never gain the respect of the other pirates. In the short time he'd spent aboard the ship, he had seen that the crew of *Poseidon's Trident* were hardened, fearless men who resolved differences with their fists rather than by complaining to their captain. Besides, Bulla was unlikely to believe his version of events over that of his trusted second in command. If he said anything to the captain, it would only make his life on the ship even more unbearable than it presently was.

'Aye, Captain. Hector's right. I slipped and fell.'

Bulla stared at him doubtfully. 'I see. Well, you ought to be more careful in future. In the meantime, get this mess cleaned up.' He turned to Hector. 'Now leave the boy to his work.'

'Aye, Captain.'

Bulla gave a curt nod then ascended the gangway, followed by the other two pirates. Hector watched them go, then looked back at Telemachus, his face contorted with anger.

'This isn't over,' he whispered icily. 'Once we've landed, the captain won't be around to save you. I'll make you pay then, boy. Mark my words. As soon as we get off this ship, you're mine.'

Telemachus finished cleaning up the mess in the hold, then headed up the gangway, a sick feeling of dread knotting his stomach. Sooner or later he would have to deal with Hector, he knew. Otherwise his days on the pirate crew would be numbered. The possibility of escape briefly occurred to him. It would be easy enough to slip away once they had landed at Peiratispolis. He could disappear inland while the rest of the crew were distracted with women and wine, hide his branding and try to make his fortune elsewhere, perhaps join a gang of brigands. But he quickly dismissed the notion. Even if he managed to avoid capture, he would stand little chance of saving enough money to purchase his brother's freedom. He thought of Nereus, and the deprivations he was having to suffer under his Roman master, and that hardened his resolve. No. He would not fail his brother now. There was nothing else for it. He would have to deal with Hector once they arrived at the pirates' base.

As he reached the aft deck, he ran into Geras. The latter climbed down from the rigging and nodded at his friend, his muscles glistening with sweat.

'What happened to your face?' he asked.

'It's nothing,' Telemachus replied sullenly.

Geras arched an eyebrow. 'In one of your brighter moods, I see. Don't worry. You'll be smiling once we land at Peiratispolis.'

'Somehow I doubt that.'

Geras slapped him heartily on the back. 'You know what you need? A good drink and the company of a cheap tart. And there's plenty of both in Peiratispolis, apparently. I was just speaking to a few of the lads, and they've agreed to show us a good time in town tonight.' He grinned. 'Maybe life as a pirate isn't going to be so bad after all, eh?'

Telemachus sighed and looked away, feeling a pang of frustration and jealousy. They had been on the crew for less than three weeks, and Geras was already making friends. If only he could be as carefree as his companion, life aboard the pirate ship would be much more tolerable.

Just then there was an anxious shout from the lookout on the mast-top. 'Captain! Dead ahead! Look there!'

The pirates dropped what they were doing and hurried over to the foredeck, jostling for space along the rail as *Poseidon's Trident* made its final approach to Peiratispolis. There was a palpable sense of unease among the crew as they stared out to sea. Telemachus sensed it as he hurried forward, squeezing into a space between Geras and Castor. Geras peered at the horizon, then glanced at the veteran pirate, frowning heavily.

'What's going on?'

Castor pointed out beyond the bows of the ship. Telemachus looked in the same direction and strained his eyes, catching a glimpse of a tall, rocky headland some miles north. Beyond the point the land rose up towards a series of low, densely forested hills.

'Peiratispolis is the other side of that point,' Castor explained. He swallowed. 'Or what's left of it.'

Telemachus looked up in alarm. 'What do you mean?'

The ship rose up on the next swell, and Castor nodded at the horizon. Telemachus narrowed his eyes, and then he saw it. Some distance beyond the headland, several thick columns of smoke swirled lazily into the afternoon sky.

CHAPTER TWELVE

A nervous silence descended over the crew as *Poseidon's Trident* approached the headland. As a precaution, Bulla ordered the men to fetch the weapons stowed in the lockers amidships in case any enemies were lurking out of sight behind the point. Telemachus grabbed a broadaxe, while Geras and Leitus wielded legionary-style short swords. Some of the pirates buckled ornate decorated cuirasses over their tunics, and others equipped themselves with helmets and armour. Those men armed with bows and slings took up their positions on the foredeck, ready to launch missiles at any enemy ships. Bulla stood next to the mainmast, his right hand resting on the pommel of his sheathed falcata as he looked out beyond the ship's bows at the grey smudge billowing into the sky ahead. Around him the pirates stood tense, anxious to see what lay on the other side of the point.

As the vessel crept round the headland, the full scale of the devastation became apparent. Three beached ships lying on their sides on the shingle had been burned and smoke still drifted up from the blackened timbers. Two more vessels had been sunk at their anchors, their shattered spars, oars and sail cloths floating in the shallows along the shoreline, together with the splintered remnants of several smaller boats. A short distance inland, Telemachus spotted a cluster of razed buildings. Fires continued to rage through the ruins of the larger structures, and a handful of figures were visible among the rubble, stopping occasionally to search for other survivors and valuables. One or two inhabitants sat staring disconsolately at the skeletal timber frames. Dozens of lifeless bundles littered the ground in and around the ruins.

'Look!' Geras cried. 'Over there!'

Telemachus followed his pointing finger towards the opposite headland, to the north of the bay. A long line of timber frames had been erected there, and he felt a tingle of horror run down his spine as he saw the bodies hanging from each one. The pirates clustered on the foredeck trembled with anger at the sight, some whispering prayers that their loved ones had not suffered the same terrible fate. Others shook their fists and vowed revenge on those responsible for the attack. Telemachus looked over at Castor and saw the stricken expression in his eyes as he surveyed the scene in front of him.

'What the hell happened?' Telemachus whispered.

'We've been attacked,' Castor replied grimly.

'The Romans?'

'Who else? Those bastards must have found our base.' The pirate shook his head in despair. 'They've destroyed everything . . . it's all gone. There's nothing left.' He clamped his eyes shut and looked away, overcome with grief.

Telemachus scanned the land and then looked out to sea, searching for any sign of the enemy. But aside from the few survivors, the base looked deserted, and he guessed that the attackers must have set sail soon after destroying the pirates' hidden lair. The ship continued to draw closer, until they were only a few hundred feet from the shoreline and he could hear the faint crackle of the flames that still consumed some of the larger buildings.

Further along the foredeck, Hector looked towards Bulla, struggling to disguise his anxiety. 'What shall we do, Captain?'

Bulla was silent for a moment before replying, 'Lower the sails. Have the men unship oars and bring us up to the beach.'

The first mate glanced nervously around the surrounding bay. 'Maybe we should leave. It's not safe here.'

'I see survivors,' Bulla said, nodding at the figures a short distance up from the beach. 'I want to know what happened, and they're the only ones who can tell us. Now give the order.'

'Aye, Captain,' Hector replied grudgingly.

He stepped away from the rail and barked at the crew. Telemachus and the other deckhands were slow to respond, distracted by the horrific scene in front of them as they moved across the deck, ascending the rigging and furling the sail. At the same time, the oarsmen strained their muscles and the heavily built steersman heaved on the tiller, pointing the ship towards an empty stretch of sand, well away from the burned ships. When they were a short distance from the bay, Bulla shouted for the crew to prepare to land, and Telemachus joined the rest of the pirates clustered near the stern. *Trident* lifted for an instant as her bows grounded on the wet sand, before shuddering to a halt.

'Ship oars!' Bulla yelled. 'Lower the gangways!'

As soon as the ramps had been lowered, the captain strode down onto the beach, followed by Hector and most of the pirates, with a handful remaining on the deck to keep watch for any approaching vessels. The men moved slowly up the sand, glancing warily at the headlands either side of the shore. An acrid stench of burned flesh and charred wood choked the air as Telemachus followed the other pirates through the ruins, taking care to step around the blackened and mutilated bodies, chunks of masonry and shattered amphorae littering the streets. Several of the victims had been decapitated. Others lay in pools of dried blood, their stomachs slashed open. A few of the pirates recognised their wives and children amid the ruins and rushed over to their bloodied corpses. One picked up his dead son and cradled him in his arms, keening like a wounded beast. Telemachus looked away, a bitter fury clenching around his heart.

'Those bastards,' Castor muttered. 'Roman bastards. I know they've always hated our guts, but in all my years I've never witnessed anything like this.'

Telemachus pursed his lips. 'How did they find the place? I thought Peiratispolis was safe from Rome?'

'It was.' The quartermaster shrugged. 'The fleet must have followed one of the other pirate ships back from a raid.'

Just then a cry pierced the air, and all eyes turned to a figure staggering towards them from the direction of a nearby latrine ditch. The man's face and tunic were smeared with human waste and dirt. Blood seeped out of a deep wound to his scalp. He stumbled forward, then let out a groan as he slumped to the ground. Bulla hurried over with the rest of the party.

'Shit,' Castor whispered. 'That's Sostratus.'

Telemachus wrinkled his nose in disgust at the putrid stench clinging to the man. 'Who is he?'

'One of the traders who made his living here. Poor bastard.'

Bulla dropped to one knee beside the wounded trader. Sostratus gripped the captain's arm tightly and lifted his head, wincing with pain.

'Help me . . . please,' he croaked. 'Water.'

Bulla gestured to one of his men. 'You. Give me your canteen!'

He hastily snatched the canteen from the pirate and pulled out the stopper, then tipped Sostratus's head back and poured a trickle of water between his cracked lips. The trader groaned as he gulped down the liquid. After a few more sips he began coughing and spluttering violently. Bulla took the canteen away, handing it back to the pirate.

'Fetch the medicine chest. See what can be done for this one. Hurry!'

The pirate turned and sprinted back down the shore towards *Trident*. Bulla lowered his gaze to Sostratus, who grimaced in pain, snatching laboured breaths.

'What happened?' the captain asked.

The trader licked his lips. 'The Romans . . . they attacked us.'

Bulla exchanged a brief glance with Hector, then looked back to Sostratus. 'The Ravenna fleet? They're the ones who did this?'

Sostratus nodded feebly. 'They arrived yesterday. At dawn.' He pointed at the headland the pirates had sailed round. 'One of the lookouts spotted the warships heading directly for the bay and raised the alarm. There was no time to prepare the defences.' His voice cracked with despair. 'We rounded up our families ready to head for the hills. But as soon as we turned to flee, their soldiers appeared on the slopes and cut us off. Before we knew it, they had us trapped.'

Hector scrutinised the low forested hills further inland from the pirate lair. 'The Romans must have landed a force on the other side of the ridge there, Captain. They would have crept into position the night before and waited for the fleet to arrive.'

The pirate chief stroked his jaw, deep in thought. 'What happened then, Sostratus?'

'Some of the pirates tried to fight their way out,' the trader murmured. 'But the Romans were too numerous. Their soldiers killed many of our lads before they had a chance to grab their weapons. A few managed to slip through the enemy lines and escape into the hills, but the other survivors retreated to the marketplace.'

'Where were you in all this?'

'One of the Romans struck me on the side of the head and left me for dead. I managed to crawl into the latrine pits behind the tavern before anyone could find me.'

'Go on.'

'Once they had us surrounded, their warships anchored in the bay. Then their officers rowed ashore in a boat to address those of us who were still resisting. One of 'em said he was the new prefect of the Ravenna fleet.'

'Tribune Canis,' Telemachus growled.

Sostratus swallowed and nodded.

'What did he want?' Bulla asked.

'To make an offer.' The trader gasped as another wave of agony racked his body. 'He said he knew that Peiratispolis was a pirates' nest. That if the remaining captains and their crews in the fort agreed to surrender peacefully, then he would spare the other inhabitants. If we refused, he promised to kill every pirate and sell the rest of us into slavery.'

'What did the captains do?'

Sostratus shook his head bitterly. 'They had no choice but to accept. The Romans had our settlement surrounded. If they had resisted, they would have been crushed. Their wives and children too. The captains discussed it and agreed to the prefect's terms and laid down their arms.' He paused. 'That's when Canis gave the order. Told his men to round up the survivors and put everyone to death.'

Bulla stared at him, eyes narrowed. 'Wait. Canis ordered their executions *after* they had surrendered?'

Sostratus nodded, his brow creasing at the terrible memory. 'The pirates begged him to spare their families. But that cold-hearted bastard refused.'

'What about the other captains? Cosicas, Socleidas, Zenicetes?'

'Dead.' Sostratus bit his quivering lower lip. 'All of 'em. Their crews too, and their families. Canis spared no one the cross. The killing went on for hours. I had to listen to their screams while I hid.'

'Roman bastards!' Hector snarled, balling his hands into angry fists. 'They'll pay for this, I swear!'

Bulla kept his gaze fixed on Sostratus. 'When did they leave?'

'Last night. At dusk.'

The man issued a groan of pain, weakened from the effort of talking. Bulla stood up and stepped back, making way for the pirate who had returned with the medicine chest. The latter kneeled down and examined the trader's injuries, while Hector gazed towards the open sea.

'They can't be far from here, Captain,' he muttered.

'No.'

'What are your orders?'

Bulla considered for several moments. 'Have the men search for any more survivors among the ruins. Find whatever supplies you can and load everything onto the ship. We can't risk staying here. We'll need to establish a new base. Somewhere the Romans won't be able to find us.'

'Where, though? It took us bloody ages to discover Peiratispolis. It could be months before we find a decent anchorage.'

'It won't be easy, I agree. But we don't have a choice. Prefect Canis and his men are clearly determined to hunt us down. Whatever base we choose, we must be able to defend ourselves. Better than our brothers were able to, at least.'

'We could try heading down to Risinium,' Hector suggested. 'We'd be close to the shipping around Dyrrachium. Lots of easy vessels for us to prey on.'

Bulla shook his head firmly. 'There are very few islands down that way. It'd be too easy for a passing navy patrol to spot us. No. We'll head north towards Flanona. That's our best bet. Plenty of places to hide up there.'

'Flanona?' Hector crinkled his brow. 'Isn't that Nestor's patch, Captain?'

'Yes. What of it?'

The first mate opened his mouth to protest, but rank got the better of him and he gave a terse nod. 'Very well, Captain. Flanona it is.'

He turned away and barked orders at the pirates. Several of the crew were detailed to look for surviving friends and family, while the remainder were tasked with foraging among the ruins for any food, wine and valuables that had survived the destruction. As the pirates spread out across the smouldering remains of the base, Telemachus stared up with a growing sense of foreboding at the timber frames lining the headland. The massacre of the inhabitants of Peiratispolis had clearly shocked the crew of *Poseidon's Trident*. Canis was certainly revealing himself as a man to be reckoned with, willing to do whatever was necessary to defeat Bulla and the other pirate captains. Even if it meant the slaughter of women and children. What other horrors was the prefect of the Ravenna fleet capable of?

Geras sighed and shook his head. 'Looks like we've joined the pirates at the worst time, lad. Our base has been attacked, the other pirate ships have been destroyed, and to top it all off, that madman Canis seems determined to hunt us down.'

Telemachus looked away from the crucified pirates and nodded. 'Let's just hope we find somewhere else soon.'

'There's hundreds of miles of coastline between here and Flanona. There's got to be a good anchorage somewhere along the way.'

'I hope you're right,' Telemachus replied. 'For all our sakes. Because if you're not, it won't be long before we all end up nailed to a cross.'

CHAPTER THIRTEEN

A sharp breeze blew in from the mainland, chilling Telemachus as he gazed out to starboard. Two miles off to his right stood the rocky mountains of the Illyrian coast. Ten days had passed since the pirates had set sail from the ruins of Peiratispolis, loaded up with provisions and the handful of survivors, and the search for a new base had so far been fruitless. Each day had followed the same routine, the vessel sailing slowly along the coast while the lookout scoured the distant shoreline. Whenever a potential location was sighted, the crew would change tack and approach for a closer look. But none of the bays or inlets they had explored were suitable for their purpose. The few good landing spots were too close to the ports and colonies near Iader, and were frequently used by merchant captains to beach their vessels for the night. Others were better concealed but lacked a water supply. An island they had explored that morning had initially looked promising, but the bay had proven too narrow and difficult to navigate.

As the day wore on, the sky and sea merged into a grey mass, and some of the crew began to openly grumble about their chances of ever finding a good anchorage. Telemachus could sense a mood of deepening despair among the pirates.

At his side, Castor stared out at the horizon with a concerned expression.

'It's bloody hopeless,' he said. 'Nothing around these parts but miles of barren shore. We'll be searching for a new home until Saturnalia at this rate.'

'How much further until we reach Flanona?' Telemachus asked.

The older pirate thought it through briefly. 'Another two days from here, I'd say.'

'There's still plenty of coastline left for us to search, then.'

'A fair amount, aye. But our problem isn't running out of places to look. It's about how long we can afford to stay at sea.'

Telemachus frowned at him. 'What do you mean?'

'We're running low on provisions. We were having to get by on half-rations even before we landed at Peiratispolis. With all those extra mouths to feed, our current supplies won't go very far. I reckon we can stay at sea for another three or four days at most.'

'What happens if we haven't found anywhere by then?'

'Fuck knows, lad. The captain could decide to raid a supply ship to top up our provisions. Or he might take a risk on a poorer anchorage so that we can go back to attacking the shipping.'

'But that's madness. We can't settle for a poorly located base, surely. Not after what the Romans did to Peiratispolis.'

'He might not have much of a choice. Quite a few of the men are already pissed off at having to go this long without a decent haul of loot. They're eager to get back to some proper pirating, and Bulla might have to compromise to keep the peace.' Castor pursed his lips. 'Although there are some aboard who'd be glad to see the captain replaced.'

'Who?'

The quartermaster glanced around, then dropped his voice to a whisper. 'It's the worst-kept secret on this ship that Hector's got his eye on the top job. He might use the discontent to his advantage and put himself forward to challenge Bulla.'

A pang of anxiety ran through Telemachus. 'Would he win?'

'Hard to say. Bulla's well liked. He treats the men fairly, and he's landed some good prizes. But if our fortunes don't improve, who knows how the crew might vote?'

Telemachus looked away, troubled by the nightmarish prospect of Hector assuming command of the ship. If that happened, his career on *Poseidon's Trident* would undoubtedly be brought to a swift and brutal end, just as he was beginning to adjust to his new life as a pirate. He shook off the unsettling thought as he stared at the coastline, suddenly yearning for dry land and the simplicity of his old life. Living on the streets of Piraeus had been a hard struggle, but at least he'd never had to worry about vengeful pirates, mutinous crews or the might of the imperial Roman navy. His old enemies of hunger, cold and misery had been relatively tame by comparison. He shook his head in frustration.

'There's got to be a good base out there somewhere,' he said.

Castor merely shrugged. 'All we can do is keep searching. And pray to Poseidon that this weather holds.'

Telemachus looked at him. 'You don't think it will?'

Castor nodded at the dense bank of clouds gathering over

the hills to the east. 'At this time of year, the weather's a fickle bitch. She changes more often than the price list in an Athenian brothel.'

Sure enough, a short while later, the clouds thickened on the horizon, darkening the sky. Angry whitecaps raced across the rising swell, causing the ship to pitch and plunge, and the wind abruptly strengthened. Telemachus could feel it stirring his hair as he stood on the deck watching the storm clouds sweep towards them.

He looked at Castor. 'How long until it hits us?'

'Soon enough, lad. The only question is whether we're caught in the middle of it or not. Either way, we're in for a rough time.'

Bulla gave orders for the crew to take in some sail, while others hurried across deck, lashing down the hatches and anything that might come loose. There was a terrible shrilling as the storm closed around the ship and the wind veered round again, tilting the vessel over so far that Telemachus had to reach out and seize hold of the handrail to save himself from being thrown overboard. A cry went up from the aft deck, and he glanced over at the stern just in time to see the steersman tumbling into the foaming mass below. Sheet lightning briefly illuminated the scene, and for one terrifying moment Telemachus glimpsed the man bobbing up and down on the waves, his arms raised as he screamed frantically for his companions to rescue him. Then another wave came surging down on him, and he was lost to the sea for ever.

'Hector!' Bulla yelled, straining to make his voice heard above the howling din. 'Take the tiller! Now!'

The first mate hurried across the slippery deck, lunging forward and grabbing hold of the tiller. He braced his feet and threw his weight against the steering paddle, steadying the direction of the ship. As the vessel righted itself, the hail came on. Stones the size of lead slingshot rattled against the deck timbers, lashing every inch of exposed skin. Telemachus gripped the rail and looked out across the waves, shielding his face from the spray with his spare hand. All around him was nothing but veiled icy rain and black clouds, with no sign of the Illyrian coast. The ship had been blown away from the shoreline, he realised bitterly. Any hope of seeking shelter in a nearby cove to ride out the storm at anchor was gone. The pirates would have to run before the tempest and try to battle their way clear of it.

'Bring us about!' Bulla yelled at Hector. Then he turned to the crew. 'Hands aloft! Two reefs in the sail!'

The hail promptly turned to rain. Glinting icy drops seethed across the deck, drenching Telemachus and the other men as they reluctantly climbed the rigging, driven on by a stream of foul-mouthed invective from their captain. They moved slowly, shivering in their rain-soaked clothes as they edged out along the yardarm. On the deck below, Bulla bellowed a command, and they began drawing the sail in to the second reefing point: all they would need when running before the storm. Too much wind might snap the mast clean off, or put *Trident* at risk of capsizing. Once they had finished fastening the ties to the yard, they made their way back down to the main deck, breathing hard with exertion.

An hour later, the rain eased to a drizzle, and although the sky remained overcast, Telemachus dared to believe that they had survived the worst of the foul weather. But the respite proved only to be temporary, and the wind veered round sharply again, as if Neptune had been taunting the pirates with the brief spell of calm. The crew braced themselves as another filthy grey squall came racing across the sea towards them.

'Captain!' Castor bellowed. 'Over there!'

Bulla and the other pirates simultaneously looked towards the stern of the ship. Through the spray Telemachus caught sight of a vast wave rolling down on them, as tall as a building. Some of the crew stood frozen with fear, momentarily transfixed. Telemachus felt the deck shifting under his feet, and he looked across at Hector, battling to turn the ship away from the onrushing monster. Bulla screamed at him to bring her around to face the wave bows-on, and Telemachus immediately realised Hector's appalling error of judgement. By steering away from it, he was presenting the side of *Trident*'s hull to the full ferocity of the storm.

Bulla's cries were lost as the wave struck the side of the vessel with savage intensity. Telemachus thrust out a hand, clinging to the mainmast with all his strength as the wave surged over him, filling his throat and nose with salty water. He coughed and spluttered, gasping for breath, and when he looked up, he saw the reefed sail straining at its seams. A flash of sheet lightning silhouetted the yardarm, almost vertical against the black sky.

'The sail's holding too much wind!' Geras cried as he hung on to one of the stays. 'We're going to lose her!'

Another wave broke across the ship, washing away two more pirates. The deck was sharply canted now, *Trident* lying on her beam ends, as the first of the shrouds parted. A handful of men held on to the mast beside Telemachus, too afraid to move. Telemachus looked across at the weapons locker amidships, instantly grasping what he had to do. There was no time to consult Bulla or any of the others. Taking a deep breath, he hauled himself up the steep deck towards the locker. Tearing it open, he seized an axe from inside, slamming the door shut before the other weapons tumbled out and over the side.

The deck sloped further as the gale strengthened, and for one awful moment Telemachus feared he might lose his grip and slip away into the raging tumult. Then the moment passed and he edged along the side rail as another wave crashed against the side of *Trident*, exploding in a burst of icy spray. At last he reached the sheets fastened to the belaying pins. Raising the axe, he hacked at the ropes, the wind snatching each one away as he cut them free. The loosened sail flapped like a flock of wild birds in the gale, and the deck shuddered as *Trident* began to right herself, to cries of jubilation and relief from the pirates. Water poured out of the scuppers as the ship settled heavily.

There was no time to celebrate. With the storm continuing to blow, Bulla shouted at the pirates to replace the damaged sheets with new ropes. Several of the crew remained huddled around the mast, shocked by their narrow escape from Neptune's clutches. Bulla kicked the nearest man.

'Move!' he thundered. 'This ship won't repair herself!'

The pirates clambered to their feet and quickly set to work. A handful of the crew retrieved spare coils of rope from a locker and carried them across the deck towards the rigging. The cut ropes swirled like severed tendrils in the wind, flogging one man across the jaw as he attempted to splice the frayed ends. A few of their comrades hurriedly unfurled the small foresail attached to the bowsprit, steadying the ship's bows. At the same time, the other pirates retrieved a pair of sweep oars stowed amidships and lashed them together to replace the tiller and rudder, which had been shattered by the huge wave.

As Telemachus finished attaching one of the sheets, he saw Lasthenes staggering over to the captain from the direction of the hold, clutching the rail as the vessel continued to roll heavily.

'What is it, Lasthenes?' Bulla asked, his voice hoarse from constantly shouting above the wind.

'It's the hold, Captain,' Lasthenes replied. 'We're taking on too much water.'

'Can we bail it out?'

Lasthenes shook his head. 'The ship's riding too low in the sea. We've got to dump some of the cargo. It's our only hope.'

Bulla was silent for a moment as he grasped the full implications of the Syrian's assessment. He pressed his lips shut, refusing to let his face betray his inner torment. 'There must be some other way . . .'

'None, Captain. Some of the seams are badly strained. We can try to repair them, but it won't be easy in this weather. If we don't lighten the hold, she'll sink.'

The captain hesitated before nodding bitterly. 'Very well then. Have the men empty the cargo over the side.'

'Aye, Captain.'

Lasthenes barked an order, and every spare hand set to work. They toiled through the gloom, heaving up the sodden sacks of grain and rice stowed below deck, along with the few possessions the survivors of Peiratispolis had taken from the wreckage of their homes. With much of the cargo disposed of, and *Poseidon's Trident* at last riding higher in the sea, the crew turned their efforts to bailing out the water that swirled in the ship's hull. At the same time, a team of deckhands made temporary repairs to the damaged timbers, wedging lengths of old tarred rope into the leaking seams. Once the men had repaired the ship as best they could, Bulla yelled for the crew to sheet home, and the pirates on deck hauled on the new ropes, tying them to the belaying pins. With the reefed sail set, the stricken vessel began pulling through the storm.

A gap opened in the distant clouds, and the wind faded as the storm slowly blew itself out. A short time later the rain died away, and as the first glimmer of sunlight appeared on the horizon, Telemachus ended his shift in the hold and slumped down on the aft deck, soaking wet and exhausted from the effort of bailing out water for hours on end.

'Bloody hell. That storm almost did for us,' Geras said, sitting down to rest beside him. 'I thought we were all going to end up in a watery grave back there.'

Telemachus simply nodded, too tired to even reply. His body ached with cold and exhaustion. Geras smiled thinly at him.

'Cheer up. You did well. If it wasn't for you, this tub would have gone down, along with everyone on it.'

Telemachus stared at the distant coastline. 'We're not out of trouble yet.'

'What?' Geras frowned. 'What are you talking about?'

Telemachus nodded towards the emptied cargo hold. 'We just had to throw away the only things of value the crew still had.' He looked back to Geras and swallowed. 'This lot were already in a bad mood. What do you think they'll be like once we reach land?'

126

CHAPTER FOURTEEN

The sun burnished the peaks of the distant mountains as *Poseidon's Trident* limped towards the coastline the following morning. As she drew nearer, the pirates slumped to the deck, overcome with tiredness. They had been working throughout the night to bail out the ship's hull, but despite their best efforts the craft had continued to take on water, slowing her to a crawl as she wallowed north on the gentle swell. Biting back his frustration, Bulla had finally decided to seek shelter so that repairs could be made to his stricken vessel. As dawn broke, he gave the command to take in the sail and use the sweep oars, and the ship drove sluggishly through the waves towards an isolated cove away from the major trade routes.

Bulla turned to Hector and indicated a strip of shingle where the cliffs curved round. Beyond the beach, there was a thin belt of pine trees before the land rose steeply towards a range of barren, unforgiving mountains.

'Steer over there,' he said. 'Have the men make the necessary repairs as soon as we land. If we drive them hard then we should be able to set sail again in another day or two.'

'What'll we do then, Captain?'

'Continue on to Flanona, of course.'

'Flanona?' Hector spluttered, looking at Bulla with a startled expression. 'But we've been searching these waters for days without finding a decent anchorage. Perhaps we'd be better off trying our luck elsewhere. I hear the Euxine Sea has some good hunting grounds.'

Bulla rounded on him abruptly. 'Are you questioning my authority, Hector?'

'No, Captain. Of course not.' Hector shrugged. 'Just saying. Maybe it's time for a change of plan, is all. The lads have gone a good while without getting any loot.'

'Tough,' Bulla snapped. 'If the men have to suffer some temporary hardship, then so be it. The future of this crew relies on us finding somewhere safe to establish a new base. Somewhere we can hide from the Romans. We will continue searching until we've tracked down a suitable location. Am I clear?'

'Aye, Captain,' Hector replied through gritted teeth.

'Good. Glad to hear it.' Bulla straightened his back. 'Now let's beach the bloody ship!'

Hector turned away and glowered at the pirates standing idly beside the mast. 'You heard the captain! Get a move on!'

The crew went about their duties in grim, weary silence as *Trident* edged around the corner of the bay and crept towards the wide beach. Hector bellowed a command, and the men shipped oars and clustered near the stern as they made their final approach. The keel lurched as it grounded, then the pirates jumped into the shallows and came ashore, trudging up the loose shingle. They immediately slumped down to rest, weakened by the long hours they had spent labouring to save the ship. But there was no time to waste, and Bulla immediately ordered a foraging party to cut wood for the fires. Hector and the other pirates were detailed to remove the remaining cargo from the hold and carry out a thorough inspection of the ship.

'Castor!' Bulla shouted, marching over to the quartermaster. In stark contrast to the rest of the crew, the pirate chief displayed no signs of exhaustion.

'Captain?'

'We need rations,' Bulla said. 'Lower the ship's boat and catch us some fish.' He nodded at Telemachus. 'Take some of the new lads with you as well.' He turned and strode further along the beach to consult with the ship's carpenter.

Castor shouted for the recruits to retrieve the casting nets, gutting knives and woven baskets from the stores.

'Wonderful,' Geras muttered under his breath. 'Just when I was looking forward to putting my feet up, we're off on a fishing expedition. Why is it always us that get the shit jobs?'

Telemachus shrugged but offered no reply. Privately, however, he was grateful for the diversion. A journey out across the bay at least meant that he could avoid Hector and his tireless bullying for a while longer.

'Maybe it'll give us a chance to escape,' Nearchus said in a low voice. 'We can make a run for it, once we're out of sight.'

Leitus laughed drily. 'I doubt it, lad. They'll be watching us carefully until they can be sure of our loyalty. Besides, even if we could get away, where would we go?'

'There must be settlements not far from here, colonies . . .'

'And what will you say when someone catches sight of that?' Leitus responded, tipping his head at the branding on Nearchus's forearm. 'We're bloody marked, lad. All of us. As soon as anyone sees that, you're as good as dead.'

'We could explain,' Nearchus said falteringly. 'Tell them we were kidnapped.'

'Good luck finding a sympathetic ear. Face it, we're stuck with Bulla and his mob whether we like it or not. All we can do is make the best of it and do our jobs. It's either that or spend the rest of our days in the shadows, hiding in some gods-forsaken corner of the Empire.'

'Sod it.' Geras climbed to his feet. 'Let's get moving. If we leave now, we might get back before this lot finish what's left of the wine.'

The boat was lowered over the side of *Trident*'s beached hull into the water, and Telemachus and his fellow recruits, along with Castor and a pair of thickset pirates, ran it out into the gentle surf. The sun continued to shine above the serrated mountain peaks as the men climbed aboard and took up the oars, propelling the boat out of the bay. Leitus worked the tiller, steering the boat around the point.

'We should find some decent fishing grounds over there,' Castor was saying, pointing out a low rocky headland two miles further along the coast. 'We'll cast there and catch what we can, then head back. But we'll have to make it quick.'

'Why's that?' Telemachus asked.

'There are a few villages scattered around these parts. We don't want to run into any of the locals if we can help it, in case they pass on word of our presence to the imperial navy.'

'Why would they do that? I thought the Romans were hated around here.'

'They are. But the locals fear the pirates more. Especially since Nestor and his gang took to preying on the shipping.'

'Nestor?' Telemachus asked. 'He's around here?'

Castor nodded uneasily. 'He's got a base somewhere in

these parts. Or so I've heard. Either way, I'd prefer not to run into him. The man's a cold-blooded killer. I'd rather face a sea monster than his mob.'

A familiar cold chill rippled down Telemachus's spine as he recalled the tales he'd heard about Nestor and his gang and the terror they inspired among the other pirates. He prayed fervently that he would never cross the path of Captain Nestor and his men.

Geras sighed. 'The sooner the captain finds us somewhere safe, the better. Personally, I'm looking forward to the day we can stop worrying about Prefect Canis.'

Telemachus pursed his lips. 'I wouldn't get your hopes up. I don't think a new home is going to solve our problems.'

'What makes you think that?'

'Wherever we go, the Romans are still going to be looking for us. We might be safe for a while, perhaps. But sooner or later we're going to have to deal with Canis.'

'Bollocks. His men have just razed our old home to the ground. Now that he's given us a good kicking, he'll piss off back to Ravenna.'

'Maybe,' Telemachus replied doubtfully. 'But I don't think he's going to stop until he's finished the job. He'll have questioned the prisoners at Peiratispolis before he killed them. He'll know that we're still operating in the Adriaticum. Which means he'll send out his squadron to look for us.'

'Let him,' Geras said. 'That high-born fool will have a hard time locating our new base, wherever we end up.'

'And what if he finds us before then? What if we run into his fleet before we can settle on a new base?'

Geras stared at his companion with widened eyes. 'By the gods, you know how to darken the mood, lad. Here we are, having just escaped a bloody horrid storm, and all you can think about is how long we've got left until Canis rounds us up and butchers us. I think you need a drink more than I do, for once.'

An hour later, the skiff rounded the headland, revealing a cove sheltered by a reef on the far side. Leitus guided the craft towards the shallows, and the pirates eased off the oars and set to work. Casting nets were thrown over the side, then closed around the catch and hauled in by the most experienced sailors among the crew. The wriggling silver fish were tossed into baskets to be brought ashore for the recruits to gut before the catch spoiled.

The sun shone brightly above the cove as Telemachus sliced open the bellies of the fish with a gutting knife, tossing the entrails to one side before placing the fish in a basket. As the sun beat down, the rancid stench quickly filled his nostrils, and he found himself longing to be back aboard *Trident*, emptying out the bilges.

'A bloody fishing trip,' Geras muttered. 'So much for the life of a pirate. All we've done since we've joined the crew is cook, clean and toil away like slaves.'

Telemachus nodded in agreement. 'Hopefully it won't be long before we take our place alongside the rest of the crew.'

'Not unless our luck changes and Bulla finds us a base. At this rate we'll be scrubbing and fishing for the rest of the sailing season.'

'Maybe that's for the best,' Leitus put in.

Telemachus looked enquiringly at the grizzled sailor. 'How do you mean?'

Leitus shrugged. 'It's not the worst idea for us to stay away from raiding the sea lanes for a while. What with Canis and his squadrons out looking for us, we might be better off lying low until things calm down.'

'I'll drink to that,' Geras said. 'Frankly, I'd be happy if we didn't put back to sea for a few months.'

'Why did you take the oath, then?' Telemachus asked.

'To get rich and drunk, of course. What other reason is there? Besides, we had no choice. If we'd refused, Bulla would've killed us or sold us into slavery. And I'd rather be dead than a slave.' He hesitated and glanced at Telemachus. 'Shit. Sorry. I didn't mean that.'

Telemachus fell quiet for a moment as his thoughts turned to his older brother. He remembered the last time he'd seen Nereus alive, the day the debt collector had arrived with his bodyguards to seize their late father's property and sell his sons into slavery. Unless he could find the money to buy his brother's freedom soon, he feared that Nereus would die at his master's hands at the forge in Thorikos.

'Don't worry, lad,' Geras added. 'I'm sure we'll be hunting for prizes again soon enough. You'll have saved up enough to pay off that Roman bastard Burrus in no time.'

Telemachus looked at his companion. 'I thought you weren't keen on going back to sea?'

'It ain't the sea that bothers me. It's running into those bloody Romans. But I could do with some extra coin myself. I plan on getting well and truly pissed once things have settled down, and all that wine isn't going to pay for itself.'

Telemachus forced a smile. 'Do you ever think about anything else? Other than wine, women and yourself?'

Geras shrugged. 'What else is there?'

Just then a cry went up from one of the pirates. Telemachus looked up at the entrance to the cove, shading his eyes against the sun. A small fishing boat was approaching. Several figures sat in it, rowing and craning their necks as they scrutinised the men on the shore. Others gripped fishing spears and casting nets. Telemachus joined the rest of the pirates as they gathered on the surf and watched the boat.

'Seems we're not alone,' Geras muttered.

'Fishermen?' Telemachus wondered aloud.

'What else could they be, in these waters? Wherever they're from, it can't be far away.'

A shout carried across the cove as one of the figures called out to the pirates. His companions stopped rowing as they stared towards the shore.

'What should we do?' Telemachus asked.

'Keep calm, boys,' Castor replied grimly. 'We'll just say we're from a cargo ship in the next bay. Give 'em a friendly smile. Find out who they are.'

'What if they're hostile?'

'Then we'll have to deal with them.' He tensed his jaw as he turned to the others. 'Keep your weapons close by. Stay on guard. If any of them get hostile, cut 'em down. Don't give them a chance to attack first.'

The men looked on in nervous silence as the other boat rowed towards the shore. Telemachus stood next to the beached skiff, watching the figures intently. Close up, they didn't look much like fishermen. They had the muscular, sunburned physique of experienced sailors, and the scars on their faces and arms suggested they had seen combat. Some rested their hands on the handles of their knives, as if expecting trouble.

'Greetings, friends!' Castor called out as the figures beached their boat a short distance from the skiff and jumped down into the surf.

The nearest figure threw up a hand and signalled for his companions to stay back. He stepped forward and inspected the pirates, his dark eyes narrowed in suspicion. Telemachus noticed that he had a tear-shaped pink scar on his left cheek.

'Who are you?' the man rasped in Greek.

Castor cleared his throat. 'We don't mean any harm,' he said in a light-hearted voice. 'Our ship was in a storm last night. She's beached nearby. We're just here to catch some fish, that's all.'

'What ship is that?' the man demanded. He caught sight of the brand on Telemachus's forearm and a look of alarm flashed across his face. 'Hang on. I recognise that mark. You're from *Poseidon's Trident*. Captain Bulla's ship.'

Telemachus exchanged a look with Geras before turning back to the man with the scarred face. 'Seems our reputation goes ahead of us.'

'How do you know about our ship?' asked Castor.

The man ignored the question. 'Where's the rest of your crew?'

'Not far from here. Close enough.'

'Is that so?' The man's lips twisted into a thin smile. 'Funny. I don't recall our captain giving permission for anyone else to fish here.'

'Permission?'

The man nodded at the surrounding cove. 'These waters belong to us. No one's allowed here without Captain Nestor knowing about it.'

Telemachus froze. 'Nestor . . .'

The scarred figure took a step closer, his companions closing ranks around him. He raised his gutting knife and bared his teeth.

'You're trespassing. Now get out of here, and tell your captain to fuck off, if he knows what's good for him.'

Castor lowered to a crouch, as if preparing to attack. Around him the other men reached for their blades. The scarred pirate glanced sidelong at his companions. There was a beat before he growled, 'Get 'em, lads!'

The two sides fell upon each other in a frenzied blur of thrusts and stabs. Telemachus stumbled backwards as the scarred pirate lunged at him. He narrowly avoided the attack, then stepped to the side and thrust at his opponent, aiming for the throat. As the pirate moved to parry the blow, Telemachus swung out with his free arm, striking the other man just below the ribs. But the blow failed to wind the pirate and he snarled in rage, lashing out at the youth before the latter could attack again, forcing him to retreat several paces. All around him he could hear the clinking clash and scrape of blades as the crew of *Poseidon's Trident* stood their ground, and the air was quickly filled with the desperate grunts of men fighting for their lives.

'Bastard!' the pirate growled. 'You're dead!'

With an angry roar, he threw himself at Telemachus, slashing wildly. The man was deceptively fast, in spite of his heavy physique, almost catching Telemachus with a vicious jab. Quick as lightning, Telemachus shifted his weight to the left before stepping into his opponent and swinging up with his free hand, balled into a fist. There was a bone-shattering crunch as he caught the man on the bridge of his nose, momentarily stunning him. The pirate stumbled back, and Telemachus lunged forward before his opponent could react, driving the blade up into the soft skin under the man's chin. The pirate grunted, his whole body squirming as the blade was forced up into his skull. Telemachus wrenched the knife free with a gurgling wet hiss, and the man's slack body toppled into the surf, blood mixing with the foaming waters.

He heard a shout, and spun to his left just in time to see a squat, bearded pirate thrusting a fishing spear at him, driving the tip at his chest. He jerked to the side, narrowly avoiding the blow as he glanced round. Across the shoreline, several bodies writhed on the sand and in the surf, most from the other boat. The determination of *Trident*'s crew had taken their opponents by surprise, and the few of Nestor's men that remained now found themselves outnumbered as the tide of battle turned against them. Telemachus snapped his eyes back to the spearman as the latter thrust again. This time he ducked low and stabbed out, trying to land a blow on the pirate's vitals. But the greater range of his opponent's weapon made it impossible to get close enough to land an attack, and in the next instant the pirate swung his spear around, striking Telemachus in the midriff with the wooden butt. The young Greek gasped, and before he could recover, the spearman attacked again, clubbing him across the jaw. The blow stunned him and sent him crashing to the sand. He tasted blood in his mouth, and looked up to see the pirate bearing down on him, eyes glowing with triumph as he prepared to make his kill.

'Got you now, scum!' Nestor's man drove the barbed spear tip towards his downed opponent. Telemachus writhed to one side and kicked out, slamming the hard ridge of his foot against the back of the spearman's heel. The man let out a surprised cry and fell clumsily forward, the fishing spear tumbling from his grip as he landed on the sand face-first. Telemachus sprang to his feet and kicked the man in the ribs before he could grab his weapon, then pressed down on his opponent's back with his knee, pinning him to the ground.

The pirate struggled, flailing in a futile attempt to free himself. Telemachus grabbed a clump of the man's hair and raised his knife arm, shaping to plunge the blade into the nape of his exposed neck.

'Don't!' Castor yelled. 'Leave him!'

Telemachus froze. He was suddenly aware that the sounds of the skirmish had died out, and as he looked up, he saw that the last few enemies had been cut down, the blood flowing freely from their wounds. Rage flared up inside him as he glimpsed the bodies of two of his comrades slumped on the sand. Their victory had come at a cost, then. He glanced over at Castor as the latter stepped forward, drops of sweat glistening on his shaven head.

'We need this one alive,' the quartermaster said between snatches of breath.

'What for?' Telemachus demanded.

'He can tell us about Nestor's lair. Has to be close by.'

Telemachus held the blade still for a moment, the blood boiling in his veins. He wanted nothing more than to drive the point into the spearman's neck and avenge his slaughtered companions. But then reason took over and he stood up, stepping away from the injured pirate. Two of the surviving men from *Trident*'s crew rushed over and hauled the man to his feet.

'Should we question him now?' Telemachus asked.

Castor shook his head. 'Put him on the boat with the fish. Captain Bulla will want to interrogate him right away.'

CHAPTER FIFTEEN

'I think he's ready now, Captain,' Castor said as he stepped back from the battered prisoner.

Telemachus watched from a corner of the cargo hold as Bulla lowered his gaze to the captured pirate and smiled. After taking the man prisoner, Telemachus and the other pirates had returned to the bay in a mood of quiet relief at having survived the brutal skirmish. As soon as they had run the small craft ashore, the baskets of silver fish were unloaded and Bulla had ordered Castor and Telemachus to bring the captive aboard *Trident* for questioning. A space had been cleared in a section of the cargo. The prisoner's wrists were bound with a length of coarse rope, with one end fastened to an iron ring fixed to the top of one of the ship's ribs. The man had resisted at first, but a few sharp blows to the face and chest had quickly subdued him. Once he had been secured, Bulla arrived with Hector and a tough-looking mate from the crew to begin the interrogation. An oil lamp had been lit and placed in one corner of the hold, bathing the captive's bruised features in a wan orange glow.

'Excellent work, Castor,' Bulla said. 'You've done well. Catch of the day. I think I'll take it from here.'

Castor nodded. 'I could rough him up a bit more, Captain? Loosen his tongue.'

'That won't be necessary. I think we can skip the pleasantries and go straight to the torture.'

A look of alarm registered on the prisoner's face. Bulla turned away from him and waved across the pirate standing next to Hector. The short, muscular man stepped forward, cracking his scarred knuckles.

'This is Sciron,' Bulla explained. 'He's something of an expert in pain. He takes great pride in his work. He has been known to keep a man alive for days in a state of unimaginable suffering. By the time he's finished with you, you'll be crying like a baby.'

The prisoner glared at the pirate chief. 'If you know what's good for you, you'll let me go while you still have the chance. Before my friends come looking for me. You won't get anything out of me. I won't talk.'

'Who said anything about talking?' Bulla smiled thinly. 'We haven't even asked you a question yet.'

There was a brief glimmer of fear in the prisoner's eyes. Then he tensed his muscles and his expression hardened. 'You're a fucking dead man. You and the rest of your crew.'

Bulla's lips curved upwards in a slight smile. 'Bravado. Always a good quality in a pirate. I'm going to enjoy this. You may begin, Sciron.'

The interrogator approached the prisoner, grinning. Without saying a word, he wound up his arm, clenched his huge hand into a fist and punched the man hard in the guts. The prisoner groaned and leaned forward, gasping in agony. Sciron struck him again before he could catch his breath, slamming his knuckles into the pirate's nose with such force that his head snapped back and struck the timber rib with a dull thud.

Telemachus looked on with a mix of horror and fascination as Sciron proceeded to lay into the prisoner with a series of vicious punches. The man said nothing as he endured the savage beating. There was no begging for mercy, no pleading with his captors to stop. He simply clamped his jaws shut on muted groans of pain.

At last Bulla cleared his throat and ordered the interrogator to step back. The prisoner took shallow breaths as he lifted his battered face to the captain. His left eye had swollen shut, and a gout of blood and snot bubbled above his cut upper lip. He spat out blood and glared at Bulla, his bruised features twisted with rage.

'Might be an idea to start talking now,' the captain suggested. 'Or do you wish Sciron to take out his fine collection of tools?'

'You'll pay for this,' the prisoner sneered. 'Once Captain Nestor finds out what you've done, you're finished. He'll track you down . . . kill you all.'

Bulla gave a dry laugh. 'I sincerely doubt it. Consider your predicament. Your comrades are all dead, and it'll be some time before your captain realises you're missing. By then we shall be gone, and it will be too late for you. Far too late. You can continue to suffer, if you prefer. Or you can spare yourself further agony. All you have to do is tell us what we need to know.'

'Like what?' The pirate scowled. 'I can't tell you anything useful.'

'Yes you can. According to what you told my men, Captain Nestor's crew is based somewhere close to here. Somewhere well hidden, presumably, since I can't recall sighting a pirate base during the many voyages I've made through these waters. As it happens, our home was recently attacked by the Romans, and we're in need of a safe new anchorage. Yours would do nicely. And you're going to tell me exactly where to find it.'

The prisoner smiled, revealing a row of broken, bloodstained teeth. 'You're a fool. Nestor would never agree to share our base with you. There's barely enough plunder on the trade routes for us as it is.'

'Oh, but I don't plan on sharing the base. No, I've got a much better idea. We're going to seize your lair for ourselves, once you tell me where to look. I want to know how many ships Nestor has under his command. How many men, how well defended his base is. Everything I need to crush him when my crew attacks. Answer my questions, and you have my word that I'll spare your life. And maybe let you join my crew afterwards. I can always use good men. Refuse, and there will be no end to the torment that Sciron will heap on you. The choice is yours.'

'Fuck you!' The prisoner spat on the floor, defiance blazing in his wild eyes.

Bulla chuckled. 'Hardly original, but I admire the sentiment. Pity. You would have made a useful addition to my crew.' He nodded at the squat pirate to his right. 'He's all yours, Sciron. Do your worst. No point holding back with this one. He's got some balls. For now, anyway . . .'

For the next hour, the ship's hold was filled with the agonised cries of the prisoner as Sciron went about his work. After administering a thorough beating with his fists, he unwrapped a set of tools and proceeded to subject the man to a series of horrific tortures, striking him with a studded club and tearing out chunks of flesh with a small iron hook. When that failed, he resorted to cutting off one of the pirate's toes with a knife. Telemachus felt a grudging sense of respect for the man in spite of his loyalties. Clearly those under Nestor's command were willing to die for one another. Even if Bulla did eventually learn of the whereabouts of their lair, seizing it would present a formidable challenge.

Finally, the prisoner broke down in tearful sobs as Sciron prepared to saw off his fingers. 'Please . . . no more,' he gasped. 'I beg you . . .'

Bulla raised a hand and moved forward. 'Just give me the word, friend. Tell me what you know, and your torture will come to an end. Surely you can see that this refusal to help us is pointless? We'll find out what you know one way or another. You will talk. It's simply a question of how much pain you wish to endure before that moment.'

The prisoner made a low keening noise, torn between betraying his comrades and the dread of suffering further agony at the hands of his interrogator.

'Why should I tell you anything? You'll kill me anyway.'

'Not at all,' Bulla replied flatly. 'If you give up the location of Nestor's lair, your life will be spared. You have my word. Now, tell me what I want to know. Or I'll have Sciron go back to work, if you prefer . . .'

The sight of the interrogator brandishing his bloodied knife finally broke the prisoner's crumbling resolve. He looked up at Bulla with pleading eyes, tears running down his cheeks. 'No! Don't! I'll talk . . .'

'Good. Now we're finally getting somewhere.' Bulla smiled and nodded at Sciron to stand down. The latter made no attempt to hide his disappointment as he stepped away from the prisoner. 'Fetch the map from my cabin,' Bulla ordered his cabin boy.

The boy, several years younger than Telemachus, hurried off towards the aft cabin. Bulla swung his gaze back to the prisoner.

'Now, tell me where Nestor's base is. But know this. If I discover that you're lying to me, or holding anything back, I'll have my men rip you to pieces. They'll cut off the rest of your fingers and toes, and then your balls. By the time they're finished with you, you'll be begging for death. But it'll take you days to die. Understood?'

The prisoner stared back, then swallowed and nodded.

'Petrapylae,' he croaked. 'Our base is at Petrapylae.'

'The Gates of Stone?' Bulla creased his brow. 'That can't be right. I'd heard there was a well-defended trading post there.'

'There was,' the prisoner replied. 'The militia garrison, along with most of the locals, left years ago, after the crops failed. We took over the port several months back. One of the hostages from a ship we raided said he was a merchant based there. He agreed to open the gate for us if we would spare the lives of his family. We captured the port, took over the citadel and recruited every man who knew how to use a sword.'

'I imagine the townspeople aren't too pleased about that.'

'Doesn't matter,' the prisoner said. 'Nestor rules them with an iron fist. He's started taxing the local traders, taking a share of their profits, and letting the lads help themselves to food and drink from the wine shops.'

Bulla frowned. 'And the locals simply accepted that, without complaint?'

'A few of 'em defied us at first, but Nestor had them put to death. Their families too. Took them up to the cliffs and had them thrown off, one by one, while the rest of the locals looked on. Everyone else was too afraid to defy him after that.' The captive groaned and lowered his head, overcome with exhaustion.

A few moments later, the cabin boy returned carrying a goatskin map. Bulla took it from him and paced over to the stack of storage chests at the side of the hold, unfurling the parchment on the surface. Hector and the other pirates moved in for a closer look, squinting in the gloom of the hold.

'Here. Petrapylae.' Bulla tapped a finger on a point not far from their present anchorage. 'Well, Nestor's certainly picked a good location for his lair. It's close enough to the major shipping routes, but well concealed. Mountains on all sides, and a narrow entrance. The Romans would never be able to surprise us there.' He shook his head in amazement. 'We must have passed the entrance to that bay dozens of times without ever sighting it. The perfect base, right under our noses.'

Hector furrowed his brow. 'If it's actually there, Captain. What if the prisoner is lying to us to protect his mates?'

Bulla considered for a beat. 'No. This is the only suitable location on this stretch of the coast. Anywhere else would be too far away from the trade routes. This has to be the place. The question is, how are we going to take it?'

He turned away and approached the prisoner. Blood dripped from the man's chin, forming a sticky pool on the timber planking. Bulla reached down and grabbed a clump of his hair, lifting his head.

'This lair of yours. How well defended is it?'

The captured pirate winced. 'There's a citadel,' he replied weakly. 'That's where Nestor has his quarters. He has a few bolt-throwers. His lookouts will see your ship coming . . . raise the alarm. Your ship will be sunk before you can reach the bay.'

'What about ships and men? How many does Nestor have?'

'Two . . . I mean, three. Nestor has three ships . . . His own flagship, plus two other crews who have agreed to sail with him. Full complement on each crew. Three hundred of us in all.'

'Three hundred?' Hector's eyes widened in alarm. 'Our lads are tough, but we'd never be able to beat those odds.'

Bulla ignored him and stared levelly at the prisoner. 'Why did you say two ships? Answer truthfully now, or you can forget about my promise to let you live.'

The man hesitated and closed his eyes briefly. 'One of the ships is away,' he said. '*Achelous*. Captain Peleus's ship. She's spent the past month raiding the coast down near Agruvium.'

'When is she due back?'

'A few days from now.' He lowered his head, too tired and battered to go on.

Bulla told the cabin boy to fetch bread and water, and gave orders for another pirate to bring the medicine chest. The prisoner would be watched over until he had recovered – *if* he recovered – and then he would be pressed into joining *Trident*'s crew. As the pirates helped the man down from the timber ribs, Castor cleared his throat and turned to the captain, rubbing his jaw.

'How are we going to defeat Nestor? We're badly outnumbered, Captain.'

Bulla stood up and looked towards his crew. 'There may be a way. *Achelous* is currently out at sea. That cuts the odds against us. We must strike now, while the citadel is under-strength. If we can find a way of surprising the two remaining crews, we can overrun them and claim Petrapylae for ourselves.'

'We'd still have to deal with the locals, Captain. They might not welcome us as their new rulers.'

'Perhaps. But if they're as unhappy as our prisoner suggests, they'll be grateful to us for getting rid of Nestor.'

Hector sucked the air between his teeth as he considered the map. 'Even so, it's going to be a bastard to take that position. Unless we tried climbing over the mountains and sneak down on the citadel.'

'Out of the question,' Bulla replied. 'I've passed those mountains before. They're too steep for our men to climb. No. We'll have to make our approach from the sea.'

'But how?' asked Castor. 'Nestor's lookouts will sight us as soon as we round the headland. That'll give him plenty of time to hit us with his bolt-throwers. We'd never make it to the shore.'

'What if we went in under cover of darkness?' Hector suggested.

Bulla shook his head. 'Too risky. There are rocky outcrops all along that stretch of the coast. We'd run aground on the shoals before we could attack, and that still leaves us with the problem of how to get into the citadel itself. No, there must be some other way to make our approach.'

Telemachus stared thoughtfully at the map. As he did so, the kernel of a plan began to take shape in his mind. It was not without certain risks, but it might allow the pirates to sneak into the citadel without raising the alarm. He cleared his throat.

'Captain?'

'Yes?' Bulla snapped irritably. 'What is it?'

Telemachus hesitated to reply. He knew that he was speaking out of turn. A young recruit had no business offering advice to his captain, and any plan he shared was likely to be dismissed out of hand. But then he remembered how he'd tried to warn Clemestes not to sail into the Adriaticum, during his time aboard *Selene*. The merchantman's captain had ignored Telemachus, and ultimately paid for his mistake with his life. He took a deep breath and decided to speak up.

'There might be another way for us to get to the citadel, Captain.'

'No one asked for your opinion, boy,' Hector snarled. 'Shut your mouth and leave the planning to us.'

Bulla raised a hand and stared curiously at the youth. 'No, I think we should hear him out.'

'Him?' Hector responded with a sneer. 'He's just a fucking recruit. What does he know about landing raids, or storming fortifications?'

'I'm not sure. But I know one thing. The lad's shown himself to be a shrewd thinker. Or have you already forgotten how he saved us during that storm?'

The first mate's nostrils flared with anger. Bulla turned away from him and nodded at Telemachus. 'Right then. Let's hear your plan. But it had better be good.'

Telemachus nodded eagerly. 'It's this third ship, Captain. The one that's out at sea right now.'

'*Achelous*. What of it?'

'The prisoner says Nestor will be expecting her to return in a few days' time. But what if she comes back early?'

Bulla scratched his cheek. 'She might . . . If her crew finds a good prize, she might return sooner than expected. Which could cause us problems.'

Telemachus gave a crafty smile. 'Then let's hope she doesn't come back early, sir.'

'What do you mean?'

'I think I might have a way of getting into the base without alerting the enemy. But first, we'll need to know exactly what *Achelous* looks like . . .'

CHAPTER SIXTEEN

'We should have sight of Nestor's base soon,' Castor said as he gazed out beyond the ship's bows.

Telemachus stood on the deck alongside his companion, the gentle breeze caressing his cheeks as *Poseidon's Trident* crept towards the shore. Ahead of them stood a long, narrow inlet with a forbidding mountain located opposite. According to the intelligence they had gleaned from the prisoner, the enemy lair was at the base of the mountain, on the other side of the headland.

'This plan of yours had better work, lad,' Castor went on. 'For all our sakes.'

'It will,' Telemachus insisted. 'You'll see.'

'Let's hope you're right. Because if Nestor's men see through our ruse, we're well and truly in the shit.'

Telemachus nodded tersely as he glanced around the deck of the ship. For the past two days the crew had been working hard aboard *Poseidon's Trident*, making the necessary changes so she could pass for *Achelous*. Bulla had seen the vessel before, during a voyage to Lissus, and together with the information given to them by the prisoner, they had made several alterations to *Trident's* rigging and sails. A close inspection of the vessel would fool no one, but Bulla had judged the likeness close enough to deceive the lookouts at the citadel, at least from a distance. After making their final preparations, the crew had left their anchorage at dawn. They had spent the past several hours crawling down the coastline of Illyricum, rounding the entrance to the inlet shortly before noon. Now they were approaching the lair at Petrapylae.

Only a handful of the pirates stood on the main deck. The rest of the crew were hidden away in the cramped hold, playing the role of prisoners. They were joined by a few survivors from Peiratispolis who had recovered from their injuries and were capable of wielding a blade. Lowering his gaze to the hatch coaming, Telemachus could see Geras and Leitus below deck amid a sea of tense faces, dressed in filthy rags and secured to one another by their ankles and wrists. Their chains were fastened with slim dowelling that could be broken in an instant. He smiled in satisfaction at their dishevelled appearance and reflected on his plan.

Once *Trident* had passed the lookout station, she would raise *Achelous*'s colours and make for the bay, grounding on the shoreline as close to the pirates' base as possible. As soon as they had landed, Telemachus and the others on deck would march the prisoners out of the hold and up the beach towards the enemy citadel. Several slave dealers were known to operate out of Petrapylae, according to the prisoner, and the sight of *Achelous*'s crew escorting a fresh batch of captured sailors into the citadel wouldn't arouse any suspicion. Once inside, Bulla would give the order and the prisoners would break out of their chains, seize the daggers concealed beneath their tunics and head for Nestor's quarters. Any pirates who resisted would be killed. The rest would be taken prisoner and given a choice between death and swearing an oath of loyalty to Bulla and his ship. Once they had captured Petrapylae, Bulla and his men could begin hunting prey again. With a few sizeable hauls, Telemachus might be able to purchase his brother's freedom sooner than he'd imagined.

But the plan was not without its risks, he reminded himself. If the deception failed before *Trident* reached the shore, the enemy would have plenty of time to prepare their defences. Even if the crew did manage to land and slip past the sentries, they still had to get inside the citadel and kill as many of the enemy as possible before the alarm was raised. What if one of the guards at the gatehouse saw through their ruse and alerted his comrades? Telemachus grimaced at the thought. Without the element of surprise, *Trident's* men would be swiftly cut down by the enemy. Nestor would be unlikely to show any mercy to his vanquished opponents. Those unfortunate enough to be captured alive would be sold into slavery, or else subjected to horrific torture before being given the mercy of death.

A shout went up from one of the crew, and all eyes on deck looked towards the small fort atop the cliff. A ripping flash of colour appeared above the lookout station as a signal flag was raised on the mast.

'Lookout must be signalling the citadel,' Hector growled.

Bulla squinted at the distant pennant. 'Yellow. That's the signal that a vessel's approaching, isn't it?'

Telemachus nodded. 'That's what the prisoner told us, Captain.'

'Unless the bastard's lying,' Hector said. 'Then we'll be sailing straight into a trap.'

The sun continued to shine in the clear afternoon sky as *Trident* approached the headland, her sail set at an angle to take advantage of the following wind. Bulla had decided against using his oarsmen under sail, not wanting to risk tiring out his men before they reached the bay, and there was an unnerving delay before the vessel rounded the headland. At last they cleared the point, and Telemachus and the other spare hands on deck lined the side rail as the pirates' lair eased into view. A mass of rock thrust out from the foot of the mountain, linked to the beach by a gravel causeway. At the end of the rocky promontory stood a fortified settlement, flanked by steep cliffs and surrounded by a crumbling masonry wall. A defensive ditch and timber gatehouse guarded the landward approach. Behind the wall Telemachus spied a cluster of rooftops lining the gentle slope, rising up to a stone-built keep overlooking the bay.

'Seems the prisoner was right,' Castor said, a note of trepidation in his voice. 'This place is bloody well defended.'

Telemachus nodded, noting the catapults mounted on platforms above the wall. 'Nestor's not taking any chances. One thing's for sure, though. It'll make a fine base for us.'

Castor grunted. 'If we can seize it.'

Lowering his gaze, Telemachus spotted a sleek-looking galley riding at anchor in the calm waters below the citadel, and from the information the prisoner had given them he realised he was looking at Nestor's flagship, *Proteus*. A much smaller vessel had been rolled on to its side on the beach, supported by sturdy timbers. Several tiny figures moved around it, applying a fresh coating of pitch to the hull. Further up from the beach Telemachus noticed a scattering of huts and several small fishing boats. The scene looked peaceful enough, and the handful of pirates on the beach took no notice of *Trident* as she glided across the water.

'Captain!' Castor cried. 'Look there!'

Telemachus followed the direction of the quartermaster's gaze and looked towards the citadel. A dark oily smudge rose above the keep, followed by a trickle of smoke swirling into the cloudless sky.

'Incendiaries,' Hector growled. 'I fucking knew it. They've rumbled us! We've got to turn around, Captain!'

'Hold your nerve, blast you!' Bulla snapped. 'They're not going to shoot. Not yet. They haven't challenged us.'

Several moments later, there was a shout from one of the crew as he thrust an arm out, and the men on deck turned in the direction indicated, towards the small fort at the top of the headland. As Telemachus looked on, the pennant dipped, and a second, dark-coloured flag was quickly hoisted in its place. Bulla tensed his jaw and stiffened.

'Right. That's the signal to identify ourselves.' He turned to Telemachus. 'Get the pennant up!'

Telemachus hurried over with Geras to the storage locker at the stern and retrieved the pile of green linen. They carried it over to the rigging and worked quickly, attaching the toggles on the end of the pennant to the newly repaired sheets before they hoisted it up the mast. The pennant lifted in the breeze, rippling out above the spar like a green tongue. If the prisoner's intelligence was correct, it would identify the vessel to the citadel as *Achelous*, signifying her return from a successful raid, and the pirates manning the incendiaries would be ordered to stand down.

'Pray to the gods that it works, Captain,' Hector muttered.

'We'll find out soon enough,' Bulla responded coolly. He cupped his hands. 'Steersman! Hold our course. Deckhands! Lower the sails! Oars out!'

Telemachus joined the others as they went about their duties as casually as possible, gathering in the sail and fastening the ties. The rest of the pirates bent at the sweep oars, maintaining a slow stroke so as not to raise any suspicions among the figures on the beach. They were only a few hundred feet from the shingle now, and with every passing moment he felt certain that the enemy would see through their disguise and unleash a barrage of incendiary missiles at the vessel, turning it into a raging inferno. All the while, Bulla paced calmly up and down the deck, occasionally stopping to glance at the columns of dark smoke trailing above the fortifications. His cool, controlled demeanour helped to reassure the crew, and for the first time Telemachus saw something of the vital leadership qualities necessary to command a pirate ship.

The captain called to the steersman to make for a strip of shingle away from the beached pirate vessel. Telemachus joined the spare hands gathered around the stern, heart thumping with tense anticipation. The other pirates anxiously watched the smoke rising above the citadel, as if expecting a shower of flaming missiles to rain down on them at any moment. But none were fired, and then the deck planking shuddered as the ship's bows lifted against the shingle before settling. There was a low rumble as the oars were shipped, and then the vessel stopped moving.

'Get the gangways down!' Bulla commanded his men. 'Prepare to disembark!'

The crew sprang into action. A pair of deckhands manoeuvred the landing ramp through the opening on the side of the prow, dropping it down into the shallows with a loud splash. Hector shouted for the rest of the skeleton crew to bring up the prisoners, and in moments Leitus, Geras and the others emerged from the dark confines of the hold, blinking beneath the harsh glare of the sun. At the same time, a trio of men marched out of the citadel to greet the new arrivals. Bulla ordered the men to disembark. Hector led the prisoners off the ship, their chains clanking as they shuffled down the gangway into the waist-high waters. Telemachus forced himself to follow at a steady pace as he waded ashore, making his way up the pebbled beach to firmer land.

He glanced warily across the bay at the figures beside the small beached vessel, watching to see if any of them approached *Poseidon's Trident* to welcome their returning friends. If they did, he knew, the plan was doomed to fail. Bulla and his men would have no choice but to try to escape from the bay before the citadel's missiles could find their range and sink them. But to his immense relief, none of the enemy moved towards them, one or two pausing only briefly to wave a greeting before they returned to work.

Once the last of the pirates had come ashore, Bulla turned and boldly led his men across the beach, heading for the thin strip of land leading to the citadel. The three men who had emerged from the gate stood at the far end of the causeway, watching the new arrivals with interest. Bulla marched along at a brisk pace, with the pirates masquerading as prisoners struggling in their heavy chains. There was a cry as Geras tripped on the loose gravel and stumbled, falling to the ground. Telemachus instinctively reached down to help his companion to his feet, drawing an angry glare from the captain.

'You there!' Bulla hissed in a low voice. 'What the hell do you think you're doing? They're not your fucking mates. They're supposed to be our prisoners. Start treating 'em that way, before that lot on the gate get suspicious!'

Telemachus swiftly withdrew his arm. After a brief pause he hardened his expression and gave Geras a swift kick in the ribs, drawing a groan from the latter.

'Get up, scum!' he shouted, just loudly enough for the sentries atop the gatehouse to hear him.

Geras rose painfully to his feet, wincing. He shot a dark look at Telemachus. 'Thanks for that.'

'Sorry.'

'Forget it.' He shook his head angrily. 'Chains and beatings. It's fair to say this isn't *exactly* how I imagined my career as a pirate panning out.'

Telemachus swallowed nervously. 'Let's just hope the enemy's buying it. Otherwise we'll all be wearing chains soon enough.'

'Shut your mouths! Keep moving!' Bulla snapped. He jabbed a finger at Geras. 'You! Back in line!'

Geras stepped back into the column of prisoners, muttering curses under his breath as they continued towards the citadel. Beyond the open gate, Telemachus could see a wide cobbled street flanked by dilapidated hovels, with a bustling marketplace located at the far end. Several wine shops lined the square, doing a brisk trade with Nestor's men. Townspeople stared warily at the pirates from across the street. Others lowered their eyes and shuffled quickly past, avoiding their gaze. One or two glared at them with open hostility, and Telemachus sensed something of the bad feeling that existed between the locals and the interlopers. In the distance he could make out the top of the stone tower where Nestor had made his headquarters.

'Almost there,' Bulla whispered. 'Stay calm, lads. Follow my lead.'

One of the figures in front of the gate, a tough-looking pirate well into his middle years, approached the new arrivals. He threw up an arm, signalling for Bulla and his men to halt. A pair of sentries stood either side of the man, their hands resting on the pommels of their falcatas. The pirate stepped forward and cocked his head at Bulla.

'You're the men from *Achelous*?' He frowned. 'I don't recognise you.'

Bulla smiled. 'We're new to Captain Peleus's crew.'

'I see.' The pirate grunted as he ran his eyes over the party. From his weathered features and greying hair, Telemachus guessed that he was one of Nestor's senior men.

'Where's your captain?' he demanded.

Bulla jerked a thumb in the direction of *Trident*. 'Still aboard the ship, gathering up the rest of the loot. He'll be up shortly. He told us to bring the prisoners first. Should fetch a good price from the slave dealers.'

'Is that so?'

The pirate's lips parted in a grin, revealing a set of stained yellow teeth. The profit from the sale of two score prisoners would represent a sizeable reward for those close to Nestor, Telemachus knew. Something that no doubt entered the man's mind as he looked over the prisoners.

'Let's have a look at what we've got here, then.' The pirate stopped in front of Geras and puffed out his cheeks. 'Fuck me, this one looks a bit dense. He won't fetch much, that's for sure. Those tight-fisted Athenians are only paying decent coin for the ones who can read and write these days. This one looks as if he couldn't say his own name, let alone spell it.'

Telemachus gave a sidelong glance at Geras and saw his friend's face bristling with indignation. While the sentries were distracted, Telemachus slowly slid his hand down to the hilt of his sword. He closed his fingers around the handle of the weapon, ready to strike at the first sign of trouble.

'He's got a bit of meat on him, though,' one of the sentries put in, prodding Geras in the stomach. 'Could sell him on to one of the gladiator schools. They'll pay a pittance, but it's better than nothing.'

'I suppose,' the older man grunted. 'Best we can probably hope for, with this sack of human shit. Better make sure he's got a full set of teeth . . .'

He reached out and grasped Geras's face with one hand before inserting a grubby finger into his mouth and rooting around his jaws. Geras abruptly recoiled, shouting angrily as he threw the pirate off and shoved him back.

'Piss off! Get away from me!'

A clatter echoed through the square as the chains around his wrists broke free, tumbling to the ground. There was a moment of stunned silence as the pirate looked down in surprise at the broken shackles at his feet. Then he lifted his gaze to Geras, and the look on his face quickly shifted from confusion to alarm. He reached down to his side to draw his sheathed weapon. In the same instant, Bulla tore his own blade free from its scabbard and turned to his men.

'*Now!*' he roared. 'Get 'em!'

CHAPTER SEVENTEEN

Bulla's voice was still echoing off the walls of the surrounding buildings as the crew of *Poseidon's Trident* burst into action. There was a chorus of rasping noises as Telemachus and the men around him unsheathed their blades, accompanied by the clatter of loosened chains falling to the ground as those men posing as prisoners broke free. They swiftly snatched out the weapons hidden beneath their ragged tunics, to the mortal horror of the three figures standing in front of them. The grey-haired pirate had just enough time to realise what was happening before Telemachus ran him through with his blade, slamming the sword deep into his midriff before angling it up into his ribs, piercing a lung. The two sentries turned to run away, shouting at their comrades gathered at the marketplace. Bulla's men quickly fell upon the pair, cutting them down before they could escape. At the far end of the street, several panicked shouts went up as a throng of pirates stood up from their dice games and drinking benches and turned towards the attackers, reaching for their sheathed weapons.

'Kill 'em all!' Bulla thundered. '*Kill them!*'

His men needed no further encouragement. They broke into a run and charged towards the market square, bellowing their war cries. All around them townspeople screamed and women grabbed their children and ran for cover as the pirates tore into their bewildered opponents. Nestor's men had no time to react and many were mercilessly slaughtered before they could pull their weapons from their scabbards. Telemachus heard an agonised cry to his right as one of the defenders drew his sword and lunged at the nearest pirate, stabbing him in the groin. The defender's joy was short-lived as Telemachus stepped into his fallen comrade's place and drove the tip of his blade deep into his opponent's guts. He gave the sword a savage twist, drawing a gasp of pain from the man as he fell away, cursing his killer as he bled out.

Telemachus stepped back from his opponent and glanced around him at the fighting, blood pounding in his veins. Only a handful of Nestor's men had managed to escape the butchery, retreating into the maze of side streets and alleys leading deeper into the citadel. Several of their defiant comrades stood their ground, but they were soon overwhelmed by their ruthless attackers. At the edge of his vision Telemachus saw four of Bulla's men swarming around a youthful-looking pirate gripping a short sword. The young man tossed his weapon aside and threw up his arms in surrender, but the crew ignored his pleas and a hideous scream pierced the air as he disappeared beneath a flurry of savage blows. At least a dozen bodies were now strewn across the market square, amid the chaos of broken clay amphorae, upturned wooden benches and abandoned market stalls, as Bulla's men took full advantage of the surprise they had unleashed on their enemy.

'Piece of piss, this,' Geras said, wiping sweat from his brow.

'Not for much longer,' Telemachus replied grimly. 'Look!'

He pointed to one of the narrow streets leading off the main square. A group of men were hurrying forward from the direction of the keep, brandishing weapons and round shields as they prepared to counter-charge the attackers.

'Shit . . .' Geras mumbled.

One of the others shouted a warning, and the men of *Poseidon's Trident* simultaneously turned to face the new threat. Nestor's men shouted their commander's name as they swept across the marketplace, leaping over their slaughtered comrades and hurling themselves at their opponents. The square soon became a writhing mass of daggers, swords and wooden clubs as the two sides tore into each other. A solidly built pirate with a buckler and a decorated linen cuirass too small for his bulk fixed his narrowed eyes on Telemachus and lunged towards him, slashing wildly. Telemachus parried the blade aside and thrust back, but the pirate easily deflected the blow with his buckler, then quickly shifted his weight and counter-attacked, aiming for his opponent's face. Telemachus threw his head to the side, and a stinging pain shot through him as the blade grazed his cheek. He stumbled backwards, hissing sharply.

'You're bleeding, boy,' the pirate sneered. 'Next one'll rip your throat out!'

Telemachus tensed his muscles and crouched low, his attention focused wholly on his opponent. The latter bared his crooked teeth and sprang forward, feinting before cutting downward at the recruit's midriff. Telemachus parried, dropping his shoulder and throwing the full weight of his body into the attack as he aimed for his opponent's head. The man frantically hefted up his buckler just in time, the blade glancing off the boss with a loud metallic ring, causing the pirate to release the shield from his numbed grip. In the next breath Telemachus drove his blade into the pirate's side where there was a gap between the front and back of the cuirass. There was a gush of dark blood as he yanked the weapon free, before the pirate slumped to the ground with a despairing groan.

Telemachus quickly reached down and seized the buckler, turning to find his next opponent. A prickle of fear ran down his spine as he saw that the enemy outnumbered *Trident's* crew. With the initial element of surprise gone, the attack had stalled, and he realised that it was only a matter of time before Bulla and his men were overrun. Across the square, he noticed a group of townsmen peering out from the gloom of a narrow side street, anxiously watching to see the outcome of the struggle.

'Don't just fucking stand there!' he shouted. 'Give us a hand! If you want to get rid of Nestor and his gang, now's your chance!'

The townsmen glanced hesitantly at one another. A few stared at the weapons scattered across the marketplace, torn between their reluctance to get involved and their desire to see Nestor defeated. One of them suddenly rushed forward, a giant of a man with a thick beard. He snatched up a gleaming sword from amid the tangle of bloodied corpses and charged at the nearest enemy, a podgy individual with curly hair protruding either side of a leather skullcap. The pirate clenched his jaw in a grimace of hatred and swung his axe at the giant. The latter ducked the blow, then thrust out, his opponent giving a bloody gurgle as the sword plunged into his chest. With a deep grunt, the giant planted a boot on his wounded enemy and tore the blade free. Then he turned away, shouting encouragement at his friends sheltering in the back streets.

More townspeople swarmed out, inspired by the giant's example. They grabbed whatever weapons came to hand and threw themselves at their oppressors, tearing into Nestor's men with pent-up rage and frustration. One grabbed a pitchfork from a nearby wagon and plunged the iron prongs into the side of a stocky pirate wielding a club. The pirate screamed in agony as the sharpened spikes pierced his guts, the shaft protruding from his wounded flank. Another local kicked one of Nestor's men in the back and sent him sprawling. He kept the pirate pinned to the ground while a companion raised a piece of masonry and smashed it down, crushing the pirate's skull. Others set upon the defenders with clubs or stones; some used just their bare fists.

'Come on!' Telemachus bellowed, clenching his fist at the townsmen who had yet to join the fight. 'What have you got to lose? Get stuck in!'

The last few onlookers hesitated for a moment longer before they rushed forward, wielding makeshift weapons and tearing into their enemies with brutal intensity. Although they were not trained killers, the sheer number of townspeople joining the skirmish quickly overwhelmed Nestor's men, forcing them to retreat. Sensing that the battle was now turning in their favour, Bulla and his men hurled themselves at the enemy with renewed effort, driving them back step by step until they had reached the far end of the marketplace. A few defenders managed to slip away from the tight press of bodies and fled down the side streets. Some of *Trident*'s crew broke off from the main attack and chased after them, slaughtering them before they could get away.

They were joined by a handful of the locals, who, carried away by their bloodlust, killed any of Nestor's men who still drew breath.

'Hector!' Bulla called out. 'Take some of our lads and go around the side of these buildings. We should be able to cut off their retreat and trap the rest of 'em.'

'Aye, Captain!'

Only a small cluster of the enemy now remained. With Hector and the other pirates cutting them off from the rear, they had nowhere left to go, and Bulla shouted for his men to pull back. The fighting stopped as *Trident*'s crew retired several paces from the melee, the clatter and thud of weapons against shields swiftly replaced by an unsettling silence, punctuated by the despairing cries of wounded men. Telemachus stood alongside his comrades, the sound of their rapid breathing filling the air as they watched the enemy closely. Nestor's men kept their weapons raised, as if preparing for one final mad charge at their opponents. A gap opened up between the ranks as Bulla pushed his way to the front.

'Which one of you is Captain Nestor?'

A tall, swarthy figure in an ornately decorated cuirass stepped forward. 'I am. Who the fuck are you?'

'My name is Captain Bulla, of *Poseidon's Trident*. I'm here to claim the citadel. Your men are surrounded, Nestor. Tell them to surrender. There's no need for any more bloodshed today.'

Nestor snorted with derision. 'Come on, Captain. We both know that isn't true. As soon as I tell them to lay down their arms, you'll put us all to death.'

Bulla shook his head forcefully. 'We don't kill for the sake of it. You and your crew will be spared. Now tell your men to drop their weapons, or I'll have my lads cut you to pieces and feed you to the dogs.'

The men either side of Nestor glanced uncertainly at each other. For a moment, no one moved. Then one pirate, bleeding profusely from a leg wound, let his sword clatter to the ground. The others quickly followed. Telemachus saw a final flicker of defiance in Nestor's eyes before he growled in bitter frustration and reluctantly tossed aside his own weapon, bowing his head.

'Hector!' Bulla called out.

'Captain?'

'Take this one away.' He pointed at Nestor. 'Stick him in one of the cells. I'll deal with him later. The rest can join our crew and replace the men we've lost.'

One of the locals stared at him in shock and disbelief. 'You're going to spare these scum? After everything they've done to us?'

Bulla nodded. 'We lost a lot of men today. I need this lot for my crew.'

'But what's to stop them from gutting us as soon as our backs are turned? We should be killing these men, not rewarding them!'

Several of the townspeople grumbled in agreement. Bulla rounded on the first man who'd spoken. 'There's been enough killing for one day. Besides, these men belong to me now. My crew have set you free.'

'Free?' The man threw up his arms and laughed bitterly. 'Load of bollocks! You just told Nestor you're here to claim the citadel for yourselves. Why should we let you rule over the rest of us?'

Others in the crowd cheered him on, and several more

shouted at the pirates to leave the citadel. Bulla ignored their voices and stared levelly at the man. 'You'll find that I'm much fairer than Nestor. I assure you, you have nothing to fear from us. I will treat you fairly, and you'll enjoy a share of our spoils.'

'We've heard that before!' The man, clearly a figure of some authority among the townspeople, looked around him as he made his plea to the others in the crowd. 'We didn't risk our lives getting rid of Nestor and his mob just to surrender to another pirate despot. I say we take back control of the citadel for ourselves!'

'Enough!' Bulla roared, silencing the dissenters. He stepped towards the man who had spoken, keeping his hand clamped tightly around the handle of his sword. 'Listen here. If it wasn't for us, you and your friends would still be living under Nestor's rule.' He paused to let his words sink in before he continued menacingly, 'Now, you can either accept our offer to enjoy a share of the riches we'll plunder when we return to the sea. Or you can join Nestor and his lieutenants and rot in a prison cell. What's it going to be?'

The man stared at Bulla, and for a moment it looked as if he might protest further. But then he turned away, muttering under his breath to his companions. The rest of the townspeople were disarmed before they slowly dispersed, and Hector barked an order at the exhausted crew. Two men stepped forward from the line and dragged Nestor away through the crowd towards the prison cells. Telemachus watched the defeated pirate chief depart, a wave of relief washing over him. At his side, Geras laughed nervously and slapped his comrade on the back.

'We did it,' he said. 'We bloody did it. Petrapylae is ours!'

★ ★ ★

Later that afternoon, the pirates gathered in the main square to celebrate their victory. Once they had rounded up the few remaining stragglers, Bulla had ordered guards to be posted to the watchtower to look out for *Achelous* in case she returned. At the same time, those pirates who had surrendered and agreed to join the crew were branded and sworn in. A handful of Nestor's men remained stubbornly loyal to their captain and refused to join *Trident*'s crew, but they soon changed their minds once Bulla threatened to sell them on to one of the slave dealers.

While the new recruits were being initiated, Bulla ordered the other pirates to help clear away the debris and bodies from the marketplace. Some of the townspeople were still apprehensive about their liberators. A few of Nestor's men killed during the fighting had left behind families in the village, and their wives and children glared at the pirates as they mourned their dead. But most of the locals were quick now to ingratiate themselves, providing Bulla's men with gifts of wine and food.

Their anxiety to please was understandable, Telemachus reflected. Petrapylae had fallen on hard times after the militia garrison had abandoned the port, and they relied on the trade with the pirates for their meagre income. With Nestor defeated, the locals desperately needed *Trident*'s crew to spend their coin in the assorted wine shops, market stalls and brothels. The pirates were happy to oblige, and helped themselves to amphorae of cheap wine in one of the village's crumbling taverns. While most of the inebriated pirates celebrated a great victory, some drank in sombre silence, remembering fallen comrades and reflecting on how close they had come to sharing the fate of the two dozen men killed during the assault on the base. As the hours passed, though, the conversation inevitably turned to cheerier subjects, the pirates eagerly discussing their next voyage and the potential riches awaiting them at sea.

Telemachus tried his best to listen to his comrades, but he found himself distracted by thoughts of his brother. Nereus remained at the mercy of his Roman slave-owner, and the very thought burned like a heated spear tip inside his heart. He knew he could never rest until he had freed him from his bonds.

'Now this is more bloody like it,' Geras announced as he refilled his wine cup to the brim. 'Cheap drink, good company, and best of all, the prospect of a modestly priced tart at the end of the night.'

'Enjoy it while you still can,' Telemachus said. 'We'll be out hunting prey soon enough.'

Geras shot him a look. 'Always have to ruin it, don't you? Can't just let me enjoy myself for once.' He sipped his wine before he went on, 'Anyway, what makes you think Bulla will be in any great rush to get back out to sea? We've barely had time to catch our breath.'

'The lad's right,' Leitus cut in. He nodded at the pirates seated at the other trestle tables. 'The captain will have to capture some valuable loot soon if he's to keep this mob happy.'

'They look content enough to me.'

'For now,' Telemachus responded. 'But their good mood won't last for long. Not unless Bulla can land a big prize or two. Remember, half this lot were ready to turn on him before he took Petrapylae. It won't take much for them to turn on him again. If that happens, we're all in trouble.'

Geras snorted. 'Gods, you two! The most depressing pirates in Illyria. There's plenty of time to worry about all that tomorrow. Right now, let's just get blind drunk, eh?'

At that moment, a gust of wind swept through the tavern as one of the ship's mates stepped inside. He glanced around before his eyes settled on Telemachus. He threaded his way across the bustling room and nodded at the young pirate.

'Captain wants to see you,' he said tonelessly.

'Me?' Telemachus looked up enquiringly. 'What for?'

The mate shrugged. 'How in Hades should I know? Now get a move on. He's waiting.'

Sighing heavily, Telemachus rose to his feet and followed the man outside. Dusk had begun to gather across the citadel, and the streets were empty except for a few locals searching the dead for their loved ones. Faces peered out from the wan glow of several doorways as Telemachus followed the mate across the courtyard towards the studded wooden door built into one side of the keep. The man swept through the entrance and up a flight of stairs, then down a darkened corridor towards a door on the left. He stopped outside the door and knocked twice.

'Come!' Bulla called out from the other side.

The mate lifted the heavy latch and gestured for Telemachus to step inside. The young man entered a square space with shuttered windows on two walls and a heated iron brazier glowing in one corner. Bulla sat at the far end of the room, behind a large wooden table with a parchment map of the coast spread out across it. He had moved into Nestor's old headquarters shortly after securing the citadel, with the other men assigned to quarters closer to the gatehouse. He waited for the mate to depart back down the corridor, then nodded towards a stool in front of the table.

'Sit down, Telemachus.'

The captain steepled his fingers, watching the recruit carefully as he seated himself opposite.

'How's the wound?'

Telemachus touched the stitches the ship's carpenter had applied to the shallow cut on his cheek. The man had cleaned the wound out and told him that it should heal in good time, although he would be left with a scar. 'It's nothing, sir. Throbs a little, that's all.'

'You did well today,' Bulla said. 'That plan of yours worked better than any of us could have hoped for. If we hadn't captured this place, one of those ungrateful bastards on the crew would have stabbed me in the back by now.'

Telemachus nodded slowly, still unsure why Bulla had summoned him. The captain grunted and took a sip of wine from a silver goblet next to the map.

'Well, I've shut them up for now, at least. Petrapylae is ours. Nestor is our prisoner.' He smiled thinly. 'When I've finished with him, I'll have him put to death in front of the townsfolk. They'll like that. There's still the problem of the real *Achelous*, of course.'

Telemachus nodded again. 'What'll we do when she returns?'

'I've already thought of that. We'll remove any signs of the struggle and trick her crew into thinking Nestor and his mob are still in control of the citadel. As soon as she lands, we'll seize the crew and make them the same offer as the others. Join us, or die. I imagine they'll surrender quickly once they realise what they're up against. We could use the extra manpower, now that we're free to hunt for prey again.'

'We're to put to sea, Captain?' Telemachus asked excitedly.

'As soon as we've established ourselves here,' Bulla said. 'A few days from now, I expect. If I delay much longer than that, the crew will get restless.'

'But *Trident* . . . she's in a bad way. We'll never get her ready in time.'

Bulla set down the goblet and ran a hand through his oily hair before he went on. 'We won't be using *Trident*. We'll use ships from Nestor's fleet instead. The carpenter tells me that two of 'em are seaworthy. The flagship, *Proteus*, and one of the smaller vessels, *Galatea*. Hector will take charge of *Proteus*. Which leaves the question of who will command the other ship.'

Telemachus arched an eyebrow in surprise. 'You're not coming with us, sir?'

The pirate chief shook his head. 'I'm needed here to keep a firm grip on the locals and Nestor's boys. Besides, we'll have to make major improvements to the citadel's defences if we're to ensure that the Romans never surprise us again.' He hesitated for a moment, then continued. 'In any case, I already have in mind the perfect captain for *Galatea*. You.'

Telemachus sat speechless for a long moment. He could scarcely believe what he was hearing. A few months ago, he had been begging for scraps on the streets of Piraeus. Now he was being offered the chance to command a pirate ship of his own.

'Me, Captain? But why?'

'Why not? You've shown yourself to be a capable seaman. More than capable, actually. And I need someone with good seafaring instincts to captain *Galatea*. Someone who can think on their feet.'

Bulla paused and leaned across the table. There was a glint in his eyes as he smiled broadly at Telemachus.

'Well?' he asked. 'Are you ready to assume your first command?'

CHAPTER EIGHTEEN

'My money's on the grey one,' Geras announced several days later. 'He'll win this fight easily.'

Telemachus glanced at his companion and frowned. 'What makes you so sure of that?'

'It's obvious,' Geras said. 'That bird's much bigger than his opponent. Besides, grey cockerels make the best fighters. Everyone knows that. Trust me, he's going to tear that other one to shreds.'

Telemachus turned his attention back to the makeshift pit as the two handlers approached, clutching their prize-fighting cockerels. A jostling crowd of pirates stood in a rough circle in the courtyard, their drunken shouts echoing off the walls as they eagerly awaited the next fight: the last of the day's entertainment. They had gathered in the gloomy corner of the citadel to pass the time laying bets on the local cockerel fights while they waited for the order to put out to sea. Captain Bulla's men were now firmly established in their new base, and there was a palpable sense of excitement at their imminent return to sea. After going weeks without a share of any loot, they were keen to resume the hunt for prey along the Illyrian coastline.

Telemachus looked on keenly as the handlers crossed the blood-splattered pit and approached the umpire. A hushed silence descended over the crowd as the man announced the competitors for the bout: a grey-feathered cockerel versus a white fowl with a bright red breast. As with the day's earlier contests, it was to be a fight to the death, with the last bird standing declared the victor. While the umpire spoke, the handlers prepared their fighters for battle, petting them and checking the curved metal spurs fastened to their legs. The spurs' sharpened tips glinted viciously in the pale light of late afternoon. The smaller of the two cockerels struggled in its handler's grip, flapping madly and drawing a curse from the man as he fought to keep it under control.

'I reckon the white one's got a chance,' Telemachus declared.

'Him?' Geras replied, raising an eyebrow. 'You must be bloody joking.'

'Why? What's wrong with him?'

'What isn't, more like!' Geras spluttered. 'Look at him! The scrawny bastard is half the size of the grey bird. You'd get better odds on me being the next emperor of Rome.'

'He's smaller,' Telemachus conceded. 'But he's got the longer reach, and he'll be faster than his opponent. He might surprise us.'

'Have it your way, lad. But I wouldn't bank on it. Especially with the way your luck's gone today.'

'What's that supposed to mean?'

'Your judgement hasn't exactly been very profitable so far, has it?' Geras gestured to his friend's leather belt-purse. 'You might be a ship's captain these days, but you've got a lot to learn about the fine art of cockerel fighting.'

Telemachus looked away, mixed emotions swirling inside his chest as he pondered his swift promotion. *Galatea* was to be his first independent command as a pirate, and he should have been thrilled at the prospect. Instead he felt a growing sense of dread. News of his rapid promotion had been greeted with hostility by some of the older hands among the crew, who resented seeing the young recruit appointed ahead of them. Unless he could quickly establish his authority, he feared his first command might also turn out to be his last.

'When are we heading back out to sea anyway?' Geras asked. 'You're close to Bulla. You must have some idea.'

'Soon enough, I should think. He won't want to delay much longer. Especially with this lot desperate for a share of some loot,' Telemachus added, nodding in the direction of the other pirates.

'Let's hope it won't be much longer. The wine and women in this village ain't exactly cheap. I imagine you could do with some coin as well.'

Telemachus felt a hot prick of anger as he thought of his enslaved older brother, toiling away in a forge in Thorikos. He consoled himself with the knowledge that as a ship's commander, he would be on a double share of any plunder they captured. Should he enjoy a successful campaign out at sea, he might be able to free Nereus much quicker than he had initially hoped. If his brother was still alive, he reminded himself grimly. It had been months since he'd heard any news, and he prayed to Jupiter, best and greatest, to spare Nereus from the terrible accidents that often befell slaves working in such dangerous conditions.

'It's about to begin,' Geras said, breaking into his dark thoughts. 'Last bout of the day. Better be a good one, this.'

Telemachus turned his gaze back to the pit as the two handlers brought their cockerels close together. The birds tensed at the sight of one another, flaring their colourful hackles and crowing wildly. With the fighters suitably provoked, the umpire – a wizened veteran called Calkas – gestured for the handlers to retreat to the chalk lines that had been marked out several paces apart, while bookies moved around the edge of the circle taking bets from the crowd. Geras placed what was left of his money on the big favourite, while Telemachus laid down a few sestertii on the white-feathered cockerel: all the money he had left from his share of the grain the pirates had seized from Captain Nestor's men. The grain had been sold on to a pinch-faced merchant in a neighbouring port and the money distributed among *Trident*'s crew, with each man due a share according to his seniority. At long odds, a big win on this last fight would cover his previous losses, and perhaps leave him with a small profit.

Once all the bets had been placed, there was a loud crack as Calkas stamped his staff on the flagstones, signalling for the handlers to release their birds.

'Begin!'

'Here we go!' Geras roared. 'Come on! Get stuck in!'

An excited chorus of cheers came from the onlookers as the cockerels charged forward, leaping at one another in a frenzied blur of flapping wings, slashing claws and torn feathers. Telemachus craned his neck, straining to get a better view of the action as the birds tore into each other again. Their handlers stood at opposite edges of the circle, clapping and shouting encouragement at their respective fighters. The grey bird feinted, stabbing out with its beak at the other cockerel's neck. The latter twisted and squirmed as it tried to shake off its bigger opponent. Then the grey-feathered cockerel snapped its head back and leaped up, kicking out with its claws and striking its opponent on its exposed flank. The white cockerel staggered backwards, squawking in pain, blood gushing out of a deep wound beneath its wing.

'Yes!' Geras shouted. He turned to Telemachus, grinning broadly. 'What did I tell you? The grey one's massacring the lightweight. This fight will be over soon now, just you watch.'

Telemachus ignored his friend's boasting and kept his gaze fixed on the pit as the fight continued. The injured bird's handler was screaming at his fighter, imploring it to attack. But the momentum of the contest was irresistibly with the grey cockerel, and it lunged again, pouncing on its stricken foe and pinning it to the bare dirt beneath its talons. The white bird thrashed about helplessly, crowing and jerking its head as its opponent stabbed out repeatedly with its beak. The ground quickly became streaked with blood, and Telemachus silently cursed himself at the thought of losing the last of his pitifully few coins.

'That's it!' Geras yelled. 'Kill him! Finish the bastard!'

The wounded bird summoned the last ounce of its strength, kicking off its opponent and hobbling back out of range before the grey cockerel could attack again. There was a brief pause as both fighters caught their breath, their chests heaving up and down. The white bird was in a bad way, Telemachus noted dejectedly. Its feathers glistened with blood, one of its wings had been damaged and there was a dark, weeping hole where its eye had been gouged out. Another blow would surely decide the contest.

There was a loud cheer among the pirates as the grey cockerel leaped forward for the kill. At the last possible moment the white bird sensed the danger and dropped its head low, ducking the attack. The grey cockerel landed and whirled around, muscles tensed as it shaped to attack again. But the white bird reacted faster, slashing open the latter's neck with one of its sharpened talons. The grey cockerel wavered on the spot for a moment as the blood flowed out of the gash in its throat. Then it flopped to the ground and went into a frenzied series of death throes, to audible gasps of disbelief from the pirates. A moment later, the white cockerel lowered its blood-soaked head and slumped beside its dead opponent.

Both handlers immediately rushed forward to attend to their stricken birds. Calkas stooped down beside the limp fighters and prodded them with his stick, checking them for signs of life. The crowd looked on in silence as they eagerly awaited his decision. After several tense moments, he stood up and pointed to the smaller cockerel's blood-soaked body, which was trembling as the bird bled out.

'The white one still lives and wins!'

'Yes!' Telemachus cried, punching the air in celebration. 'I knew it!'

'Unbelievable.' Geras shook his head ruefully. 'I thought that bird was surely done for.'

Telemachus grinned. 'Guess I know a thing or two about cockerel fighting after all.'

'Beginner's luck,' Geras replied in a deep growl. He shook his head. 'Come on. Grab your winnings then let's get out of here. I need some wine.'

The crowd began to thin out as Telemachus hurried over to one of the bookies. As he approached, Hector stepped forward from the throng, shoving aside a couple of men and marching across the pit towards the umpire. He glared at Calkas, his twisted expression simmering with rage.

'The fight's a draw!' he bellowed, gesturing towards the cockerels being carried away by their handlers. 'Both of them birds are dead. The result shouldn't count!'

'The grey one died first,' Calkas said in an officious tone. 'Therefore he's the loser.'

'I don't give a toss,' Hector snapped. 'Neither bird's alive. That means the result don't stand.'

'I can't help you. The rules are clear.'

'Fuck your rules!'

The umpire swallowed nervously as Hector took a step closer to him, jabbing a meaty finger at his chest. 'You just cost me a lot of money, old man. Now, I want the coin I bet, or you and me have got a problem.'

Telemachus looked round the sea of faces in the crowd. No one moved to intervene. That was understandable, he knew. Among the pirates Hector had a reputation as a dangerously violent man, accomplished with his fists and skilled with a sword, and most of the crew knew it was unwise to challenge him.

'I said, give me my money back,' Hector demanded. 'You'll do it if you want to keep your teeth.'

'Please,' Calkas begged. 'Be reasonable . . .'

'Leave him alone, Hector,' Telemachus said in a firm voice as he stepped forward. 'Calkas is right. Your bird lost.'

Hector turned his back on the umpire and slanted his pitiless gaze towards Telemachus. The corners of his thick lips curled upwards in a cruel smirk.

'Look who it is! The boy who calls himself a fucking pirate.' He hardened his expression. 'Nobody asked for your judgement on the fight. Now piss off out of my sight.'

Telemachus forced himself to stand his ground as the first mate approached. All around, the other pirates looked on silently, taking a keen interest in this unexpected sequel to the afternoon's entertainment.

Hector snarled and spat on the ground. 'You deaf, boy? I said fuck off.'

Telemachus looked at him steadily. 'I'm not a boy.'

'Is that right? You could have fooled me.' Hector chuckled and stepped closer. 'Look at you. Think you're so tough, just because the captain gave you command of that stinking little tub, eh? Just wait until we head out to sea. We'll soon see that you're nothing more than a boy playing at being a pirate.'

He balled his hands into huge fists, and for a moment Telemachus thought the older pirate might throw a punch at him. Then he stepped back and looked across the crowd as a space opened up between the onlookers. Telemachus followed his line of sight just in time to see one of the ship's boys approaching from the direction of the citadel. The freckled youth stopped at the edge of the pit and nodded at Telemachus and Hector in turn.

'Captain's respects, and he wishes to see you both. At once.'

Hector shot a final glare at Telemachus, then nodded at the boy. 'Fine. Let's go. Me and the lad have finished our little chat anyway.'

'My winnings?' Telemachus asked, looking round for the man who had taken his bet.

'I'll hold on to 'em for you,' Geras said. He placed a hand on his friend's shoulder and waited until Hector had started to follow the boy out of the courtyard before he leaned in close.

'Word of advice,' he whispered. 'Watch yourself around Hector.'

'Tell me something I don't know.'

'I mean it. You just challenged him in front of the other lads. He won't be forgetting that in a hurry. Just be careful, all right?'

'I'll try.' Telemachus sighed, then turned and hurried out of the courtyard after the first mate and the ship's boy. No matter how hard he tried, he never seemed to be far from trouble.

CHAPTER NINETEEN

The sun was already dipping behind the mountains as Telemachus and Hector followed the boy along the thoroughfare leading towards the main square. They moved at a brisk pace through the citadel's cobbled streets, passing several run-down watering holes, gaming places and brothels vying for the custom of the new occupiers of the settlement.

'This place stinks,' Hector grumbled as he stepped round a small midden buzzing with flies. 'I'll be glad to put to sea again.'

Telemachus nodded, though he was even more glad at the thought of getting away from Hector. The boy led them under a crumbling arch and across a small courtyard towards the stone keep. A pirate stood guard outside the main entrance and lifted the heavy iron latch as the small party approached. The ancient hinges protested as the door opened and the boy stepped across the weathered sill and escorted Telemachus and Hector up the stairs. He stopped outside the door at the far end of the corridor and rapped with his knuckles. There was a pause before a gruff voice called, 'Enter!'

The boy lifted the latch with a grating rasp and Hector

swept through the door first. A moment later Telemachus followed him into the captain's quarters.

The room had been lavishly furnished in the days since *Trident*'s crew had taken possession of the citadel. Thin shafts of twilight crept through the shuttered windows, revealing a luxurious couch to one side of the room, next to a woven rug. A silver platter of honeyed figs, olives and cheeses lay untouched on a side table beside the couch. At the opposite end of the room, Captain Bulla stood hunched over the wide table, his brow wrinkled in concentration as he studied a large goatskin map of the coastline. As his guests entered, he looked up from the map and nodded at the boy.

'Leave us now.'

The boy bowed his head obediently, then hurried back down the corridor. Bulla turned to acknowledge the two pirates standing in front of him, nodding stiffly at both men.

'Your ships are ready to set sail, I presume?'

'Aye, Captain,' Hector replied. 'The lads on the *Proteus* are raring to go.'

'And you, Telemachus? How's *Galatea* looking?'

Telemachus cleared his throat. 'She's fully provisioned, sir. I've had her rigging checked and replaced a few worn ropes. Her sails have been patched up, but they'll need replacing soon too.'

'Good.' Bulla ran a hand through his dark locks before he continued. 'You'll set sail tomorrow. Now that the weather's cleared, there should be plenty of nice fat cargo ships venturing out.'

'What about *Achelous*, Captain? What if she returns while we're out hunting?'

Bulla frowned. For the past few days he had ordered his

men to keep a constant watch for the rival gang's ship, but there had still been no sign of her.

'I'll have more than enough men here to hold the citadel if she returns,' he replied. 'But it's unlikely that she'll come back now. She's long overdue. Probably lost at sea.'

'Or she might have run into a naval patrol,' Telemachus speculated.

'It's possible,' Bulla replied. 'That bastard Canis seems determined to wipe us all out, that's for sure. You'll have to be extremely vigilant out at sea now that the Romans are running extra patrols on this side of the Adriaticum.' He smiled faintly. 'I suppose we have the previous occupants of this citadel to thank for that. It's a pity Nestor and his mob weren't less successful in attracting the attention of the imperial fleet. That would have made our lives considerably easier.'

Hector shrugged. 'A few biremes roaming the coast never stopped us before, Captain.'

'No. But avoiding the Romans may well be the least of our problems.'

'How do you mean, sir?' asked Telemachus.

'I spoke with our friend Nestor shortly before his execution.' Bulla flashed a cruel smile. 'The fool believed I would spare his life if he answered my questions. He confirmed what we had already suspected: his men have struggled to find any trading vessels to attack of late, and most ships are too terrified to sail along the coast in case they run into his men. It's going to be tricky finding enough plunder to keep our crews happy. The dogs are already mutinous.'

Telemachus arched an eyebrow. 'Mutiny, Captain? The lads look like they're in good spirits, if you ask me.'

'Right now, perhaps,' Bulla conceded. 'But it won't be

long before they grow restless. Seizing Petrapylae has bought me some time, nothing more. Unless the men get their share of some loot soon, my rivals among the crew will turn against me. But finding enough prey in these waters is going to be difficult.'

'What's to be done then, Captain?' Hector asked.

'There's only one thing for it. We'll have to seek out some new hunting grounds.' Bulla waved a hand at the map spread out on the table. Telemachus and Hector leaned in to study the coastline more closely as their captain continued. 'You will patrol the areas to the north and south of Petrapylae, taking any vessels you encounter. We need whatever loot we can find; we can't afford to pass anything up. Hunting separately will give you both the best possible chance of finding prey.' He tapped his finger on the coastline some distance to the north of the citadel. 'Telemachus, you'll take *Galatea* and head north, hunting along the sea lanes of the Liburnian coast, between Ortopla and Nesactium. Since *Galatea* has a small hold, you'll need to keep any ships you capture and put a prize crew on 'em.'

Telemachus nodded.

'What about me, sir?' Hector asked.

Bulla turned to the first mate and traced his finger down to another point on the map. 'You'll take *Proteus* and head south towards Tragurium.'

Hector lifted his gaze from the map and stroked his weathered brow. 'Tragurium, Captain? But that's not far from Salonae.'

'What of it?'

'We recently passed through there without encountering so much as a sniff of another ship. No merchant captains have risked sailing along there for a while now.'

'That was nearly a month ago. The situation may well have changed. I expect Prefect Canis will have been bragging about his attack on our old base. The merchant captains will have heard news of it by now. Some of them may consider it safe to return to the area.'

Hector looked unconvinced. 'Even if that's true, I'll be competing with all the other pirate crews operating down that way. I'll be hunting for scraps.'

'Perhaps. But we won't know for sure until you have a good look.'

The first mate shook his head. 'Let me go north instead of the boy, Captain. There's plenty of thriving ports up that way, and *Proteus* has got a bigger hold than *Galatea*. I could land a lot more plunder than him.'

'Out of the question. Nesactium is much closer to the imperial base at Ravenna, which means there's a greater risk of running into a Roman squadron. Since Telemachus has the faster craft, he's best placed to search that area of the coast and avoid trouble.'

'But the lad's got no experience,' Hector rasped. 'He's never even boarded a ship, for Jupiter's sake!'

'I've made my decision,' Bulla responded firmly. He shot a challenging look at Hector. 'Of course, if you don't want to obey my orders, then I'm sure I can persuade one of the other mates to take your place.'

Hector lowered his head. 'No. It's fine, sir. Tragurium it is.'

'Glad to hear it.'

Telemachus had been staring intently at the map, lost in his own thoughts. Now he looked up, a question forming in his head. 'How long are we to remain at sea, Captain?'

'As long as it takes to catch some good prizes. It's vital you do not return empty-handed. There must be spoils for the men to share . . .' Bulla stared hard at them to emphasise the point before turning his attention back to the map. 'There's one other thing.' He indicated one of the mass of small islands not far from the citadel. 'Insula Pelagus. There's an abandoned trading post there. Nothing except some crumbling ruins nowadays. You'll meet there every ten days and exchange whatever intelligence you may have gleaned from your voyages. That should give you plenty of time to hunt between each meeting.'

Hector scratched his cheek. 'Going to be bloody hard to get there at the same time, Captain. What if one of us is delayed? Or runs into trouble? How will we let the other know?'

'Simple. Whoever arrives first will wait a full day for the other ship. If there's still no sign of it on the second morning, then you're to continue raiding as per my orders. Any questions?'

'What about the sailors on any ships we take?' Hector said. 'Do we kill 'em, or take 'em prisoner?'

'Kill anyone who resists you. The rest you are to take captive and bring here. Those who wish to join us will be given the opportunity; the others should fetch a decent price in the slave markets.' Bulla hesitated. 'There is one more thing. You are under strict orders not to raid any settlements.'

'The men won't like that,' Hector said, a trace of disappointment in his voice. 'Fewer opportunities to grab loot.'

'Tough. We can't afford to anger the Romans further. Not with Canis breathing down our necks. The last thing we want to do is give those bastards a reason to reinforce the Ravenna fleet. You're to refrain from anything other than stealing cargo, at least until Canis loses interest in hunting us and turns his attention elsewhere. Understand?'

'Aye, Captain,' Hector replied moodily.

Bulla nodded and straightened his back. 'You'll need to brief your officers. In the meantime, I'll arrange for replacements to be assigned to your crews. Some of the men from Nestor's ranks will be sailing with you. You'll have to keep a close eye on them, of course.'

Telemachus nodded slowly. Even among the pirate crews of Illyricum, Captain Nestor's crew were renowned as a ruthless gang of cut-throats, seemingly as interested in torture and butchery as in earning booty. The thought of several of Nestor's pirates serving on *Galatea* added to his growing list of concerns.

'They've all sworn the same oath as the rest of us,' Bulla went on. 'But a few of them may still be loyal to their old captain. They might be difficult to bring into line.'

Telemachus frowned at him. 'Why press them into our ranks then, sir?'

'We don't have any choice. We have few enough good seamen, and without the new additions from Nestor's ranks we wouldn't have enough hands to run both ships and defend this place. We need these men, whether we like it or not. The situation is hardly ideal, but you're just going to have to make the best of it. Got it?'

Telemachus and Hector nodded. Bulla stared at them for a moment.

'Do not take too long before you return with the spoils. Any delay may encourage my enemies to move against me.

My . . . our future depends on you returning to this base with as much loot as you can carry. Otherwise there may not be a safe base for you to come back to. Now, unless you have any other questions . . .'

'No, sir,' Telemachus said.

'Then I suggest you both get moving. You sail at dawn.'

CHAPTER TWENTY

'So much for this area being a good hunting ground,' Geras complained as he stood on *Galatea*'s cramped foredeck. 'We'll have more chance of running into a sea nymph at this rate.'

Telemachus ran his fingers over the fresh scar on his face as he gazed out at the azure expanse. A breeze gusted in from the land off to starboard, humming through the rigging as *Galatea* made her way along the Liburnian coast. Ahead of him, he could see nothing except the line of the horizon and the white-capped waves, glinting under the brilliant midday sun. He searched in vain for any sign of a sail and then looked away, thumping a fist against the carved rail in frustration.

'I don't understand. We should have encountered something by now. That's what Bulla reckoned.'

'Maybe the captain's wrong,' Geras said. 'Or maybe the merchant captains are more afraid of us than we thought.'

'But there's no one else operating this far north. Not as far as we know, anyway. The captains here have got nothing to be afraid of.'

Geras shrugged. 'Well, something must have scared them away from the sea lanes. It's been six days now and we've hardly seen a thing. Captain Bulla ain't going to be happy.'

Telemachus grimaced at the reminder of his ultimate responsibility as the commander of *Galatea*. A responsibility that had weighed heavily on his shoulders ever since they had set sail from Petrapylae. As *Galatea* had rounded the headland and made her way north, her hold filled with supplies, he had felt his initial unease give way to a surge of excitement. With a favourable wind at their backs he'd experienced something of the exhilarating power of being in command of a pirate ship, and he'd soon forgotten about his troubles with Hector. Even the regular bouts of seasickness that afflicted him during those first few days at sea could not dampen his enthusiasm.

But his hopes of capturing an early prize had been swiftly dashed. The crew had sighted only a handful of vessels since leaving their base. The few ships they did encounter turned and fled at the first sight of another sail, without waiting to see if they were friendly. Each passing day added to the pirates' boredom and frustration, with the men carrying out an endless routine of keeping watch, bilge-emptying and sail-mending.

To add to Telemachus's woes, several of the amphorae of wine stored in the hold had turned out to be rancid. He had been forced to empty the offending wine into the sea and had been left with no choice but to put the crew on reduced rations, further worsening their mood. The failure of *Achelous* to return to Petrapylae weighed heavily on the minds of the men, and some of them were openly wondering whether *Galatea* might suffer the same fate as the missing vessel, lost to the sea or captured by the imperial navy.

At least he had a friendly face to sail with. Bulla had allowed both commanders to appoint their own ship's mates, and Telemachus had been secretly relieved when Geras had agreed to join him as first mate aboard *Galatea*. His easy-going nature and quiet courage made him a popular figure among the men. Appointing him as first mate had been an easy choice. He was one of the few friends Telemachus had, and he depended on Geras's loyalty and comradeship.

'Perhaps Hector's had better luck than us,' he muttered.

'Down to the south? I wouldn't get your hopes up. Every sailor from here to Dyrrachium knows to avoid that stretch of the coast. He'd have more luck finding a hen with a decent set of dentures.'

'Then it's down to us, I suppose.'

Geras shrugged. 'Either way, one of us is going to have to land a prize soon. Otherwise we'll have to cut the rations again, and frankly I don't fancy telling this lot we're out of wine.'

'No,' Telemachus replied quietly. 'Me neither.'

They were interrupted by a heated exchange of shouts from across the deck. Telemachus looked towards the stern just in time to see Leitus barking orders at a heavily scarred pirate with dark flowing locks. In an instant the pirate rounded on him and tore into him with a mad flurry of blows. A crowd of deckhands quickly gathered as the man swung a fist, striking Leitus on the jaw and sending him crashing to the deck.

'Shit,' Geras muttered. 'What now?'

Telemachus sighed. 'Come on. We'd better sort this out.'

He pushed away from the rail and marched aft along the narrow deck, Geras hurrying after him. Telemachus shoved aside one of the cheering onlookers and stepped forward, filling his lungs.

'That's enough!' he roared. 'Break it up!'

There was still time for the dark-haired pirate to deliver a swift kick to Leitus's ribs. Telemachus snapped an order to a pair of deckhands, and they sprang into action, grabbing hold of the man and dragging him away. They kept a firm grip on him while Leitus rose groggily to his feet, pawing a hand at the blood streaming out of his nose.

'What's going on here?' Telemachus demanded.

'Bastard hit me,' Leitus growled.

'He deserved it,' the other pirate rasped. 'Called me a lazy Thracian dog.'

'Only because it's true.' Leitus spat out blood. 'This scum ain't been pulling his weight. I told him it was his turn to scrub down the decks, and he refused. I threatened to cut his rations if he didn't do as I said, and the bastard just came swinging at me.'

'Bollocks!' The Thracian glared at him, shaking with anger. 'Ain't my job to swab the decks. It ain't what I signed up for!'

Telemachus slanted his gaze to the man who'd spoken and recognised him as one of the recruits who had joined from Nestor's defeated crew. He was an impressively built figure, the veins on his muscular arms as thick as ropes. As with all those who had been pressed into the pirates' ranks, he carried the mark of a trident branded onto his left forearm.

'Bassus, isn't it?'

The Thracian nodded. 'Aye. That's me.'

'You have a problem with following orders?'

Bassus snorted. 'I have a problem with being told to clean decks and empty bilges all day, that's what. I'm a pirate. I joined this ship to get plunder, not clean on my hands and knees like some fucking slave.'

Telemachus took a step towards the scarred Thracian and looked him hard in the eye. 'You'll do your job the same as everyone else on the crew.'

'And what job is that? Pissing about on the sea instead of hunting prey?'

'We'll take some prizes soon. Very soon.'

'Is that right?' Bassus glanced at the faces surrounding him. 'And why should any of us believe a word you say? It's been six days and we ain't had so much as a sniff of loot. If we can't find any ships then we should be out raiding one of them rich ports, not sitting on our arses.'

Several voices murmured their support for the Thracian. From the corner of his eye, Telemachus glimpsed some of the older pirates staring keenly at him, curious to see how the young commander would respond to this challenge to his authority. He tensed his muscles and took a step closer to Bassus.

'Our orders are to stick to attacking merchant shipping,' he responded in a firm voice. 'Not to antagonise the Romans any further.'

'Fuck our orders! Captain Nestor never would have stood for this. If he was our commander, we'd be up to our eyeballs in wine and plunder by now.'

'*Silence!*' Telemachus shouted at the top of his voice.

The muttering around the deck fell quiet. For a moment there was no sound except the soft moan of the wind through the rigging and the hiss of the sea passing alongside, as the captain sought out a familiar face in the crowd.

'Castor!'

'Aye, sir?'

'Flog this man,' Telemachus ordered, tipping his head at Bassus.

The Thracian's jaw slackened. 'What?'

'Striking a superior. Twenty lashes. Rules of the ship.'

Bassus's face darkened. 'You can't do that.'

'Yes, I can,' Telemachus replied, his voice growing bolder. 'You agreed to the rules when you joined our band. And you'll follow them now, or I'll make it forty lashes. Your choice.'

Bassus instinctively opened his mouth before quickly clamping it shut again.

'Bind him!' Telemachus ordered the nearest deckhands, two men from Bulla's original crew whose loyalty he could rely on. They manhandled the dark-haired pirate over to the standing rigging in preparation for his flogging. Meanwhile Castor hurried to one of the storage lockers located amidships. A few moments later he returned gripping a short leather whip, a smile creasing his weathered face. The deckhands stripped Bassus to the waist and bound his hands to the shrouds, presenting his exposed back, then Telemachus nodded at Castor to begin.

He forced himself to watch as Castor lashed the pirate, drawing a howl of agony from the man with each blow. When the flogging had finished, Bassus was dragged off to have his lacerated back treated with vinegar. Geras shouted at the rest of the crew to return to their duties, and they quickly dispersed across the deck, muttering among themselves.

'That was well handled,' Geras said as he drew up alongside *Galatea*'s commander. 'Harsh, but it'll do the trick. A good flogging always does. It should keep 'em quiet.'

'For now, maybe,' Telemachus said.

'Captain?'

'I hate to say it, but Bassus is right. These men joined us to fight and get rich. Discipline's all well and good, but it won't keep them in line for ever. We can only do that by taking some prey.'

'And if we don't capture any? What then?'

Telemachus shrugged. 'More of the crew will turn against us. And a flogging won't be enough to stop them next time.'

Geras shook his head. 'So much for the life of a pirate. Hardly any wine, no plunder, and a mutinous crew. It's almost enough to make you yearn for the days aboard old *Selene*.'

Telemachus smiled weakly at his comrade. Less than two months had passed since *Selene* had been attacked by *Poseidon's Trident*, but already it felt like a lifetime ago.

'Having second thoughts, Geras?'

'Course not, Captain. Just saying, life was simpler back then. Being a sailor wasn't easy, but at least we didn't have to worry about keeping half the crew from our throats.'

Telemachus looked away, gripped by an intense feeling of helplessness. Perhaps if he had been a more experienced commander, the men might not have been so quick to question his judgement. But as a novice on his first independent command, he knew he had everything to prove. Which was why he'd punished Bassus so severely, he reminded himself. His limited experience as a pirate had taught him that the best captains rarely resorted to the whip, but he'd had no choice but to flog the man. Some of the crew were already sceptical of their young leader, and were ready to pounce on the slightest hint of weakness. He could not allow them to think of him as a soft touch.

A shout went up from the lookout sitting astride the yard.

'Deck there! Sail sighted!'

Telemachus and Geras both tilted their heads up at the boy on lookout duty. He sat on the spar, one arm wrapped around the mast while he pointed with the other off to the port bow, further out to sea. Telemachus looked in the same direction, peering at the horizon, but he could see nothing. He called up.

'Where away, Longarus?'

The boy paused before making his reply. 'One sail, sir. Hull down. Six, maybe seven miles off.'

'What's her heading?'

'North, sir.'

'Could be a merchantman,' Geras speculated.

Telemachus nodded absently, recalling the map of the coastline he'd pored over the night before they had set sail. 'Whoever she is, she must be making for Tarsatica. That's the only port for miles in any direction.'

Geras frowned. 'Why hasn't she shown us her heels yet, I wonder? She must have sighted us by now.'

'Not necessarily.' Telemachus pointed to the midday sun. 'She's to the north of us, which means the sun will be in her lookout's eyes.'

Geras squinted out at the horizon and grunted in agreement.

'I can see her hull now!' Longarus called down again. 'It's a merchantman. A big one, by the looks of it!'

'At long last!' Geras thumped his fist into the palm of his other hand. 'With a bit of luck, she'll have some decent wine on board as well.'

'We'll find out soon enough,' said Telemachus. 'Call all hands and put us on a course to intercept. We'll close at an angle and cut her off from the coast. There'll be no escape for her then.'

CHAPTER TWENTY-ONE

The merchantman made no attempt to flee and struck her sails as soon as she was within clear view of the pirates and their black pennant. As *Galatea* ploughed through the swell, Telemachus gave the order to approach the cargo vessel on her stern quarter, and the sturdy timbers shifted beneath him as the steersman adjusted course. While the men in the boarding party fetched their weapons, he looked back across the sea and cautiously surveyed the other ship. She was riding high, with none of the usual sluggishness of a bulky vessel loaded down with cargo. Then he noticed something else and turned to Geras, frowning.

'Where's the rest of the crew? There's hardly a soul on her deck. She should have more sailors than that, surely?'

Geras shrugged. 'Probably below in the hold, shitting themselves. Who cares? This is the easiest ship we'll ever catch!' He was grinning with excitement. Geras had been a reluctant pirate in the past, claiming to be more interested in sating his Epicurean desires than in hunting prey. Now he shared the mood of anticipation among the pirates as they closed in on their prize.

Telemachus looked back towards the merchantman, squinting beneath the noon sun. Only a handful of men were visible on her deck. None of them appeared to have any weapons, and they had seemingly made no effort to arm themselves or prepare their ship for boarding. Their lack of fight was puzzling. Bulla had taught him that even the meekest crews would offer some token resistance before eventually laying down their arms. But these sailors had surrendered without a fight. He shook his head and wondered again why the ship hadn't tried to evade capture. If her captain had fled at the first sight of the pirates, she might have had a chance of escaping, or at least of prolonging the chase in the hope that she might slip away under cover of darkness. But there was no prospect of that now.

At his side, Geras kept an eye on the horizon, searching for any hint of an abrupt change in weather, but the sky remained blissfully clear. When they were less than a hundred paces from the merchantman, Telemachus nodded at the first mate.

'Ready the men, Geras. We'll be boarding her shortly.'

'Aye, sir!'

Geras turned to shout at the crew. The pirates hefted shields and weapons as they massed around the mast, while several pairs of deckhands sprinted over to the boarding grapples tethered to cleats along the sides of the ship, ready to throw them over to the merchantman once the order was given. Telemachus yelled at the steersman to bring *Galatea* up on the merchant's starboard side. Then he grabbed a falcata and a small buckler and took his place forward with the rest of the boarding party. Although the cargo ship had struck her sails, he was taking no chances and wanted his men ready to attack in case the sailors were waiting to spring a trap.

Shortly after, the two ships slowly drew level and Telemachus called out across the deck, 'Ready grapples!'

Several pirates braced their feet on the planking and began to swing the iron hooks with lengths of rope attached. Telemachus carefully judged the gap between the two vessels as *Galatea* began to pull ahead of the merchantman. Then he shouted, 'Tiller, steer to port!'

Calkas heaved against his handle and the bows of *Galatea* angled towards her prey. The veteran pirate was an accomplished steersman and one of several men who had volunteered to serve with Telemachus, with many of *Trident*'s crew keen to avoid sailing with Hector.

'Grappling hooks . . . away!' Telemachus yelled.

The hooks arced up and over the side of the merchantman's deck. The men pulled hard on the ropes, drawing the two vessels closer together. As soon as they were directly alongside, Telemachus barked an order and the deckhands hastily lowered the mainsail. Then he clambered over the rail and leaped across to the cargo ship. The other pirates threw themselves across after him, thudding down on the smooth timbers and spreading out across the deck.

At the sight of the onrushing pirates, the handful of sailors immediately threw up their arms.

'Don't!' one cried out. 'We surrender! Please!'

Telemachus's blood was up, and it was with some difficulty that he lowered his weapon. 'You, there!' he shouted at a skinny older pirate. 'Sirras! Round this lot up!'

'Aye, sir.' A cruel smile lifted the corner of the pirate's mouth, before Telemachus remembered that nearly half of his men were from Nestor's crew, and were accustomed to dealing ruthlessly with the prisoners they captured.

'I want them alive, Sirras . . . for now. They might prove useful.'

The pirate nodded grudgingly and gestured to several of his companions. They shoved the terrified sailors towards the base of the mainmast, shouting at them and brandishing their weapons. Telemachus looked away from them and beckoned Castor over.

'Captain?'

'Take a few of the lads and search the hold. Look for any sailors hiding below and find out what she's carrying. Make sure no one keeps any plunder for themselves. Any man caught doing so will be flogged.'

The bald-headed veteran nodded and set off with several of the crew for the aft hatch leading down into the cargo hold. As they disappeared from view, Telemachus looked slowly around the deck. There were clear signs of a struggle aboard the merchantman. The cargo hatches had been dragged open, and several empty boxes and chests were strewn across the deck, while in places the planking was streaked with blood.

A few moments later, Castor returned from the direction of the aft hatch, looking grim-faced. 'Hold's empty.'

'Empty?' Telemachus repeated.

Castor made a helpless gesture with his hands. 'Nearly everything's been taken. There's not much down there except rats and a few old sailcloths. Whatever this old bird was transporting, she ain't got it now.'

Telemachus frowned deeply, struggling to hide his disappointment and frustration as he turned his attention to the sailors huddled beside the mast. A handful of passengers stood among them, their paler complexions and less well-defined physiques marking them out from the weathered-looking ship's crew.

'This lot probably dumped their cargo overside when they

saw us coming,' Sciron snarled, pointing at the sailors with the tip of his sword. 'I say we gut some of the spineless bastards.'

'Don't!' one of the sailors protested. 'We didn't dump anything, I swear to the gods! We were attacked!'

Telemachus turned his attention to the speaker, a swarthy, Eastern-looking man wearing a Phrygian cap. He was the same sailor who'd pleaded with the pirates when they had swarmed aboard, Telemachus noticed. He narrowed his eyes at the man. 'And who might you be?'

'Amyntas, sir,' the sailor replied nervously. 'First mate aboard *Artemis*.'

'Where's your captain, Amyntas?'

'He's dead, sir. Him and most of the others. They killed 'em.'

'Who did?'

'The men who attacked us, sir. The pirates.'

Telemachus exchanged a surprised glance with Geras. Then he returned his icy stare to the sailor. 'Pirates attacked you?'

'Aye, sir, I swear it.'

'Tell me what happened, Amyntas. The truth, now, or I'll gut you and your friends right here.'

The sailor met his glare anxiously and quickly composed himself. 'We was making our usual run up from Ephesus to Pula in the company of another ship, the *Skamandros*. Most of the captains won't risk sailing alone these days, on account of all that pirate activity that's been going on.'

Telemachus nodded slowly. He knew from his own experiences aboard *Selene* that merchant captains were wary of sailing up through the lower Adriaticum due to the fear of running into a pirate gang, and it was no surprise to hear that trading vessels had taken to making the voyage in pairs.

'Go on.'

'That's when we spotted them, sir. The other pirates. Big ship, she was. Came out of nowhere and swooped down on us. *Skamandros* made a run for it, but we had no such luck,' he added bitterly. 'Our captain knew we didn't stand a chance, so he agreed to surrender, but the pirates cut him down anyway. They took all our cargo, and most of our provisions as well. Meanwhile their captain questioned us. Demanded to know what we knew about any other shipping in the area. Then he started killing the rest of us. We begged him to spare the women and children among the passengers, but he was a cold-hearted bastard. Would've killed us all if it weren't for that Roman patrol showing up when it did.'

Telemachus felt a chill on his neck. 'Romans?'

'Aye, sir.' The man sniffed. 'They've had patrols running up and down this area of the coast for the past few weeks.'

'I see. What happened then?'

'The pirates abandoned our ship and fled before the navy could give chase. One of the Roman officers boarded us to take stock. He advised us to head for the nearest port and not put to sea again until the threat had been dealt with. We took shelter last night in a bay and were hoping to make Tarsatica before nightfall. That's when we saw your sail. We knew we couldn't outrun you, so we decided to surrender, sir. We ain't got nothing left worth looting anyway.'

The sailor lowered his head, his shoulders slumped in despair. Telemachus left him to his private grief and turned to Geras. 'What do you think?'

Geras pressed his lips together as he considered. 'His story adds up. At least we know why we've hardly sighted a sail for the past few days.'

'I agree. But it doesn't make any sense. There aren't supposed to be any other crews operating this far north. Unless there are some pirates in the area that Bulla doesn't know about.'

'There must be, sir. Who else could it be?'

Telemachus stared out across the blood-splattered deck, a troubling thought forming inside his head. He swung back to face Amyntas. 'These other pirates,' he said. 'What did they look like?'

The sailor looked up, scratching his elbow. 'Just pirates, like you. Their ship was bigger, mind.'

'Anything else? Think hard, Amyntas.'

The man paused for a moment, his face scrunched in thought. 'There was one other thing, come to think of it.'

'What? What was it?'

'Their leader. Big bloke, he was. He had a mark on his forearm. I didn't get a proper look at it, but it looked like some sort of spear.'

'A trident? Like this?' Telemachus drew his sleeve back and extended his left arm towards the sailor, revealing the mark that had been branded into his flesh several weeks earlier.

Amyntas studied it for a beat. 'Aye,' he said. 'That's it. That's the same mark, sir.'

'Hector . . .' Telemachus hissed through gritted teeth.

'What's he doing up here?' Geras wondered, his brow heavily creased. '*Proteus* is supposed to be down to the south.'

Telemachus shook his head angrily. 'That lying bastard never intended to follow orders. Don't you see? He knew there would be slim pickings down that way. He must have cut round us not long after we set out from Petrapylae.'

'Hector must have had his reasons,' Castor interjected. 'Maybe one of the navy patrols chased him this way.'

'But if that's the case, why is he butchering the crews of the vessels he takes? Think about it. He's only doing that so there aren't any witnesses to the raids, in case we discover what he's up to.'

Telemachus looked away, trying to conceal his emotions as a bitter rage flared inside his chest. His hated rival had bested him, he realised. He had been a fool to believe that Hector would ever follow Bulla's orders, and the men would think of him as incompetent for allowing the other captain to outwit him so easily.

But then he reminded himself that he was the commander of a pirate vessel. He had an unhappy crew to deal with, a ship low on provisions, and a Roman naval squadron scouring this side of the Adriaticum. A lifetime of hardship and day-to-day survival had inured him against dwelling too long on misfortune, and he forced himself to shove aside his frustration as he turned back towards the sailor.

'When did this attack happen?' he asked.

'Yesterday afternoon. Not long before dusk, sir.'

'Whereabouts exactly?'

'Not far from Senia. A few hours after we'd passed that colony.'

Geras rubbed his jaw in thought. 'That puts Hector half a day ahead of us. *Proteus* isn't the quickest ship. We can still overhaul her with this following wind and raid the shipping before she does.'

'Assuming there's any prey still to be had,' Castor pointed out.

'What do you mean? Of course there will be.'

The quartermaster shook his head. 'It's been days since we started hunting in these waters. We have to assume that

Hector's had more successes than this one ship. If that's the case, the other vessels might be wise to our presence by now. And according to this lot, the navy's telling every captain to avoid putting to sea. There'll be fewer ships chancing a voyage, and those that do will probably turn at the first sight of us.'

'Shit!' Geras shook his head angrily. 'There must be something we can do. We can't let that bastard get away with this.'

Telemachus thought for a moment. He knew he couldn't return to Petrapylae empty-handed. To do so would incur Bulla's wrath and signal the end of his short career as commander of a pirate vessel. He needed a victory. One that would prove to the rest of the crew that he deserved to be their leader. He cocked his head at the sailor.

'This other ship . . . *Skamandros*. Where is she headed?'

The sailor shrugged. 'I don't know. Our captain knew, but he's dead.' He looked away and shifted uneasily on the spot.

Telemachus saw the flicker of defiance in the man's eyes. 'You're lying, Amyntas.'

'It's the truth, sir,' he replied meekly.

Telemachus glanced over his shoulder. 'Sciron! Cut this liar's tongue out.'

The stocky pirate grinned wickedly as he stepped forward and unsheathed a dagger from his belt. Two other men clamped their hands around Amyntas's arms, holding him in place as Sciron brought the dagger up towards his face. At the sight of the gleaming blade, the sailor's resistance crumbled.

'Flanona! She'll have headed for Flanona! That's where she'll be now.'

'You're sure?' Telemachus demanded.

'It was an agreement between our captains,' Amyntas

responded quickly. 'If either of us ran into trouble, we'd make for Flanona and wait until it was safe to return to sea.'

'Makes sense,' Castor put in. 'It's not too far from here. It's as good a place as any to seek shelter.'

'What's she carrying?' Telemachus demanded, his piercing blue eyes fixed on the sailor.

'Spices mainly. Some camphor and sandalwood. Ivory too.'

'Spices!' Geras whistled. 'Neptune's cock! That lot would be worth a small fortune if we could get our hands on it.'

'That's if she's still at the port,' Castor observed. 'Flanona is a day's sailing from here. She might have moved on by now.'

The sailor shook his head. 'She'll be there for a couple of days at least. Her captain's a cautious old sea dog. If I know him, he won't want to return to sea again until he's sure it's safe.'

'That settles it, then. We'll return to *Galatea* at once. Leitus, round up the prisoners and put them in the hold. Transfer whatever supplies are left to our ship.'

The sun was already dipping towards the horizon as the civilians trudged disconsolately across the deck towards the hold.

'Is this wise, Captain?' Geras asked quietly. 'We're low enough on supplies without having extra mouths to feed.'

'Bulla's orders. Besides, we'll get a decent price for them on the slave market.'

Telemachus was mildly surprised at how little he cared about condemning these people to a lifetime of misery and servitude while his own brother remained a slave. But he had lived a hard life, and he had long ago grown accustomed to the outrageous injustices and cruelties of the world. Since he could not change them, he might as well profit from them instead.

'Have the others return to the ship,' he said to Geras determinedly. 'We'll set sail for Flanona and take *Skamandros* at her anchorage. If we move now, we'll be able to seize her before she has a chance to move on again.'

Castor overheard and sucked the salty air between his teeth. Telemachus stared at him. 'Is there a problem?'

'It's going to be difficult to cut her out,' Castor replied. 'I've been to Flanona a few times, back when I served on merchant ships. That place is well defended. Steep cliffs on both sides, and there's a garrison there too.'

'Militia?'

'Auxiliaries. The authorities reinforced the garrison after the last pirate raids a few years back. They've got a watchtower and catapults as well. We'd never be able to get close enough. Not with that lot guarding the port.'

'We could go in at night,' Geras suggested. 'They wouldn't see us then.'

Castor considered, then shook his head. 'Won't work. We'd still have to take the ship without raising the alarm. It's hopeless.'

'Maybe not,' Telemachus mused.

Geras stared enquiringly at his commander. 'Captain?'

Telemachus grinned as the outline of a plan began to take shape in his head. 'If we can't go in to take *Skamandros*, then we'll just have to bring the prize out to us instead . . .'

CHAPTER TWENTY-TWO

'Are you sure this is a good idea?' Geras asked as he stared out at the black mass of the mountains rising above Flanona.

Telemachus had given the order to heave to near the mouth of the bay shortly after night had fallen over the coastline. *Galatea*'s sails had been lowered and her yard had been taken down to reduce her chances of being seen from the land. Beyond the bows, he could hear the soft lapping of the waves against the hull.

He smiled grimly. 'Ask me again in another hour.'

'Perhaps we're better off looking elsewhere,' Geras said. 'Head back out to sea. We'll snap up something sooner or later.'

'I've made my decision,' Telemachus replied firmly. 'We can't pass up this opportunity. Now remember. If I don't return within the hour, you're to assume command of the ship and leave the bay at once. Head to the meeting point and stop for nothing.'

'You'd bloody better come back.'

'I will.' He attempted a smile. The look of unease on his companion's face was barely discernible beneath the loom of the stars. Behind Geras, the men in the boarding party were assembling near the mast. They whispered softly as they made their final preparations ahead of the night's surprise attack on *Skamandros*.

The pirates had arrived at Flanona several hours earlier, having raced down the coast under full sail. Approaching the bay, Telemachus had ordered the crew to bring *Galatea* as close to the port as possible to reconnoitre the defences before moving away again in the gathering dusk. With luck, the lookouts would have seen the pirates disappearing over the horizon and might be lulled into thinking they had gone off in search of easier prey. Telemachus's plan depended on the merchantman's captain assuming that no pirate commander would be reckless enough to try to steal her from under the noses of the local auxiliary garrison.

His careful study of the port had confirmed his initial calculation that a direct approach was impossible. A watchtower guarded the entrance to the harbour, ready to alert the local garrison at the first sign of trouble. Bolt-throwers had been mounted on the town walls to protect the local cargo ships and fishing boats, and any raiding parties would be sunk long before they could reach the quay. Even if they managed to sneak past the defences, seizing the merchantman would not be easy. Amyntas had readily identified *Skamandros* at her mooring, warning that the cargo ship's crew was fiercely loyal to their captain and would put up a tough fight if anyone attempted to capture her by force.

Twenty men would accompany Telemachus on the raid: close to half the ship's crew. He had picked the most capable sailors to seize and then sail *Skamandros* out of the port in the dark. He himself would go ahead with three others in the small skiff *Galatea* carried on her deck. The rest of the boarding party, under the command of Castor, would follow at a distance in a mackerel boat they had captured earlier that day.

'The lads are ready,' Castor announced in an undertone, approaching from the direction of the side rail.

Telemachus nodded. 'Get them aboard the boats. Remember, no one's to make a noise. I'll have the hide off any man caught talking once we set off.'

'Don't worry. They won't make a peep. I'll make sure of it.'

Castor turned away and issued a hushed order to the boarding party. His men climbed down first, lowering themselves into the fishing boat bobbing alongside *Galatea*. Then several deckhands yanked on the pulley ropes and raised the skiff from its platform while others eased it over to the side. Telemachus descended the rope ladder last, dropping down gently behind Bassus, Longarus and Leitus. The latter had objected vehemently to bringing Bassus on the mission, but Telemachus had overruled him, arguing that the surly, recalcitrant Thracian had performed his duties without complaint in the days since his punishment. Besides, Telemachus reflected, as a former gladiator, Bassus's skill with a sword would come in handy during the expedition.

The two boats shoved off, the men straining at the muffled oars. Telemachus softly called the time as the skiff slowly drew ahead of the men in the mackerel boat and rowed towards the shore. All seemed quiet and still, but he could feel his heart beating faster in his chest as they neared the bay. The plan depended on the men in the skiff creating a diversion before the rest of the boarding party could attack *Skamandros*. Without it, the pirates would never be able to overrun the cargo ship's crew before the auxiliaries arrived on the scene. Any of the men unfortunate enough to be taken alive would be crucified, the punishment inflicted on those who dared to defy Rome's command of the high seas.

With a great effort of will, Telemachus shook off his doubts as the skiff crept into the bay. He glanced over his shoulder for any sign of Castor's boat, but it was far behind now, lost to the darkness as its crew waited to play their part in the attack. He looked ahead again and caught a glimpse of the ships moored bow to stern along the stone quay, their masts silhouetted against the warm glow of the lights in the town.

He whispered an order and the skiff altered course, gliding towards the stone ramp at the far end of the quay. As they drew near, he ran his eyes over the wharf. To one side stood a row of large timbered warehouses, with several narrow streets leading off the quay. Most of them were deserted, but a distant hubbub of voices came from the direction of the town as the sailors caroused at the local taverns.

A few moments later, the skiff drew alongside the quay and Telemachus whispered for his men to ease at their oars. The small craft bumped lightly against the ramp as Bassus took the painter and fastened it to one of the stone posts, steadying the skiff on the calm water. Once it was secure, Telemachus slowly rose to his feet and motioned to his crew.

'On me,' he said quietly. 'And remember, boys, don't rush, or we'll draw attention to ourselves. If anyone approaches us, I'll do the talking.'

The other three pirates nodded, then followed Telemachus as he mounted the steps leading up to the quay. All four of them were dressed in plain tunics and cheap sandals similar to those worn by *Artemis*'s crew. If they were challenged, they would claim to be sailors from one of the cargo ships moored along the quay. The ruse might buy them a few moments to spring a surprise and make their escape.

Telemachus forced himself to walk at a casual pace as he moved towards the cluster of warehouses located to the side of the harbour. He could feel the sheathed falcata he had concealed beneath his cloak tapping against his thigh as he crossed the wide thoroughfare separating the quay from the warehouses. A pair of sailors passed them, grinning drunkenly as they stumbled back towards their vessel. Telemachus nodded a greeting and carried on, his heart quickening. At any moment he expected to be challenged, but the handful of people out in the streets were drunk and too busy swapping jokes or fighting each other to pay him any attention.

He stopped abruptly in the shadows and scanned the warehouses. Amyntas had told them that one of the buildings stocked cargoes of flax. After a few moments, he found the place he was looking for.

'There,' he said quietly, pointing to a warehouse off to the left. 'That's the one.'

The other three men concentrated their gazes in the direction he'd indicated. A painted sign above the entrance to the yard announced that the warehouse belonged to Vibius Draco. Beside the gate sat a thickset guard, his features illuminated by the wan glow of a burning lamp. A studded wooden club hung from his leather belt.

'What now?' Leitus asked.

'We get inside and torch the place.'

'How? If we try and force our way in, he'll raise the alarm. Them auxiliaries will be on us before we can get the fire going.'

'I've got a better idea,' Telemachus replied. 'Come on. Follow me.'

Taking a deep breath, he strode casually up to the gates with his men either side of him, glancing around to make sure that no one was watching them. As they drew near, the guard rose from his stool and blocked the entrance, folding his thick arms across his chest. His small, dull eyes considered the four men in front of him.

'The fuck do you want?' he growled.

'We're looking for the Drunken Dolphin,' Telemachus said, holding up his hands. 'Supposed to be meeting some friends there.'

The guard narrowed his eyes in suspicion. 'The Dolphin? That's the other side of town.'

Telemachus made an exaggerated show of cursing under his breath. 'Typical of Galabrus. Giving us the wrong directions, as bloody usual. How do we get there, friend?'

The guard relaxed his stance slightly as he gestured down the street. 'It's a bit of a walk. You'll have to head down that way, see, take the second turn on your right and follow it all the way along . . .'

As he pointed out the route, Telemachus snatched out the dagger from under his cloak and brought it up to the guard's neck, pressing the tip against his soft flesh.

'Make a sound,' he hissed under his breath, 'and I'll gut you like a fish. Got it?'

The guard lowered his arm and nodded quickly. Telemachus nudged him through the gap into the yard, with the other three men following close behind. Once they were inside, he stopped and turned to his companions.

'Get the torches lit,' he ordered. 'Hurry.'

Leitus hurried out of the yard, returning a moment later with the oil lamp removed from its bracket. At the same time, Bassus and Longarus fished out the torches they had been carrying under their cloaks. Leitus grabbed the first torch and carefully touched the lamp flame to the tallow-soaked cloth wrapped around one end of the wooden shaft. It took a moment for it to flicker into life. He lit the second torch, then set down the lamp and returned to the gate to keep watch. Telemachus took Bassus's torch and gave him orders to bind and gag the guard, and slit his throat if he caused any trouble. Then he padded over to the warehouse alongside Longarus, the flickering glow of the torch flames illuminating the sturdy-looking doors facing the yard.

Glancing around, he saw that all the doors were secured with iron bolts. He approached the nearest one and tested it. The locking mechanism made a grating noise as he tried to heave it out of the receiving bracket. He whispered for Longarus to help him, and they gently shifted the bolt free, working slowly to make as little noise as possible. Then he pulled the door open and stepped cautiously inside, with Longarus following close behind.

They entered a wide chamber with a stone floor. Bales of flax were stacked along either side, some of the stacks so tall that they almost touched the timber beams running along the tiled roof. Telemachus moved over to one of the bales on the right, tugged it apart and held the torch to the loosened material, whilst Longarus did the same on the other side of the room. As soon as the flames spread, they moved on, circling the chamber and torching several more bales. The fire quickly took hold, crackling furiously as bright yellow and orange tongues of flame spread from one bale to the next.

'Come on,' Telemachus said. 'Let's get out of here.'

Plumes of acrid black smoke billowed into the night air as they made their way back outside. Bassus had tied up and gagged the warehouse guard and dumped him beside the handcarts to one side of the gate. The man's muffled cries for help were soon drowned out by the roar of the blaze as it rapidly consumed the warehouse. There was no need for stealth now, and the four men hastened out of the entrance and moved quickly along the quay. Already several of the sailors on the decks of the moored ships were rousing their comrades, gesturing frantically towards the flames.

Telemachus squatted down with his comrades beside a pile of grain baskets heaped near one of the cargo vessels and looked back towards the warehouse as a handful of auxiliaries rushed forward from the garrison to deal with the blaze. By now it was raging uncontrollably, and as the flames spread to the neighbouring building, one of the guards shouted at the onlooking sailors to help them. No one moved at first, many of them paralysed by the sight. At last some of the ships' captains ordered their crews to action, no doubt grasping that their own supplies and goods were in danger of being destroyed. Soon only a few men remained on the deck of each vessel.

'Where are the others?' Leitus muttered under his breath. 'They should have seen the signal by now.'

Telemachus turned his attention to the placid waters of the harbour, undisturbed by the rhythmic motion of muffled oars, and for a few anxious moments he wondered if the second boat had gone astray. Then he saw her dark shape emerging from the blackness as her crew rowed straight for *Skamandros*. Just as Telemachus had anticipated, the handful of crew remaining on the cargo ship's deck were transfixed by the flames engulfing the warehouse and were completely unaware of the small boat steering towards them. It abruptly disappeared from his field of vision as it closed fast on *Skamandros*. There was a long, tense pause, and then several panicked cries pierced the air as the pirates scrambled up the side of the hull and swarmed across the deck, weapons gleaming.

'Now!' Telemachus said, moving out from behind the cover of the grain sacks. 'On me, lads!'

He raced down the quay with his three companions, heading for the gangway leading up to *Skamandros*'s deck. Ahead of him he could hear a chorus of shouts as a desperate struggle unfolded aboard the cargo ship, but with the fire continuing to rage across the harbour, no one else was paying attention. Telemachus gripped his falcata as he sprinted up the lowered boarding plank, his three companions wrenching their own swords free from their concealed scabbards as they hurried after him.

He reached the foredeck in a few more strides and looked towards the dark mass of bodies tearing into each other by the mainmast. In the glow of the distant flames he could see a small knot of sailors standing their ground against the boarding party, armed with belaying pins and boathooks and whatever other makeshift weapons they had been able to find. They were putting up a determined fight against their better-armed opponents, but they were oblivious to the four men rushing towards them from the foredeck.

'Get 'em!' Telemachus roared.

He charged towards the nearest sailor, a squat figure gripping a spear. At the last instant the sailor heard the pounding footsteps behind him and whirled around to face the onrushing pirate. The man thrust out with the spear, driving the point at his opponent's throat. Telemachus desperately parried the attack and responded with a feint, but the sailor stepped out of range before he could land a blow with his falcata. Snarling, the sailor stabbed out again. This time Telemachus sidestepped the attack, throwing himself to the side to avoid the leaf-shaped point as it hissed savagely through the night air. He snatched hold of the shaft with his spare hand and pulled hard, jerking the sailor towards him. The man gasped in dumb surprise as Telemachus slashed the edge of his falcata across his front, just below the ribcage, opening up a deep wound to his guts. Trembling hands reached down, pawing at his glistening intestines as they bulged out of the gash, and the man sank to his knees, mouth gaping in shock.

Telemachus heard cheering, and looked up to see that the few remaining sailors were throwing down their makeshift weapons in surrender. Others were leaping into the water in a bid to escape the pirates. But there was no time to celebrate, as the noise of the attack had drawn the attention of the crews on other moored ships. Some of them sprinted down the wharf, shouting in panicked voices at the auxiliaries tackling the fire at the warehouse. Telemachus turned back to his men.

'Slip the moorings!' he bellowed. 'Get us moving! *Now!*'

One party of men hurriedly loosened the mooring cables and tossed them over the side, while others grabbed the ship's sweep oars and used them to ease *Skamandros* away from the quayside. As soon as they were in open water, Castor shouted an order and the rest of the crew hurriedly set down their weapons and rushed to help with the sweeps, thrusting the ship's bows towards the mouth of the bay.

Telemachus glanced anxiously over his shoulder as they

got under way. By now, the auxiliaries and the rest of the crowd near the warehouse had grasped what was happening, and he spied tiny figures scrambling up the ramparts enclosing the town, their shapes illuminated by the apricot glow of the flames. The fire lit up the surrounding harbour, reflecting off the gently lapping water, and several of the pirates crowded the aft deck as they gathered to watch the spectacle.

A challenge was shouted from one of the watchtowers as the captured cargo ship edged across the harbour. Then Telemachus saw a shimmer of movement atop the town walls, swiftly followed by the distinctive crack of a bolt-thrower. There was a loud splash as the bolt fell short of its target and struck the water behind *Skamandros*. Telemachus wheeled round to face Castor.

'They'll have our range soon. Can't we go any faster?'

The quartermaster shook his head. 'The lads are rowing as hard as they can.'

Telemachus muttered a curse to himself. A series of cracks sounded across the bay as more bolts arced invisibly through the dark sky. The next shot landed in the ship's wake, but the third scored a direct hit on the men gathered on the aft deck, skewering two of the raiders. Their hideous cries split the night air as the bolt tip ran through them, lodging in the planking in a vicious shower of splinters. As the barrage continued, the other hands scrambled along the deck or dived for cover in a desperate attempt to avoid the same fate as their comrades.

Telemachus felt a puff of air on his cheek.

'Get the mainsail raised!' he bellowed at Leitus. 'We'll use the land breeze to increase our speed. Hurry!'

Leitus relayed the order, and those men not straining at the oars hurried up the ratlines and spread out along the yardarm, working as fast as they could to undo the leather ties around the linen sail. Below them, on the deck, the others worked frantically to haul in the sheets and fasten them to the side rails. The breeze filled the mainsail with a dull thud, and under the increased pressure *Skamandros* quickly picked up speed, her bows surging through the water towards the entrance to the bay.

Telemachus and Castor both glanced back at the port as several more cracks signalled another barrage of missiles arcing towards them, in a last attempt to hit *Skamandros* before she could make her escape. But she was steadily drawing out of range and the bolts missed their target, dipping into the water astern of the ship as she reached the safety of the open sea.

An excited cheer went up from the men working the oars as Telemachus told them to ease off and take them in. Castor went down into the hold and reappeared moments later, grinning widely.

'Her cargo's all there,' he said. 'A bloody fortune in spices and ivory. Just like that sailor from *Artemis* said.'

'And supplies?'

'Ship's been freshly provisioned, by the looks of her. Bread, water, cheese and barrels of salted pork. Plenty of wine down there too.'

Telemachus nodded and felt an enormous sense of relief. His daring plan to seize *Skamandros* had worked. With his double share of the plunder they had taken, he would be closer to buying his brother's freedom. Much closer. But the scheme had cost the lives of some of his men, he reminded himself bitterly. And they were not entirely safe yet. Not while they remained in the area, with the garrison hurrying to alert the rest of the coastline to their presence. He turned to Sciron.

'Round up a prize crew. I'm placing you in command of this ship. We'll heave to once we reach the open sea and set sail for Insula Pelagus as soon as it's light enough.'

'Aye, aye,' Sciron replied.

Telemachus stared ahead as they sailed towards the waiting *Galatea*, smiling to himself. For the first time since taking command, he felt the wild thrill of leading a hardened pirate crew on a successful raid. It was a sense of achievement and pride beyond anything he'd ever known before. At his side he noticed Castor grinning at him, rubbing his hands expectantly.

'Now that's what I call a good cutting-out,' he said. 'The men will be toasting you tonight.'

Telemachus nodded and looked back towards Flanona. 'The lads did well,' he said at last. 'Now we've just got to deal with that bastard Hector.'

CHAPTER TWENTY-THREE

'Seems we're the first ones here.' Leitus nodded at the distant shore and Telemachus followed his gaze, shading his eyes as he searched for any sign of *Proteus* and her crew.

The sun beat down from a cloudless sky, and a warm breeze was blowing as *Galatea* steered towards the meeting point. In her wake a pair of prize crews sailed the two ships Telemachus had captured: *Skamandros*, and a smaller cargo vessel they had intercepted on their way back from Flanona. The latter had been caught fleeing a squall further up the coast and had stood no chance against the far speedier pirate craft. Her cargo of cloth, glass and Samian ware would fetch a decent price with the merchants at Petrapylae. With each man due a share of the profits from the captured hauls, the crew were in good spirits and chatted and laughed as they went about their duties.

Geras scanned the unbroken shoreline and frowned. 'Where's *Proteus*? Hector and his lads should be here by now.'

'Who knows?' Telemachus shrugged. 'Perhaps they ran into another naval patrol. Or they might have been blown off course in that last squall.'

'Or maybe the bastard simply wants to keep us waiting. That'd be just like him.'

Telemachus sighed wearily. 'Either way, there's nothing for us to do except heave to and wait for him to arrive. Bulla's orders.'

'Since when did Hector give a toss about following orders? Anyway, we'll have the last laugh. Just wait until he sees all the loot we've plundered. I bet his lads won't have captured anything as valuable as a shipload of spices. That'll put the bastard in his place.'

Castor pressed his lips together. 'I wouldn't be so sure.'

'What's that supposed to mean?' Telemachus asked, turning to the veteran pirate.

'Hector's been on the crew for a long time. Longer than most. He might not be a skilled sailor, but he's tough and he knows how to survive. He's seen off plenty of challenges to his authority over the years. Once he finds out how well we've done, he'll see you as a threat. Mark my words.'

Telemachus shook his head. 'I'm just following orders. At least Bulla will be happy.'

'Try telling that to Hector.'

Geras snorted noisily. 'Pirates. More bloody politics than an Athenian debating society. Frankly, I'm just looking forward to getting back to the base with all this loot. There's enough here to keep us drunk and laid for months.'

'For the other lads, perhaps,' Telemachus remarked. 'Somehow I doubt your share will last that long.'

Geras looked at him, grinning. 'Maybe not. But what's the point in capturing all this booty if you can't enjoy it?'

Telemachus looked away, listening in silence as Geras and the others lapsed into an excited discussion about how they would spend their fortunes once they returned to Petrapylae. His own thoughts turned to his brother. Even with his double share of the profits, he might not have enough coin to purchase Nereus's freedom. According to one of the merchants he'd spoken to at Petrapylae, Decimus Rufius Burrus had a reputation for driving a hard bargain, and Telemachus could expect to have to pay a hefty sum if he wanted to free his brother. A bitter frustration took hold of him. Despite his best efforts, his brother was still a slave, at the mercy of his Roman master. Unless he could capture an even greater prize than *Skamandros*, he might never see Nereus again.

Two hours later, a shout sounded from the masthead. 'Deck there! Sail sighted, Captain!'

Telemachus tilted his head up at the lookout. 'What can you see, Longarus?'

'Too small to be a merchantman, sir.'

'Could be a Roman patrol,' Geras commented.

Telemachus shook his head. 'I doubt it. We're off the main trade route.'

'I can see her more clearly now,' the lookout called down. 'She's flying a black pennant. Looks like *Proteus* all right, sir.'

Geras grunted. 'About bloody time.'

Telemachus nodded and turned his attention back to the horizon. *Galatea*'s mainsail had been furled and a small foresail had been set to steady her bows as she rode on the gentle swell. An hour later, he spotted the black pennant. As he looked on, the larger pirate vessel closed in slowly. She moved sluggishly, wallowing along through the calm sea, and as she turned on the final tack, Telemachus saw that a spar had been lashed to the broken stump of the mainmast. A stained and streaked spare sail had been set in an irregular fashion.

'Looks like she's been damaged,' Leitus said. 'No wonder it took her so long to get here.'

When *Proteus* was a mile away, a handful of figures carefully lowered the sail and spar. Then the crew ran her sweep oars out and they rowed the remaining distance to *Galatea* before heaving to fifty paces away. A few moments later, one of the crew appeared on the foredeck and called out across the swell.

'Captain Hector wants to speak with you, Telemachus!'

Telemachus shouted a response and then turned to the ship's mates. 'Right. I'd better find out what's going on. Lower the skiff. Geras, come with me. Leitus, you're in command here until we return.'

The skiff rocked as it bobbed across the gap between the two ships. Telemachus sat in the stern, with Geras in front of him, two other pirates straining at the oars as they propelled the boat towards *Proteus*. When they had drawn alongside the galley, Telemachus gave the order for the men to rest at their oars. Geras fastened the boathook to *Proteus*'s side rail, and then someone threw down a rope. Telemachus got awkwardly to his feet, waited for the boat to rise on the swell and then grabbed hold of the rope and scrambled up the side of the vessel. Geras swiftly followed, joining him on the main deck several moments later.

Glancing around, Telemachus could see the full extent of the damage. *Proteus*'s shrouds and sheets had been improvised with numerous splices, and some of the timbers around the hatch coaming had splintered. A chain of men emptied buckets of water over the other side. They went about their duties with dejected expressions, muttering among themselves.

'What happened here?' Geras asked the deckhand who'd thrown down the rope.

'What the fuck does it look like?' the man said in an under-tone. 'We got caught in a storm last night. Took our mast clean off.'

Telemachus pulled a face. 'We passed through that same storm. It wasn't that dangerous. Not enough to take away a mast, anyway.'

'It was the captain's fault,' the hand replied bitterly. 'He refused to take in any sail before the storm hit. Wind put us right over. It's a miracle we didn't capsize. We lost three men, and the rest of us have been bailing out water for most of the night.'

'What about your cargo?' Telemachus asked.

The hand shrugged despondently. 'We had to dump most of it overside.'

'Can't imagine Hector's happy about that.'

'Ask him yourself.'

He nodded towards the gangway leading down to the stern cabin. *Proteus*'s captain had emerged alongside a taller, sinewy pirate, his matted dark locks flecked with grey. Telemachus vaguely recognised him as Virbius, the ship's first mate.

Hector scowled at the deckhand and the latter hurried off, leaving the four men to confer in as much privacy as could be permitted on the cramped deck. Hector glanced briefly at the two merchantmen floating alongside *Galatea* before looking at Telemachus.

'I'll make this quick,' he snapped. '*Proteus* is in no state to hunt for prey. She's barely staying afloat.'

'What are you going to do?' Geras asked.

'What choice do I have? I'll have to take her back to Petrapylae for repairs. With this rigged mast we should just about make it back there in one piece.'

Virbius cocked his head at *Skamandros* and the smaller cargo ship. 'At least you've had some luck.'

'We've done all right,' Telemachus said, turning to Hector. 'No thanks to you.'

'What's that supposed to mean, boy?'

'I know what you've been playing at.' Telemachus stared coldly at *Proteus*'s commander. 'We came across one of the ships you and your men looted the other day. Their survivors told us the whole story. You never went south. You've been chasing down prey in our area of operations, against orders.'

Hector smiled arrogantly and spread his arms. 'So what if I have? Any fool could see there was no point in going south.'

'You disobeyed Bulla's orders.'

'I didn't have a choice. Me and the lads would've spent weeks down there without finding a fucking thing.'

'Tell that to Bulla when we return.'

Hector chuckled. 'And whose side do you think the captain will take? I'm his second in command. He'll trust my judgement over yours any day.' He folded his arms across his chest and grinned.

Telemachus clenched his jaws in anger, but he knew Hector was right. The first mate had plenty of allies among the crew, and Bulla would not want to risk provoking them. Not when his own position remained under threat.

'Besides,' Hector continued, 'if we hadn't been hunting to the north, we wouldn't have found out about the convoy that's sheltering not far from here.'

Telemachus furrowed his brow. 'What convoy?'

'There are three merchant ships anchored in a bay about half a day's sailing away. Ripe for plucking.'

'And I'm supposed to take your word for that, am I?'

Hector shook his head. 'Not mine. We ran into some fishermen yesterday. They're the ones who told us about it.'

Geras looked at him closely. 'What did they say?'

'Apparently a naval squadron's been going up and down the coast telling every ship they run into to anchor somewhere safe until they've sunk us, or driven us off. The fishermen reckon the bay the convoy is sheltering in is undefended. Anyone attacking them would have the pick of their cargo.'

'How do we know those fishermen are telling the truth?'

Hector shrugged. 'I'm just telling you what I know.'

'If these ships are such an easy target, why haven't you gone after them yet?' Telemachus asked.

'We were going to,' Virbius replied in his rasping voice. 'We were planning to reconnoitre the bay when that bastard storm struck. There's no way we can go ahead with it now, not with *Proteus* in the state she's in. But there's nothing to stop you taking it on.'

'Where exactly is this bay?'

'No more than thirty miles up the coast from here,' Hector said. 'Should be easy enough to find. You could scout it and see if it's worth attacking.' He paused a beat. 'I could take them vessels you've captured back to Petrapylae with me.'

Geras laughed. 'Bollocks! Why would we agree to that?'

Hector stared hard at him.

'You must think we were born yesterday,' Geras continued. 'We'd rather die than hand over our spoils to you.'

Hector shrugged indifferently. 'Have it your own way. Of course, if you don't fancy it, then you're welcome to return with us. You can explain to Bulla how you let those fat prizes get away.'

Telemachus rubbed his jaw as he considered his response.

He was suspicious of Hector's motives, and he knew there was a reasonable chance that the first mate might be deceiving him. The report could be nothing more than a ruse, designed to trick him into handing over his hard-won spoils. But on the other hand, it was possible that Hector was telling the truth. If the three merchant ships were indeed sheltering to the north, the potential riches on offer were too great to ignore. A lightning raid on an unprotected bay would further strengthen his reputation among his crew. And with the extra profits from the plundered merchantmen, he might finally be able to afford to purchase his brother's freedom.

He nodded at Hector as he made his decision. 'Fine. We'll do it.'

Hector grinned. 'I'll make my report to Bulla once we get back to the base. Tell him about the extra loot that'll be coming his way.'

Virbius hurried off to the captain's quarters, returning with a papyrus map. Hector laid it out and pointed out the location of the bay. A short time later, Telemachus climbed back down into the skiff with Geras and returned to *Galatea*, where he gave the order to draw alongside *Proteus* so that some of her cargo could be transferred to the larger ship. He wanted his vessel as light as possible in case she needed to chase down the merchant ships, and with Hector's crew having thrown most of their cargo into the sea, they were in dire need of additional provisions. A modest amount of food and wine was left in *Galatea*'s hold, along with the spare fishing gear from the mackerel boat used in the raid on Flanona. The equipment would be useful if there was an opportunity to top up their rations.

As the deckhands toiled away, Geras joined Telemachus

beside the mast. He wore a troubled expression as he watched the men carrying barrels of salted beef across the deck towards *Proteus*.

'Is this wise?' he said. 'I don't trust Hector.'

'Me neither,' Telemachus replied. 'But we don't have much of a choice. Apart from *Skamandros*, we've hardly found a ship worth taking. If there's some more loot to be had, we can't afford to ignore it.'

'Maybe not,' Geras conceded. 'But it's not like Hector to help us out. That back-stabbing bastard never lifts a finger unless there's something in it for him. What if he tries to take the credit for seizing the booty we've captured?'

'Then we'll set the record straight when we return to port.'

'And what if Bulla takes his side? What then?'

Telemachus sighed wearily. 'Look, we can't worry about what Hector might or might not do. Our orders are to capture as much loot as possible. That means heading north and at least reconnoitring this bay. If it looks promising, we'll have the opportunity of a lifetime.'

'And if it looks suspicious?'

'Then we'll turn around and sail back to the base immediately. Either way, it can't hurt to take a closer look.'

Geras nodded slowly. 'As you wish.'

'Good.' Telemachus stiffened his back. 'Once we've finished transferring the cargo across, I want the prize crews on both ships to return to *Galatea*. Hector will put his own crews on them. Then we'll set sail for the bay. By this time tomorrow, we could be rich men.'

'I only pray you're right, Captain.'

CHAPTER TWENTY-FOUR

'We should reach the entrance to the bay within the hour with this following wind,' Castor said as he pointed towards the headland.

The first hint of dawn glimmered across the eastern horizon as *Galatea* crept towards the shore. Her pennant had been lowered to reduce the chance of alerting any lookouts on the headland, and the men chosen for the boarding party were huddled below deck, ready for the signal to attack. Only a handful of the pirates remained visible, dressed in simple tunics to pass themselves off as sailors on a merchant vessel. Telemachus stood among them, scrutinising the bay opening up beyond the headland as he looked for the first sign of the cargo vessels riding at anchor. They were still too far away to make out anything except the pale shadow of the distant mountains.

Galatea had reached the area the previous evening, heaving to a few miles further down the coast. In the fading light, Telemachus had ordered Castor to take a small party of men aboard the skiff to reconnoitre the bay. The quartermaster had returned a few hours later to report that they had sighted the three ships riding at anchor, their dark hulls lit up by several small fires on the beach. In the gloom it had been impossible to make out any details, but Telemachus had been satisfied that the intelligence Hector had obtained from the fishermen was accurate. All that remained was to decide on an approach that would allow *Galatea* to take the three merchantmen by surprise.

As darkness gathered, he had explained his plan to his men. After a supper of bread, cheese and dried beef, they had bedded down on the deck to catch some precious sleep. He wanted them fed and rested before they launched their attack on the unsuspecting merchantmen the following morning.

'Looks quiet enough from here,' Geras commented, craning his neck at the bay. 'Seems Hector was right after all.'

Telemachus nodded. 'Then I pray the gods smile on my plan.'

'No need to worry, Captain,' said Castor. 'We'll look harmless enough. Those merchant crews won't suspect a thing. Until it's too late. Besides, if they get suspicious, we'll turn around and leave. *Galatea*'s built for speed. We'll be able to escape any danger long before they can catch us.'

'I hope you're right.'

Telemachus smiled grimly and turned his attention back to the bay in front of them. His plan depended on getting close to the three cargo ships without their crews raising the alarm. From a distance, the pirate ship would hopefully pass for an innocent vessel. With *Galatea* blocking the only way out of the bay, there would be no escape. The capture of three more merchant vessels would cap a successful voyage and surely end any threat of mutiny against Captain Bulla.

As they neared the headland, Telemachus could hear some of the men speculating about how they intended to spend their share of the profits once they returned to the base, and he reflected on the difference between himself and his crew. While they gave no thought to anything beyond the immediate future, content to squander their money on jars of cheap wine and wagers on games of dice, he himself was motivated by a greater purpose: buying Nereus's freedom. But he was also driven by something else, he realised in a rare moment of self-reflection: a desire to prove himself a worthy pirate commander. The success of the mission and the thrill of capturing prey mattered to him even more than the potential riches to be had.

The wind picked up and *Galatea* increased her speed as she cleared the point. Now Telemachus could see the three ships riding at anchor half a mile away, below the cliffs just inside the headland. One of the vessels was smaller than the other two, with an ornate sternpost and a lateen rig. The larger ships were anchored either side, their dark hulls reflecting off the shivering surface. Both had two banks of oars. Gleaming bronze rams extended from their prows.

The colour drained from Leitus's face. 'Shit . . .'

'Those aren't merchantmen, Captain,' Geras growled. 'They're Roman warships!'

As they looked on, a cluster of ant-like figures appeared on the decks of the biremes, helmets and weapons glinting sharply under the clear morning sun. There was a sudden flurry of activity as the marines took up their stations, with a handful of Romans armed with bows assembling on the foredecks. Then the oars were run out and the anchors hauled in before the two biremes headed directly for *Galatea*.

'I don't understand,' Leitus said. 'How did we fail to spot them?'

Castor shook his head bitterly. 'They weren't there last night when we scouted the place. I swear it!'

Bassus, the powerful Thracian, looked away from the biremes and turned to Telemachus, eyes bulging with horror. 'What are we going to do, Captain?'

Telemachus watched the biremes for a moment longer, teeth clenched in anger. Then he called out to the steersman, 'Turn her around!'

'Aye, sir!'

The steersman heaved the tiller over to the starboard side, swinging the bows away from the advancing biremes. As several deckhands raced aloft to shake out the last reefing points, a shout went up from one of the men.

'Two more ships closing fast, Captain!' he yelled, pointing towards the entrance to the bay.

Telemachus glanced round and saw another pair of warships rounding the opposite headland. A third bireme, and a much larger vessel that he readily identified as a trireme. A long purple pennant fluttered atop the masthead, and catapults had been mounted on the bow and stern. The men below in the hold had heard the commotion, and he sensed a wave of alarm quickly spreading through the crew as the Romans completed the trap. Geras stood beside him, shaking his head disbelievingly.

Telemachus looked back at the two warships surging past the headland and saw at once that there was no hope of escape. With *Galatea* surrounded, it was only a matter of time before the Romans closed on them and swarmed the deck. He could count on his men to put up a hard fight, but there were too few of them to hold the enemy off for very long. All they could do was take down as many of the Romans as possible before they were overrun.

'We'd better give the order for the men to form up on deck,' Geras said grimly.

Telemachus nodded. He was about to shout the order down at the pirates in the hold when he froze, his mind racing as an idea suddenly occurred to him. A plan that might yet avert disaster and save his imperilled ship. He cupped his hands and called across the deck, 'Heave to! Take the sail in.'

Bassus stared at his commander in horror. 'What the fuck are you doing? We have to escape while we still have the chance.'

Telemachus shook his head. 'We'll never make it out of the bay.'

'But we can't stay here. They'll kill us!'

'Not if they don't think we're pirates.'

Several of the crew looked at him questioningly. Telemachus waved a hand at the cargo hatch as he continued.

'We've still got all the mackerel boat's fishing gear,' he explained. 'We'll hide the weapons and the rest of the lads below, and pretend to be fishermen.'

'You can't be fucking serious,' Bassus spluttered. 'What if they see through us?'

'They won't. Look, this is our only chance of getting out of here alive.' Telemachus stared a challenge at the Thracian. 'Unless you've got a better idea?'

Bassus stared at him but made no reply. Telemachus turned away from the Thracian and issued instructions to his men. The crew worked fast, hurriedly passing up the light casting nets, wicker baskets and fishing lines stored in the hold. At Geras's command, two of them covered the hatch opening with a length of tarpaulin tied around the cleats, hiding the pirates in the hold from view, while the men on deck concealed the brands on their forearms with leather bracers, cloaks and long-sleeved tunics taken from the ship's slop chest. By the time they had finished their work, Telemachus was satisfied that he and his crew could pass themselves off as fishermen. Then he gave the order for *Galatea* to heave to, and the pirates settled down to wait for the warships to approach.

The two biremes ahead of them eased oars as the trireme closed on the pirate vessel, with the fourth vessel blocking the exit to the open sea. When the largest warship was within hailing distance, the oars were taken in and figures ran aloft to take in the sail. Several moments later, a figure in gleaming armour appeared on the foredeck clutching a brass speaking trumpet. Beside him the crew were winding back the arms on the fore-mounted catapult, ready to turn the pirate ship into a splintered wreck at the slightest provocation.

'You there!' the figure called out in Latin. 'Identify yourselves!'

Although Telemachus had grown up on the streets of Piraeus, he had picked up a smattering of Latin from the sailors on the Roman ships that frequently docked at the port, and he was confident enough to reply in the tongue of the Empire. He drew a deep breath and replied, 'Don't shoot! We're fishermen! Crew of the *Galatea*!'

There was a pause while the officer with the trumpet conferred with his subordinates. Then he turned back to the pirate vessel. 'Wait there! I'm sending a boat over. Any tricks and we'll sink you.'

Someone barked a command and several of the crew heaved on the pulley rope attached to the warship's tender, lowering it into the sea. As four sailors readied the oars, a pair of officers descended the rope ladder and lowered themselves into the stern seats. Telemachus looked on as the boat shoved off and the small craft bobbed along, steering towards *Galatea*.

'The moment of truth,' Geras muttered.

'This was a bad idea,' Bassus said, panic rising in his voice. 'They'll see through us, I bloody know it.'

Telemachus glared at the Thracian. 'Shut up! That goes for everyone else. Leave the talking to me.'

As the boat came alongside, a rope ladder was lowered down *Galatea*'s side. The two Romans clambered up and rose to their feet on the unsteady deck with as much dignity as they could muster. One of them stiffened his back and stepped forward. He was a tall, lean man, well built, the crest on his helmet indicating that he was an officer. He had the unmistakable air of arrogance of a high-born Roman. Telemachus recognised him instantly.

'Canis,' he whispered.

He felt a stab of anxiety as he recalled seeing the imperial navy prefect aboard *Selene* several weeks earlier. Telemachus had been a mere ship's boy then, and Canis had paid him no attention. But if the prefect recognised him now, his suspicions would be raised. News of *Selene*'s capture would have undoubtedly reached the naval headquarters at Ravenna, along with details of the capture or death of her full complement of sailors. The unexpected sight of the ship's boy on the crew of a fishing vessel would be difficult to explain.

The prefect cleared his throat. 'My name is Caius Munnius Canis, prefect of the Ravenna fleet. Which one of you is the captain of this ship?'

'I am,' Telemachus said, keeping the hood of his cloak pulled over his head. The long period he had spent at sea had subtly altered his appearance, tanning his skin and adding muscle to his once scrawny frame. The stubble on his face had thickened into a scruffy beard, covering the knotted scar tissue on his chin. Even so, he feared that Canis might recognise him, and he offered up a silent prayer to the gods as he bowed slightly before the Roman. 'Captain Telemachus at your service, sir.'

Canis regarded him curiously. 'Telemachus, you say? You look familiar . . . Have we met before?'

Telemachus stared blankly back at the prefect. 'Can't say that we ever have.'

'How old are you?'

'Seventeen, sir.'

'A little young to be a captain, aren't you?'

'This is my father's ship, sir. I took over from him after he died.'

Canis stared at him for a moment longer. 'Perhaps you'd care to explain what you're doing in these waters?'

'Me and the lads came here for the fishing, sir. We'd heard there might be some decent mackerel grounds around here. Thought we'd try our luck.'

'I see.' Canis glanced down at the pile of fishing gear beside the mast. 'You must be aware that pirates have been sighted along this stretch of coast in recent days?'

'Pirates, sir?' Telemachus repeated, feigning ignorance.

'They've been menacing this side of the Adriaticum for months now. As a matter of fact, we intercepted one of their ships in this very bay a few days ago. My men moved in swiftly to deal with them.' Canis thrust out an arm towards the shore.

Squinting hard in the pallid early morning light, Telemachus could just about discern a long line of wooden stakes planted in the ground, with severed heads impaled on the sharpened tips. He failed to suppress a shiver.

Canis smiled coldly at his reaction. 'We've been waiting here to trap the others when they return.'

'Others?'

Canis nodded. 'Two of their ships happened to be out at sea when we attacked. My lookouts sighted your sail and assumed you were one of the returning crews. You're the first friendly ship we've encountered in days, as it happens.'

'There's not been many ships around here, then?'

Canis laughed bitterly. 'That's a bit of an understatement. Pirates have been plundering the entire stretch of coast between here and Ortopla, and no merchant ships have risked putting out to sea in the area for weeks. Frankly I'm surprised you haven't heard. Where did you say you were from again?'

'I didn't, sir. We're from . . . Colentum.'

'Colentum? That's rather a long way to come just to do a spot of fishing.'

Telemachus thought quickly. 'We haven't had any luck with a catch closer to home, sir.'

The suspicious look lingered on the prefect's face for a moment longer before his expression cleared. 'Then you should thank the gods you didn't run into any pirates on the way. They're getting bolder all the time, especially now that the sea lanes are emptying of merchant ships.'

'Is that so, sir?'

'Oh yes. The vermin are having to take more risks, and some of them have even resorted to cutting-out expeditions. Only a few days ago they stole a valuable cargo ship out of the harbour at Flanona. Still, it's only a matter of time before we discover where they're hiding. And once we do, we'll move in and put every last one of them to death. There'll be no escape . . . no mercy. Those scum will be sorry they ever defied Rome.' There was a look of iron determination in the prefect's eyes that unnerved Telemachus.

'Good on you, sir,' Geras put in after a moment's silence. 'It's about time someone taught them pirates a lesson. They deserve to be crucified, the lot of 'em.'

'Quite.' Canis glanced at Geras then nodded stiffly at Telemachus. 'You're free to go on your way, Captain. I suggest you find a safe anchorage for the night and return to Colentum as soon as possible. There's still a risk of running into those pirates. Best to stay in port until we've dealt with them.'

'Aye, sir. We'll be sure to do that. We'll turn about the moment you're finished here.'

Canis straightened his back and turned to leave. He stopped by the rail as he remembered something. 'One more thing, Captain.'

'Sir?'

'Those pirates who attacked Flanona. The owner of the cargo ship they stole happens to be a good friend of mine, so I'm putting up a reward for any information that leads to their capture.'

'How much, sir?' Geras asked.

'Ten thousand sestertii. I intend to make a special example of them when we capture them. Their insolence will not go unpunished. If you hear anything, be sure to report it to the fleet.'

Telemachus swallowed hard. 'I'll do that, sir.'

'Make sure you do.'

The prefect nodded again before climbing back down the

side of the ship into the waiting boat. Telemachus watched the tiny craft bobbing up and down as it made its way back to the trireme. At his side, Geras breathed a deep sigh of relief.

'That was bloody close. I thought we were done for back there.'

'Me too,' Telemachus replied quietly as he looked away from the trireme. 'This is all Hector's doing. He knew the Roman navy was here. That bastard stitched us up.'

'I knew we shouldn't have trusted him,' Geras hissed. He shook his head angrily. 'And he's got his hands on our plunder. I bet he's back at the base right now, taking all the credit.'

'Not for much longer.' Telemachus turned to his comrade. 'Get us out of here, Geras. We'll set sail for Petrapylae as soon as we're clear of the coast. Once we return, there's going to be a reckoning . . .'

CHAPTER TWENTY-FIVE

Dusk began to settle across the bay as *Galatea* glided slowly towards Petrapylae. On the deck the crew carried out their tasks in weary silence. Their narrow escape from the clutches of the imperial navy had strained their nerves, and many of them were simply relieved to be returning to the relative safety of the citadel. Only once they had cleared the headland did the anxious mood finally begin to lift.

'Looks like they've been hard at work,' Geras said as he joined Telemachus and Castor on the foredeck. He nodded beyond the bows at the mass of rock extending from one end of the narrow beach.

In the fading light, Telemachus could just about see the improvements that had been made to the citadel's seaward defences. Repairs had been made to the damaged masonry wall that enclosed the small village, and a large bolt-thrower had been mounted on a wooden platform above the watchtower overlooking the bay. Several more platforms were being constructed across the citadel to carry further artillery pieces, ready to sink any approaching hostile vessels.

'Impressive,' he admitted. 'But we've got more immediate

matters to worry about than an attack from the Romans, I think.'

Geras shot him a questioning look. 'You mean the small matter of Hector trying to get us all killed?'

'It's not just that.' Telemachus lowered his voice so that the rest of the crew wouldn't overhear. 'You heard what Canis said. There's hardly any trade left on this side of the Adriaticum. And it's going to get worse. If only a handful of merchant captains risk going to sea, it'll be tough for us to find any more prey.'

'So? We'll just find new waters to cruise.'

'But where? Bulla's already told us that there's too much competition to the south.'

'I don't know. That's not our problem, though, is it?' Geras sighed. 'What are you going to do about Hector?'

'Nothing,' Telemachus replied. 'Once Bulla finds out that he lied to us and disobeyed orders, Hector will be finished.'

'I wouldn't be so sure,' Castor said. 'He's wriggled off the hook before.'

'Not this time. He won't get away with this, I swear it.'

They were interrupted by a shout from the lookout. 'Watchtower's signalling!'

Telemachus glanced in the direction of the watchtower on the headland. A dark-coloured strip of cloth fluttered in the gentle breeze as it was hoisted up the mast.

'That's the challenge,' he said, turning to Geras. 'Make the recognition signal.'

'Aye, Captain.'

Geras barked an order, and a moment later the vessel's pennant rose to the masthead, identifying it to the citadel's lookouts.

Dusk gathered, merging with the black mountains in the distance as *Galatea* continued into the bay. On the narrow strip of shingle directly above the shoreline Telemachus noticed the dark shapes of three beached vessels. *Proteus* had been rolled onto her side for repairs and propped up with timber supports. The pair of trading vessels that Telemachus and his men had seized were sitting next to the storm-damaged galley. A cold rage spread through his guts at the sight of the merchantmen, and he vowed to the gods that he would have his revenge on Hector, whatever it took.

As they neared the beach, Geras shouted a series of commands. While the rest of the crew gathered near the stern to lift the bows, a small crowd of figures emerged from the citadel, marching down the gravel causeway to greet the new arrivals. Telemachus searched for Hector among them, but in the gloom, and at this distance, he couldn't make out individual faces. There was a jarring noise as the keel lifted briefly before the ship shuddered to a halt. Once the vessel had been secured, Telemachus led his crew down the lowered gangway and trudged towards the reception party waiting for them a short distance further up the beach. Bulla was at the head of the crowd, wearing a look of confusion. Hector stood by his side, Telemachus noticed. The first mate fixed his cold, piercing gaze on *Galatea*'s captain, his expressionless face giving nothing away.

Bulla stepped forward as the rest of *Galatea*'s tired crew disembarked and made their way up to firmer ground.

'Telemachus! I must admit, this is something of a surprise. I wasn't expecting to see you again. Hector reckoned you must have fallen foul of the Romans.'

Telemachus glanced quickly at *Trident*'s first mate and

tensed his jaw. He forced himself to control his temper before looking back to the pirate chief. 'You were misinformed, Captain.'

'So it appears. Well, never mind that. Your crew and ship are safe, that's the main thing. You're back just in time for the celebrations, as it happens.'

'Celebrations?' Telemachus spluttered.

Bulla gestured to the pair of merchantmen beached next to *Proteus*. 'Hector returned with a small fortune in captured loot.'

Telemachus bit back on his rage and shook his head. 'Hector lied to you, Captain. Those are our prizes. Me and the lads captured 'em.'

Bulla creased his features into a bemused smile. 'What are you talking about?'

'Hector betrayed us, sir. At the meeting point at Insula Pelagus. He sold us a tale about a merchant convoy hiding out in a bay, then took our prizes back with him. When we got to the bay, we ran into an imperial navy squadron. He almost got us all killed.'

'The boy's lying, sir!' Hector rasped. 'The cargo's ours. Ask any of my lads, they'll tell you the same.'

'I'll vouch for him, Captain,' Virbius cut in, drawing up alongside Hector. 'I was there. The boy's full of shit.'

Bulla glanced quickly at his second in command before he turned back to Telemachus with a puzzled expression. 'Why in the name of Neptune would Hector want to set you up?'

'He lost most of his cargo in a storm,' Telemachus explained calmly. 'The same one that damaged his ship, sir. One of his men told us about it when we arrived at the meeting point.

Hector didn't want to return here empty-handed, so he hatched a plan to get rid of us and claim the merchantmen we'd taken as his own.'

'Bollocks!' Virbius exclaimed. 'Lying bastard!'

Bulla ignored him and cocked his head at Telemachus. 'Do you have any proof to support these claims?'

'One of my men was with me at the time.' Telemachus nodded towards Geras. 'He'll back up what I say.'

'It's the truth, Captain,' Geras said. 'Hector led us into a trap. If it hadn't been for Telemachus's quick thinking, the Romans would've done for us.'

Bulla stared at him for a moment, then looked towards Hector. 'Well? Is this true?'

The first mate snorted his contempt. 'Course it ain't, sir. I didn't know about any navy squadron, I swear. I just told 'em what I'd heard, like. It's not my fault the information turned out to be wrong.'

'Fair enough,' Bulla said after a pause. He slid his shrewd gaze back towards Telemachus. 'You can't hold Hector responsible for second-rate intelligence. Perhaps you should have scouted the bay properly before recklessly endangering your ship and crew.'

'I know what happened, sir,' Telemachus said. 'Hector lied to me. Give me the chance and I'll make him admit it, in front of the whole crew.'

Hector's eyes bulged with fury. 'Never! I ain't admitting a thing to you, you little streak of piss.'

'That's enough!' Bulla roared. 'Both of you.'

The two commanders fell quiet. Bulla stiffened and cleared his throat.

'Your accusation is serious, Telemachus. You claim that

Hector has betrayed you. There's nothing worse than a man who schemes to send his comrades to their deaths. But the decision as to what to do about it rests with me. In accordance with our rules, accuser and accused will settle their dispute with blades. A fight to the death.'

A silence descended over the beach. Surprise momentarily flashed across Hector's face, and then his fat lips twisted into a vicious smile. 'Fine by me, Captain. I look forward to gutting this miserable wretch.'

'Telemachus?' Bulla stared hard at the young commander. 'Do you want to withdraw your accusation? I'll give you one last chance . . .'

Telemachus tried not to look nervous as he replied. 'No, Captain. I stand behind my words.'

Bulla nodded curtly at both men. 'It's decided, then. The fight will take place tomorrow morning, at dawn. I'll instruct one of the ship's mates to make the necessary preparations. In the meantime, you're both to return to your quarters. I expect no trouble from either of you until the duel.'

He turned on his heel and strode back across the causeway. The rest of the crowd slowly dispersed, the conversation already turning to the duel as they wandered towards the citadel. Geras watched them for a beat before he turned to face Telemachus. He regarded his comrade with an expression of deep concern.

'I hope you know what you're doing.'

'What choice do I have? It's the only way to settle things between us.'

'Maybe so,' Castor put in. 'But Hector's not going to be an easy opponent. He might be a useless sailor, but he can handle himself in a fight. I wouldn't fancy myself against him.'

Telemachus looked up just then and saw Hector approaching, his lips parted into a wicked grin. 'You're a dead man tomorrow. Just you wait. You won't be able to escape this time, boy.'

Telemachus stood firm and met his opponent's menacing gaze. 'I'm not afraid of you, Hector.'

The first mate chuckled. His thick, fleshy muscles rippled. 'Then you're a fool. I was fighting with a blade before you learned to walk. Come tomorrow, I'm going to cut your heart out.'

'We'll see about that.'

'Aye. We will.' Hector smirked as he took a step closer. 'I'll make yours a nice slow death. Mark my words, boy. You'll regret the day you ever crossed me.'

CHAPTER TWENTY-SIX

The pirates gathered in the main square as the pale dawn tinged the sky. Telemachus approached the shadowy throng from the direction of the shore, a sick feeling of fear seeping like acid into his guts. Geras had been sent to fetch him from his berth and now marched alongside *Galatea*'s captain. In accordance with the rules that Bulla had explained the previous evening, the quarrelling parties had been confined to their quarters until the hour of their fight and were to arrive separately at the appointed spot. Telemachus had spent much of the night lying awake on his palliasse, unable to relax as he counted down the moments until his duel with Hector. It had almost been a relief when Geras had come for him shortly before first light.

'How are you feeling?' his friend asked softly.

Telemachus forced a smile. 'Never felt better.'

'That's the spirit.' Geras tipped his head at the crowd. 'Just remember. Most of this lot hate Hector almost as much as you do. They'll be cheering you on.'

'Really? It doesn't look that way to me.'

He nodded at the large crowd forming a rough circle around the edge of the square. The pirates closest to the action jostled for the best view, while those further back craned their necks or stood on wooden benches as they waited in eager anticipation for the fight to begin. In the middle of the make-shift arena stood Bulla. Hector was there too, along with Calkas, the white-haired steersman whom Bulla had chosen to umpire the morning's duel. Several figures near the front of the crowd were chanting Hector's name, interspersed with obscenities directed at his opponent.

'Hector has got a few hardcore supporters,' Geras conceded. 'Noisy bastards. Take no notice of them.'

'Easy for you to say. You're not the one about to fight.'

'No.' Geras paused. 'Still, at least there's a big crowd. Everyone in the citadel is keen to watch, by the looks of it.'

'Is that supposed to make me feel better?' Telemachus growled.

'Just saying. You're the main entertainment around here.'

Telemachus swallowed nervously. He had faced danger many times before and he wasn't afraid of dying, but the thought of losing to Hector in front of the entire crew filled him with shame. Hector would be a tough opponent, he knew. Tougher than anyone he'd yet faced in battle. He would need to draw on all his resourcefulness and natural fighting instincts if he was going to stand any chance of defeating him. He closed his eyes for a moment and promised to make a votive offering to Neptune if he won. Then he remembered something else and turned to Geras.

'If Hector wins, I want you to promise that you'll see to it that my share of the booty goes to my brother.'

Geras nodded. 'Of course.'

'It won't be enough to buy his freedom, but he might be able to hide it and save up the rest himself. It's better than nothing. I'd be grateful if you could find some way of getting it to him.'

'You've no need to ask. I'll find him, if it comes to it. But promise me something in return.'

'What's that?'

'You do us all a favour and cut the head off that scheming bastard.'

Telemachus half smiled at his friend. 'I'll try.'

When they reached the cobbled square, Telemachus composed his face as he pushed his way through the men and out into the open ground where the fight was to take place. Hector stood opposite him. The first mate showed no sign of fear, his eyes glinting meanly as he glared at his younger opponent. Bulla barked an order at the crowd, demanding silence. All conversation ceased as the onlookers turned towards the pirate chief.

'When I give the order, you will fight.' Bulla looked keenly at Telemachus. 'Unless you're willing to withdraw your accusation? This is your final chance.'

Telemachus shook his head. 'I've told the truth. I swear by Jupiter, best and greatest, that I'll make the bastard confess before I'm done with him. But I'll offer him one last chance to save his honour and his life by speaking the truth himself.'

That drew a withering look from Hector. He spat on the ground. 'I piss on your honour, you jumped-up little runt!'

Bulla nodded. 'As you both wish. Calkas!'

The umpire stiffened to attention. 'Captain?'

'You ready?'

'Aye, Captain.'

Bulla retreated towards the edge of the circle while Calkas beckoned a pair of men standing to one side of the ring. They marched over carrying the weapons the two men had chosen for the fight. Hector had opted for a heavy sword almost three feet in length, while Telemachus had chosen the shorter, lighter falcata he favoured in battle. Another two pirates then approached and handed each combatant a buckler.

At the umpire's command, they took up their weapons and moved back until they were a few sword lengths apart. Telemachus clasped his fingers around the falcata handle and hefted it in readiness. Hector gripped his long sword and sneered at his younger opponent. Then Calkas addressed them both.

'You know the rules. This is a fight to the death, so anything goes. Are you ready?'

Hector grunted a response. Telemachus nodded and tensed his muscles, recalling all the petty cruelties and humiliations that he'd suffered at the hands of the first mate since joining the crew. He felt his pulse quicken at the prospect of revenge and cutting down his tormentor.

'Begin!' Calkas yelled.

As soon as the word had left his mouth, Hector charged forward, roaring as he thrust out at Telemachus with his long sword. The speed of his attack caught his younger opponent off guard, and there was just time for him to duck behind his small shield before the blade hissed through the air. He stabbed out with his falcata, but Hector stepped effortlessly out of range, the longer reach of his weapon allowing him to strike and quickly retreat before his opponent could land a telling blow. He paused to catch his breath and licked his lips.

'You're mine now. I'm going to enjoy watching you bleed to death.'

'You tried to kill me once before, Hector,' Telemachus

muttered. 'You failed. Now it's my turn.'

Hector bared his stained teeth in rage and lunged again. He feinted before raising his blade, then slashed down at Telemachus's skull. Telemachus threw up his buckler to deflect the blow, and there was a jarring metallic ring as the blade clattered off the shield boss. Hector followed up swiftly, punching out with his buckler and slamming it into Telemachus's midriff. The impact drove the breath from the younger pirate's lungs and he staggered backwards, gasping as his own buckler's handle slipped helplessly from his grip. Hector grinned.

'Got you now, scum.'

He paced forward and swung at Telemachus with a flurry of slashes and thrusts as he moved in for the kill. Telemachus parried the blows with his falcata, his arm muscles burning with the strain of deflecting his opponent's attacks. Sweat glistened on Hector's face and flowed freely down his arms, his shoulders heaving with exertion. Telemachus continued to edge away from him, using his lighter footwork to stay out of his opponent's reach. A glance over his shoulder told him that he had retreated almost to the edge of the ring. Several figures were cheering Hector on, spurred by Virbius, urging their man to cut Telemachus down. Others responded by roundly booing the first mate and shouting their support for the younger man.

Out of the corner of his eye, Telemachus noticed Bulla shifting uneasily on his feet as he scanned the crowd. He shot his gaze back to Hector as the latter launched another attack, the brittle clash of blades echoing off the walls of the square. The first mate's thrusts were becoming increasingly ragged as the effort of fighting with the heavy sword took its toll, and

Telemachus sensed that he must be tiring. He leaped backwards, parrying a stab aimed at his throat, and it brought him right to the edge of the ring. Hector stopped a sword's length away, a triumphant look flashing across his coarse features.

'Nowhere left for you to run, boy. It's over. Time for you to die.'

Telemachus ignored the furious beating in his chest and dropped to a low crouch, watching his foe closely. Hector hefted up his sword arm and lunged. Telemachus jerked to the side, the blade missing him by inches as it cut through the air. Momentum and fatigue carried Hector forward, throwing the overweight pirate off balance. He drew his arm back and lumbered round to face his opponent, a fraction too late. Telemachus brought his blade down in a blur and slashed Hector across the thigh, slicing through flesh and muscle. Hector hissed through gritted teeth, stumbling backwards as his shield tumbled from his grip.

'Bastard!' he rasped.

He stabbed at Telemachus again, his face trembling with rage and hatred. Telemachus easily evaded the blow, then dropped to his knee and struck out with a savage backhand. There was a sharp crack as the pommel of his falcata cracked against the side of his opponent's jaw. Hector's head snapped back, then his legs gave way and he tumbled heavily to the ground. Telemachus rushed forward, kicking away the sword before Hector could snatch it up. Around him he heard the cheers and boos of the crowd as he raised his falcata above his head and shaped to deliver the killer blow.

'Confess, Hector!' he demanded.

'Fuck you, boy.'

'Kill the fat bastard!' someone yelled.

Telemachus ignored the shouts around him and fixed his gaze on his defeated rival. Hector looked up at him, and now there was a flicker of fear in his expression.

'Wait!' Bulla called out.

Telemachus froze. He held his weapon in place and looked over his shoulder as the pirate captain stepped into the ring, glancing anxiously around the square before resting his gaze on the duelling parties.

'That's enough,' Bulla announced, shouting to make himself heard above the noise of the crowd. 'We have seen an honourable fight. Now lower your blade.'

The excited shouts died away, replaced by a ripple of murmuring voices. Hector spat out blood and rose stiffly to his feet, grunting with pain. Telemachus stared at Bulla, unable to conceal his bitter frustration.

'But this is a fight to the death. You said so yourself, Captain.'

'Both of you have fought well,' Bulla replied firmly. 'There will be no killing today.'

A chorus of protest went up at the decision. Telemachus bristled with indignation.

'But Captain—'

'I'm doing you a favour, you fool,' Bulla hissed sharply as he stepped closer. 'Kill Hector and you'll make enemies of half the crew. You've proved your point. Now lower your sword or you'll answer to me with your life.'

There was a moment's hesitation before Telemachus reluctantly dropped his sword arm to his side. Bulla breathed in relief before he turned to address the crowd. 'The fight is over! Honour has been restored.'

Around the square, the spectators jeered in bitter

disappointment. A few men shouted for the fight to be allowed to continue, while further away a handful of pirates were angrily demanding their money back from those who had been in charge of taking bets. Two of the pirates came to blows, shoving then kicking and punching one another. Bulla bellowed an order at the pirates who had armed the fighters, and the nearest pair rushed over, separating the two men. Others in the crowd had turned to witness the dispute unfold and no one was watching the middle of the arena any more.

Amid the confusion and noise, Geras's voice called from across the square. 'Telemachus! Look out!'

As soon as he heard the warning, Telemachus glimpsed a movement out of the corner of his eye. He whipped round and saw Hector charging towards him, gripping the sword he'd snatched from the ground while his minders had been distracted. The younger pirate quickly jerked his sword arm up and parried the thrust aside, then jumped backwards as Hector stabbed low. Some of the crowd had realised what was happening and shouted at their companions, who turned round to see Hector rushing forward to strike again. As he raised his weapon, Telemachus saw his chance and lunged forward, punching out with his falcata. The blade slammed into Hector's midriff and cut up at an angle, tearing into his chest. Hector let out an explosive cry as Telemachus twisted the weapon, skewering the first mate's vitals. He yanked the falcata out and it came free with a sucking hiss before Hector slumped to the ground, gasping in agony.

There was a stunned pause, and then a cheer went up around the square. Most of the crowd chanted Telemachus's name, while several spectators condemned Hector as a back-stabber. Those who had been yelling their support for the first mate shot icy glares at his triumphant rival.

'Cheating snake!' one man shouted as he pointed at Hector. 'Good fucking riddance!'

'Murdering bastard!' Virbius yelled, gesturing at Telemachus.

Bulla stared at his first mate for a moment, a look of contempt in his eyes. Then he beckoned to Calkas, and the umpire came hurrying to his side. 'Have this lot dispersed before things get any uglier. We've had enough trouble for one morning.'

'What do you want us to do with this one, Captain?' Calkas asked, nodding at Hector, who groaned and writhed as he bled out.

'Take him away. I don't care where you dump him. Just get rid of him and let him die where he lies.'

'Aye, Captain.'

Calkas bellowed orders at the crowd and they reluctantly trudged out of the square in small clusters, heading back to their billets or their guard duties. As the pirates dispersed, the sentries got to work. A pair of them dragged Hector's body out of the square, while their comrades snatched up the weapons and shields used for the fight and dumped them in a handcart.

'Telemachus!' Bulla yelled out as he marched over.

'Captain?'

The chief looked the younger pirate up and down. 'You come with me.'

'It's not the outcome I'd hoped for,' Bulla said as Telemachus stood before him in his quarters a short time later. 'You fought bravely and well. There are few men in this crew who would have given Hector such a tough challenge. Still, it would have been better for you if he had lived.'

The flattery had no impact on Telemachus as he replied coldly, 'He tried to kill me. I didn't have a choice, Captain.'

'I know. I was there,' Bulla snapped. He shook his head. 'Hector was always too arrogant for his own good. I knew there was a chance he might do something foolish once I called a halt to the fight. But I had to try.'

Telemachus pursed his lips. After the duel, he had wanted nothing more than to return to his quarters, change out of his bloodstained tunic, close his eyes and rest his weary body. Instead he found himself standing in front of Bulla, exhausted and hungry, while the captain criticised him for killing a man who had sent dozens of his fellow pirates into the teeth of a Roman trap.

'That snake had it coming,' he said angrily.

'That may be true. But Hector had lots of friends on this crew, including some of the senior mates.'

'You mean Virbius? The one who claimed I was a liar?'

'Among others. They won't take kindly to seeing their comrade killed by a young upstart. By taking down one enemy, you've surely made yourself several more.'

'Then I'll fight them too,' Telemachus replied defiantly. 'I cut down Hector. I'll take my chances against any of the others.'

'No, you won't.' Bulla glared at him, daring Telemachus to defy his will. Then he sighed. 'We've had enough disputes for a while. Understood?'

'Aye, Captain,' Telemachus replied sullenly.

'Good.' Bulla relaxed into his throne-like chair. 'Anyway, Hector's reckless attempt on your life may have worked in our favour.'

'How so?'

'I've known for a while that he had an eye on my position. And he wasn't alone in conspiring against me. With Hector dead, there's less chance of the rest of the crew turning against me.'

'But that would be mutiny. Why didn't you just do away with him, and the other conspirators?'

'I couldn't.' Bulla sighed heavily. 'A good captain rules by the example he sets, not by fear. Or at least not just by fear. Sometimes it's better to humiliate a man rather than kill him. That's why I was prepared to spare Hector's life. His defeat would have been humiliation enough.'

'Not in my book.'

'Don't act so offended,' Bulla replied dismissively. 'You got your wish. Hector's dead. The crew will know that he wasn't to be trusted, after the coward tried to stab you in the back. And the others will think twice before crossing you in the future. That will prove useful, I think, in your new role.'

Telemachus knitted his brow. 'What do you mean, Captain?'

'I would have thought that was clear enough. From now on, you're my second in command.'

Telemachus looked at the pirate chief in open-mouthed surprise. Bulla leaned forward, clasping his hands in front of him on the table.

'I'll need someone to replace Hector,' he went on. 'There are more experienced candidates than you, of course, but right now I need someone I can trust. Besides, you did a fine job of giving the imperial navy the slip. You've clearly got what it takes to help run a ship. I'd like you to take over as my lieutenant.'

Telemachus smiled in spite of himself. He had been quietly wondering why Bulla was so concerned about him making more enemies. Now he understood. His new position would make him second only to the captain in terms of authority. Bulla would not want to risk angering the men by promoting someone who was deeply unpopular with *Trident*'s crew.

'You will be expected to serve me loyally and ensure the crew carry out my orders,' the captain added. 'The day-to-day running of the ship while we're at sea will be your responsibility, and you'll also be required to keep a close eye on the mood of the men. Any hint of unrest, you are to report it to me, in private. Is that clear?'

'Aye, Captain.'

Bulla nodded. 'Then I suggest you return to your quarters. We'll set sail as soon as we've sold off the loot and divided the spoils. We'll put to sea on *Poseidon's Trident* now that she's been repaired. And this time, I'll be leading the hunt.'

'Where are we headed, Captain?'

Bulla smiled, his eyes glinting. 'There's plenty of prey if you know where to look for it. It's time for us to start hunting down some nice fat prizes from right under the nose of that bastard, Prefect Canis . . .'

CHAPTER TWENTY-SEVEN

Twenty days later

Standing on the main deck of *Poseidon's Trident*, Telemachus gazed out towards the shimmering horizon. Less than two miles away, a cloud of spray went up as the small cargo vessel they were pursuing ploughed through the swell.

Four hours had passed since the lookout had first sighted the merchantman's sail, near the port at Vegium. The chase had been long and hard, with the prey's captain taking desperate measures in his attempt to evade the pirates. Her spare anchor, cordage and deck cargo had been dumped overside, and the last reefing points had been taken out of the sail, exposing every stitch of her sailcloth to the land breeze whipping in from the Illyrian coastline. But even with her lightened load, the merchantman was no match for the pirates' sleeker craft. As the afternoon wore on, *Trident* had steadily drawn nearer to her prey.

'We'll be closing on her soon,' said Castor, staring out to sea, shading his eyes beneath the blinding sunshine.

Telemachus turned to him. 'How long?'

'An hour, I'd say. Not much more than that. Either way, she's ours.' Castor nodded confidently. 'We're miles from the nearest safe anchorage. She won't get away from us. Not if this weather holds.'

Geras grinned. 'Finally, some booty. About time. The way our luck's been going, I was beginning to think we'd be returning home empty-handed.'

Telemachus glanced at his comrade. 'It's been slim pickings,' he admitted.

'Slim?' Geras raised an eyebrow. 'That's putting it mildly. This is the first bloody sail we've seen in weeks. This area is more barren than a roomful of old crones.'

Telemachus nodded with feeling. Three weeks had passed since the crew had set out from their base at Petrapylae, the ship freshly revictualled and ready to loot the northern Adriaticum. They had quickly discovered that the coast was bereft of shipping, with the few sails they had encountered turning out to be fishing boats – hardly the lucrative plunder they had been promised by their captain. Bulla had worked the men hard to guard against idleness, ordering them to clean out the hold and practise running aloft to give chase to imaginary prey. But the threat of mutiny was never far away, and Telemachus had heard the first murmurs of discontent a few nights ago as the men went ashore for their evening meal. The sighting of the merchantman shortly before noon had provoked a sense of quiet relief in the young first mate.

'I don't get it. What's happened to all the other shipping?' he wondered aloud.

'Staying in port, I expect,' Castor responded gruffly.

'But why?'

'I should have thought that's obvious,' the veteran said. 'We've been hunting in these waters for a while now. Word's bound to have got around about our presence.'

'Perhaps they're waiting for the Romans to clear the sea,' Geras speculated.

'Maybe,' Telemachus said. 'Or maybe something else has persuaded them to play safe.'

'Like what?'

'I'm not sure. All I know is, the captains wouldn't stay ashore without good reason.'

'Who cares?' Geras gestured at the vessel ahead. 'Our luck's about to change. As long as she's carrying some decent cargo, I'll be happy. So should you, seeing as you're first mate.'

As second in command, Telemachus would be due a double share of any plunder they captured while at sea. With a few more successful raids, he reminded himself, he would soon have saved enough money to make a generous offer to Nereus's Roman master at the forge in Thorikos.

'Just as long as we don't run into any more warships,' Castor muttered.

Geras nodded uneasily and looked away. Twice in the past few days the pirates had sighted imperial navy squadrons. On both occasions the men of *Poseidon's Trident* had changed course and fled under full sail, seeking anchorage in the remote islands and inlets scattered along this side of the sea. The Roman biremes had made no attempt to pursue them, but the incidents had unnerved some of the crew, and they cast wary glances at the horizon as they sailed on.

'Canis certainly seems determined to hunt us down,' Telemachus said quietly.

'He'll give up sooner or later,' Castor replied confidently.

Telemachus shook his head. 'Canis is different. You were there, Castor. You heard what he said. He won't rest until he's put us all to the sword.'

'I'd say you've got more pressing concerns than running into the Romans again,' Geras cut in.

'What's that supposed to mean?'

The stocky pirate tipped his head in the direction of a cluster of older men near the foredeck. One or two of them glanced at Telemachus as they waited for *Trident* to draw close to her prey.

'Hector's mob aren't exactly thrilled about your promotion.'

Telemachus nodded tersely. Although he had worked hard since the duel to demonstrate his loyalty and earn the respect of the crew, several of Hector's companions continued to harbour a grudge towards him. They had made no attempt to disguise their feelings, glaring at him and muttering behind his back as they went about their duties.

'I'm not worried about a few disgruntled hands,' he responded sternly. 'I've faced worse enemies.'

'Look, all I'm saying is, you'd do well to watch yourself around that lot. Especially Virbius. He's a mean bastard, that one. Not the type to let go of a grudge.'

'They won't try anything. Not after what happened to Hector.'

'I wouldn't be so sure.'

Telemachus noticed the pirate staring at him with a contemptuous sneer. He shook his head, turned away and let out a sigh. He'd assumed that his problems aboard the ship had ended with Hector's death, but now he would have to be wary of Virbius and the other men looking for a chance to avenge their fallen comrade. And then there was the constant threat of capture by the Romans. With the increased patrols along the coast, there was a greater possibility of being captured by the enemy, and the grim prospect of torture followed by an agonising death. Life as a pirate was far more perilous than he'd ever imagined.

He swung his gaze back to the fleeing merchantman. The sun was already low in the sky, the sea glittering beneath its warm rays as *Poseidon's Trident* bore down on her prey. No more than half a mile separated the two vessels now. The cargo ship continued stubbornly on her present course but *Trident* was closing fast and Telemachus could see that the merchantman's dash for freedom was doomed to end in failure.

'Reckon her crew will put up a fight?' Geras asked.

Telemachus paused as he ran his eyes over their prey. Even at this distance he could see that the sailors on the other ship were outnumbered by at least four to one. Against the well-armed fighting men of *Poseidon's Trident* they would stand no chance.

'If her captain's got any sense, he'll surrender to save his men,' he said. 'But if they resist, it'll be over quickly.'

As he spoke, a cry went up from one of the men near the foredeck. All eyes looked in the direction he was pointing. Telemachus followed his finger and spied a handful of figures on the merchantman scrambling hurriedly across her deck, sunlight flashing off weapons. Castor narrowed his eyes at the sight and grunted.

'Seems they want a fight after all,' he growled.

'Telemachus!' Bulla bellowed from across the deck. 'On me!'

At the sound of his captain's voice, Telemachus wheeled around and marched briskly over to the stern. Bulla stood next to the steersman, dressed in his leather breeches and black linen cuirass, a curved sword dangling from his belt. There was a calculating glint in his eyes as he judged the distance to the prey.

'Captain?' Telemachus bowed his head.

'We'll be overhauling her shortly,' Bulla said, gesturing to the merchantman. 'Have the men form up. If she won't drop her sails then we'll have to take her by force.'

'Aye, Captain.'

Telemachus turned away from the captain and took a deep breath.

'All hands! Prepare to engage!'

CHAPTER TWENTY-EIGHT

As soon as Telemachus had shouted the order, the crew ran to take up their positions. Those men selected for the boarding party gathered their weapons and assembled beside the mast, their armour and sword points glinting beneath the sharp glare of the early summer sun. Others seized slings, javelins and broadaxes, while the spare hands on deck readied the grappling lines, ready to launch them towards the other vessel. The men went about their duties with renewed vigour, fired by the prospect of action and loot after the long days of boredom on the sea with nothing to occupy them except the dull routine of keeping watch, setting the sails and scrubbing the decks.

Telemachus sought out a face among the men rushing about on the deck. 'Bassus!'

The huge, heavily scarred Thracian hurried over. He had recently been promoted to the rank of ship's mate, on Telemachus's recommendation. Despite his limited seafaring skills, Bassus had proved himself to be a ferocious warrior, and Telemachus had not regretted his decision for one moment. He nodded at the burly pirate and pointed at the foredeck.

'Form up the bowmen and wait for my command. Any

man who looses an arrow before I give the order will forfeit his share of the loot. Got it?'

'Aye, sir!' Bassus turned to address the archers. 'Take up your places! You lot, make room!'

The other pirates stepped aside for the archers as the latter snatched up their quivers and bows and massed on the foredeck, ready to unleash a hail of missile fire. Telemachus waited until the rest of the crew had taken up their positions. Then he grabbed his falcata and buckler and joined Castor and the others by the mainmast. The veteran pirate nodded at the cargo vessel, his weathered face glowing with anticipation.

'Won't be long now.'

Telemachus swung his gaze back to the merchantman. The sailors were forming up across her deck, some gripping a variety of makeshift weapons: belaying pins, fishing knives and boathooks. Their captain shouted at the crew, his voice carrying distinctly across the water as he implored them to resist the pirates.

'Braver than some of the crews we've faced,' Castor noted.

Geras snorted. 'Let's see how tough they are when that lot get to work.' He waved a hand in the direction of the archers. 'They won't know what's hit 'em.'

'Let's hope so,' Telemachus said.

The first mate, along with the rest of the men, had spent the evenings ashore practising with slingshot and bows under Bulla's watchful eye.

The land breeze increased, vibrating through the rigging as *Poseidon's Trident* clawed her way through the sea. Telemachus took in a breath, easing the tension in his muscles as they drew up on the merchantman's stern quarter. He felt the familiar quickening of his pulse and the dryness in his mouth at the prospect of an imminent fight. Around him the men shouted taunts and abuse at the sailors, while others brandished their swords threateningly. With their wild hair, savage cries and gleaming weapons the pirates were a terrifying sight. Only a fool would dare to resist them, Telemachus thought. He felt a sudden pang of contempt for the merchantman's captain, risking the lives of his men in a futile gesture of defiance.

As they carried on down the starboard length of the ship, Bulla turned to the steersman. 'Bring us closer, Calkas.'

The steersman braced his legs and pulled on the giant paddle, angling *Poseidon's Trident* towards the merchantman. They were close enough now that Telemachus could make out the individual faces of the sailors grouped around the other ship's mainmast. Some of them stared back at the pirates on *Trident*'s deck as she drew near, while a few glanced nervously over at the horizon, as if hoping for some nearby Roman squadron to save them. Telemachus could easily imagine the terror they were experiencing; he had known it himself as a ship's boy aboard *Selene*. But he was a pirate now, and he felt no sympathy for their plight. Only a burning desire to force them to submit and loot their cargo, before continuing in search of another victim . . .

'Ready arrows!' he roared at the men on the foredeck.

The archers fitted their arrows to their bowstrings and took aim. No more than a hundred feet separated the two crews now. Some of the sailors had taken notice of the archers and shouted panicked warnings to their companions, but most of the deckhands were without shields and were terribly exposed. Once Telemachus decided they were easily within range, he roared at the archers.

'Release! Take 'em down!'

The air was filled with a deadly hiss as the arrows arced out and plunged down towards the merchantman's deck. A few fell short and splashed into the churning water between the two ships, but most found their target. Agonised cries split the air as the barbed missiles tore into the sailors. One arrow struck the steersman through the neck and sent him stumbling backwards, hands pawing at the shaft protruding from his throat. Another sailor heard his comrade's guttural cry as he fell over the side rail. The man scurried to the stern, but an arrow hit him in the left shoulder, knocking him down before he could take control of the tiller.

'Keep it up!' Telemachus thundered. 'Let 'em have it!'

More arrows plummeted down on the cargo ship's deck, studding the planking and impaling flesh in a chorus of dull raps and thuds, the terrified cries of the crew reaching the ears of the men of *Poseidon's Trident*. Further aft, a trio of sailors hurried towards the cargo hatch in an attempt to seek cover below deck. Some of the archers spotted them and loosed their arrows, cutting down two of the sailors before they could disappear from sight. At Telemachus's command, others in the boarding party reached for their slings and unleashed a ragged volley of lead shot at the merchantman, striking down two more men. Under the relentless missile fire, the few remaining sailors dropped their weapons and shouted their surrender, drawing a lusty cheer from *Trident*'s crew.

Telemachus glanced over at Bulla. 'Shall I give the order, Captain?'

Bulla stared at the cargo ship, then nodded his assent. 'I'd say they've had enough.'

'Cease!' Telemachus bellowed. 'Cease shooting!'

The bowmen lowered their weapons but kept a careful eye

on the merchantman as the two ships continued to draw closer. The cargo vessel wallowed on the swell, the sound of the water lapping against the hull intermittently drowned out by the cries of the wounded.

'That's put paid to those fools,' Geras chuckled.

'They shouldn't have resisted us,' Telemachus replied quietly.

Unlike some of his comrades, he took no pleasure from the merciless slaughter of poorly armed seamen, and he cursed their arrogant captain for forcing them to defend their ship. Had the captain surrendered at the first sight of *Trident*'s black pennant, he might have spared his men. They would have been sold as slaves to one of the traders at Petrapylae – a better fate than death, surely? A few might even have been persuaded to join the pirates' ranks. Instead, they had died needlessly.

'Get us alongside!' Bulla called out to the steersman before turning to face Telemachus. 'Have the men round up the survivors as soon as we board. Check the hold as well. No quarter for anyone who tries to resist. Once we've secured the ship, we'll take her cargo.'

The mainsail sheets were let fly and flapped in the breeze as the cargo ship lay tethered to *Poseidon's Trident*. With the barrage of missiles having cleared the merchantman's deck, the pirates were free to sweep aboard the vessel without a fight. Bulla's men were quick to deal with the rest of the crew, marching them over to the bows while others rushed down the aft hatch to bring up the few sailors hiding below deck.

Telemachus stood alongside Captain Bulla near the bows, watching over the terrified prisoners. All around him lay devastation caused by the missiles. Dead bodies were sprawled across the deck, and in places the planking glistened with blood. Some of Bulla's men crouched beside the lifeless corpses, searching them for rings, jewellery and anything else of worth. The valuables would be added to the pirates' haul and sold on their return to their base. Any man caught trying to steal or hide valuables for himself, in violation of the pirates' sworn oath, would be bound with rope, tied down with weights and thrown overside.

Castor emerged from the gangway leading down to the cargo hold and hastened over.

'Well?' Bulla demanded.

The quartermaster shifted on his feet. 'Cargo is grain and olive oil, Captain. Not much of it, either. Only a few sacks and amphorae.'

Bulla furrowed his brow. 'That's it? There's nothing else?'

'There's a few bales of cloth too, but that's the lot. Nothing that'll fetch a decent sum, like.'

'Where's the rest of it?' Telemachus cut in. 'That can't be all she's carrying.'

Castor spread his hands. 'That's all the lads have found. Ain't nothing else down there.'

The note of frustration in his voice was obvious. Without any lucrative cargo, *Trident*'s crew would be left with only a small share once the loot had been sold off to one of the merchants back at Petrapylae. A paltry haul of grain and oil would hardly cover the ship's costs, let alone silence the dissenters.

Bulla tried to suppress his disappointment. 'Fetch up the supplies, Castor. We'll take whatever she's carrying.'

'Aye, Captain.'

The veteran promptly marched off towards the hatch. Bulla turned away and ran his eye over the prisoners: the few

273

surviving sailors and a handful of terrified passengers. Many of them were injured, some bleeding heavily from their wounds. They stared back at their captors with a mixture of fear and apprehension.

'My name is Bulla,' he rasped. 'Captain of *Poseidon's Trident*. Which one of you is the captain of this ship?'

There was a moment of silence as the prisoners exchanged anxious glances, the sound of their shallow breathing punctuated by the groans of their dying companions a few paces away. Bulla settled his gaze on the nearest sailor – a dark-featured man well into his middle years, grizzled and sinewy from a lifetime of hard toil at sea – and gestured towards Bassus.

'You there! Speak now, or I'll have Bassus cut your throat.'

At the sight of the Thracian lowering a hand to his sword, another prisoner raised an arm and stepped forward. 'Please, sir. There's no need for that.'

Bulla narrowed his eyes at the man who had spoken. He was older than the other prisoners, with thinning hair and a beard flecked with grey. He lifted his head and stared guardedly at Bulla, meeting the pirate captain's piercing dark eyes.

'And who might you be?'

The man fought to control his trembling voice as he spoke. 'Titus Lucullus, sir. Captain of *Delphinus*. From Arausa.'

'Is that so?' Bulla stepped closer to the captain. 'Tell me, Lucullus. Where's the rest of your cargo?'

Lucullus hesitated, his eyes wide with fear. 'That's all there is. We were carrying goods up the coast, and passengers on the return trip.'

'I see. And there's nothing else on board . . . nothing of value that you might want to tell us about? Think carefully,

Lucullus. If I find out you're lying, I'll have you dragged under the keel. It'll take you hours to bleed to death.'

The merchant captain spread his hands in a show of pleading.

'That's all we were carrying,' he said. 'Grain and olive oil. It's the other ships that were loading cargo at Arausa. They were waiting for the order for the convoy to set sail.'

'Convoy?' Telemachus asked. 'What convoy?'

Lucullus looked surprised. 'Haven't you heard? The navy's been offering a convoy service, sir. To escort merchant shipping along the coast.'

Telemachus and Bulla exchanged a puzzled look. The captain swung his gaze back to Lucullus, his expression darkening. 'When did this happen?'

'Some weeks ago, sir. There was an announcement at the forum at Arausa. The same one was made in ports up and down the coast, apparently.'

'What did it say, exactly?'

Lucullus shrugged. 'Just that Prefect Canis had ordered the Ravenna fleet to increase their patrols between Ruginium and Salonae. Any merchant ships wishing to make a voyage should wait for a Roman squadron to accompany them before leaving port.'

'But there are dozens of ports along this side of the coast,' Telemachus said. 'The Ravenna fleet isn't big enough to provide an escort to all of them. Not at the same time, anyway.'

'That's what some of the merchants said. Everyone knows that the navy has gone to shit since the days of Actium. It ain't fit for purpose. But the worthies kicked up a fuss and demanded something be done. So now half the merchant fleet is sitting around in port while they wait for a Roman escort to show up.'

Telemachus nodded, quickly grasping the implications of the convoy service Canis was offering. Sailing under the protection of a navy escort was undoubtedly safer, but it would severely disrupt trade up and down the Illyrian coast. The constant flow of shipping on which the merchants depended to carry their goods from one corner of the Empire to another would be reduced to a slow trickle. Prices would rise as supplies became scarce. Goods in the warehouses and markets along the Adriaticum would rot while they waited for the next convoy to arrive. The prefect was taking a big risk in implementing such a drastic policy.

Bulla stabbed a finger at Lucullus. 'So if the other merchant captains are staying ashore, what are you doing out here?'

'Some of us weren't happy about the arrangement, sir. It's all well and good for the wealthier captains, but us smaller vessels can't afford to be laid up for weeks or months on end. Me and the lads talked it over and decided we'd risk sailing up to Parentium.' Lucullus let his shoulders sag, overcome with despair at his misfortune.

A question occurred to Telemachus and he jerked his chin at the broken captain. 'Did the announcement say how long the navy would keep this up?'

'Until the sea's been cleared of the likes of you. That's what we heard in the forum.'

'For a while, then,' Bulla mused as he turned away from the man. He looked at Telemachus. 'What do you reckon?'

'Sounds truthful enough, Captain,' Telemachus replied after a moment's consideration. 'It would explain why we keep running into those Roman warships.'

Bulla nodded. 'Canis must be even more desperate to wipe us out than I thought.'

That drew a derisive snort from Virbius. 'So what? We've nothing to fear from those Roman bastards, Captain. A few biremes on patrol ain't stopped us before.'

Bulla shook his head. 'We can't continue to hunt around here. Even if we manage to avoid the Romans, there won't be many vessels who'll risk sailing alone. Not if they can help it.'

Virbius threw up his arms in protest. 'What are we supposed to do, then? The lads won't be happy about going home without some plunder.'

'We could try heading further south,' Telemachus suggested. 'Between Epidaurum and Dyrrachium, perhaps. The convoy service only extends as far south as Salonae.'

'According to that worthless shit,' Virbius said, jerking a thumb at Lucullus. 'Besides, it ain't gonna be much easier finding prey down there. The word is, that's where Agrius has based himself.'

'Agrius?' Telemachus raised an eyebrow.

'One of the other captains in our trade. Commands *Pegasus*.'

'He's a bloody madman,' added Leitus. 'Worse than that bastard Nestor. The watering holes at Piraeus were full of tales about him. He led a mutiny aboard the merchantman he was serving on. Skinned the captain alive and had the mates hacked up and thrown to the fish. After that he took to cruising along the Illyrian coast. His men slaughtered villagers, crucified any Romans he encountered. They say he cuts out the heart of any man who refuses to join his crew.'

'Rumours,' Bulla responded dismissively. 'There's stories about every crew in our trade. Agrius is no different to the rest of us.'

'How do we know he's based himself to the south?' Telemachus asked.

'One of the mates on Nestor's old crew told us,' Virbius said. 'One of the lads who served with me and Hector on *Proteus*.'

'What did he say?'

'Not much. Just that he'd heard that Agrius had given the Romans the slip and moved his operations close to Dyrrachium.'

'He might be wrong,' Bulla said.

'And if he ain't?' Virbius countered.

'Then it's only one crew. There'll still be plenty of prey left for us to hunt.'

Leitus shook his head. 'Agrius is no ordinary captain. If he's based himself near Dyrrachium, the merchant ships will think twice before they put to sea. I know I would, sir.'

'Perhaps,' Bulla said after a pause. 'But we won't know for certain without patrolling the area ourselves. Unless anyone has a better idea?'

He glanced around him, searching the faces of the other pirates. But no one dared to question their captain's judgement, and after a pause he gave a nod.

'It's settled, then. We'll make for Dyrrachium. Telemachus!'

'Aye, Captain?'

'Take the spare hands and help Castor load the supplies into the ship's hold. Make it quick. We'll need to set sail before the wind changes.'

'What about this lot?' Leitus asked, waving a hand at the prisoners hunched together near the bows.

Before Bulla could reply, Virbius stepped forward, clearing his throat. 'Perhaps we should let them go, Captain.'

Bulla creased his brow. 'What for?'

'They're no fucking use to us. Look at them. Most of 'em are just passengers. Hardly a decent seaman among them. We could do without the extra mouths to feed as well. Given the situation with our supplies.'

'It would be easier to kill them,' Bulla mused.

'Aye, Captain. It would,' Virbius continued. 'But why risk pissing off the Romans more than we have done already?'

Bulla thought briefly, then nodded. 'Fine. Take the pick of the sailors from 'em, anyone with a skill. We'll leave the rest.' Without another word, he wheeled away and moved off towards *Poseidon's Trident*.

Virbius watched the captain for a moment before he turned to one of the mates and ordered him to round up the merchantman's sailors. Then he grabbed Lucullus and marched him towards the aft cabin. 'Come on. Let's see if you have any useful charts, my friend.'

Geras moved alongside Telemachus. 'What's his game, I wonder?'

Telemachus glanced at his comrade. 'Virbius? What do you mean?'

'He's one of Hector's cronies. It's not like any of that lot to go easy on prisoners.'

'You think he might be up to something?'

'No idea. But I trust him about as far as I can spit a scorpion.'

'We can't worry about him now.' Telemachus exhaled irritably. 'We've got bigger problems to consider.'

'Like running into Agrius? He sounds like a right nasty piece of work.'

'I was thinking more about our chances of finding a prize.'

Geras gave his friend a questioning look, waiting for him to elaborate. Telemachus glanced around, checking to make sure no one was listening before he went on.

'You heard what their captain said. Canis is closing off our hunting grounds. If he keeps this up, our days of snatching easy prizes will be over.'

'We'll find something, lad. We always do.'

'And if we don't? What then?'

'I don't know.' Geras sighed. 'But you're right. We're running out of options. Let's just pray to Fortuna that Bulla knows what he's doing. Otherwise we're all in the shit.'

CHAPTER TWENTY-NINE

The early summer sun had already risen above the horizon and shone down brilliantly, clearing the watery mist to reveal a series of imposing grey cliffs in the distance as the pirates neared Dyrrachium. Telemachus leaned against the rail and gazed out towards the jagged shore. *Poseidon's Trident* had slipped out of her anchorage at dawn, before continuing her journey south, never venturing far from the coastline. By staying just within sight of land, *Trident*'s crew stood the best chance of sighting a merchantman hugging the shore, or sailing out from a remote anchorage.

'We'll be approaching Dyrrachium soon enough,' Leitus announced as he narrowed his eyes at the rocky hills to the east. 'Another day or so, I reckon.'

'Think we'll have better luck down there?' Telemachus asked, turning to Geras. His comrade stood beside him, forehead creased into a deep frown as he scanned the horizon.

'Who knows?' Geras replied in an undertone. 'Can't be much worse than what we've had so far.'

Telemachus nodded. Ten days had passed since they had set sail for Dyrrachium. The longer summer days meant the pirates could spend more time at sea, and they had made good progress down the coast, reaching the port at Agruvium on the third afternoon. But they had sighted precious few sails since then. The previous afternoon, two vessels had been spotted, but both had gone about and fled before the pirates were able to give chase.

The men were kept busy running aloft to repair sails and replace frayed ropes, while others scrubbed down the deck and washed the tunics in seawater. But despite Bulla's best efforts, the crew were restless, and their mood had been made worse by the water shortage. There had been little rainfall recently, and with most of the streams and rivers drying up, the crew had been unable to replenish their water supply when they went ashore each night. The butts were dangerously low, and after consulting Castor, the ship's quartermaster, Bulla had been forced to impose a strict ration.

'Why would those ships turn and run without even bothering to find out who we were?' Telemachus wondered.

Geras shrugged. 'Merchant captains are a suspicious bunch. Goes with the territory, especially when they know there are pirates operating up the coast.'

'No. There's more to it than that. They don't usually cut and run without at least checking to see if the other sail is friendly or not. Something has got them panicked.'

'What do you think that might be?'

'Perhaps some of the other pirate crews have had the same idea as us. The ones operating to the north will have heard about the convoys by now. Some of them might have beaten us here. Enough to scare off the merchant ships, at least.'

'There's a simpler explanation, of course.'

Telemachus gave his friend a considered look. 'Agrius?'

Geras nodded. 'I hate to say it, but Virbius might be right. If Agrius is as feared as everyone says he is, he'll have cleared the sea of any decent prey.'

'Do you really think so?'

'I've served on enough trading ships in my time. I know how the captains think. They won't risk the voyage if there's a chance of running into some murderous pirate chief.'

'We'll find something. We have to.'

'Let's hope so,' Castor muttered. 'We've already had to halve the lads' water ration. Another few days without prey and we'll have to give up and piss off back to the citadel.'

'And that's not going to please Bulla.'

Castor opened his mouth to reply, then abruptly closed it again, familiar enough with the first mate's temperament by now to recognise when it was better to leave him alone. The failure to snare a prize was beginning to affect Telemachus, and he was acutely conscious of the fact that it had been he who had suggested sailing towards Dyrrachium.

He was not the only one feeling the strain. Bulla had also been in a black mood for the past few days. Earlier that morning Telemachus had made his usual report to the captain, and in the gloom of his private cabin he'd been struck by how tired Bulla looked. He felt a sharp pang of anxiety as he realised that the pirate chief might lose his command unless the ship's fortunes improved. If that happened, there would be a bitter contest to decide who replaced him. The frightening idea that one of his enemies might become the new captain darkened his thoughts as they sailed on through the day.

As night closed in, the crew anchored in a narrow bay south of the steep mountains around Olcinium. Fires were lit across the beach and the men chewed sullenly on their meagre rations of salted mutton and hardened bread while the sailors taken prisoner aboard *Delphinus* were drilled in basic swordsmanship by Virbius. The impressed men could not yet be trusted with real swords and had been given wooden training weapons to practise with until Bulla could be assured of their loyalty.

Geras and Leitus drank thirstily from their leather tankards, but Telemachus was in a thoughtful mood and stared absently into the flames as he sat beside his two companions.

Geras drained the last of his wine and smacked his lips. 'At least that tub we ran into had some decent drink on board. Can't beat an amphora of the Mendean stuff.'

'If you say so,' Telemachus said.

Geras tilted his head to one side and regarded his friend. 'Something wrong? You've hardly touched your wine.'

'Here. You have it.'

'You sure?'

Telemachus nodded.

'Don't mind if I do. Cheers.' Geras accepted the tankard and took a long swig. Then he studied his friend closely. 'What do you think will happen if we don't find anything over the next few days?'

Telemachus considered for a moment before he made his reply. 'There's only one thing for it. We'll have to find some other waters to hunt in.'

'But where? We've already established that there's hardly any prey to be had in these parts, what with Canis running that convoy service. Where could we go?'

Telemachus shrugged. 'I don't know, Geras.'

Leitus looked down at his cup. 'Perhaps it's time to find a new base. Somewhere far from that bastard Canis.'

'Leave Petrapylae?' Geras looked startled. 'You must be bloody joking.'

'What choice do we have? You said yourself we're running out of options along this stretch of coast.'

Telemachus sighed and shook his head. 'It's not that simple. It took us ages to find Petrapylae. If we leave, how long do you think it'll take before we find another decent spot? It could be months. Longer, even.'

'It's got to be better than sticking around here,' Leitus said.

Geras puffed out his cheeks. 'So we're fucked if we stay and fucked if we don't?'

'That's about the size of it,' Leitus replied.

'Gods, it's times like this that I wish I was back on *Selene*. The food was shit and the pay was crap, but at least it was regular. No wonder the men are grumbling.'

'That's the captain's problem, not ours,' Leitus responded. 'That's why he gets paid the biggest share. It's up to Bulla to make the tough calls.'

'For now,' Telemachus said quietly.

Geras looked at him. 'You think the captain's in danger?'

The young first mate considered before he replied. 'I think there are some on the crew who are itching for a chance to challenge his authority. Right now they're biding their time, but the only way he can keep 'em quiet is to land a big prize. If he doesn't . . .'

He hesitated. Geras stared down at his wine cup and nodded solemnly. 'Let's hope his luck changes soon, then. For all our sakes.'

Just then Telemachus heard a torrent of curses from further along the beach. He looked across the shingle to see Virbius shouting angrily at one of the sailors fighting in pairs.

'Call that a stab?' The sinewy pirate gestured at the wooden training sword the man was holding. 'I've seen armpit-pluckers fight better than that, you useless shit!'

As Telemachus looked on, Virbius thrust out an arm and shoved the sailor backwards. The portly young man lost his footing, grunting as he landed on his back on the shingle. Before he could scrape himself off the ground, Virbius swept forward and kicked him in the ribs and face.

'Scum!' he rasped. 'You ain't fit to be no pirate!'

Telemachus clenched his jaw as he watched. Virbius had been bullying the new recruits from the outset, beating them as they scrubbed down the decks or hauled in the sheets. But he had been careful not to be too hard on them in front of Bulla. Glancing around, Telemachus realised that the captain had already returned to his cabin to sleep. He rose wearily to his feet and crunched across the shingle towards the pair, as Virbius unleashed another series of blows on the sailor.

'He's had enough,' he said, nodding at the recruit. 'Lay off.'

'This ain't none of your business,' Virbius snarled.

'You're supposed to be training these men, not beating them to within an inch of their lives.'

Virbius snorted in disgust. 'This worthless twat needs a good kick up the arse. He's too soft. Should've tossed the prick overside when we had the chance.'

Telemachus glanced at the sailor as the latter rose weakly to his feet. He had several bruises on his arms and face in addition to the blows he'd just sustained.

'Proculus, isn't it?'

'Aye . . . sir,' the man responded weakly.

'How did you get those other injuries, Proculus?'

There was a pause as the sailor glanced over at Virbius. He scratched his elbow and shifted uneasily on the spot. 'I slipped, sir. On cleaning duties, like.'

'I see,' Telemachus said. He slanted his gaze back to Virbius and studied him closely. 'You'll train him up properly from now on. That goes for the rest of the recruits as well. These men are no good to us if they're too badly injured to fight.'

'You're forgetting yourself, boy,' Virbius countered. 'I'm in charge of training these bastards. I'll treat 'em how I see fit.'

'You'll do as I tell you, or we'll see what Bulla has to say about it.'

Virbius chuckled. 'You threatening me, boy?'

'No,' Telemachus responded tonelessly. 'I'm giving you an order.'

'Bollocks. I don't take orders from kids.'

'I'm the ranking mate. You'll do as I say, or I'll have you in chains for insubordination.'

'I don't think so,' Virbius sneered.

Telemachus stood his ground and tensed his muscles. 'Want to try it on? You saw how that worked out for Hector. Or perhaps you're keen to suffer the same fate?'

For a moment Virbius wavered. Then he saw the determined look in Telemachus's eyes and stepped back. 'All right. Have it your way. But I wouldn't get too used to being Bulla's favourite if I were you. There's plenty on the crew who ain't forgotten what you did to Hector.'

'Is that supposed to frighten me?'

'Just telling you how it is. You want to watch yourself, boy. One of these days someone will get you back.'

'You think so?' Telemachus smiled coldly.

'We'll see, won't we?' Virbius shot him a final glare then swung back round to face the new recruits. 'What are you women looking at? Back to sword drill, the lot of you!'

The recruits hurriedly resumed their individual combats while Proculus picked up his fallen sword, nursing his bruised ribs with his other hand. Telemachus watched them for a moment longer before he beat a path back over to the cooking fires. The dull crack of wood against wood echoed across the beach as he sat down beside his companions.

Geras stared at him with concern. 'Making friends again?'

Telemachus shrugged helplessly. 'We're short-handed as it is. No point letting him make the situation worse.'

'That may be so, but you'd do well not to piss Virbius off. Any more than you already have, at least.'

'If you're worried for my safety, don't bother. I can look after myself.'

The following morning, *Poseidon's Trident* steered out of the bay and continued on her course towards Dyrrachium. A warm northerly breeze was blowing, filling her sail as she rose and fell on the swell. The men had been permitted a light breakfast of bread and a cup of water, and every spare hand now lined the rails, eager to claim the prize of an extra half-share that Bulla had promised to the first man who sighted a sail.

As the sun continued to climb, the wind strengthened and grey clouds thickened the sky, and Bulla called for the crew to take in a reef. Leitus stood beside Telemachus, keeping a wary eye on the rigging.

'We'll have to pray this weather doesn't get any worse. We'll be passing Cape Timoris soon.'

Telemachus glanced over at the older pirate, recalling the name from his days as a ship's boy. 'Is the Cape as bad as everyone says?'

'Bad?' Leitus laughed. 'It's the worst area for shipwrecks along the Illyrian coast. Every captain worth his salt knows the danger of running too close to that point.'

'What'll we do?'

'What every ship does when passing the Cape. We'll have to stand far out to weather it, and hope we don't run into a squall.'

'Sail ho!' the lookout cried. 'I see one, Captain! Over there!'

All hands on the deck simultaneously looked up towards the young pirate perched atop the yard. He pointed enthusiastically off to the horizon, barely able to contain his excitement. Bulla tipped his head back and shouted up.

'What do you see, Longarus? Make your report calmly, boy.'

There was a pause before Longarus called down again, this time in a more even tone. 'She's off the port bow, Captain. Three miles away maybe, and heading right across our bow.'

Bulla strode over to the rail, with Telemachus moving alongside him. Bassus and several others joined them a few moments later, stretching up on their toes as they stared out across the sea. At first Telemachus could see nothing. Then Bassus thrust out an arm.

'There!' he cried.

Telemachus strained his eyes in the direction the Thracian had indicated. As he stared out across the swell, he caught a glimpse of a tiny dark shape, barely discernible on the horizon.

'Roman warship?' Geras wondered.

Telemachus shook his head. 'Not here. The patrols will be busy to the north.'

'Can you see anything else?' Bulla called up.

Longarus watched the horizon for several moments before replying, 'She's hull up now. Too big to be a fishing boat. Looks like a merchantman, Captain.'

Excited voices rippled across *Trident*'s deck. Castor grinned. 'Seems the gods are favouring us after all.'

'Lucky bastard,' Geras muttered as he glanced up enviously at the lookout. 'He'll be getting an extra half-share for spotting her.'

A moment later Longarus yelled down, pointing in the same direction as the unseen merchantman. 'Captain, another sail!'

The chatter on the deck ceased as Bulla stared out towards the horizon. After several moments, he gave up and angled his head up at the lookout again. 'What can you make out?'

'She's perhaps a mile beyond the first ship, Captain. On the same heading.'

Geras's face lit up. 'Another cargo vessel?'

Before anyone could reply, Longarus called down once more. This time there was a clear note of anxiety in his voice. 'I can see her more clearly now. She's smaller than the merchantman, Captain. Flying a black pennant.'

'Black?' Bulla's eyebrows came together. 'Are you sure?'

'Aye. It's black all right.'

'Pirates.' Geras glanced over at Telemachus. 'Seems you were right. We're not the only ones hunting around these parts.'

Telemachus nodded, thoughts racing through his mind. 'They must have come from further along the coast of

Illyricum. They'll have seen that merchant ship standing out to weather the Cape and given chase to her.'

'Whoever they are, the bastards are driving her right into our path,' Bulla said. He stiffened his back. 'Call all hands, Telemachus. We'll head to cut her off before that other crew can catch up with her.'

Telemachus turned and shouted at the crewmen gathered on the deck to take up their positions. Then Bulla barked an order at Calkas, and the steersman heaved on the tiller, swinging *Trident*'s bows towards the merchantman. At the same time, the deckhands untied the sheets and braced the yard round until the wind was directly astern. Telemachus yelled at the hands to sheet her home and the vessel promptly surged forward as *Trident* gave chase to her prey.

'Merchantman's changed her course, Captain!' the lookout yelled.

Bulla automatically looked out towards the horizon. Telemachus followed his gaze. Far off, he spotted the cargo ship lurching round, her bows swinging away from *Trident*.

'Her captain's running before the wind, Captain,' he observed.

'She won't get very far,' Bulla said, his face set in a determined expression. 'We're too fast for them.'

Telemachus nodded, quickly grasping the situation the merchantman found herself in. With the other pirate ship cutting her off from the safety of the coast, her best chance had been to flee across to the Apulian coast, seeking refuge at Brundisium. But with *Poseidon's Trident* closing on her from the direction of the sea, she was now hemmed in on both sides.

'The other ship's altered her course as well!' the lookout

cried. 'Closing to intercept the merchantman from landward, Captain.'

'Very well. There's nowhere for her to run to now.' Bulla swung round to face Telemachus. 'We'll need to board the prey as soon as we're alongside. I want the crew dealt with and the cargo safely aboard *Trident* before that other pirate can intervene. Get the men ready.'

'Aye, Captain.'

Telemachus bellowed orders and the boarding party hastily assembled on the foredeck. Those pirates equipped with missiles gathered close by, while others took up their stations beside the grappling hooks. Bulla moved to his post beside the steersman, from where he could keep a careful eye on *Trident*'s course and the distance to her prey. With the crew in position, Telemachus joined the rest of the spare hands along the rail as they looked for the first sign of the other pirate craft.

A short while later, there was a cry from one of the mates, and Telemachus caught a glimpse of a triangular sail far off to landward. He looked over at Leitus. 'Think we'll reach her before that other ship?'

The veteran scratched his grey-flecked jaw. 'It'll be close. But we're nearer than that lot and she ain't likely to be as weatherly as this bird. I'd bet my share on us getting to her first.'

The chase continued. Soon *Poseidon's Trident* had closed to less than half a mile from the merchantman, and the two ships were slowly converging. Telemachus felt a warm prickle of excitement at the prospect of some booty after weeks of hunting without success. He glanced across to landward and was surprised to see that the other pirate ship had drawn much closer to the prey, her dark sail taut as a drum in the failing breeze as she continued on her course. Her crew had run the sweep oars out in an attempt to close the gap more quickly, but despite her captain's best efforts, it was obvious to Telemachus that *Trident* would reach the merchantman first.

Geras was rubbing his hands with anticipation. 'We've got them by the balls now. There'll be some good loot on her as well, by the looks of it.'

He nodded beyond the bows. Telemachus looked ahead at the prey and saw that she was riding low in the water, and realised that her hold must be weighed down with cargo.

'What do you think she might be carrying?' he asked.

'Whatever it is, we'll have to capture her before the other crew catches up.'

The sun broke through the scattered clouds and there was a chorus of frantic shouts further forward of the mast. As Telemachus studied the merchantman, he caught sight of several helmets glinting dully on her deck, and he turned to Geras.

'Look! Over there!'

Geras saw them too, and his face registered shock. 'Fuck . . .'

A throng of heavily armed men dressed in plain tunics and carrying legionary-style short swords and shields teemed on the cargo ship's deck. Javelins were being issued to some of them, while others were organising the defence of the ship, yelling orders and shouting their encouragement at the sailors. Telemachus counted at least twenty armed men. More than enough to make a determined stand against *Trident*'s crew.

'Marines?' he wondered aloud.

Geras peered at the figures, then shook his head. 'Some kind of soldiers, I'd say.'

'What are they doing on a trading ship?'

'Hired guards, maybe. We'll find out soon enough.'

Bulla yelled at the steersman and Calkas threw his weight against the tiller. Telemachus heard the grinding of timbers as the sweep oars were run out, and a few moments later the blades began churning through the sea, manoeuvring *Trident* closer to the merchantman's right side. A glance eastward told him that the other pirate ship had also changed her course, intending to take the cargo ship on the left side.

The merchantman abruptly changed direction and came up towards *Trident* at an angle. She was less than fifty paces from the pirate ship now, Telemachus estimated.

'What's her captain up to?' Geras asked. 'Why is she steering towards us?'

A voice carried across the sea as an order was shouted on the merchantman's deck. Telemachus grasped the defenders' intentions an instant before a shower of dark shafts rose into the sky.

He cupped his hands to his mouth and bellowed, 'Take cover!'

CHAPTER THIRTY

There was a terrible pause as the volley of missiles seemed to hang in the air for a moment before they clattered down on the deck, splintering the facing on the pirates' shields. Past the rim of his shield Telemachus saw one man drop to the deck as a javelin struck him below his buckler and the iron tip skewered his thigh. Two of the hands scrambled over to their comrade and dragged him away moments before another javelin struck the spot where the man had been slumped, quivering as it bit into the planking. Cries rose into the air as more men were hit by the lethal shafts or crippled by slingshot, but most of the pirates had taken shelter behind their shields before they could be struck down.

Bulla's voice carried across the deck, above the screams of the wounded. 'Put our archers to work!'

Telemachus relayed the order to the bowmen, shouting to make himself heard. The archers notched their arrows, took aim and loosed shafts at the men on the other deck. Several missed their targets, splashing into the narrowing stretch of water between the two vessels. But most found their range and thudded against the shields that the defenders had hurriedly raised above their heads. Two sailors were cut down, drawing a ragged cheer from *Trident*'s crew.

The two sides continued to exchange volleys as Bulla gave the order to take in the sweep oars and *Trident* carried on down the starboard beam of the merchantman. When the two ships had nearly drawn level, he moved forward from the stern and called out, 'Cast grappling lines!'

The hands scrambled back to their stations and snatched up the pointed hooks, launching them through the air. Once the spikes had bitten into the merchantman's side rail, the men began to haul on the lines, drawing *Trident* closer. Behind them the boarding party crowded around the mast, awaiting the moment they could leap across to the other ship and tear into the defenders.

'Pull, you useless bastards!' Telemachus roared. 'Pull!'

A whirring noise split the air as a group of slingers loosed a deadly hail of shot at the pirates heaving on *Trident*'s grappling lines. The men were unable to defend themselves against the barrage, and the pirate directly in front of Telemachus toppled backwards as a shot struck him on the side of his head, shattering his jawbone. The man let out a guttural moan of pain, the line he had been holding slackening as his arms fell away.

Telemachus turned to the bowmen on the foredeck. 'Over there!' he bellowed, thrusting out his sword arm at the slingers. 'Take that lot down!'

The bowmen adjusted their aim and released a torrent of arrows at the targets Telemachus had pointed out, striking down one of the men and forcing others to dive for cover. Under the torrent of missiles the slingers were gradually forced to retreat to the ranks of the other defenders. The moment the rain of lead shot had lessened, Telemachus looked round to the crewman on his right.

'Bassus!' he yelled, indicating the grappling line in front of the man with the shattered jaw. 'Take that man's place. Move!'

The burly Thracian hesitated briefly before scurrying forward and snatching up the line, driven on by the prospect of a share of the merchantman's spoils.

The bowmen kept up their steady shower of missiles as Bassus and the others strained at the grappling lines, pulling them tight. Once the ships were side by side, the pirates fastened the lines to the wooden cleats and grabbed their weapons, joining the rest of the boarding party, while the spare deckhands let the mainsheets fly. There was time for the archers to launch one final volley at the defenders before Bulla brought up his curved sword and shouted at the boarders, 'Go! GO! Move yourselves!'

The boarders swarmed forward. As the first man climbed over the side rail, a javelin was hurled at him by one of the sailors aboard the merchantman. The pirate let out a gasp of pain as the shaft punched through his guts, and he fell forward, tumbling into the narrow gap between the two vessels. Proculus and the other new recruits froze at the edge of the rail and looked down in terror as the pirate's body was crushed between the hulls.

Gritting his teeth, Telemachus climbed up on to the side rail as a stray arrow hissed narrowly past him. 'Come on! What are you waiting for, an invitation from the emperor?'

He launched himself across the gap, landing with a heavy thud on the merchantman's deck. Proculus and the other boarders began leaping across after him, inspired by the first mate's fearlessness. Telemachus straightened up and immediately charged at the defenders. No longer pinned down by missile fire, they were rushing forward to meet the boarding party at the rail. The soldiers were leading from the front, with the less well-armed sailors behind them. The defenders showed none of the usual fear or trepidation of seamen when confronted with a wave of pirates, and Telemachus knew that the men of *Poseidon's Trident* were going to be in for a hard fight.

'Don't stop!' he yelled at the others. 'Them or us, lads!'

He dropped his shoulder and charged at the nearest defender, a barrel-chested figure with close-cropped hair, who was gripping a short sword and a legionary shield. The Roman lowered his head and stepped towards his younger opponent, and Telemachus felt a shuddering impact as the man's shield slammed against his smaller buckler, robbing him of momentum. He stumbled backwards, recovering just in time to see a gleaming tip of steel as the Roman stabbed at his throat.

Telemachus jerked up his right arm, parrying the blow with the edge of his falcata. The Roman snatched his sword back, a brief look of surprise crossing his face at his opponent's quick reflexes. Then he thrust out again, stabbing down at Telemachus's midriff. This time Telemachus read the move and punched out with his buckler, deflecting the blow and lunging forward before the Roman could retreat, slamming the rim of the shield into the man's face. The Roman let out a grunt as the metal rim smashed the bridge of his nose. He staggered backwards, dazed from the impact and the pain, and Telemachus slashed down, cutting deep into his opponent's neck. The Roman slumped to his knees, jets of blood squirting out of the wound.

Telemachus stepped away from the Roman and glanced around him. The air was filled with curses and shouts and the sharp crack of blades clattering against shields, and amid the melee he glimpsed the bodies of several of *Trident*'s crew sprawled on the deck. The contest had been fairly even so far, with the defenders more than holding their own against the pirates. One or two of the sailors threw darting glances at the second pirate vessel as it closed in on the port side, but most paid it no attention as they fought for their lives.

Telemachus heard a challenge to his right. He wheeled round and came face to face with a short, overweight Nubian armed with an axe charging towards him. Blood glistened on the axe head as the Nubian swung it round, bringing it down towards his opponent's skull. At the last moment, Telemachus dropped to his haunches and hefted his buckler. A burning pain shot down his arm as the axe buried itself in the shield rim, biting deep into the wood. Gritting his teeth through the pain, he slashed out with his sword, slicing through fabric and flesh as he opened up a shallow wound to the Nubian's stomach. But the cut only seemed to enrage the sailor, and he tore his weapon free from the buckler before edging away, his features twisted with rage.

The Nubian swung again, throwing all his weight into the blow as he brought the axe down in a two-handed grip. Telemachus sidestepped just in time and the axe head slashed down, glancing off the edge of the buckler before splintering the deck. The Nubian wrenched his weapon back and slammed his shoulder into Telemachus's chest so that he was pressed up against the side rail. A triumphant smile played on the Nubian's lips.

'Nowhere for you to go now, scum!'

Just then a dark shadow passed over the merchantman as the other pirate craft came up alongside, and the timbers shuddered as the vessel crashed into her beam, knocking over some of the men on the deck. Caught by surprise, a nearby sailor lost his footing and fell against the Nubian. Both men crashed to the deck in a tangle of limbs and weapons, the Nubian's axe skimming along the planking out of reach. A pair of pirates descended upon the sailor before he could snatch it up, hacking savagely at his torso.

An instant later, the hooks on the second pirate ship were released, flying across the narrow gap between the vessels before being hauled back and lodging into the merchantman's side rail. Some of the defenders shouted warnings at their comrades as the other ship's crew pulled their vessel closer. Then the leading pirates vaulted over the rail and charged towards the defenders in a howling mass. Several of the Romans spun away to deal with the new threat, but many others were slow to respond and were cut down in a frenzy of flickering sword points and spear thrusts.

'That's it, men!' Bulla roared. 'We've got 'em now! Let's finish the job!'

Confusion and panic seized the defenders, and they fell back around the mast as both pirate crews pressed home their advantage. More armed men were pouring over from the other pirate ship now, slaughtering anyone who tried to resist. Soon only a handful of defenders were left, and most threw down their weapons as they realised that there was no possibility of victory. A couple of those who surrendered were cut down by men still in the grip of fighting madness, and only a shout from Bulla finally persuaded *Trident*'s crew to spare the survivors.

His men reluctantly pulled back from the mast, leaving a space between *Trident*'s crew and the men from the second pirate vessel. The two crews eyed each other with mutual suspicion, neither side daring to lower their weapons. Then one of the pirates on the other crew shouted for his men to make way. The ranks swiftly parted, and a lean, dark-haired figure stepped forward. Gold earrings glinted on either side of his face, beneath his black skullcap. He scanned the men opposite for a beat before he addressed them.

'Who is your captain?'

'I am,' Bulla announced as he pushed to the front. 'My name's Bulla, captain of *Poseidon's Trident*.'

'Bulla?' The other pirate pursed his lips and nodded. 'Yes, I've heard the name. You're the captain who knocked Nestor's mob on the head.'

'Aye. That's us. And who might you be?'

The other captain smiled thinly. 'Perhaps you've heard of me as well. My name is Agrius. Commander of *Pegasus*. At your service.'

A look of surprise flickered across Bulla's face at the mention of Agrius's name, and several of *Trident*'s men exchanged anxious glances.

Telemachus kept a wary eye on *Pegasus*'s crew as their commander took a few paces forward. Agrius glanced around at the pile of bodies on the deck, then returned his gaze to Bulla. 'It appears we got here just in time, Captain. Any longer and you and your men might well have been finished.'

'We had the beating of them,' Bulla responded. 'But I'll admit they gave us a hard fight.'

'Not surprising, now that we're up against mercenaries.'

'Mercenaries?' Telemachus raised an eyebrow.

Agrius waved a hand at one of the dead Romans. 'The ships around these parts have taken to travelling with protection. Retired marines, legionaries, gladiators . . . anyone who can handle a sword. I've lost quite a few men myself taking vessels lately.'

'Seems that we need to choose our victims more carefully from now on,' Bulla remarked.

'Indeed, Captain. Now, kindly tell your men to lower their weapons and return to your ship. We'll be on our way as soon as we've transferred the cargo to our hold.'

Bulla stared at him. 'This is our prize. We boarded her first. The cargo belongs to us.'

'You're mistaken, Captain. We were hunting this bird long before you showed up. Just because you tried to steal her from under us doesn't give you the right to the spoils.'

'Who said anything about stealing? We seized the ship fair and square.'

Agrius's eyes narrowed to slits. 'I won't ask you again, Captain. Tell your crew to leave this ship at once.'

'No.'

A tense silence hung over the merchantman, broken only by the cries of the injured and dying. The pirates either side of Agrius raised their weapons, waiting for the signal from their captain to attack. Ahead of them, the survivors from the merchant ship edged closer to the mast, their eyes darting anxiously from one pirate crew to the other. From the corner of his eye, Telemachus saw some of his companions hefting their shields as they prepared to fight a new enemy.

Agrius took another step forward, his gaze fixed on Bulla. 'Last chance, Captain. Retreat, or you will regret it.'

'Wait!' Telemachus cried, stepping into the space between the two crews. Every pair of eyes on the deck swung towards him.

'And who might you be?' Agrius demanded.

'Telemachus, sir. First mate on *Poseidon's Trident*.'

'This skinny runt is your second in command?' Agrius laughed. 'You must be a desperate man, Captain.'

Several of *Pegasus*'s crew chuckled among themselves. Telemachus shot them a hard look before he continued to address both captains. 'Why don't we share the loot between us, rather than fight over it?'

Agrius frowned at him. 'Why would we agree to that?'

'We both have a claim to the cargo. Maybe neither one of us would have succeeded in capturing it alone. Seems to me a division of the spoils is the best way to settle matters.'

'Bollocks!' the thickly bearded man to the right of Agrius growled. 'We shouldn't strike a deal with these scum! Ain't right, Captain. I say we cut 'em down! Take what's ours.'

'Silence!' Agrius hissed at his lieutenant. Then he turned back to Telemachus and gave him a considered look. 'What terms do you suggest, boy?'

'Fifty–fifty. An even split. That seems fairest, seeing as we both played a part in capturing the ship.'

'And if we refuse?' Agrius asked.

'Then you'll have to fight us for the booty. If you're lucky, your crew might win the day. But many of your men would die. This way, we both get to walk away with something, without having to shed any more blood.'

'What about the survivors?'

'We'll take half each, same as the rest of the loot.'

'Sounds reasonable to me,' Bulla announced after a brief pause. 'Well, Agrius? What do you say?'

Pegasus's captain pulled at his chin in thought. 'It's tempting. We could certainly do without losing any more of our men . . . Very well. You've got yourself a deal, Captain. This time.'

Bulla nodded with relief. 'I'll give the order for my lads to bring up the cargo. We'll distribute the spoils on the deck, along with the ship's stores and the survivors.'

'Demetrius will accompany your men.' Agrius waved a hand at the bearded figure at his shoulder. 'Make sure that everything is above board, so to speak.'

'As you wish.'

The merchantman was alive with activity as the two pirate crews bent to their tasks. *Pegasus*'s men rounded up the surviving sailors while several of *Trident*'s hands made their way over to the hatch to bring up the ship's cargo. The bales of cloth, fine wool and leather hides were taken from the hold and carried up to the deck, where a separate team led by Demetrius and Castor divided the loot equally into two piles, one destined for each ship. The sight of the valuable goods had put both sets of pirates in good spirits, and the earlier animosity between them was quickly forgotten.

As the last bales were brought up, Demetrius made his way over to the two captains. 'That's all of it. There's some blocks of marble down in the hold, but they're too heavy to shift.'

'Pity,' Agrius said. 'Marble's worth a small fortune these days. Still, it's a sizeable haul. Tell the men to begin transferring our share, Demetrius.'

'Aye, Captain.'

The bearded man turned on his heels and marched back over to the cargo hatch, shouting at the other hands. Agrius watched them thoughtfully as they began transporting the first goods over to *Pegasus*.

'Perhaps this might become a more profitable partnership,' he mused.

Bulla looked curiously at him. 'How do you mean?'

'We trapped one ship by cornering it between us. Why don't we repeat the trick?'

'You're proposing that we hunt together?'

'Of course. We'd have a better chance of catching victims than we would by sailing alone.'

Bulla shook his head. 'My men would never agree to joining forces with you.'

'I'm not suggesting a permanent arrangement,' Agrius said. 'We'd merely sail together for the rest of the season. Until winter, at best.'

Bulla peered at the other captain. 'And who would be in charge of this partnership?'

'Both of us, of course. We'd have to agree which ships we go after, which ports we raid, and fix on a meeting point in case our ships got separated. Whatever we take together, we split down the middle.'

'That could work,' Bulla replied, scratching his jaw. 'But we'd still have the problem of finding ships to attack. Anywhere north of Epidaurum is out of the question.'

Agrius listened attentively as Bulla explained about the convoy scheme Canis had instigated.

'You're right, Captain,' he said when Bulla had finished. 'There's no chance of us raiding the northern coast. And there's not much in the way of prey around here either. But perhaps there is one other area we could try.'

'Where?'

'Italia.'

A look of alarm flashed across Bulla's face. 'Why would

we want to raid closer to the enemy?'

'Because the Italian coast is ripe for plundering. Now that Canis is busy pursuing our kind on the other side of the Adriaticum, there's bound to be some rich pickings to be had.'

'The Romans won't have left their own coast undefended,' Telemachus interrupted. 'Even Canis isn't that foolish.'

Agrius sneered at him. 'You clearly don't understand the Romans, boy. They're an arrogant race. They would never imagine that anyone would dare to raid so close to home. Besides, I have it on good authority that Canis has left only a small force behind to guard the shipping there.'

'Who told you that?' Bulla demanded.

'My men captured a vessel a week ago. A naval packet. Not much of value on board, but one of the marines was very helpful. Once he saw his friends' throats being cut, he couldn't wait to cooperate.'

Telemachus suppressed a shiver. 'What did he say?'

'He told us about Canis's plan to offer a convoy service. He also said that the Ravenna fleet is in far worse condition than I'd thought. The shortage of seaworthy vessels is so severe that Canis has been able to leave only a handful of ships to defend Ravenna. Half a squadron, to be precise. Five biremes, plus the flagship.'

'Six? To defend the whole coast?'

'That's what the Roman told us.' There was a calculating glint in Agrius's eyes as he went on. 'Those biremes are under strict instructions not to venture more than a day out from Ravenna. The coast to the south is ripe for the plucking.'

Bulla frowned. 'If Italia is so lucrative, why haven't you sailed down there already?'

'We've been trying to gather more intelligence. Make sure

that Roman was telling us the truth and not leading us into a trap. What you've just told me confirms his story.'

'But word would get back to the navy if we raided Italia,' Telemachus cautioned. 'They'd take action against us. They wouldn't stand for their own coastline being attacked.'

'So what? By the time the Romans get their arses together, we'll be long gone.' Agrius smiled, then turned to Bulla. 'Well, Captain? Are you in?'

Bulla glanced back over at the cargo, his brow crinkled and eyes narrowed in thought. 'We'll have to put a prize crew on this bird to take our wounded and our share of the booty back to base. *Trident*'s the slower ship, and she won't handle as well with a full hold.'

'By all means. The ship is yours.'

There was only the briefest hesitation before Bulla made his decision. 'In that case . . . I accept. We'll go along with your plan, Agrius.'

'Excellent. We'll set sail for Italia as soon as the rest of the goods have been transferred to our ship. In the meantime, I'll brief my men. I suggest you do the same.'

'We'll need to agree on a meeting point,' Bulla pointed out. 'In case we lose sight of one another at sea.'

'Of course. I'll have Demetrius bring up the maps from my cabin. We'll choose a suitable location, decide on the signals to communicate with each other, and settle any other questions before we part.'

Agrius gave a cursory nod, then marched over to his lieutenants. Telemachus turned towards Bulla, struggling to mask his unease. 'Are you sure about this, Captain?'

'Agrius is right,' Bulla responded grudgingly. 'If what he says is true, Italia is too good an opportunity to pass up.'

'But we'll provoke the navy. They'll come after us.'

'With what? You heard what he said. There are hardly any warships down there to protect the sea lanes. We can seize a fortune.'

'Right now, maybe. But this is going to make us plenty of enemies in Rome. More than we have already.'

Bulla exhaled irritably. 'I can't worry about that. My responsibility is to this ship and crew, and as far as I'm concerned, this is our best hope of finding some loot.'

'But Captain—'

'Enough!' Bulla snapped. The impatience in his voice was clear as he went on. 'I've made my decision. Now find Castor and tell him to pick a prize crew for this ship. The wounded are to be taken back with him. The rest are to return to *Trident*. Then we'll make for Italia.'

CHAPTER THIRTY-ONE

A month later

'Quite the welcome party waiting for us,' Geras said, pointing towards the far end of the bay.

Telemachus followed his gaze and spied a crowd of figures gathering on the beach, a short distance away from the causeway leading up to the citadel. Fires glowed from beyond the walls of Petrapylae, illuminating the mounted catapult platforms. As soon as *Poseidon's Trident* had rounded the headland, the crew had made the recognition signal, announcing their arrival to the lookout station. The signal had been relayed to the pirates inside the citadel, and the men manning the catapults had stood down from their posts. Now they were making their way down to the shore to await *Trident's* return.

'We've been gone a while,' Telemachus commented as he stood on the foredeck, shading his eyes against the setting sun. 'I imagine the others are desperate to see how we've fared.'

Geras's face broke into a wide grin. 'They'll owe us a drink or two tonight, once they find out how much booty we're carrying.'

A month had passed since the men of *Poseidon's Trident* had set sail for Italia, in partnership with the crew of Agrius's ship, *Pegasus*. The raid had been a success, Telemachus reflected, as

Poseidon's Trident glided towards the beach. Between them, the two pirate vessels had captured an impressive haul. After closing on the Apulian coast, they had made their way north, snatching up a pair of merchantmen near the port at Sipontum. Another vessel had been captured several days later at Histonium. Between them, the crews of *Trident* and *Pegasus* had plundered a small fortune in silk, spices and other luxuries that fetched premium prices across the Empire.

After dividing the spoils, Bulla had decided to return to Petrapylae before resuming the hunt for prey. Agrius had insisted on pursuing further victims, but with *Trident* heavily weighed down with loot and in need of additional supplies, Bulla had argued that he had no option but to head back to base. Once they had sold on the merchandise and revictualled their ship, they would meet *Pegasus* at a secluded anchorage away from the main trade route. Meanwhile, Agrius would continue to search the area, gathering intelligence on possible targets for the two ships.

The only dark note had been the brutal treatment Agrius and his men had inflicted upon the sailors they had taken prisoner. After capturing each vessel, Agrius had called the seamen forward in turn, demanding they join the pirates' ranks. Any who refused were put to death on the spot, beheaded or thrown overside with bound hands and feet. Telemachus had looked on in horror as a tearful cabin boy, no older than ten or eleven, had begged for his life, moments before Demetrius struck the child down. Such cruelties would only further inflame Roman anger at the pirates, but Bulla seemed reluctant to upset his fledgling partnership with Agrius, and he had done nothing to intervene.

'Pity we're not staying here for longer,' Geras muttered.

'Two nights ain't much time for celebrating. I could do with putting my feet up for a bit.'

Telemachus shrugged. 'Bulla knows we can't afford to waste time ashore. Especially after that last vessel got away.'

Geras nodded. A few days earlier, *Trident* and *Pegasus* had chased down a small coastal trader some miles north of the port at Mirenum. Although the trader had been damaged with missile fire, she had eventually managed to pull away from her pursuers, escaping as night fell.

'I wonder how the Romans are going to react?' Geras asked.

Telemachus rubbed his chin. 'Canis won't stand for Italia being attacked.'

'All the more reason for us to enjoy it while it lasts.' Geras slapped his friend cheerfully on the back. 'Come on. Things are looking up for us for a change. We've got enough loot to keep this mob happy, and there's plenty more where that lot came from. It's not all bad.'

'I suppose not.'

'That's the spirit! In the meantime, I plan to enjoy myself with a jar of reasonably priced wine and the company of a plump tart. There's plenty of both waiting for us there.' Geras pointed at the citadel. 'What do you say? A toast to our success?'

'Tempting.' Telemachus smiled. 'But I've got another matter to attend to.'

'Nereus?'

Telemachus replied with a nod, turning his thoughts to the double share of the spoils due to him. Once the merchants had bought up the captured cargo, he would have a substantial fortune from the proceeds of the sale: enough finally to allow him to purchase his brother's freedom. He had chosen two of his most reliable men on the crew to safeguard his money, with orders to travel to Thorikos and negotiate a fair price with Burrus, the metalworker who had purchased Nereus to work in his forge. He was at last on the cusp of freeing his brother, and his heart swelled in his chest at the thought of seeing him again.

The ship made a final approach to the shore, and a few moments later, the bows shuddered to a halt against the loose shingle. Telemachus followed Bulla down the sturdy lowered gangway and spotted Castor approaching from the throng of pirates further up the beach. The quartermaster flashed a worried glance at Telemachus, then turned to Bulla.

'Captain,' he began. 'Thank the gods you're back. Me and the lads was starting to get worried.'

'No need,' Bulla replied airily. 'We didn't run into any trouble. We're back to revictual, that's all. And to empty *Trident*'s hold.'

'You had a profitable voyage, then?'

'More than you could imagine. We'll discuss everything later. Then we're leaving again in a couple of days.'

'So soon?' Castor arched an eyebrow.

'Agrius is keen to snap up more ships while our Roman friends are still preoccupied on this side of the Adriaticum. I'm minded to agree. Now, is there anything to report? Any trouble with the men?'

'It's been fairly quiet here, like. One of the guards got into a scrap with a moneylender. Had to give him twenty lashes. Other than that, it's just been the usual complaints from the locals about the lads drinking and fighting.'

'And the wounded you returned with?'

'Four of 'em died. Three others are crippled and ain't no good for service at sea. The rest are fit for duty.'

'See to it that the dead men's families are paid in full,' Bulla replied grimly. 'A full share for each one. That ought to see them through the winter. As for those no longer fit to go to sea, we'll find work for them ashore.'

'Aye, Captain.' Castor shifted uncomfortably. 'There is something else . . .' He pursed his lips, evidently reluctant to go on.

'Well?' Bulla snapped. 'What is it? Out with it, man.'

Castor glanced warily around. 'Perhaps we'd better discuss it in private, like. You, me and Telemachus.'

Bulla let out a breath of impatience. 'Fine. Leitus!'

The grizzled sailor came running over from *Poseidon's Trident.* 'Captain?'

'You're in charge here,' Bulla announced. 'Have the men begin unloading the cargo. None of 'em are to sneak off until everything is accounted for. Make a list of any supplies we'll need while you're at it. I want us ready to sail again in two days' time. Understood?'

'Aye, aye, Captain.'

Leitus hurried back off towards the beached hulk, barking orders at the crew. The crowd on the beach drifted away while the spare hands stayed back to help unload *Trident*'s cargo. Bulla strode further up the beach until he reached the edge of the causeway leading to the timber gatehouse. When they were out of earshot of the men on the beach, he turned to Castor.

'What's going on? Speak up now.'

Castor scratched at his elbow. 'It's like this, Captain. While you was away, me and some of the lads took out that ship we'd captured to purchase some supplies from Ortopla. That last voyage had nearly cleaned out the citadel, and the locals have barely got enough grain and meat to keep themselves from starvation, let alone to sell to us.'

Telemachus gave a faint nod. Ortopla was the nearest friendly port to Petrapylae, a den of corrupt merchants who had few scruples about who they did business with, asking no questions as to the provenance of the goods they purchased or the identities of the men they sold to. *Trident's* crew had often anchored there when they needed to buy in extra supplies and equipment.

'I see,' Bulla said. 'Go on.'

'We'd just finished negotiating a price with that snake Lycinius when one of the lads overheard an announcement being made in the forum. One of them heralds what reads out the gazette. It was the usual gossip, mostly. There was a report that the Romans had captured a pirate crew operating to the north of here and put the lot of 'em to death.'

'One less crew for us to compete with, then,' Bulla said grimly. 'Anything else?'

'Aye. An announcement from that imperial navy prefect, Canis. Regarding the lad here.'

Telemachus felt his guts turn to ice. 'What did it say?'

Castor turned to address him directly. 'Canis has your brother. He's being held hostage.'

'Nereus? No. That can't be.'

'I'm just telling you what we heard, lad.'

'But . . . how did the Romans come to know about me and my brother in the first place?'

Castor shrugged. 'I don't know. People talk, word spreads . . .'

314

Telemachus stared unblinking at the quartermaster. 'What else did you hear?'

'That the Romans have given you until the end of next month to give yourself up. If you refuse, Nereus will be crucified.'

Anger swelled inside Telemachus, burning in his veins. He clenched his fists tightly and closed his eyes for a moment, overcome with rage and grief. For the past months he had been afraid that Nereus might succumb to some dreadful accident at the forge. He had never imagined that his efforts to free his brother would place him in even greater peril. He took a deep breath and forced himself to think clearly. 'How long ago was this?'

'Five days back,' Castor replied.

A rush of hope flooded through Telemachus. 'Then there's still time to save him. Captain, we have to rescue him.'

'We can't.' Bulla shook his head. 'We don't know where they're holding him.'

'Then I'll hand myself in at Ravenna. My life for my brother's.'

'Don't be a fool! Do you really think Canis would honour his word and spare Nereus? He'd simply execute both of you.'

'I have to try. If there's a chance of saving his life, I'm willing to risk it.'

'And I'm not,' Bulla replied firmly. 'What do you think would happen if you agreed to Canis's terms? The Romans would torture you the moment you gave yourself up. Their interrogators have a talent for making men talk . . . Some of them are even better at it than we are. You'd tell them everything you know, eventually. Including the location of our base. I can't allow it.'

'But we can't just abandon him!' Telemachus exclaimed. 'There has to be something we can do, Captain. There has to be.'

'There isn't.' Bulla saw the distress in the first mate's expression and softened his tone. 'Look, I'm sorry. But we can't risk the lives of the crew blundering around in some hopeless search for your brother. Surely you can understand that.'

Telemachus forced himself to take a breath. Through the haze of anger and despair he could see the logic of Bulla's argument. He had to find some other way of persuading the captain. 'I'm not asking you to endanger the crew. Just promise me one thing.'

'What's that?'

'If there's an opportunity to rescue Nereus, you'll let me take it.'

Bulla sighed. 'I won't ask my men to lay down their lives for the sake of your brother. But if there's a chance of getting him back, and if there's no danger to the men, then yes. We'll do what we can to rescue him.'

Telemachus nodded. 'That's all that I ask, Captain.' A troubling question still prodded his mind. 'There's something I don't understand. No one knew about my brother other than the lads I've told on this crew. No one else.'

Bulla was looking at him with interest. 'What are you implying?'

'Someone must have told the Romans about him. Someone who knew where he worked, who his master was. Someone here betrayed me.'

Bulla arched an eyebrow. 'I doubt it. My men can be cruel bastards when the mood takes them, but they wouldn't do that to one of their own.'

'What other explanation could there be?'

Bulla stared at him. 'But why would anyone tell our enemies about your brother?'

'To get rid of me. Whoever did this knows I'd do anything to save Nereus.'

There was a pause before the captain responded. 'If that's true, we'll find the man responsible. You have my word. Any traitor in my crew will be rooted out. I'll deal with them personally.'

Telemachus nodded his gratitude.

'What'll we do now, Captain?' asked Castor.

'We carry on with our plan,' said Bulla. 'See to it that Trident is provisioned and ready to set sail. We'll head straight for the meeting point with Agrius and decide our next steps.' He strode off down the causeway, abruptly ending the discussion. A moment later, Castor followed him into the citadel to organise the necessary supplies for Trident's next voyage.

As Telemachus turned to head back down the beach, he felt a black despair engulf him. Geras marched over from the direction of the ship, cocking his chin at the departing captain.

'What was all that about?' he asked.

He listened silently as Telemachus told him about his brother's capture.

'Shit. I'm sorry . . .' He frowned. 'What are you going to do?'

'There's nothing I can do right now. But I'll find a way to save him once we return to the coast of Italia. We'll be hunting along the main Italian trade routes, which means there'll be plenty of prizes to snatch up. Someone we run into might know where he is.'

'It's a long shot.'

'I know. But it's the only hope I've got.'

Geras furrowed his brow. 'Even if you find out where the Romans are keeping him, how are you going to rescue him? He's bound to be closely guarded.'

'No doubt. But there will be plenty of time to worry about that later. Right now, I need to find out where Canis is keeping him prisoner.'

'Well, you don't need to persuade me. I'll help you in any way I can if it means getting one over those Roman bastards.'

Telemachus smiled warmly. 'Thanks.'

Geras stared at his friend. 'Any idea who sold you out?'

'It's got to be someone on the crew,' Telemachus said. 'Someone who knew about Nereus and was in a position to get a message to the Romans.'

'Sounds like you know who it might be.'

'I have an idea. But I can't act. Not until I'm certain.' He looked over at the pirates unloading the goods from *Trident*, hatred clenching like a fist around his heart. 'Whoever betrayed me will suffer for what they've done. I swear it before Jupiter, best and greatest.'

CHAPTER THIRTY-TWO

Three days later, Telemachus stood with Bulla and Agrius in the tiny cabin built into *Pegasus*'s stern. A roughly drawn goatskin map of the Italian coastline had been placed on the desk occupying the middle of the captain's quarters, the details illuminated by the light coming through a grille in the deck above. Around them the timbers groaned as the vessel rocked gently on the sea.

Poseidon's Trident had arrived at the meeting point in the early afternoon, her stores fully provisioned and her ranks swelled by Castor and the rest of the prize crew. After coming within a hundred paces of her consort, the oars had been taken in and the sail lowered, then Bulla and Telemachus had gone across in the ship's boat to consult with Agrius in his cabin.

'We should hunt here,' Agrius said as he tapped his finger on a section of the map. 'Between Ancona and Ariminum. I reconnoitred the area closely while you lot were away. Looks promising. Plenty of vessels making landfall on the main trade route, and not many coves for them to hide in. Should be easy enough for us to snap up a few more prizes. Who knows, with all those pleasure boats and passenger ships travelling between the colonies, we might even net ourselves a high-born Roman

319

or two. Could bring us a hefty ransom. Once we've had some fun with their womenfolk, of course.' There was a dangerous gleam in his eyes as he spoke.

Bulla scrutinised the map for a moment, his face scrunched up in thought. 'If we sail here, it'll bring us close to Ravenna.'

'Aye.' Agrius nodded. 'What of it?'

'There are many ports on the coast, and not many safe anchorages. What happens if we run into trouble?'

'We won't,' Agrius responded confidently. 'Besides, moving further north is our best bet. We can't continue operating to the south. Not any more.'

'Why not?'

'We sighted a pair of biremes on the way back. They looked like they were heading south.'

'Romans?' Telemachus struggled to contain the alarm in his voice. 'Did they see you?'

'Of course not.' Agrius smiled. 'We were sheltering in a cove from a storm when one of my lads spotted 'em. We'd lowered the main spar and sail to the deck. Stupid bastards sailed right past us.'

'But if they're sending out patrols, they must know we're here,' Telemachus remarked. 'They're on to us.'

'Relax, boy. It's a couple of patrol ships, not the entire imperial fleet. The rest of the squadron is still hundreds of miles away, running Canis's convoy service.'

'There's the five biremes at Ravenna,' Bulla pointed out.

'They're under orders not to venture far from the port. Besides, Canis won't dare to use those ships. He can't risk leaving Ravenna undefended.'

'But if the Romans are moving back down to Italia, they'll be sending more reinforcements across soon,' said Telemachus.

'If they haven't done so already. What happens if we run into another warship?'

'Then we'll give them the slip, like we always do. Our vessels are more than capable of outrunning their ancient tubs.'

Telemachus took a breath and fought to control his rising temper. Much as he wanted to remain close to where his brother was held prisoner, that had to be weighed in the balance against the lives of the crew he had sworn to serve with. He turned and made his appeal directly to Bulla instead. 'Maybe we should turn around and move back across the Adriaticum, Captain. Try our luck closer to home. It's almost autumn, and some of those ships are bound to risk another trip before the season is over.'

'Why bother when there's still plenty of riches to be found here?' Agrius countered.

Telemachus shook his head. 'It's too risky.'

'We're pirates. Taking risks is what we do.'

'Not like this we don't. There's too much chance of getting caught by the navy.'

Agrius sneered at him. 'Scared of ending up like your brother, boy?'

Telemachus stared at the pirate chief. 'How do you know about Nereus?'

'Why, every port up and down the coast has heard the news. Even the local fishermen have been discussing you.' Agrius smirked. 'It seems you're the most famous pirate in all of Illyricum, rather than Bulla, or even me. Quite the achievement, some might say. And all thanks to your brother.'

'Nereus is none of your business.'

'He is if he's clouding your judgement. If you haven't got

the balls to attack the shipping here, perhaps you're in the wrong profession. Pirating ain't for those who shit themselves at the first mention of the Romans.'

Telemachus shook his head. 'If we continue to hunt in these waters, we'll be putting the lives of the men in danger.'

Agrius shrugged. 'It's a risk I'm prepared to take.'

'I've heard enough,' Bulla announced as he looked up. 'I agree with Agrius. We'll head north, and strike before Canis has a chance to reinforce Ravenna.'

He stared at Telemachus, daring him to defy his authority. Telemachus briefly considered protesting further, but thought better of it. He knew his captain well enough to know when a matter was decided. 'Aye, aye, Captain.'

Bulla's eyes returned to the map, his frown lines deepening. 'What about a meeting point? There's not many safe havens on this side of the sea.'

'I've thought of that,' said Agrius. 'There's a bay here, near an abandoned colony. Quiet, and far enough from the major ports. If we lose sight of each other, we'll both head there and wait for the other to arrive.'

'Is it safe?'

'As far as I know. One of my men used to work on the fishing boats around here. He tells me no ships have risked anchoring there for years. Too many shallows for a coasting vessel.'

'Let's hope your man is right.'

'Oh, he is, Captain. He'll pay with his life if he's wrong.' Agrius nodded at *Trident*'s captain and first mate in turn. 'Now, unless there's anything else? Then you'd best return to your ship. We leave at once.'

★ ★ ★

Pegasus and *Trident* set sail a short time later. They encountered no cargo ships that afternoon, and anchored for the night in a small cove before continuing north at first light. As the day wore on, the sky became grey and overcast and the wind increased, forcing the crew to trim the sail. By the middle of the afternoon, Castor announced that they would shortly be in sight of Ancona, and the men talked excitedly among themselves about the riches awaiting them on the Umbrian coast.

Telemachus stayed quiet, tormented by thoughts of his brother's captivity. The image of Nereus hanging from a cross filled him with a despair beyond anything he'd ever known, and he clung to the faint hope that if he found out where his brother was being held captive, he might still be able to free him before the date of his execution. It was the slenderest of chances, he knew, but he refused to give up. Nereus was the only family he had left, and he would not rest until he had done everything in his power to save him, even if it meant sacrificing his own life. But he would not risk the lives of his comrades as well.

While the other deckhands carried out their duties, Geras joined him forward of the mast. He nodded at the horizon. 'No sign of anything yet?'

'Nothing,' Telemachus said.

'That'll soon change. We're about to attack the busiest trade route this side of the Adriaticum. We'll be drowning in spoils before long.'

'Unless we stumble upon a patrol first.'

Geras glanced at his friend. 'Do you really think we're in danger?'

Telemachus pressed his lips together. 'The Romans know

we're operating here. It's only a matter of time before we run into them.'

'That's not the only thing we've got to worry about.'

'What do you mean?'

Geras inclined his head at the darkening clouds. 'Looks like we're in for a patch of rough weather.'

Telemachus glanced at the horizon. From experience, he knew that summer storms were a common danger in the Adriaticum: short-lived but violent squalls that struck with almost no warning. 'You think it will hit us soon?'

'Aye. Looks like a nasty one too. Heavy winds, rain. The only question is which direction the bastard will come from.'

'*Pegasus* is signalling, Captain!' the lookout shouted down.

Bulla strode over from the aft deck and squinted off to starboard at the other pirate vessel, a mile further out across the choppy sea. Telemachus gazed in the same direction and saw a strip of brightly coloured cloth hoisted atop the masthead, rippling out across the steely grey sky.

'Green,' Virbius reported. 'Agrius has sighted a sail, Captain.'

'I know what it means, damn you,' Bulla growled. 'Masthead! What can you see up there?'

'Nothing yet, Captain. Must be further out to sea . . . Wait. No, I can see her now. Hull down and nearly right ahead of us.'

Telemachus fixed his gaze on the horizon as *Trident* pitched up on the crest of the next wave. Across the rising swell, he glimpsed the faint impression of a sail.

'Merchantman?' asked Leitus.

'Most likely. There are no other pirate crews operating here.'

Geras grinned widely as he nudged Telemachus. 'What did I tell you? Looks like we'll be netting some prey today after all.'

Bulla turned away from the rail. 'Telemachus, call all hands. And make the signal to *Pegasus* to give chase.'

Telemachus took a deep breath and shouted across the deck. While the men made *Poseidon's Trident* ready for action, a pair of youthful hands fetched a bundle of red cloth from one of the side lockers and raced over to the rigging. They worked quickly, attaching the toggles on one end of the pennant to the mast halyard before they hauled on the coarse rope. The cloth rose up the mast and shook out with a crackle in the blustery wind. An identical pennant rose up *Pegasus*'s mast, acknowledging the signal, before dipping down again.

'Calkas!' Bulla called out. 'Change our course! Close to intercept!'

The steersman heaved on the oar shaft, while a roar from Telemachus sent the deckhands pouring up the ratlines to take a reef out of the sail. As the loosened canvas fluttered wildly in the wind, the men on deck strived to haul the sheets in, urged on by the young first mate. *Trident* lurched round, and Telemachus looked across and noted with professional satisfaction that *Pegasus*'s crew was taking longer to alter her course. A short time later, her bows were pointing straight at the merchantman as both vessels closed on their victim, cutting her off from both sea and coast.

As soon as the sail was clearly in view, Longarus yelled down again. 'Deck there! Chase has altered course, Captain!'

'She's seen us,' Bulla muttered.

Virbius snorted. 'Won't do her much good. Ain't nowhere for her to run around these parts. And we've got the wind gauge. She's as good as ours, as long as that weather holds.'

'Let's pray that it does.'

The captain glanced over at the rigging, eyes narrowed as he used all his wealth of experience to determine how long he could wait until taking in a reef. Telemachus shifted his attention back to the prey and saw that both pirate ships had gained ground rapidly on their victim. *Trident* held a slender lead over her consort, but as the lighter of the two ships, *Pegasus* was coming up fast. Ahead of them the cargo ship continued to flee downwind, but he could see that they would close on her long before she could reach the safety of Ancona. Then he spotted a band of dark grey cloud bounding towards them from the horizon.

'Squall's coming in, Captain.'

Bulla frowned. 'Bastard's heading right for us. We'd better take in a couple of reefs.'

'Aye, aye.'

A shout from Telemachus sent the deckhands scurrying aloft to draw in the sail to the first reefing point. As they raced back down to the deck, Telemachus glanced back out to sea and saw *Pegasus* and the chase swiftly disappear from view as the filthy veil closed around them. Then the wind freshened, and Bulla yelled a warning as the grey haze came racing down upon *Poseidon's Trident* with astonishing speed.

'Here it comes!' Castor roared.

A moment later, the squall struck. The wind howled through the rigging, rapping the halyards against the mast as the ship listed dangerously to port. Every pirate on the deck clung to the nearest handhold to stop himself falling overside before the vessel slowly righted herself. Then the rain came on. Big icy shimmering drops slanted across the deck, soaking the sailcloth and stabbing like needles against the pirates' exposed skin. Bulla shielded his face from the freezing torrent as he bellowed at the steersman to hold their course.

Then the squall closed in, and Telemachus felt a powerful urge to vomit as the ship pitched and shuddered sickeningly on the swell. It lurched again, and he promptly leaned over the rail and emptied his guts downwind. He held grimly on to the wooden surface, his head pounding, powerless to do anything except endure Neptune's fury and wait for the weather to pass.

As suddenly as it had struck, the squall was gone. The wind died down to a soft breeze and the rain ceased, and the first shaft of golden sunlight broke through the dense clouds overhead. Telemachus wiped salty spray out of his eyes, his damp hair clinging to his face as he glanced round. To the south he could see a curtain of dark grey pulling away from *Trident* as the squall receded towards the horizon. The deck was now eerily quiet except for the coughs and splutters of the men and the soft splash of water lapping against the hull. Then Leitus gave a shout.

'Look, Captain!'

Telemachus and Bulla followed his pointing finger, fixing their gaze on the horizon. *Pegasus* had vanished from sight, along with the large cargo vessel she had been chasing. Bulla stared closely at the sea for a moment longer, then pounded a fist against his thigh.

'Shit!' he muttered.

'What happened to them, Captain?' Telemachus wondered. 'Where are they?'

'We must have lost 'em in the squall. They'll have been blown off course, the same as us.'

'Can't we go after them?'

Bulla shook his head. 'There's no way of knowing which way they'll have gone. That squall could have scattered them for miles in any direction. Gods only know where they are now.'

'What's to be done, then?'

Bulla scanned the coastline as he reviewed his options. 'We've lost the chase. It could take us hours before we find *Pegasus*, and it's not long until dusk. We don't want to be caught out at sea at nightfall. Not with all the shoals in this area. We'll have to head to the meeting point. Agrius is bound to sail there as well, once he realises we've been separated.'

'Unless he goes after the prey first,' Leitus pointed out.

'Then we'll wait for him to arrive. That's all we can do.' The captain looked at Telemachus. 'Check the ship for damage. Then have the men turn us around and set a course for the meeting point.'

'Aye, Captain.'

As *Trident* got under way, Geras smiled weakly at Telemachus. 'Not the best start to our voyage.'

'No,' Telemachus replied glumly. He gazed back in the direction of the Italian coastline. The sun was already beginning to sink towards the horizon, and even if both ships arrived at the meeting point, there would be no time to set sail again before darkness closed in. The thought of anchoring for the night in hostile waters troubled him, but there was nothing else that could be done.

In the gathering dusk, *Poseidon's Trident* approached the entrance to the small bay Agrius had marked on the ship's map. The sea was calm and the setting sun bathed the land in a warm glow as the pirates rounded the headland and rowed slowly towards the shore. A pair of low cliffs rose either side of a curved strip of fine sand, half a mile wide. Casuarinas grew a short distance from the sea, and to one side stood the rubble of some long-abandoned village. Telemachus surveyed the ruins carefully but saw no evidence of recent habitation. Apart from the main entrance to the bay, the only other approach was through a narrow channel running between the nearest headland and a large tumble of rocks. A patch of shallows was just about visible around a sandspit.

'Seems we're the first ones here,' Castor said as he glanced round the deserted bay.

Telemachus nodded. 'Agrius must have gone after that ship we were chasing.'

'Either that, or his ship was damaged in the squall and he had to find refuge somewhere else. Still, his man picked a good hiding spot. There's little chance of the Romans finding us here.'

Telemachus looked back at the entrance to the bay. The low headlands either side would shelter the pirates from view of passing vessels, while any approaching ships would be forced to pick their way through the offshore sandbars, giving Trident's crew plenty of time to prepare in case of an attack.

'It looks quiet enough,' he said. 'Let's just hope we don't have to wait here for long.'

Castor dismissed his concerns with a wave of his hand. 'Agrius will make his way here as soon as he can. Even he's not mad enough to hunt along the coast of Italia by himself.'

'I'm not so sure.'

The quartermaster smiled. 'Not an admirer of our new partner, I assume?'

Telemachus was about to reply honestly when he remembered that he was first mate now and it would be wrong to openly question Bulla's judgement in front of the other men. He coughed. 'Agrius has his qualities. But his methods aren't going to win us any friends. It's bad enough that we're operating close to Ravenna, but butchering the crew of every ship we take is only going to make the Romans more determined to hunt us down.'

'That's one way of looking at it.'

'You don't agree?'

'Agrius might not be everyone's cup of Falernian, but he gets the job done. There's plenty to be said for that, given our recent difficulties.'

Telemachus shrugged. 'I just hope Bulla knows what he's getting into.'

'Don't worry about the captain, lad. I've known him for as long as anyone on this crew, and he's no fool. He'll turn us around before things get too hot.'

'I hope you're right,' Telemachus replied quietly.

Castor changed the subject and leaned in closer. 'What about the man who betrayed your brother? You any closer to finding out who it is?'

'Not yet.'

Telemachus had been keeping a close eye on the crew over the past several days, watching for any hint of suspicion or guilt. But there had been nothing to point to the traitor's identity, adding to his intense frustration. Neither was he any closer to discovering the whereabouts of his brother. Time was running out, and in less than a month, Nereus would be killed, condemned to suffer an agonising death at the hands of his Roman captors.

He pushed aside his troubled thoughts and looked ahead as they glided past the channel. Beside the mast, Bulla straightened up and shouted across the deck. 'Make for the shallows, Calkas! Telemachus, prepare to drop anchor!'

'Aye, Captain!'

At the first mate's command, Bassus and three other well-built men hurried to the anchor locker and fetched up the stout wooden anchor weighted with iron flukes and rope, hauling it over to the stern. Then Telemachus shouted for the crew to ship oars, and the sweep blades were hastily withdrawn through their slots. There was a splash as the anchor was dropped overside and the cable rasped out through the hawse, tethering *Trident* a short distance from the shore.

Once the ship had been secured and a watch had been set, the men were finally able to relax. They took their supper on the deck, eating cold rations since Bulla had forbidden the lighting of cooking fires, which might betray their presence to any passing vessels or travellers on the mainland. The night passed peacefully, and shortly before dawn, the crew stirred and set about their duties while they waited for Agrius to arrive. A dense bank of fog hung over the surface of the sea, hiding the entrance to the bay behind a pale grey mist. There was no sign of *Pegasus*, and some of the men began to openly grouse about the delay to their plans.

Telemachus made his way on deck after his morning inspection of the hold and found Geras by the taffrail, staring out beyond the stern.

'What's taking Agrius so long?' Geras muttered. 'He should be here by now.'

'Maybe he had to beach somewhere and make repairs,' Telemachus suggested.

Geras shook his head. 'We won't get much hunting done today anyway. Not if this bloody fog don't clear.'

They were interrupted by a shout from one of the hands. 'Sail approaching!'

Telemachus swivelled his head back round to the bay as Bulla and the senior hands stopped what they were doing and hurried over. As they crowded *Trident*'s stern, Telemachus strained his eyes and saw the faintest outline of a ship emerging from the mist a quarter of a mile away. Her dark pennant flickered above the mast in the gentle breath of air blowing across the bay.

'That's *Pegasus* all right,' Bulla said.

'About bloody time,' Virbius grumbled. 'Been sitting on our arses here for long enough. Let's hope they're bringing back some loot and all.'

'We'll find out soon.'

As Telemachus looked on, barely visible figures spread out across *Pegasus*'s yard and furled the mainsail. The oars slid out, and after a few moments to get the rhythm, the blades settled into a repetitive stroke, propelling the ship slowly forward. Several men were hauling up the anchor from below deck, ready to drop it over the stern, while the free hands lined the rail and waved greetings at the pirates on the other ship. The crew seemed to be in a relaxed mood, and there was no obvious sign of damage to *Pegasus*'s mast or rigging.

Telemachus scanned the vessel, but in the dawn fog he couldn't see Agrius, so he climbed a short distance up the ratlines for a better view. Among the figures on deck he noticed one man, burlier than the others, stealing an anxious glance at the aft cargo hatch. Telemachus stared in the same direction, and felt a sudden tremble run down his spine. He yelled down at Bulla. 'Captain, it's a trap!'

Bulla frowned as he looked up at the first mate. 'What the hell are you talking about?'

'There!' Telemachus pointed at the other ship. The plume of a Roman officer's helmet rose above the hatch coaming. Dozens more auxiliary helmets and sword points gleamed there. 'Those are Romans in the hold!'

Before Bulla could respond, a shout went up on *Pegasus*'s deck. Telemachus looked back across and heard the burly man yelling in Latin as he snatched out a sword from beneath his cloak. Across the deck the other figures also drew their weapons, and the next moment, a deep-throated roar echoed across the bay as a wave of heavily armed figures poured out of the cargo hold, dressed in white tunics and brandishing their auxiliary swords and shields. Bulla looked on in horror, mouth agape, as he realised what was happening.

'We're fucked.'

CHAPTER THIRTY-THREE

As soon as the words had left Bulla's mouth, the Roman officers on *Pegasus's* deck yelled a series of orders and the oarsmen picked up the speed as they rowed towards *Poseidon's Trident*. In the same breath, the marines swarmed across the deck, some already readying their grappling lines. For an instant no one on *Trident* moved as the crew stared dumbfounded at the warship sweeping towards them. Then Bulla shook himself out of his stupor and spun away from the rail.

'All hands! Form up! *Now!*'

There was almost no time to organise themselves, and the crew raced across the deck as they made desperate preparations to face the oncoming enemy. Telemachus scrambled down the rigging and snatched up a falcata and a small curved dagger from one of the side lockers, slipping the latter into his belt as he rushed over to join his comrades assembling at the foot of the mast. Scores of marines had emerged from the other ship's hold, spreading out across the length of the deck. Although the numbers were evenly matched, the Romans had the superior training and equipment and Telemachus knew they would be in for a hard fight.

Leitus stood to his right, shaking his head in disbelief. 'How did the bastards find us?'

'Agrius must have run into one of their patrols after we were separated.' Telemachus gritted his teeth. 'And you know how good Roman torturers are at getting information.'

'Either way, now they've got us trapped.'

The enemy had executed their plan perfectly, Telemachus realised bitterly. By making their approach on the captured vessel and concealing the marines below deck, they had been able to draw close to *Poseidon's Trident* without raising any suspicion among her crew. Only when they were nearly upon *Trident* had their ruse become apparent. By that point it was too late for the pirates to attempt to slip away to the open sea. He briefly wondered what had become of Agrius and his men, then shook off the grim thought as he concentrated his mind on the approaching Romans.

Some men came up from below clutching bundles of javelins from the ship's stores. Telemachus grabbed one, sighted it at the marines on the other deck and hurled it across the narrowing gap between the two vessels. At such close range it was almost impossible to miss, and one of the Romans let out a shrill cry as the shaft ran through his guts. Others followed Telemachus's example. The Romans responded with a barrage of missiles of their own, and the air was filled with the hiss of arrows and the whir and crack of slingshot as the two sides exchanged desperate volleys. Then *Pegasus* nudged up against *Poseidon's Trident* with a jarring blow that trembled through the ship, and those marines with grappling lines launched them across, hauling them tight before cleating them and seizing their weapons.

Before they could charge aboard, Bulla clambered up the

side rail and filled his lungs. 'Don't just fucking stand there! Kill 'em! Kill the bastards!'

The pirates let out a deafening roar as they followed their captain, throwing themselves across to the other ship.

Telemachus landed on *Pegasus*'s deck, determined to cut down the first Roman he saw. Snatching out his dagger with his left hand and raising his falcata, he plunged into the melee. A grizzled marine shouted at him, and Telemachus sprang forward at the man, stabbing out with his falcata. The marine met the attack with his shield, the curved blade glancing off the boss with a sharp metallic ring. Even so, the blow stunned the marine, and before he could recover, Telemachus thrust with his dagger and stabbed him just below the armpit. The marine swayed, then tumbled away with the dagger still buried in his flesh. Telemachus snatched up the man's shield, his heart pounding.

'Watch out!' someone yelled close by.

He whirled round to see a squat, stocky marine thrusting his sword at him. Months of fighting at sea had sharpened Telemachus's reflexes, and he reacted in an instant, jerking up his shield. The Roman's blade clattered against it with a solid thud, and the man snarled as he came forward, feinting for the throat then cutting downward. His sword ripped through a fold in Telemachus's tunic, narrowly missing the bunched muscles of his thigh.

Telemachus punched his shield forward an instant before the marine thrust out at him once more. The blow knocked the Roman back a couple of steps, bringing him up against the writhing mass of bodies behind him. Telemachus shot forward again, this time sweeping his falcata beneath the Roman's shield. The marine read the move, but as he jumped back, his heel caught on a body sprawled across the deck. He lost his balance and fell backwards, landing on the planking with a heavy thud. As he tried to scramble to his feet, Telemachus raised his falcata overhead and brought it crashing down on the Roman with such force that the blade cut through the man's helmet, cleaving his skull in an explosion of blood and bone.

The young first mate swiftly retreated behind his shield, catching his breath as he looked round. Most of the fighting was concentrated about the mast, the two sides tearing into one another in a shimmering flicker of hacks and stabs. Although the pirates were less well armed than the Romans, they were more than holding their own, and the deck was littered with the dead from both sides.

Above the cries of the wounded and the ring of clashing blades Telemachus heard someone calling out to him. He wiped the blood from his eyes and saw Castor thrusting out an arm towards the mouth of the bay.

'Look!' he cried. 'Over there!'

He glanced in the direction Castor had indicated. Through a thinner patch of fog he spied three Roman warships gliding in from the sea. Two biremes were leading the way, with a larger trireme lagging some distance behind. He recognised the trireme by its ornately decorated bow and the purple pennant flapping atop its mast. The flagship of the Ravenna fleet.

'Canis . . .' he muttered.

A current of despair welled up inside Telemachus as he realised that the three other warships must have been hiding in the fog while they waited for the first wave of marines to take *Poseidon's Trident* by surprise. Now they were rushing in to complete the trap. Boarding parties had already formed on the prows of both biremes, armour and sword points catching the light breaking through the streaky mist as they closed in on the pirate vessel. Most of *Trident*'s crew were fighting with their backs to the sea and had not yet spotted the approaching threat. Unless they retreated soon, he foresaw, they would be fatally overrun.

As Telemachus turned to warn the others, he saw that Bulla had been pressed back to the stern by a pair of marines and was cut off from the rest of the crew. Two other pirates lay squirming on the deck as the marines fell upon the captain. Bulla parried the first thrust, but the second struck below the rim of his shield, and he curled forward as the blade punched deep into his stomach.

'Captain!' Telemachus cried.

With a mad roar, he charged towards the stern. A marine moved to block his path, but Telemachus dropped his shoulder and slammed shield-first into the man, knocking him aside. One of the two marines standing over Bulla shouted at his comrade, and the other man spun round to face Telemachus as he bore down on them. Even as the Roman raised his sword, Telemachus cut down with a chopping motion, slicing the man's arm just above the wrist and almost severing his hand. Droplets of blood sprayed from the wound as he kicked the man aside and turned towards the second marine.

The tip of a blade flashed towards him as the Roman thrust out with his short sword. Telemachus desperately hefted up his shield and the blade glanced off the rim with a splintering crack, numbing his arm and shoulder muscles. He stabbed out with his falcata, trying to strike down at the marine over the top of his shield with the curved tip, but the Roman ducked low and in the same move hooked his shield around the edge of Telemachus's buckler, wrenching it from his grip. The marine grinned as he shaped to attack his defenceless foe.

From the corner of his eye, Telemachus caught a gleaming movement as an axe blade scythed through the air and crunched into the man's neck, parting his head from his shoulders in a clean blow. Warm blood splattered against him as the Roman folded at the legs and collapsed to the deck. He looked up to see Bassus standing behind the slumped figure, holding a bloodstained axe in a two-handed grip. Telemachus nodded his thanks and then dropped down beside his captain. Bulla was clutching a hand to his stomach, blood pulsing between his fingers as he groaned in pain.

'You there!' Telemachus shouted, grabbing hold of the nearest pirate. 'Get the captain back to the ship. Right now!'

The man hesitated for a moment, reeling in shock at the sight of his wounded chief. Then he bent down and helped Bulla to his feet, half carrying him towards *Poseidon's Trident*. On the deck of the other vessel, a trio of young hands saw the pair approaching and hastily lowered a gangplank between the two ships. Castor watched them for a beat, then turned back to Telemachus.

'What are we going to do?'

Telemachus risked a glance over his shoulder and with a sick knot in his stomach saw that the two biremes had drawn much closer to *Pegasus*. The fight was lost, he knew. As soon as the marines from the biremes joined the struggle, the pirates would be overwhelmed. There was no time to lose if the remaining men from *Poseidon's Trident* were to stand any chance of survival.

He called out across *Pegasus*'s deck. 'All hands! Fall back!'

At his command, the first men turned away from the melee and retreated towards the side rail. Those closer to the mast were pushed back as the Romans attacked with renewed vigour, encouraged by the imminent arrival of the other warships. The nearest of the two biremes had raced ahead and was only moments away from *Pegasus* now, her marines ready to sweep aboard and join the fight. Some of the pirates had become separated from their companions as the fight dissolved into pockets of brutal combat. A cluster of *Trident*'s men had been pressed back into the bows, while others were being surrounded about the mast. Twisted, tangled bodies were strewn across the blood-splattered planking.

'Back!' Telemachus thundered at the men. 'Back, now!'

As the pirates leaped back over the side rail, one of the Romans shouted at his comrades, pointing furiously towards *Poseidon's Trident*. A section of marines, led by an officer with a red-crested helmet, broke off from the fighting and rushed across the deck to cut off the pirates' retreat. Telemachus turned away and launched himself across the short gap between the two vessels, landing awkwardly on *Trident*'s deck. Behind him, the marines quickly spread out across the length of *Pegasus*'s side rail, hurling their remaining javelins at the pirates.

'Get down!' Telemachus shouted. '*Down!*'

At a roar from their centurion, the marines released their missiles at almost point-blank range, striking down several of *Trident*'s men. A javelin struck the pirate next to Telemachus, bursting through his eyeball. His head snapped back and the axe he had been wielding slipped from his grip as he fell senseless to the deck. Two other pirates were too slow to react, and their pained cries split the air as dark shafts skewered their torsos. There was another ragged volley and then the Roman centurion bellowed at his men and the marines charged across the gangplank before it could be raised.

'On me!' Telemachus called out to his men as he raised his sword. There was a brief hesitation before the pirates around him fell upon the marines jumping down from the gangplank. Gritting his teeth, Telemachus stepped over the body of a slain pirate and lunged at the closest marine, slashing low at the man's legs. The Roman roared as the falcata smashed into his kneecap. Telemachus swept aside the man's desperate parry and punched out with his shield, striking the Roman on the jaw and sending him tumbling over the rail into the water below.

He drew his shield arm back and glanced around the gore-drenched deck. To his right, Geras was bellowing encouragement at the others, urging them to give the enemy no quarter. The handful of marines who had swept aboard *Trident* were surrounded, and most of them were swiftly killed as the pirates swarmed over them, cutting them down in individual skirmishes. Amid the slain corpses Telemachus spied the blood-soaked body of the Roman centurion. Only the marines' optio and a few of his men remained standing, their shields raised as they fought desperately for their lives on the mist-wreathed ship. The optio bellowed at his men, urging them to resist the fury of the pirates' attack. Beyond them Telemachus could see more marines on *Pegasus*'s deck peeling away from the main fight as they rushed over to help their stricken comrades. As he looked on, the nearest bireme drew level with the other side of *Pegasus*. Grappling lines were hurled and the first marines shouted their battle cries as they leaped down to her deck, overwhelming Leitus and the others fighting around the mast.

Telemachus turned and cupped his hands. 'Cut the cables!' he roared. 'Cut 'em!'

Castor looked aghast. 'But the others?'

'There's nothing we can do for them. Cut the lines, now!'

Several pirates hurried over to the grappling lines and began hacking away at them with their axes and swords. With a dull twang the last of the cables parted, and Telemachus shouted over at the steersman. 'Get us moving, Calkas! Hurry!'

The pirates closest to the oars heaved them up and fended off from the side of *Pegasus*. As they edged away, the gentle swell lifted *Poseidon's Trident* and swung her bows away from the other ship.

'That's it, lads!' Telemachus shouted. 'Now get us out of here!'

The crew ran out the sweep oars as *Trident* got under way, heading for the entrance to the bay. A cluster of marines on *Pegasus* hurled javelins, discarded weapons and anything else to hand at the fleeing pirate ship. There was no time to aim and most of the missiles fell harmlessly into the widening gap between the two vessels. *Trident's* motion steadied as she pulled ahead, and the last marines, realising that they had been fatally cut off from their comrades on *Pegasus*, threw down their weapons as they tried to surrender. One of the pirates moved forward to cut down the optio, but Telemachus stopped him with a shout. 'No! I want them alive!'

The pirate reluctantly lowered his axe. Several of the others stared with looks of murderous intent at the three Romans.

'Take them down to the hold,' Telemachus snapped. 'We'll deal with them later.'

Geras barked an order, and the nearest pirates grabbed hold

of the optio and his comrades and shoved them towards the cargo hatch. As they headed below deck, Telemachus glanced back at *Pegasus* and saw Leitus and the last of the boarders disappearing beneath a relentless flurry of blows as the marines from the nearest bireme swarmed over them. A few of the pirates had been forced back against the bows, and several of them leaped overboard, preferring to take their chances in the water rather than be captured by the enemy. They were quickly cut down as the marines on the furthest bireme crowded the stern and flung missiles down at them. A moment later the ship was lost as a thicker skein of fog rolled in between the ships.

'Bastards killed Leitus,' Geras growled softly. 'He didn't stand a fucking chance . . .'

The loss of so many men was a bitter blow. Telemachus gripped the rail tightly and swore to the gods that he would do everything he could to avenge his fallen comrades. Rome would pay, one way or another. If the pirates made good their escape.

Already the marines aboard *Pegasus* were shouting at the trierarchs on the two biremes, pointing furiously at *Poseidon's Trident* as the latter pulled clear. At once the grappling lines on the nearest bireme were cast off and the warship lurched heavily away from *Pegasus*, slewing round the stern of the captured pirate ship as she gave chase to *Trident*. The second bireme, further away from *Pegasus*, also changed her course, while further out across the bay, the flagship closed at an angle, blocking the pirates' escape.

'We're trapped,' Castor spat. 'We've bloody had it now.'

Telemachus cursed through gritted teeth. Then a thought struck him. He swept his eyes round to the opposite headland.

Through the thinning mist he glimpsed the narrow channel running between the sandspit and the rocks beyond. He pointed it out to the steersman.

'There!' he shouted. 'Calkas, steer for the shallows!'

CHAPTER THIRTY-FOUR

At Telemachus's bellowed order, the wiry steersman braced his legs and leaned into the tiller, lining up *Trident*'s bows with the patch of shoal water extending between the headland and the rocks further out to sea. The change in course prompted several startled looks from the crew, and a number of the men glanced anxiously at one another before Virbius stepped forward, his face screwed up in disbelief. 'What do you think you're doing?'

'Getting us out of here,' Telemachus replied firmly. 'We'll escape across the shallows and lose the Romans in the fog.'

'But we'll never make it. We'll run aground, for fuck's sake.'

'*Trident* draws less water than those warships. Her draught should be shallow enough for us to make it through.'

'And if it ain't, we'll be bloody stranded. The Romans will pick us off like rats in a barrel.'

'Maybe. But if we don't try it, we're done for. At least this way we've got a chance.'

'You're sending us to our fucking deaths.'

'There's no time for this,' Telemachus growled. 'I'm in charge of this ship while the captain is down. I've given the

345

order. Now get back to your duty, or I'll throw you in chains.'

Virbius went to protest, but then he saw the look on Telemachus's face and pressed his thin lips shut. Telemachus turned away from him and beckoned to Castor. 'Get a man forward. Someone with a keen eye. We'll need a lad to watch for any rocks.'

Castor hurried off, yelling at the crew. They rushed to their stations while Telemachus took up his position aft of the mast. Geras stood beside him, his face grave with anxiety as they steered away from the sandspit and rowed towards the shallows. Astern of them, the flagship had changed her course as she closed on *Poseidon's Trident*. The two biremes were some distance behind the trireme, their progress slowed by having to manoeuvre around *Pegasus*. All three warships were rowing hard, and Telemachus calculated that *Trident* would reach the shallows just ahead of the trireme.

Geras stared doubtfully ahead. 'You really think this will work?'

Telemachus pursed his lips. 'There's a chance that the water is deep enough, but I can't be sure until we're passing over it. And we'd better pray that it is too shallow for our pursuers.'

'And if it ain't?'

'Then Virbius is right. We're dead meat.'

'Well, one thing's for sure. I'll not let those Roman bastards take me alive. I don't know about you, but I don't plan on leaving this life nailed to a cross.'

'Me neither.' Telemachus smiled grimly. 'Don't worry. If it comes to that, we'll take as many of them as possible with us as we go down fighting.'

But as they approached the channel, he felt a tingle of

uncertainty at his plan. A vivid mental picture flashed in front of him, of *Poseidon's Trident* striking a submerged rock. As Virbius had pointed out, a grounded vessel would be easy prey for the Roman flagship. The trireme would be free to move to within a safe distance and smash the pirates' small ship apart with the artillery mounted on her foredeck. There would be no escape for *Trident* and her crew then. Those who survived the wreckage would be picked off in the shallows by the enemy, or worse, captured and crucified.

A dull crack abruptly pierced the air. Telemachus looked aft as a rock shot up from the catapult on the flagship's foredeck. It soared through the air and seemed to hang suspended for a dreadful moment before it plunged into the foaming white wake ten or twelve feet behind *Trident*'s stern.

'By the gods, that was close,' Geras muttered.

'A lucky shot,' Telemachus growled. 'They won't have our range yet. She's too far away from us.'

'Aye, but for how long?'

The trireme was drawing steadily closer, Telemachus realised. At her current speed she would easily catch up with the pirates before they could escape across the channel. He called out to Castor, 'Have the men increase our speed!'

The quartermaster shook his head. 'They're going as fast as they can, but this ship ain't no galley. She ain't built for rowing.'

Telemachus clenched his jaw tightly in frustration and looked away. He knew Castor was right. *Trident* could outsail most other vessels, but without even the slightest puff of wind, she was forced to rely on her twelve pairs of sweep oars to propel her forward, whereas the trireme could draw on the strength of far more oarsmen. The warship was gaining fast, blades cutting through the water, and with a hollowing sensation in his guts he realised that *Trident* would soon be within missile range. The lighter biremes were also steadily closing in and would reach the channel a short time after the flagship. He tried desperately to think of some way to increase his ship's speed, but there was nothing he could do now except pray to the gods for a sudden gust of wind. Only then would *Trident* have any hope of outrunning her enemy.

He swept his gaze round to the shallows again. From his perspective the gap between the rocks and the sandspit looked frighteningly narrow, and he felt sure the ship would run aground at any moment. Over the side he could see the dark shapes of rocks not far beneath the surface. Further forward, one of the deckhands was leaning over the bows, calling out to the steersman whenever he sighted shallow water or any rocks that might imperil the ship. There was now only a few hundred feet to go until they reached the freedom of the open sea beyond the headland, and Telemachus willed the men at the sweeps to row faster.

There was another crack as a dark shaft leaped from one of the trireme's bolt-throwers, followed by a shrill scream as the iron point burst through the chest of a pirate in front of him. Another bolt thudded into the rail, throwing up an explosion of splinters. One man staggered backwards, groaning, a jagged piece of wood protruding from the side of his face. When Telemachus looked back again, he saw that the flagship had almost caught up with them.

'We'll never make it!' Virbius shouted. 'Bastards are going to sink us!'

Suddenly a faint trembling carried across the water. Geras cried out as he pointed aft. 'Look! Look there!'

Telemachus glanced back and saw the Roman trireme shuddering as she ran aground. Her oars snagged and clattered against the rocks, and then the mast pitched forward with a shattering crack. A chorus of panicked screams and cries went up as the tangle of timber, rigging and sailcloth came crashing down on the deck, smothering the artillery and knocking marines off their feet. The damaged warship's bows lifted briefly before she stopped moving, prompting delirious cheers from the men on *Trident*.

'Bastards!' Geras roared, punching a fist in the air. 'That showed you! Won't be catching up with us now!'

Telemachus saw several figures darting across the trireme's deck to hack away at the broken mast and rigging. The two biremes abruptly veered away from the grounded flagship to avoid a collision and set off on a new course towards the main entrance to the bay. With their trierarchs unwilling to risk the treacherous passage through the shallows, they would have to skirt around the rocks and take the longer route out to sea before resuming the chase. Telemachus watched them for a moment longer, and then looked ahead as *Trident* ploughed on through the gap, drawing steadily ahead of the warships.

Geras exhaled with relief. 'Thank the gods.'

'It's not over yet,' Telemachus warned. 'We've still got to lose those biremes. Once they're out of the bay, they'll be able to keep up the chase and close on us.'

'Better hope this fog holds, then.'

The men at the oars summoned one final effort and *Trident* surged forward, then suddenly they had cleared the shallows and there was deeper water around them. Telemachus lifted his head, feeling a soft breeze coming off the land. Strong enough to raise the sail. He gave the order to Geras, and the exhausted deckhands climbed aloft and unfurled the mainsail. With the following wind, *Poseidon's Trident* quickly picked up speed and soon she was pulling away from the coastline. The men who had been straining on the oars were finally able to rest, and they slumped back on the deck, their faces and arms glistening with sweat.

As *Trident* clawed her way further out to the open sea, a shout went up from the stern. Telemachus snapped his attention back to the entrance to the bay, already far behind them. Amid the wisp-like tendrils of mist the masts and spars of the biremes were barely visible as the warships rounded the point. For a moment he thought Fortuna might play one last cruel trick on him and the fog would clear just in time for the Romans to chase them down. Then another dense bank of mist swept in from the headland, and the warships were swiftly lost from sight. The tension among *Trident*'s crew lifted at last, replaced by a nervous relief at their escape.

Once Telemachus was certain that they had lost the biremes, he gave the order for Castor to set a course for Petrapylae. The wounded were carried down into the hold, while Bulla was taken to his private cabin. The captured optio and marines were shackled in chains, and Telemachus placed two men on guard duty to watch over them.

As the morning wore on, the mist thinned out and the sun struggled to break through. Telemachus continually searched the horizon for any sign of the Roman warships, but the sea remained mercifully clear, and for once he was grateful that no sails were sighted by the lookout. The men were in a sombre mood, relief at their escape mixed with despair at the heavy losses they had suffered, and as *Trident* continued north, he reflected on the scale of the pirates' defeat.

One ship had been captured, and another had lost half its men. Canis's trap had paid off handsomely. Dozens of *Trident*'s crew had been killed, with many more injured. And her captain had been badly wounded. Worse still, Nereus's fate was all but sealed. After such a crushing defeat, the crew would have no choice but to spend the next few months ashore in hiding, hoping that Canis would eventually grow tired of chasing the pirates and seek out a new posting. Perhaps then they would be free to return to the sea.

He quickly dismissed the thought. Canis was more ruthless than any man he'd known. He would never accept anything less than the total annihilation of the pirates. The capture of *Pegasus* and the heavy casualties he had inflicted upon *Poseidon's Trident* would not sway him from his goal. Indeed, his victory might embolden him to launch a new wave of attacks, pressing home his advantage over his demoralised enemy. Perhaps his men were already questioning any survivors from the two pirate ships, demanding to know the whereabouts of their hideout.

As they sailed through the afternoon, Telemachus's mood darkened. He knew that unless they defeated Canis and his fleet, the men of *Poseidon's Trident* could never rest.

CHAPTER THIRTY-FIVE

'How is the captain?' Telemachus asked. He had been pacing up and down the courtyard outside the citadel's watchtower, waiting for Proculus to finish his examination of Bulla's wound. The round-faced recruit stood outside the door and wiped his hands with a soiled cloth as he considered his reply. Although the new ship's carpenter was a reluctant pirate, he had proved himself useful in dealing with the wounded. After a long pause, he shook his head.

'It ain't good, sir. The wound's corrupted. Awful smell coming off him, like. I'm no expert, but once the blood gets poisoned, they've had it. That much I know. I'm sorry, sir, but even Asclepius can't save him now.'

'I understand,' Telemachus replied softly. It was no less than he had expected, after watching Proculus inspect and dress the captain's wound the previous day. The Roman blade had punched through a weak point in Bulla's linen cuirass and torn deep into his stomach, piercing his vitals. Regular changing of the dressing had failed to stem the bleeding, and a sickly yellow pus had begun seeping out of the gash.

Five days had passed since the ambush. The survivors aboard *Poseidon's Trident* had returned to Petrapylae, reaching the anchorage at dawn on the third morning. Once the ship's bows had been grounded on the shingle, the wounded had been unloaded. Those who were able to walk made the short trip along the causeway leading to the citadel gates, while the rest were placed on makeshift stretchers and carried down the gangway. As they were brought through the gatehouse, their comrades who had been left behind remained anxiously at their stations overlooking the bay, watching for any sign of an approaching enemy fleet.

The mood of relief among the pirates' families and friends at the ship's return had soon turned to despair as they frantically searched among the wounded for their loved ones. The wails of grieving wives, lovers and children lasted throughout the day, while the rest of *Trident*'s crew drowned their sorrows in drink and swore they would have their revenge on the Romans. The prisoners had been taken away to be sold on to the slave traders, with the Roman optio placed in one of the cells in the citadel while the interrogators went to work on him.

'How long has the captain got?' Telemachus asked.

Proculus shrugged. 'Another day or two, I'd say. Could be more. Depends on how long he can fight the fever, sir.'

Telemachus nodded slowly. 'What about the other men?'

The recruit wrung his hands. 'I'm doing my best, but there's a lot of lads who are in a bad way. I can stitch a wound up nice and proper, but I ain't got no experience of setting bones and the like. Some of them are beyond my help, sir.'

Telemachus nodded again. 'Patch up those you think you can save. That's all I ask of you, Proculus.'

'And the others, sir?'

'Make them as comfortable as possible. Do whatever you can to ease their suffering. Understood?'

'Aye, sir. I'll do that.'

Proculus strode off across the courtyard, heading towards the cluster of buildings near the gatehouse where the rest of the wounded were billeted. Telemachus turned away and ducked through the iron-studded door built into the side of the watchtower, climbing the stairs to the rooms on the upper floor.

A guard was stationed outside the captain's quarters at the far end of the gloomy corridor. At the sight of the approaching first mate he stepped aside, and Telemachus lifted the latch with a grating rasp. A thick, cloying odour of vomit and corruption hung in the air, violating his nostrils as he entered the room. Bulla's tunic and sword hung from a pair of hooks fixed to one wall, next to a large table holding a pitcher of water and a silver goblet. The captain lay on a couch to one side of the room, sweat glossing his forehead and matting his dark hair. A bloodstained bandage was wrapped around his stomach, covering the wound. His heavy-lidded eyes slowly focused on Telemachus as the latter squatted beside him.

'Captain,' Telemachus said softly.

'Not for much longer, I fear.' Bulla smiled half-heartedly, then winced with pain. His skin was waxy and pale, and Telemachus was shocked to see how rapidly his condition had deteriorated since he had last visited him the previous afternoon. He cleared his throat.

'Can I get you anything, Captain?'

'Water.'

Nodding slowly, Telemachus moved over to the table and poured the captain a goblet. As he set down the pitcher, he spotted a small clay vial with a wax stopper in it, next to a bundle of scrolls and maps. He regarded the vial for a moment before he took the cup and kneeled down beside Bulla, pressing the rim to his cracked lips. Bulla leaned forward, groaning as he gulped down the water. He took a few more sips before he coughed and spluttered and signalled for Telemachus to take the cup away.

'Thanks,' he said in a hoarse, rasping voice. 'Needed that. At least I won't be dying of thirst.'

Telemachus opened his mouth to respond, but Bulla raised a weak hand, cutting him off.

'It's all right, lad. I've gutted enough men in my time to know how this ends. This is it for me. I'm not long for this world.'

Pity welled up inside Telemachus and he felt his throat constrict. 'I'm sorry, Captain.'

'Sorry? You have nothing to be sorry for. You're not the one who led the men into a trap.'

'You weren't to know. The Romans tricked us nicely.'

'Perhaps. But if I had listened to you instead of going along with that fool Agrius, we wouldn't have been anywhere near Ravenna to begin with . . . Oh fuck, that hurts.'

Bulla clamped his eyes shut, teeth clenched in a grimace as a fresh wave of pain knifed through him. His whole body tensed in agony, before his breathing settled into a shallow, fitful rhythm. He smiled weakly at the young first mate.

'You're a good leader, Telemachus. Better than I ever was. Don't forget that.'

'I learned from the best.' Telemachus forced himself to smile. 'You should rest now, Captain. Save your strength.'

'Bollocks to that. I'll have plenty of time to rest later. Right now, I need you to do something for me.'

'Yes, Captain?'

'Summon the other mates. Bring them here. There is something I must tell them.'

Later that afternoon, the ship's mates gathered around their captain in his quarters. Bulla sat upright on his luxurious couch, a pale hand pressed to his blood-soaked dressing. Although the windows at the back of the room had been opened, the air was filled with the foul stench from the infected wound. Sweat trickled down the pirate chief's brow as he addressed his men.

'You all know why I have asked you here,' he began. The rasp in his voice was more noticeable now, and Telemachus could see the strain on the captain's face as he spoke. 'I shall be blunt. I am done for, boys. My days as captain of this crew are over.'

The mates heard his words in silence. Then Bassus cleared his throat. 'Let us send for a surgeon, Captain. Me and some of the lads can sail to Ortopla and find one there. We'll kidnap the bastard if we have to.'

'It's too late for that . . . too late for me. You must look to the future.'

Castor knitted his brows together. 'What do you mean, sir?'

'Before I die, a new man must be chosen to take over from me.'

The mates exchanged uncomfortable glances. No one said anything for several moments as they digested Bulla's announcement. Then Virbius spoke up.

'Do you have someone in mind?'

Bulla nodded slowly. 'That is why I have called you here.

So you can bear witness to me formally handing over command to your new leader.'

'Who is it?'

'Him.' All eyes turned towards the man Bulla had pointed to. 'Telemachus. From this moment on, he shall be the captain of *Poseidon's Trident*.'

'Me?' Telemachus was stunned. 'But Captain—'

'I am not your captain any more. That is your responsibility now.'

Around him the other mates reacted with a mix of surprise and envy. Telemachus was aware of several of his comrades staring at him as if they were sizing him up for the first time. Virbius shook his head slowly, then returned his gaze to Bulla.

'Is this really wise, sir?'

'You disagree?'

'With all due respect, the lad ain't experienced enough. He's only been with us for a few months. Why not give it to one of the older hands? Someone who knows what the job is all about.'

Bulla managed a smile. 'Someone like yourself, you mean.'

Virbius shrugged. 'My only concern is what's best for the crew.'

'I don't doubt that. But Telemachus has proved himself worthy of command. He has captured numerous ships, evaded the Romans more than once and proved himself to be a skilled seaman. More than that, he has a cool head. I think we can all agree on that.'

'Captain's right,' Bassus cut in. 'If it weren't for Telemachus, we'd never have escaped from that bay. The Romans would have cut every last one of us to pieces.'

'He's impressed us all, sure enough,' Virbius responded

coolly. 'But is this really the time to take such a risk? The Romans have just given us a good kicking. Maybe we'd be better off with a wiser pair of hands on the tiller.'

'No,' Bulla groaned, the veins on his neck bunched as another wave of pain racked his body. He slumped back, exhausted from the effort of sitting upright. His breathing grew more erratic, and it was only with great difficulty that he was able to continue. 'My decision is final. Telemachus shall assume command of this crew. I expect every man here to serve him loyally . . . as you once all served me. That is, as long as you accept, my young friend?'

Telemachus was momentarily lost for words. He nodded slowly. 'Aye, Captain. I accept.'

'Good.' Bulla closed his eyes. A kind of calm settled over him and his breathing reduced to a faint rasp. 'Then perhaps you might stay behind. I would like a word with you in private. The rest of you can go.'

The other mates filed out of the room in stunned silence. Bulla watched them depart, then drew his gaze back to Telemachus. His dim greying eyes struggled to focus on the new pirate captain.

'You are surprised?' he asked.

'Surprised, sir,' Telemachus said, 'and honoured.'

'You will make a fine captain, Telemachus. I can rest peacefully. The crew will be in safe hands. Now, there is one last thing I must ask of you.'

'Yes, sir?'

Bulla gestured towards the table. 'The vial. I had one of my guards acquire it from a merchant in the village, in case the pain became too great. A few drops should do the trick. Then you can bury me at sea, where I belong.'

Telemachus stared at him, swallowing hard. 'If that's what you really want, Captain.'

'My time is up. No use in delaying my journey across the Styx. But promise me something.'

'Sir?'

Bulla summoned one final act of strength and reached out, gripping Telemachus by the forearm. His skin was cool and his hand was shaking as he stared levelly at the younger man.

'When the time is right, you make Canis pay for what he's done to us. Him and all those other Roman bastards. And save that brother of yours.'

'I will, sir,' Telemachus replied. 'By the gods, I swear it. I'll teach the Romans a lesson they won't ever forget.'

A short while later, Telemachus made his way across the courtyard towards the dank cell adjacent to the stables. He had left the vial of poison with Bulla and instructed the guard outside his quarters not to disturb the captain, respecting the latter's dying wish to spend his last moments alone.

As he crossed the cobbled square, he felt a swirl of conflicting emotions inside his chest. Bulla had been more than a captain to him. Far more. He had recognised the potential of the young recruit early on and had taken a keen interest in him, becoming something of a father figure to him over the past few months. Even so, the news of his sudden promotion had come as a shock to Telemachus. There would be time later to properly grieve for Bulla, he decided. He was keenly aware that some of the older pirates might disregard or oppose the captain's decision, men such as Virbius, and he would not be able to put off a confrontation with any troublemakers for very long. But first he must focus his mind on his responsibilities to the crew. Canis's ambush had severely damaged their morale, and he knew what had to be done.

A pair of sentries armed with spears stood in front of the door of the crumbling cell. At the sight of Telemachus they straightened their backs and stepped aside. One of them lifted the latch and the door grated on its hinges as it swung inwards. Telemachus stepped into a cramped space that had once served as the stable master's quarters.

The Roman prisoner, a scrawny veteran optio named Calidus, lay on a bed of straw to one side of the room, his ankle and neck chained to a pair of iron rings fixed to the far wall. At the sound of the door opening, he slowly lifted his head, squinting in the gloom. He cut a miserable sight. His tunic was streaked with filth, his hair matted with dried blood and his arms were purpled with bruises. At first he had struck an air of defiance with his captors. Even when Telemachus had threatened to cut his thumbs off, the man had refused to cooperate. But then the interrogator had been put to work. Sciron did not need long. Two days of beatings and torture had been enough to break Calidus's will. The man in front of Telemachus was now a wretched imitation of a Roman officer. He flinched as Telemachus took another step towards him.

'Sciron tells me you're ready to talk.'

Calidus stared at the pirate determinedly. 'First I want assurances.'

Telemachus smiled. 'You're in no position to negotiate, Roman.'

'I'm no fool, either.' The prisoner winced, chains clinking as he shifted. 'Once I've told you what I know, what's to stop you from killing me? I'm no use as a hostage. Canis would never negotiate for my release.'

That much was true, Telemachus thought. 'Tell me what I want to know, and you will be spared. You have my word.'

'You'll let me go free?'

Telemachus almost smiled, surprised at the man's naivety. But a broken man would believe anything if it gave him hope of survival. He shook his head. 'That I cannot allow. You've seen our base. If I let you return to your people, you'd give us up. But you will be allowed to live, if you talk.' He waved a hand at the door. 'Otherwise I'll send for Sciron again. Perhaps you'll be more agreeable once he's gouged your eyes out.' He half turned to leave, and the Roman stared at him in panic.

'No! Wait. Your brother! I know where he is!'

Telemachus whipped round, pulsing with anger as he glared at the prisoner. 'You know about Nereus?'

'Of course I do. Everyone in the fleet has heard the news about him being held captive. It's no big secret.'

'Where is he?'

'Ravenna,' Calidus said quickly. 'He's being held at the naval base there.'

Telemachus felt his chest hitch up. 'Are you sure?'

The prisoner nodded. 'I've seen him being flogged in the parade ground a few times. He's there all right. Him and all the pirates we've taken prisoner. Canis is interrogating them personally. He wants to get every scrap of information out of them while the rest of the fleet is laid up for repairs.'

Telemachus cocked his head to one side, looking carefully at the prisoner. 'Canis is repairing his warships?'

'All the ones that ain't seaworthy, aye. Which is most of them. Some of those vessels at Ravenna haven't been out of the harbour for years. The prefect has got the shipyards working day and night to get them up to scratch, scraping off the barnacles and repairing rotten timbers.'

'Why doesn't he send for reinforcements from Misenum?'

'He can't. Word is, the Misenum fleet is nearly as run-down as ours and they've got enough problems to deal with, what with having to guard the Eastern Mediterranean. So it's up to Canis to get the Ravenna fleet up to scratch, and he's not mucking about. He wants every ship in the fleet ready to put to sea before the sailing season is over.'

'What for? Why the rush?'

'He's desperate to hunt you lot down. Especially with all them local worthies protesting to Ravenna. The merchants' guilds and shipowners have been stirring things up, demanding that the prefect does something about the damage to their trade. Canis has even had to send up one of the biremes from the convoy service to Senia, to ease the tensions with the town council.'

'I see. And what is Canis planning to do once he's built up his fleet?'

Calidus shrugged. 'He's going to sweep this side of the Adriaticum and burn every pirate nest to the ground. None of you will be left alive, or so he reckons. It's all anyone in Ravenna is talking about.'

'How long until the repairs are completed?'

'Last I heard, they'll be done before the end of the month.'

Telemachus fell quiet for a moment. An icy feeling travelled down from the nape of his neck. Once Canis had the full power of the Ravenna fleet at his disposal, the navy would have a decisive advantage. The prefect would be free to maintain his convoy service whilst simultaneously launching raids up and down the Illyrian coast, destroying one pirate hideout after another. It would only be a matter of time before they discovered the base at Petrapylae.

He glared at Calidus. 'Who told the Romans where to find my brother?'

Calidus shook his head weakly. 'I don't know anything about that.'

A hot rage clenched around Telemachus's heart. He thrust out an arm and grabbed hold of the prisoner's tunic. 'You're lying, Calidus. Answer me honestly. Before I call for Sciron again.'

'It's the truth, I swear it!' the optio said pleadingly, his lips quivering. 'Look, all I know is that someone handed in a scroll at Ravenna addressed to the prefect.'

'Who?'

'Some merchant captain. He showed up at the gate about a month ago demanding to see Canis. He was carrying a scroll he'd been told to hand in to the top brass at Ravenna. Said Canis would find it interesting.'

'Who gave him the scroll?'

Calidus shrugged. 'I don't know. Canis asked him the same question. He just said that his ship had been attacked by pirates some days earlier. One of them took him to one side and said to see to it that the scroll was delivered to Ravenna. That's why the pirates spared his life, or so he claimed. That's all I know, I swear by all the gods.'

Telemachus released his grip on the soiled tunic, and the prisoner collapsed to the straw bed on the floor. Calidus was telling the truth, he decided. He could learn nothing more from him. He stiffened his back and inclined his head at the dishevelled figure at his feet.

'You've been useful, Calidus. Very useful indeed. As a reward, I'll make sure your death is a quick one.'

Calidus lifted his eyes in terror. 'But . . . you can't. We had a deal!'

'Do you really trust the word of a pirate? You fool. There's no reason to spare you. As you pointed out yourself, you carry no value as a hostage. You've outlasted your usefulness.'

'Please!' the Roman begged. 'You can't do this. You can't kill me!'

'Why not?'

A thought flashed behind the prisoner's eyes. 'There's more information I can give you. The layout of the base, the cell where your brother is being held . . . I can help!'

'Is that so?' Telemachus paused as he smiled. 'Then perhaps you still have a chance to save yourself, Roman. I'll send for my interrogators shortly. But a word of warning. If you fail to tell my men everything you know, or if they suspect you're misleading us, I'll have you fed to the wolves in the nearest forest.'

He turned and headed out of the cell, leaving the prisoner whimpering pathetically behind him. His younger self might have spared Calidus, and perhaps found some use for him around the citadel. But he was in no mood to be merciful. Not after what the Romans had done to his comrades and his brother. He had already decided on Calidus's fate. As soon as the optio had given up every last scrap of information, he would have the man put to death.

As his eyes adjusted to the light, he noticed Geras approaching him from the direction of the watchtower.

'Bulla's dead.'

Telemachus stared at him and felt his throat constrict.

'One of the guards found him,' Geras added. 'Seems the old boy ended it before it got too painful. Can't say I blame him. Bloody horrible way to go, though. Looks like you're in charge now . . . Captain.'

'Yes,' Telemachus replied. It felt strange to have Geras address him by his new title. 'I'll need you to pick four good men for funeral duty. Have Bulla wrapped in linen and then take him out in one of the fishing boats tomorrow morning. We'll bury him at sea, in accordance with his wishes.'

'What about our friend in there?' Geras asked, tipping his head at the cell.

Telemachus explained what he had learned from the Roman prisoner. When he had finished, Geras pulled at his chin, his face scrunched up in thought. 'Reckon he's telling the truth? About them warships being repaired?'

'We'll find out soon enough.'

'What does that mean?'

Telemachus sidestepped the question. 'First I want you to prepare the two smaller ships, *Proteus* and *Galatea*. They are to be provisioned and ready to set sail first thing tomorrow. Skeleton crews. I want two suitable experienced mates as captains, but you are to stay here. Is that clear?'

Geras lifted his eyebrows in surprise. 'No offence, but is this really the best time to go hunting?'

'Those ships aren't going out to look for prey,' Telemachus explained. 'I want them to sail up and down the coast, from hideout to hideout, spreading the word among the Illyrian pirate crews. We'll summon every gang and ship this side of the Adriaticum to a meeting. Here at Petrapylae. Ten days from now.'

Geras's eyebrows arched higher. 'What do you want to invite them lot here for?'

'To make them an offer.' Telemachus paused, a trace of mischief on his face. 'I'm going to propose that we attack Ravenna.'

Geras stared at his friend, as if trying to decide whether he was serious. He caught the hard gleam in Telemachus's eyes and puffed out his cheeks. 'You've got a pair of balls on you, I'll give you that. But you'll have a bloody hard time convincing the other lads to go along with your plan. Especially after we've just had our arses thrashed by the Romans.'

'Which is why we need to act now. Canis will be busy congratulating himself on his latest victory. He won't be expecting an attack. We can catch him by surprise.'

'You really think that'll work? Attacking Ravenna?'

'It's our only chance of ending this once and for all. If we attack before the fleet has been repaired, we can destroy the base and cripple their naval operations. It'll be a long while before they're able to resume operations on our side of the sea.'

'And if there's an opportunity to rescue your brother at the same time . . .'

'Then I'll find him,' Telemachus said. 'I'll bring him back. And Canis will be dealt with. Mark my words. After I'm done with him, he won't be troubling us ever again.'

CHAPTER THIRTY-SIX

It was late in the afternoon when the first pirate ships sailed into the bay. Telemachus stood a short distance up from the beach and gazed out at the sleek vessels as they rounded the headland, their black pennants fluttering like crows in the breeze. A small party of pirates had gathered beside him, their cloaks pulled tight across their chests as they waited to greet the new arrivals. Some of the crew muttered among themselves, while others wore looks of apprehension at the prospect of welcoming strangers to their base. Despite the oppressive heat of the late summer, the sky was grey and forbidding.

'Are you sure you know what you're doing, inviting this lot here?' Geras asked, waving a hand at the approaching vessels. 'How do we know we can trust any of these other gangs? You know as well as I do that some of 'em would sooner slit each other's throats than work together.'

Telemachus pursed his lips and returned his gaze to the bay. Ten days had passed since he had sent out the two ships to summon the pirate gangs to Petrapylae. A feast was to be held on the beach, and then he would detail the latest incursions on their trade by the Roman navy, together with his thoughts on how they should respond. The decision to invite the other captains had been met with disbelief and anger by some of his men, but Telemachus had argued that they had no choice but to try and recruit further ships to their cause. Between them, should they agree to work together, they would have enough vessels to take on the Roman squadron at Ravenna. As soon as the first sails were sighted, Telemachus had left his private quarters in the watchtower and made his way down to the beach to greet his fellow captains.

Now, as the ships neared, he glanced anxiously over his shoulder at the crumbling citadel. Tendrils of smoke rose from the incendiaries mounted on platforms above the battlements, whirling into the late-afternoon sky. Although the pirate captains had correctly identified themselves to the lookout station, Telemachus was taking no chances and had ordered the artillery crews to remain ready to shoot at the first sign of treachery.

'What exactly are you hoping to achieve, Captain?' Geras asked.

'I've explained already,' Telemachus replied, a trace of irritation creeping into his voice. 'We can't take on the Romans by ourselves. We need the support of the other crews.'

'That may be so, but these self-interested bastards ain't likely to go along with our proposal. Not unless there's something in it for them. Besides, it didn't end well the last time we worked with another crew.'

'Thanks for reminding me,' Telemachus replied tersely.

'Just saying, Captain.'

Telemachus turned his gaze back to the horizon and sighed heavily. 'We've got to try, at least,' he said at last. 'Building up a fleet is our only hope of reclaiming the Adriaticum from that bastard Canis. If we allow him to seize control of the sea lanes, our days will be numbered.'

'Are you sure that's your only reason for trying to recruit this lot to our ranks?'

Telemachus gave his friend a searching look. 'What's that supposed to mean?'

Geras glanced around, then leaned in closer so that the other mates wouldn't overhear. 'Everyone knows it ain't long until the Romans execute that brother of yours. I know you're desperate to free him, but some of the lads are starting to wonder whether you're putting his rescue over the needs of the crew. At the moment it's only a few of 'em who are saying anything, but I thought you should know.'

'What are they saying, exactly?'

Geras shrugged. 'Just that we might be rushing into this whole business of building up a fleet. Some of them think we might be better off lying low for a while. Waiting until things calm down, like.'

'And what do *you* think, Geras?'

'Maybe they've got a point.' The first mate saw the dark expression on Telemachus's face and raised his hands. 'Look, I'm as keen as you are to give the Romans a good kicking. Gods know they deserve it, after what they've done to us. But have you considered what will happen if this plan of yours fails? Any support you've got among the crew will disappear faster than an empty seat at the Circus Maximus.'

'I swore I'd do everything I could to rescue Nereus,' Telemachus replied firmly. 'If there's a chance to save him, I have to take it.'

'Assuming he's still alive.'

'He is. I know it.'

'Even if that's true, you've got a fight on your hands persuading this lot that you're not needlessly risking their lives for the sake of your brother.' Geras jerked a thumb in the direction of *Trident*'s crew.

'I'll handle the men. Leave them to me.'

'Gladly.' Geras puffed out his cheeks and shook his head. 'Leader of a pirate gang. More bloody trouble than it's worth if you ask me. Give me the simple pleasures of life any day.'

Telemachus looked back towards the bay as the crew on the nearest vessel took in the sail and ran out the sweep oars to make their final approach. After a few moments the blades began rising and dipping in a steady pattern, driving her towards the shingle. Half a dozen sails were in sight now, with the more distant ships only just visible as they cleared the point.

As Telemachus watched, the closest ship reached the waters of the anchorage and a series of orders were shouted across the deck. A moment later, the sweeps were taken in and the anchor was dropped over the stern. There was a brief pause before the ship's boat was lowered overside and a pair of oarsmen rowed the short distance to the shoreline. The boat ground to a halt and the four men in the rear clambered down into the shallows. Telemachus watched them disembark and then straightened his back, nodding at Geras.

'Time to greet our guests.'

'Great,' Geras muttered. 'Can't bloody wait.'

Telemachus led the welcoming party down the beach, the shingle crunching beneath their soft leather boots. Ahead of them, the new arrivals made their way through the gentle surf, looking around the beach with suspicion. Three of the burly pirates stopped a few paces away from *Trident*'s crew and spread out, their hands clasped around the handles of their belted swords and daggers. An older man stepped forward, dressed in a leather jerkin and breeches. Gold rings gleamed on each of his gnarled fingers.

'Welcome, friend!' Telemachus declared as he extended his hand to the grey-haired figure. 'Welcome to Petrapylae.'

The pirate eyed Telemachus's hand warily without shaking it. Behind him, two more ships had drawn nearer to the shoreline and were also lowering their sails.

'Who the fuck are you?' he rasped.

'My name is Telemachus. Captain of *Poseidon's Trident*, and chief of the pirates here. Since the death of Bulla.'

'Bulla's dead?' A look of surprise flashed across the pirate's face. 'And now you're the new captain?'

'Aye. That's me.'

The older man looked *Trident*'s captain up and down, regarding him the way a trainer might assess a prospective gladiator. 'I wasn't expecting someone so young. I thought Bulla would have had more sense than to appoint a mere child as his successor.'

Telemachus stared hard at the pirate. 'I'm no child. And you'll address me as your equal, Captain . . . ?'

'Criton, commander of *Lycus*. You know the name, I'm sure.'

Telemachus nodded. Although he had never met the other pirate captains of Illyricum, he had been fully briefed by his lieutenants on his potential allies. From what he had been told, Criton was one of the oldest pirates still at sea, and a few of *Trident*'s crew had even sailed alongside him before he had assumed an independent command. His support would be crucial to winning over the other crews.

Criton's dark eyes narrowed as he scanned the citadel's

defences. 'Quite the operation you've got here,' he said. 'Wish I'd thought of it myself. Although I must admit, I was under the impression this was Captain Nestor's hideout.'

'It was. It's ours now.'

'I see.' Criton stared intently at the younger man for a moment before straightening up. 'Well, it's been a long journey. My men and I are in need of refreshment.'

'Of course.' Telemachus gestured towards the cooking fires being lit further up the beach, near a sprawl of huts. 'There's plenty of wine and meat, and the rest of your men are welcome to join us later on.'

'No need. I've ordered them to stay aboard *Lycus*. They'll be keeping watch throughout the night, just in case.'

'You don't trust us?'

Criton gave a dry laugh. 'How do you think I've survived as long as I have? A cautious pirate captain lasts a lot longer than a reckless one. You'll learn that yourself in time. Anyway, we'll be leaving again as soon as it's light.'

'Wait. You're not staying?' Telemachus asked in surprise.

'What for? Whatever hare-brained scheme you're proposing, these captains won't agree to it.'

'Why did you bother coming, then?' asked Geras.

'I came under the impression that we'd be speaking with Bulla. Me and some of the lads sailed alongside his crew once or twice, hunting in consort before we went our separate ways. He was a good man. If you've got something to say then I'll hear you out. I owe Bulla that much. But if you think any of the captains are about to start taking orders from you, you're mistaken.'

'This isn't about giving orders,' Telemachus said. 'It's about the survival of our crews.'

'Says you.' Criton moved in closer, parting his lips in a smile, and Telemachus caught the whiff of garlic on his breath. 'A friendly word of advice. You might call yourself a captain, but I've been hunting in these parts for twenty years. I know most of the other captains well enough, and it'll be a cold day in Hades before they agree to work together.'

He turned and barked an order at his men, then marched off up the shingle, brushing past the rest of the welcoming party and drawing several hostile glares. Telemachus stared after him guardedly until he was out of earshot.

'Looks like it's going to be harder to convince this lot than I thought.'

Geras nodded slowly. 'Perhaps the other captains will be more agreeable.'

'Let's hope so. Because if we don't make common cause, Canis will be free to build up his fleet and hunt us down. And we'll be finished. Us and every other pirate crew along the coast of Illyricum.'

CHAPTER THIRTY-SEVEN

As evening approached, the last of the pirate ships anchored in the bay, their dark hulls silhouetted by the setting sun. The captains disembarked and gathered with their trusted lieutenants in a semicircle around the cooking fires, while the rest of their crews stayed aboard their ships, ready to respond at the first sign of danger. Those captains who operated out of the same bases sat together, chewing on hunks of meat and eyeing the other crews with looks of mutual suspicion. Jars of fine wine were brought down from the citadel, along with platters of cheese, bread and figs.

Telemachus sipped on a cup of wine and studied his fellow captains. They were all much older than him, their faces weather-beaten from the hard years at sea, and their dislike of each other was readily apparent. It was clearly going to be difficult to unite such unruly men. Once he had judged that his guests had consumed enough wine to ease the tension, he set down his cup and stepped forward to address the gathering.

'Brothers,' he began, waiting until they were still and silent before he continued. 'Thank you for coming here. I know that for some of you, this was not an easy decision.' His gaze lingered on Criton for a moment before he went on. 'I know too that there has been much ill-feeling between our crews recently, and I hope that this meeting will be the first step in bringing us closer together. Perhaps in time we will enjoy many more nights as brother captains, like the crews who once dominated the Adriaticum, celebrating great victories together with wine and meat and song. But tonight, there is a more pressing issue we must deal with. I speak, of course, of our common enemy – the Romans.'

He paused and ran a hand through his hair while he glanced around at his audience. The captains and their lieutenants listened in silence, their faces illuminated by the glow of the cooking fires. The senior mates from *Poseidon's Trident* had also been invited to the gathering, and they sat in a tight knot to one side, clutching their leather drinking cups. Telemachus took a breath and continued.

'For months now the Roman navy has made life intolerable for us. We've all suffered. Rome and her warships have attacked our bases wherever they have found them, intercepted our ships and put our comrades and families to death. Recently the Ravenna fleet has started providing an escort to merchant convoys in these parts. I don't need to remind you how hard that has hit our trade. Some of us have been driven to the brink of ruin.'

'So what?' someone said. 'Things have always been like that between us and Rome. You'd understand that if you'd been a captain for more than a bloody day.'

Several figures around the fires grunted their agreement. Others chuckled heartily. Telemachus shifted his gaze to the man who'd spoken, a sinewy pirate dressed in a flamboyant silk tunic. He had been one of the last captains to come ashore, complaining loudly about the loss of trade he'd suffered by attending the gathering.

Telemachus waited for silence to settle again before he responded. 'Gentius speaks the truth. Rome has always been determined to combat piracy. In the past, they might have sent out a patrol or driven us from one of our havens. But this time it is different. This time they plan to wipe us out.'

Gentius smiled thinly. 'And what makes you such an expert on Rome's intentions?'

'Because I have met their commander, Prefect Canis. I have heard him vow to hunt down every one of us, until the entire coastline of Illyricum is cleared of pirates. More than that, I have seen with my own eyes the destruction Canis and his squadron inflicted on our old base at Peiratispolis. He will stop at nothing in his quest to defeat us. Indeed, three days ago I received disturbing news that another hideout at Terra Cissa has been razed to the ground.'

Criton's eyes widened. 'Terra Cissa? That's been a pirate haunt for decades.'

'It was. There is nothing left of it now.'

'How did you hear of this?' Gentius demanded.

'One of my ships found the ruins of the base while they were getting word out about this gathering. They picked up a few survivors, who told us their story. The pirates were attacked at their base and beheaded, their ships were burned and their families taken prisoner to be sold as slaves or to work in the mines.'

Shocked gasps went up around Telemachus's audience. Some of the men stared back at the young captain, unable to conceal their stunned expressions. Criton clenched his fist, trembling with rage.

'Clearly we cannot afford to ignore such a serious threat,' Telemachus went on. 'Unless we act now, Canis and his fleet will eventually hunt us all down and destroy our bases. Not one of us will escape his wrath.'

'We shall have to settle elsewhere, then,' another pirate suggested. 'Sod Canis and his mob. We'll find new havens to hunt from.'

'I only wish it was that easy, Scylla. But where could we go? Pickings are slim around the Ionian Sea, and there are hardly any islands to hide in further to the south. No, my friends. There is only one option for us, and that is to fight back against the Romans and drive them from our waters.'

'And risk our necks? Bollocks to that!'

Telemachus looked across the circle. It was Virbius who had spoken. His heavily scarred features glowed in the flames as he glanced round at the other pirates, gesturing at *Trident*'s captain. 'Our great leader here says there is nowhere to go,' he went on. 'Well, that ain't true. We could head east, brothers. To the Euxine Sea.'

'The Euxine?' one pirate called out. 'Why the fuck would we go there? It's the absolute arse end of the Empire. It'd take us a month to sail there and longer to find a good anchorage, and there's not much rich shipping that far from Rome.'

'But there are no Roman fleets to bother us either. And there ain't many pirate gangs out that way, last I heard. We'd have the area to ourselves.'

'You're suggesting we abandon Illyricum?' Gentius asked.

'Why not?' Virbius shrugged. 'What's keeping us here, after all? The sea lanes are closely guarded, there's fuck all prey to be found and we're living in constant fear of death or capture. Anything has got to be better than that. At least in the

Euxine we could get back to what we're good at: hunting down fat merchant ships.'

'I agree with Virbius!' one pirate called out. 'Let's head east!'

'Fuck Illyricum!' another yelled.

More of the captains joined in, shouting their support for Virbius's plan. Others reacted to the suggestion with anger. A din of competing voices went up as the pirates squabbled with one another and traded insults. Telemachus clenched his jaw, sensing that he was in danger of losing the argument, and with it any hope of persuading the captains to form an alliance. He filled his lungs and bellowed, '*Enough!*'

Most of the captains quickly fell silent. After a pause, the few remaining voices died away and a stony silence fell over the beach.

'Virbius is right,' Telemachus continued. 'On the face of it, sailing east would be the easiest choice. We'd leave our problems behind, and none of us would have to live in fear of Rome.'

'So what are we waiting for? Let's go!'

Several men murmured their support. Another pirate opened his mouth to speak, but Telemachus raised his hand, cutting him off. 'If we left Illyricum, we might be safe for a year or two. Until the Romans came after us again. Then where would we go? Ask yourselves this: why did we choose to hunt in these waters in the first place? What brought us all here?'

'Good anchorages!' one captain shouted.

'Cheap tarts!' another joked, to peals of laughter.

'Aye, there's that,' Telemachus replied. 'But the Adriaticum is also where the richest pickings are to be had. If we sailed east, we might be safer. For a while, at least. But we'd also be a lot poorer. Are you really prepared to give up the best hunting grounds in the Empire and settle for living on whatever scraps we might find in the Euxine?'

He paused while he searched the faces of his audience. No one answered his question, and he went on, his tone growing bolder as he warmed to his subject.

'This is not just about plunder, brothers. This is about claiming what is rightfully ours. I may not have been a captain for very long, but this much I know: the pirate brotherhood has always worked this area of the coast. Why, even Pompey the Great failed to crush us, despite his boasts to the Roman people. We survived him, yet we are ready to surrender meekly in the face of Canis. And Canis is no Pompey, whatever he may think.' He glanced around the fires and pointed to one of the captains. 'Are you forgetting, Scylla, that your father hunted in this area, and his father before him? What about you, Perimedes? Are you willing to surrender your birthright so easily, without putting up a fight?'

The captains he had named shifted awkwardly, unwilling to meet his gaze. There were more heated exchanges as the pirates resumed arguing among themselves. After a few moments, a swarthy figure with a straggling beard and wild white hair stood up. He cleared his throat and waited for his comrades to fall silent.

'Quiet there!' one man shouted. 'Birria wishes to speak!'

The others stopped arguing and looked towards the captain in question. Telemachus could see the respect and fear on everyone's faces as Birria addressed them.

'You all know me, brothers. As captain of *Olympias*, I have hunted in these parts for as long as any of you, and I have the scars to prove it. And I say Telemachus is right. For too long we have let the Romans hunt us down like dogs, killing us and driving us from home and hearth. And what have we done in response? Bicker among ourselves while we fight over the scraps! I say it's time we stopped running. Let's give the Romans a taste of their own medicine. Let's kill the bastards!'

A few loud murmurs of assent went up around the beach. Several of the pirates roared their support, and soon a chorus of lusty cheers filled the air. Telemachus noticed Virbius glowering at him, his thick arms folded across his chest.

'This talk of brotherhood is all well and good, Birria,' Gentius cut in. 'But we're thieves first and foremost. Why should we risk everything by plunging into a reckless conflict with Rome?'

'We already *are* in conflict,' Telemachus said. 'I thought that much was clear from Canis's actions in Terra Cissa and elsewhere.'

'Even so, we should be careful before we commit to action. The situation is bad enough. Who knows how Canis will react if we attack him? It could make the situation even worse than it is.'

Telemachus sucked in a breath. 'And if we do nothing, he will come after us anyway. Either we take a stand against the Romans and regain control of this side of the sea, or we sit back and let our enemy grow more powerful. That's the choice we face.'

'Suppose we join you in this venture,' Criton said cautiously. 'What do you propose, exactly?'

'Canis knows that we're wary of attacking his fleet,' Telemachus explained. 'For obvious reasons. Our ships are fast and light, but they wouldn't stand a chance against his heavily armed warships. Which is why we must destroy the fleet in stages. Beginning with an assault on Ravenna.'

'The naval base?' Gentius's eyes widened. 'But that will be heavily defended.'

'Usually, yes. But Canis has sent most of his fleet over to this side of the sea, to escort the merchant convoys. There are only a few seaworthy tubs left at Ravenna.'

'How many?'

'Five biremes and the flagship, plus a handful of scout ships and transports.'

Gentius gave Telemachus a sceptical look. 'Six warships? That's all?'

'Six seaworthy vessels, aye. There are several more liburnians and triremes beached in the dockyard, but many of them date back to the Battle of Actium, and with the cuts that the emperors have made to the service, they've been left to run down. Some of 'em haven't left the port in years.'

'Tell us something we don't know, lad. Every pirate captain from here to Piraeus knows that the Ravenna fleet is in a piss poor state.'

'But it won't be that way for much longer,' Telemachus cautioned. 'Indeed, I've recently learned that Canis is making repairs to the rest of his fleet, in order to hunt us down and destroy us once and for all.'

'How do you know this?'

'Fifteen days ago, we captured a Roman marine during an ambush. An optio based at Ravenna. He told us about the enemy's plans to search the coast for our bases. He also told us that Canis has got his men working hard to refurbish the rest of his fleet before the end of the sailing season. If he succeeds in building up his forces, we'll be done for. But if we strike now, we can burn the ships in the docks, plus the stores at Ravenna. We can use that victory to rally more pirates to our cause. Then we'll take on Canis and what remains of his fleet in battle, and crush him.'

'Your prisoner might be lying.'

Telemachus permitted himself a smile. 'Clearly you haven't met my interrogators, Gentius.'

'The optio's story makes sense,' Criton said. 'It would explain why Canis hasn't been able to launch a full campaign against us yet. He can carry out the odd foray, but for anything else he needs more ships.'

Gentius looked unconvinced. 'But would an attack on Ravenna really drive the Romans away? What's to stop them from simply sending reinforcements from Misenum?'

'They won't.'

'Forgive me, Telemachus, but I will need a firmer guarantee than that.'

Telemachus gritted his teeth as he fought to control his rising temper. Gentius was obviously one of those pirate captains who cared nothing for the brotherhood, and who coldly assessed every decision according to how much he stood to profit personally from it. In another life he might have flourished as a moneylender at Piraeus, Telemachus reflected wryly. But he knew he had to win over the likes of Gentius if his argument was to carry the day.

'According to our prisoner, the Misenum fleet has suffered from the same lack of investment as at Ravenna. Which means it would take a long while for the Romans to rebuild the service here. In the meantime, our ships would be free to plunder this side of the sea without any fear of Roman attack. Does that satisfy you?'

A greedy look flashed in Gentius's eyes. Around him the other pirate leaders grinned at one another, licking their lips at the prospect of plentiful booty.

'There is something else.' Telemachus hesitated as he chose his next words carefully. This was the part of the meeting that he had been dreading. 'Some of you may have heard that a few weeks ago my brother, Nereus, was captured by the Romans. Canis has threatened to crucify him unless I hand myself over to the authorities by the end of the month.'

Criton stared warily at him. 'We'd heard the news, aye. What of it?'

'Several days ago, I found out where Nereus is being held,' Telemachus said. 'The optio we took prisoner claims that my brother is in a cell at Ravenna, along with some captured pirates who are awaiting execution.'

A groove formed above Birria's brow. 'How did Canis know where to find your brother?'

'Someone tipped the Romans off. A traitor among our ranks. The prisoner told us that a merchant captain arrived at Ravenna the month before last carrying a scroll addressed to the prefect. A scroll he had been ordered to deliver by a pirate on a ship that had attacked them. That's how Canis learned about Nereus.'

'And you think it was someone on your crew who sold you out to the Romans?' Birria asked. 'But who?'

'I don't know. I'll find that out soon enough, I assure you. And when I do, they'll be dealt with. One way or another, I'll have that traitor's head . . .'

'There's nothing worse than a pirate who betrays his own kind.' Criton's expression tightened. 'And I suppose you intend to rescue your brother, when we attack?'

'Yes. But I won't ask any man among us to risk his life to save him or the other prisoners. That responsibility, and risk, is mine and mine alone. I want to be very clear on that.'

'Bollocks!' Virbius spat. He glared at Telemachus with a stony expression. 'This ain't about getting one over on the Romans, or defending the brotherhood. You're desperate to attack Ravenna just so you can rescue your brother.'

Telemachus shook his head firmly. 'It isn't about me or my brother. My friends,' he added, sweeping his eyes across his audience, 'I would be arguing for an attack on Ravenna even if those Roman dogs weren't holding Nereus prisoner. What I said before still stands. The imperial fleet must be destroyed if we are to survive. The fact that my brother is being held there only gives me greater motivation to see that we succeed.'

'If he is still alive,' Gentius pointed out. 'How do you know the Romans haven't killed him already?'

'Because Canis is a cruel bastard. If I know him as well as I think I do, he'll want to prolong my brother's suffering – and mine – for as long as possible before he puts him to death.'

'That sounds like Canis all right,' Birria growled.

'How do you plan on rescuing him, though?' Criton asked. 'Surely the Romans will execute the prisoners as soon as we attack?'

'I'll explain that later,' Telemachus replied. 'I'm telling you all this in the new spirit of cooperation between our crews. Brothers, we cannot fight together if we cannot trust one another. But know this: if you decide to walk away, there is no future for us in the Adriaticum. The great brotherhood of pirates will be wiped out. Only if we work together will we stand any hope of surviving.' He paused and straightened up. 'Now, who will fight with me?'

There was a brief silence. Several of the captains muttered among themselves before Birria spoke up.

'It's about time we took on the Romans. They've had it their own way for too long. Every one of us has lost a loved one to those bastards. A wife or a son, or a friend . . . or a brother.' He looked Telemachus hard in the eye. 'I'll sail with you.'

'Thank you, Birria.' The words caught in Telemachus's throat. He looked round at the remaining captains. 'Who else will join us?'

There was a long pause as the pirate leaders glanced at one another. Then Criton cleared his throat.

'Brothers, this is not an easy decision to make. Like many of you, I am reluctant to take on the Roman navy. But if what Telemachus says is true, then it seems to me that we have no choice but to set our differences aside and fight together. I agree to the plan.'

After a few moments, Scylla too declared in favour, and one by one the others swiftly followed until only Gentius remained undecided. Telemachus looked hard at him.

'Well, Captain? What do you say?'

Gentius pursed his lips. 'You're asking us to commit to an extremely dangerous plan of action, young man. If this attack fails, you'll be sending us to our deaths.'

'And if we do nothing, we'll be as good as dead anyway.' Telemachus threw up his arms. 'This is our only chance of success. Surely you can see that? Or would you prefer to abandon these rich waters and leave the profits to your brother captains?'

The overweight pirate commander hesitated moment-arily before he nodded. 'Very well. We'll join you on this endeavour.'

Telemachus drew in a deep breath and breathed a sigh of relief.

'We'll begin our preparations immediately. Castor is our quartermaster. He'll tend to any supply needs your ships may have. In the meantime, enjoy the rest of the feast. We have a long fight ahead of us. Now, unless you have any other questions . . .'

'I have one,' Criton said. 'How do you plan to get us into Ravenna without raising the alarm?'

Birria nodded. 'Criton has a point. Even if Canis has got most of his fleet running the convoy service, we'll still have to deal with those warships. I used to sail out of Ravenna myself, back in my trading days, and the bastards have got catapults and heated shot. As soon as we're in sight of the lighthouse, they'll head straight for us. They'd sink our fleet before we could get anywhere near the harbour.'

'Then we'll have to lure them out,' Telemachus said.

Criton snorted. 'And how do you plan on doing that, exactly? Canis won't dare leave Ravenna undefended.'

'He might,' Telemachus said, 'if we give him a good reason to.'

Silence descended along the beach as the pirates stared at him with puzzled looks. Telemachus took a deep breath and smiled. 'Listen carefully, my brothers. This is what we're going to do . . .'

CHAPTER THIRTY-EIGHT

'This had better work,' Geras muttered as he gazed out beyond the treeline.

Telemachus and his first mate were crouching beside a small rocky outcrop near the edge of a sprawling olive grove close to the Liburnian coast. The first light of pre-dawn was thickening on the horizon, revealing the stretch of open ground beyond the grove. Ahead of them, no more than a quarter of a mile away, stood the small Roman port of Senia. The town had been constructed on flat ground at the entrance to the bay, with a crude defensive ditch dug around the surrounding wall and a gatehouse overlooking the main entrance. Three bored-looking sentries stood in front of the gate, while further away Telemachus spied the watchtower guarding the entrance to the tiny harbour. A handful of merchant vessels were moored along the pier, the slanted lines of their masts like grounded spears against the gathering dawn. Further away, beached on the shingle for repairs, was the single Roman bireme that guarded the shipping.

Geras sniffed irritably. 'Still no sign of our fleet. What's taking 'em so bloody long?'

'It's too early,' Telemachus replied. 'They won't be long now.'

He glanced at his friend and noted the strained expression on his face. Behind him, the rest of the landing party was just out of sight, hidden from view behind the densely covered treeline. They had come ashore under cover of darkness, landing in a small cove a few miles down the coast from Senia. The pirates wore dark cloaks to make themselves less visible, and carried only their weapons, with the rest of their equipment and anything that might make a noise left behind on the ships. Two hundred men had been picked for the landing party: more than enough to deal with the small militia garrison and the marines. Even so, Telemachus had ordered the boats and their skeleton crews to remain at the cove in case they needed to make a swift retreat.

The pirate fleet had reached Senia the previous afternoon, having set sail from Petrapylae three days ago. Shortly before dusk they had snapped up a small fishing vessel making its way back to the harbour. Then the interrogators had gone to work on the boat's captain. He had readily confirmed what Telemachus had previously learned from the optio they had taken prisoner, adding that Senia had poor walls and the townsfolk had neglected to adequately invest in the defences. The local militia was severely depleted, with much of its equipment missing or in poor condition, and it would present no great threat to the pirates. The marines were a different proposition, but Telemachus aimed to establish a foothold inside the town before they could mount a proper defence. To make sure the captain did not attempt to mislead them, Telemachus had ordered his crew be kept hostage aboard *Trident*. If the information he gave turned out to be incorrect, he had explained, the fishermen would be put to death.

'Still nothing,' Geras growled softly as he scanned the coast, searching for the first glimpse of a sail.

'Patience,' Telemachus replied. 'They'll get here soon enough. Then the town will be ours. And that Roman bireme too.'

'Assuming the defenders fall for it.'

'They will. Trust me. They'll be too busy dealing with our fleet to notice us. Not until it's too late, anyway.' Telemachus smiled cruelly. 'We'll cut them down before they have a chance to react.'

'And if you're wrong?'

'I'm not. Think about it, Geras. This is a port town. These people are worried about the threat from the sea. They won't be anticipating an attack from the landward side.'

'Let's just hope our new friends play their part,' Geras muttered.

Telemachus shot him an inquisitive look. 'What do you make of them?'

Geras paused briefly and considered. 'Criton is all right. He's an old salt, but he's steady enough. Same goes for most of the others. They can be tetchy but they won't back out of a fight. Gentius is a greedy bastard, and he'll only stick with us as long as he stands to profit. As for Birria, he's a bit mad and the most ruthless of the bunch, but he'll be useful in a fight.' He dropped his voice. 'But it ain't the new pirates I'm worried about, Captain. It's some of our own that concern me most.'

'You're talking about Virbius?'

'Aye. We both know he won't ever accept you as commander. That snake will do his duties well enough, but he'll be plotting behind your back to get rid of you.'

Telemachus grinned. 'I'd like to see him try.'

'I'm serious. This business about rescuing your brother has got him and some of the older pirates worked up. They're not happy about risking their lives for a family reunion.'

'Freeing Nereus has nothing to do with saving the pirate brotherhood.'

'I know that, Captain. But some of the other lads ain't as easy to persuade, and you can be sure that Virbius will be looking to take advantage.'

'You may be right.' Telemachus sighed. 'Look, we can't move against Virbius now. We need every man on our side if we're to destroy Ravenna. Besides, he won't try anything yet. He's got just as much interest in defeating Canis as the rest of us.'

'For now, maybe,' Geras conceded. 'But you can't put off dealing with him for ever.'

'I know.'

Telemachus returned his gaze to the town as the band of light on the horizon slowly thickened. Everything depended on the pirate ships playing their part in the attack. Somewhere over the horizon, out of sight of land, lurked *Lycus* and the rest of the fleet. Shortly before dawn, they would make directly for the port under full sail. As soon as they swept into view, the landing party, led by Telemachus and Birria, would move forward from the olive grove and rush the town's defences. With the defenders' attention drawn to the seaward threat, they would enter the port before the enemy became aware of the danger. The militia forces would be swiftly overrun, along with any marines who tried to resist.

News of the attack on Senia would soon reach Canis, compelling the Roman prefect to take out the remainder of his fleet to hunt down the pirates, leaving Ravenna undefended. Meanwhile, Telemachus and his fellow captains would bide their time in a small cove down the coast from the naval base. Once the Roman fleet left, the Illyrian pirates would launch their surprise attack on Ravenna, using the bireme they planned on capturing from Senia to disguise their approach. If everything went to plan, the fleet would be destroyed in detail, and Telemachus could finally free his brother from captivity.

Geras suddenly stirred, squinting at the horizon. He nudged his captain, grasping the latter's arm. 'Over there!' he whispered. 'Look!'

Telemachus swung his gaze forward, straining his eyes at the open sea a mile or so from the coastline. At first he saw nothing except the shreds of mist clinging to the surface of the water. Then the last streaks cleared and he glimpsed something close to the horizon: the shapes of several ships racing towards the harbour. He had instructed each vessel to approach with its dark pennant atop its masthead and its crew amassed on the foredeck, making as much noise as possible to spread fear and panic among the locals.

For a moment, the quiet before dawn was unbroken. Then a trumpet sounded the alarm and the faint cries of terrified sailors and civilians carried across the air as the menacing fleet bore down on the harbour. At the town gate the sentries turned their backs on the road and glanced anxiously at one another. A few moments later, a series of shouts went up from inside the town and the guards along the battlements rushed over to help their comrades prepare the defences. Telemachus watched the scene for a moment longer before he turned to Geras.

'Come on. Let's go.'

Flat on their stomachs, the two pirates crawled back through the olive grove. The rest of the landing party was lying in wait twenty paces away, concealed behind the treeline as they waited for the seaward attack to commence. Many of them wore tense expressions at the thought of action, with none of the usual excitement the men felt before attacking prey. And with good reason, Telemachus reasoned. Today they would be facing a much more dangerous foe than a few unarmed sailors. Although the pirates despised Rome, many of them feared and admired her soldiers for their skill and courage, and none relished the prospect of facing them in a land battle.

Birria edged forward from the main party, alerted by the shouts and cries coming from the port. He crept over to Telemachus, inclining his head in the direction of the sea.

'Is that our fleet?' he asked.

Telemachus nodded. 'We need to get moving. Tell your men to form up.'

'At last. Time to kill some Romans.' Birria smiled grimly.

Telemachus stared levelly at the captain. 'Remember. Kill the garrison, but leave the local people out of it. Everything must be focused on the soldiers.'

Birria nodded and dropped back to pass the word down the line. A few moments later, there was a ripple of movement as his men rose to their feet. At the same time, Telemachus formed up his own men to the right. The pirates carried a variety of short swords, boarding axes and javelins, while some were equipped with grappling lines taken from *Trident*'s storage lockers. When they had finished assembling, Telemachus glanced round at the sea of faces in front of him. Dawn was coming up fast now and he could make out their expressions of grim determination as he drew a deep breath.

'Ready, lads! On me!'

At his command, the landing party swept forward, the grass rustling as they moved steadily through the olive grove. Telemachus led the way, his heart beating fiercely inside his chest. Through a gap between the trees he spied the sentries at the town gate. They were still focused on the chaos of activity down by the port and had not yet spotted Telemachus and his men. A handful of merchants and travellers who had been waiting to gain entry to the town had wisely abandoned their plans and were hurrying back down the road with their baggage-laden mules and wagons. Telemachus raised his eyes to the battlements but saw no sign of any archers as the defenders concentrated their meagre resources on the threat from the sea, and his heart lifted at the realisation that his plan was working.

A moment later, the pirates emerged from the treeline and one of the sentries glanced over, alerted by the sound of pounding footsteps. There was a pause as he stared at the shadows spilling out of the olive grove. Then he spun away, shouting at his comrades, thrusting an arm in the direction of the pirates. The others turned to look, and there were cries of alarm from the traders and merchants as they caught sight of the mass of armed men charging towards them. Telemachus drew his falcata and pointed his blade in a broad sweep at the gate.

'Now!' he yelled over his shoulder. 'Charge!'

As soon as the words left his mouth, the pirates rushed forward across the open stretch of stunted trees, scrub and rocks between the olive grove and the town walls. No more than a hundred paces away, the sentries quickly recovered from the shock and ran through the gates. A moment later, the studded timbers slammed shut and a handful of figures appeared along the wall, alerted by the sentries' warnings. Those merchants and traders outside the walls turned and fled in every direction, abandoning their carts and wagons in their desperation to escape. Others threw themselves to the ground, hoping to be spared the pirates' fury.

'Leave them!' Telemachus roared. 'Follow me!'

He sprinted forward, leading his men towards the section of the wall to the left of the gatehouse. Around him the pirates were breathing heavily as they ran for all they were worth. Birria led a separate section of his men, armed with boarding axes, over to the sally port built at the foot of the guard tower at one end of the wall. In the next instant the defenders on the parapet above loosed off a ragged volley of arrows at the onrushing pirates and Telemachus heard a howl of agony from a man to the right as he was struck down by a pair of dark shafts to his breast, while another pirate fell away, pawing at an arrow protruding from his thigh. He ignored their despairing cries and in another breathless stride had reached the ditch.

'Over to the wall!' he shouted, waving his men on. 'Hurry!'

The first pirates poured over the edge, sliding down the slope before they rushed across the uneven ground. Telemachus followed them close behind, almost losing his footing on a clump of rocks and exposed roots before he reached the far side of the escarpment and hauled himself up to the ledge above, joining the other pirates around the base of the wall. From above came frantic shouts as the sentries on the battlements called out to their comrades on the far side of the town, alerting them to the new danger.

'Get those fucking lines up!' Telemachus yelled.

The pirates sprang into action, reaching for their grappling hooks. The man to the right of Telemachus flung up his line and gave a cheer as the iron tips snagged on the parapet. He tugged on the line, testing to make sure it was secure before he began scaling the wall. By now the defenders were aware of the threat, and as he climbed, a figure appeared above and hurled down a javelin. The heavy point punched through the pirate's chest and burst out of his lower back, and the man groaned as he tumbled into the bottom of the ditch. The other pirates who had been wielding lines hesitated at the sight of their impaled comrade. Telemachus sheathed his falcata and grabbed the slackened rope, turning to his men.

'What are you lot waiting for? Get up there!'

Gritting his teeth, he pressed his feet against the side of the wall and began climbing. From the other side of the ditch Geras shouted an order, and those men armed with slings aimed them at the guards on the parapet, driving them back. Others followed Telemachus's lead, throwing up their lines and hastily starting to ascend. Telemachus scrambled towards the parapet, his heart pounding furiously. In the next breath he reached the surface and secured a decent purchase, the crumbling stonework shifting beneath his callused hands. He swung his legs over and dropped down to the timber walkway.

He recovered to see a stick-thin guard charging at him with a spear. He had no time to parry the blow, and he twisted at the waist, narrowly evading the tip as it blurred past his torso. There was a cry of pain as the spear struck the pirate who had been climbing up immediately behind him, piking him in the guts. The Roman tore his weapon free with a grunt, but before he could strike again, Telemachus unsheathed his blade and sprang to his feet, slashing horizontally at his

395

opponent's legs. The guard hissed through his teeth as the falcata cut into his shin bone, and he staggered backwards. With an incoherent roar, Telemachus lurched forward again, slamming shoulder-first into the guard. The man stumbled back and fell screaming to the alley below.

Looking over his shoulder, Telemachus saw that more pirates were crowding the walkway now as they hurried up the ramparts, and the bloodied corpses of two other guards lay slumped along the parapet. Dozens more pirates had succeeded in reaching the battlements on the opposite side of the gatehouse, and they hacked and stabbed at the few guards blocking their path, swiftly cutting them down. He spun round and nodded at his men, indicating the gatehouse.

'This way! Don't stop!'

The pirates ran on, their feet drumming on the weathered walkway. Telemachus glanced down and saw the last militiamen fleeing down the side streets. Further away, a section of marines came rushing over from the quayside, boots pounding on the cobblestones as they hurried forward to deal with the landward attack. He looked up again as the gatehouse door was flung open and a pair of guards came charging out, brandishing short swords. They stopped in momentary surprise, and before they could bring up their weapons, he crashed into the nearest man, knocking him back against the gatehouse. The Roman grunted as the air was expelled from his lungs, and Telemachus followed through with a quick downward stab, sinking the blade deep into the guard's guts.

He tore his weapon free, snatched up the Roman's oval shield and wheeled round to face the second guard. The next two pirates had already swarmed forward, cutting the Roman down in a flicker of vicious thrusts. Telemachus barrelled past them and hurried through the doorway, the blood rushing in his ears as he sprinted down the narrow stairs that led into the town. Moments later, he emerged into a wide street and turned right, racing over to the main gate. Behind him three more pirates came storming out of the gatehouse, panting heavily as they searched for the next enemies to kill. Telemachus called out to them.

'You men! Over here! Get this gate open!'

They set down their weapons and hurried across, working quickly, hauling the heavy locking bar into its receiver before they grabbed hold of the iron rings and heaved on the timbers. The doors swung inward with a protesting groan, scraping across the flagstones. As soon as the gate was fully open, those pirates who had not yet breached the walls sprinted over from the ditches and swept into the town with a great cheer. Telemachus snatched up his weapon and shield and then pointed his sword at the loose section of marines advancing towards them from the main thoroughfare.

'Kill them!' he ordered. 'Kill the bastards!'

CHAPTER THIRTY-NINE

The dull thud of swords cracking against shields and the ring of clashing blades echoed off the walls as the two sides met along the thoroughfare. Telemachus pushed his way to the front of the skirmish, keeping his oval shield at chest height as his eyes flickered from left to right along the line of fighting men. Unlike the poorly trained militia, the marines had been drilled to a much higher standard, and they would pose a stern challenge to the pirates. He looked ahead and saw a marine in a leather cuirass step towards him. At the sight of the youthful captain, the Roman broke into a vicious grin and drew back his arm as he shaped to thrust at his opponent's throat.

'No you don't!' Telemachus growled.

The Roman was slow and Telemachus read the blow easily, deflecting it with an upward flick of his shield. His forearm trembled as the blade clattered against the curved surface and glanced off at an angle. Then he lunged forward, stabbing at the Roman in the style he had been taught during his early days aboard *Poseidon's Trident*. The blade found its way beneath the man's cuirass and sank a few inches into his stomach, piercing his vitals. The Roman made a keening noise in his throat as Telemachus kicked him aside and left him writhing on the ground.

The pirates either side of him were pressing forward, forcing the marines back. Already a dozen bodies littered the ground, and even as Telemachus looked on, one Roman screamed in pain as a pirate swept down with his broadaxe, severing the man's arm in a single blow. Another staggered away from the fight, clawing at a dagger protruding from his throat. The marines and the militia had been caught by surprise and many wore no armour or helmets, having hurried from their barracks to fight the savage horde of pirates that had burst into the port. They were quickly cut down.

As the fighting continued, a roar erupted from one of the side streets and Telemachus looked over to see a wave of cheering pirates rushing forward. Among them he spotted Birria, flanked by the party of axemen who had been sent over to breach the sally port entrance. They immediately threw themselves into the skirmish, sweeping out across the thoroughfare and charging at the marines, who were momentarily stunned by this new swarm of pirates.

With the attack on their flank, the last embers of resistance among the marines died out. A few men to the rear broke off and retreated down the thoroughfare, but Telemachus ordered a party of pirates to hunt them down through the side streets. Soon only a small number of Romans were still fighting, spurred on by a stocky centurion.

'Stand and fight, you curs!' he raged. 'Don't yield to these scum!'

Despite his pleas, the remaining marines grasped that there was no hope of victory, and there was a clattering of swords against the flagstones as they surrendered. Finally the centurion was the only one left gripping his weapon. One of *Trident*'s mates hefted up his sword and approached the man, poised to strike him down. Telemachus ordered the mate to halt before he turned to address the officer.

'It's over, Roman. Throw down your weapon.'

The centurion stood firm for another moment, glaring defiantly at the pirates. At first Telemachus thought he might refuse to yield, preferring death over the indignity of defeat. Then his shoulders slumped and he tossed aside his blade with a bitter sigh.

Telemachus left a group of men to watch over the prisoners and then sought out Birria. The pirate captain wiped the sweat from his eyes as he surveyed the bloodstained street.

'A good victory, brother,' he said. 'The Romans will fear us after this.'

'It's not over yet.' Telemachus beckoned to Geras and pointed at the tower guarding the small harbour. 'Take some of the lads and destroy the bolt-thrower before the fleet is in range. A dozen men should do it. If there are any defenders holed up inside, tell them that the commander of the marines has surrendered.'

'And if they resist?'

'Then kill 'em.'

Geras barked an order at several of *Trident*'s crew and they set off down the thoroughfare at a steady trot. Most of the residents had fled indoors to escape the bloodshed, and Telemachus could see their anxious faces peering out through the bars of their windows or from the shadows of rubbish-strewn alleyways. He sent another party of his men over to the quayside to clear the warehouses and search for any more marines. Those pirates not on guard duties wasted no time in plundering the more affluent houses, as well as the merchants' stalls and wine shops lining the main street, tearing open money boxes and helping themselves to jars of wine.

As dawn spread across the sky, a thin column of smoke drifted up from the beacon atop the watchtower, signalling to the pirate fleet that the town had been taken and it was safe to enter the harbour. A short time later, the first ships edged round the mole and disgorged their crews along the pier. While the men raced ashore to indulge themselves in an orgy of looting and violence, the pirate captains marched down the thoroughfare to confer with Telemachus. Gentius led the way, stepping carefully around the corpses sprawled across the flagstones as he approached *Trident*'s captain.

'It appears you made short work of this mob, brother,' he said. 'I'm impressed.'

'Nothing we couldn't handle. Any trouble at the port?'

Gentius shook his head. 'The governor and some of the quality tried to flee on a yacht, with a few of the marines. We intercepted them before they could slip out of the harbour. Should fetch a tidy sum from their relatives when we ransom 'em.'

'And the bireme?'

'Captured. Along with the sailors. They surrendered quickly enough. Our lads snapped up the merchant ships too. Some of the captains tried to rally their crews, but they were no match for our ships. My men are transferring their supplies as we speak.'

Telemachus nodded. 'Take whatever we need, but let the sailors go free.'

Gentius snorted with derision. 'Why would we do that?

They could fetch a decent price in the slave markets. We'd be turning down a small fortune.'

'They're no use to us. We can't take prisoners, and our ships are full as it is. Besides, our quarrel is with Rome, not the people of this town.'

Criton cleared his throat audibly. 'With all due respect, Gentius has a point. Our men took a risk attacking this place. They'll want what's due to them.'

'And they'll get it,' Telemachus responded firmly. 'Once Canis is out of the way, we'll have the pick of the shipping to help ourselves to. But until then, we leave the locals out of it.'

'What about this lot?' Geras asked, gesturing to the prisoners.

Telemachus turned to face them. The marines stared back at him with a mixture of fear and hatred, and he felt a strange thrill at his ability to provoke such a reaction in the battle-hardened soldiers of Rome. Only the centurion retained a posture of defiance. Telemachus stepped towards the man and looked him up and down. Four silver medallions gleamed on the harness he wore over his scale armour. Awards of some kind, Telemachus realised.

'I take it you are the ranking officer?' he asked in Latin.

'That's right!' The officer stood erect. 'Centurion Ligarius, commander of the marines aboard *Osiris*.'

Telemachus cocked his head in the direction of the beached bireme. 'That's your ship, I presume? You're a long way from Ravenna, Centurion.'

'The prefect sent us up here.' Ligarius stared back at Telemachus unflinchingly. 'Ordered us to keep an eye out for any pirates looking for trouble. Should've known you bastards would attack us sooner or later.'

'Yes, you should.' Telemachus smiled thinly. 'That's an impressive array of medals you have. I'm sure they'll be worth a decent sum once they've been melted down.'

'Fucking pirates.' Ligarius spat on the ground. 'You might have beaten us here today, but your days are numbered. Once Canis finds out what you've done, he'll come after you. And he'll get the job done properly this time. You can count on it.'

Telemachus narrowed his eyes. 'What do you mean, "this time"?'

Now it was the centurion's turn to smile. 'I was there when our ships attacked one of your bases. That stinking nest at Peiratispolis.'

A hot rage flared up inside Telemachus as he recalled the devastation that *Trident*'s crew had discovered at their old lair. He glowered at the centurion, his fists clenched so tightly he could feel his fingernails digging into his skin. 'You were part of the squadron?'

'Aye. Me and the lads here. Cut them pirates down like they was rats. Them and their scum families.'

'Those families were no threat to you.'

'They were vermin. Nits breed lice. Some of them would have grown up to follow in their fathers' footsteps. Why take the risk? So Canis gave us the order to kill them. Once we had persuaded them to lay down their weapons, of course.' Ligarius gave a dry laugh. 'Easiest day's work I've ever had. You should've seen the looks on their faces when they realised they were going to die. Fucking priceless. Especially the women. Offered us every sexual favour under the sun to spare their babies' lives.'

'You murdered innocent women and children, you cold-hearted bastard.'

'Do me a favour. Those families were as guilty as the pirates. They had it coming. And so do you and your gang. You might have slipped away last time, but Canis will have your heads soon enough.'

'We'll see about that.' Telemachus stepped away from the centurion, his blood burning in his veins. He had never known such rage as he experienced at that moment. 'Castor!'

The quartermaster marched over. 'Aye, Captain?'

'Take these men outside the town walls and impale them.' He pointed to a stretch of open beach beyond the port. 'Do it there, so that every passing ship can see how these Romans died.'

The prisoners reacted with shouts of despair and abject terror. Castor glanced at his commander, unable to conceal his shock. Nor could the other pirate captains hide their surprise and unease at his ruthlessness.

'So much for pirate honour,' Ligarius sneered. 'You were never going to spare us, were you? Even though we surrendered.'

'So did the families at Peiratispolis,' Telemachus answered coldly.

Gentius took him to one side with his fellow captains so they would not be overheard by the prisoners. 'Is this really necessary?'

'It's what they deserve. And it will send a message to Rome. One our enemy won't forget.'

'That's my worry. Look, we've already accomplished our mission here in Senia. Canis will have every reason to come after us with what's left of his fleet once he learns of our raid. Why anger Rome more than we need to?'

'We should spare them,' Criton added. 'I don't want to

spend the rest of my life being hunted down by the imperial navy.'

Telemachus took a deep breath to hide his growing frustration. 'Brothers, these men are responsible for the massacre of our families. They must suffer for it. Or have we decided that the murder of our women and children should go unpunished?'

'No one's suggesting we let them go,' Gentius countered. 'But impaling them will only enrage Rome.'

'Rome wouldn't hesitate to do the same to us, if the boot was on the other foot. Ask yourself this, Gentius. If Canis captured our ships, do you think he'd show us any mercy?'

'I agree,' Birria interjected. 'Nothing is guaranteed to lure Canis out more effectively than the execution of Roman soldiers.'

Criton shook his head. 'This isn't what we agreed to.'

'You don't have to like it,' Telemachus replied. 'I wish there was some other way too. But we need to send a message to Rome, one they cannot ignore. This is the only way.'

He glanced round at the others, but none offered any further protest. Satisfied that his argument had carried the day, he beckoned to Castor. 'Get on with it!'

There was a flicker of hesitation on the veteran pirate's face before he shouted orders at the men guarding the prisoners. They dragged the marines to their feet and ripped off their helmets, armour and tunics, stripping them down to their loincloths and binding their hands behind their backs with lengths of rope. Some of the Romans begged for mercy, while others shouted vile curses at the pirates. Those who struggled or resisted were quickly subdued beneath a flurry of punches and kicks from their captors. The rest of the pirates, their bellies filled with drink from the looted wine shops, jeered loudly and taunted the condemned men.

'Fucking bastards!' Ligarius spat above the lurid abuse. 'You'll be hanging from a cross soon enough. All of you! You'll be screaming then, just like them pathetic wretches we put to death!'

'Take them away!' Telemachus ordered.

Several onlookers stood around the edge of the thoroughfare to watch the Roman marines being marched out of the gate. Many of the prisoners were shaking pitifully, trembling at the prospect of their grisly fate. Their deaths would bring no satisfaction to Telemachus, but he consoled himself with the knowledge that he had no choice. A brazen raid on a minor Roman port might not be sufficient to lure Canis out of Ravenna. The prefect would be reluctant to take out his fleet and leave the base undefended. Only by wiping out the garrison could the pirates be certain of tempting the Roman fleet into battle.

As the last marine was hauled to his feet, Telemachus called out for the pirates to wait, and beckoned the man over. Two of the guards dragged the prisoner away from his companions and marched him to their captain. Telemachus studied the Roman closely before he addressed him.

'What's your name?' he asked in Latin.

'Pullus, sir,' the prisoner replied anxiously. 'Quintus V-Vedius Pullus.'

'Do you want to live, Pullus?'

'Yes, sir.'

'Then listen carefully. You're going to deliver a message to Prefect Canis in Ravenna. Tell him that the days when Rome considered herself master of the Adriaticum are over. The brotherhood of the coast will no longer submit themselves to the authority of the emperor and his lackeys. Tell Canis that we challenge him to a battle. Our fleet versus his. Tell him that we look forward to avenging our dead brothers and will wait for him ten miles off the coast of Parentium, five days from now. If he refuses to give battle, we will continue to sack Roman towns and ports until every building has been razed to the ground and every man, woman and child cut to pieces. Can you remember all that?'

'I th-think so, sir.'

'You need to do better than think, Roman. Otherwise I'll choose another messenger, and you can join your friends on the stakes.'

'No! Please!' Pullus answered hastily. 'I'll remember, I swear it!'

'That's better.' Telemachus cocked his head at the pirates standing either side of Pullus. 'Take this pathetic creature down to the wharf. Find him a small boat. He's to set sail at once.'

As the pirates marched the terrified marine down the wide thoroughfare towards the harbour, Geras drew up beside his captain, frowning heavily. 'Do you really think Canis will take the bait, Captain?'

Telemachus shrugged. 'We can trust our friend Pullus to report back to him with our challenge. I believe Canis will accept. His pride will demand it.'

Geras glanced anxiously at the beach as the distant cries of the Romans drifted across to the port. 'One thing's for sure, Captain. If this doesn't lure him out, nothing will.'

'It will,' Telemachus replied. 'I'm sure of it.'

'So that's it? We wait for the Romans to act?'

'Not quite. There's one more thing we must do.' Telemachus's eyes wandered down to the strip of shingle, and the beached warship. 'Round up the carpenters from every crew and send them down there. We'll need that bireme ready to put to sea as soon as possible, if our plan is to succeed. Then we'll make for the Italian coast and wait for Canis to take the bait.'

CHAPTER FORTY

The pirate fleet reached the Umbrian coastline two days later. After leaving Senia, the fleet had divided. Birria had taken *Olympias* north to Parentium, along with the three other fastest sailers, where they would anchor and wait for the first sign of the approaching Roman squadron. The rest of the pirate ships continued on to the cove Telemachus had previously scouted, half a day out from Ravenna. They made landfall shortly before dusk, beaching in the bay as the last glimmers of sunlight dipped beneath the horizon. Lookouts were posted to the ruins of a farmhouse on the nearest headland, while the mast of each ship was unstepped to reduce the possibility of being spotted from the sea. Telemachus gave strict instructions forbidding the lighting of any cooking fires, and the men were ordered not to venture far from the beach in case they needed to make a swift escape.

Over the next three days, the pirates toiled to make their preparations for the attack on Ravenna. Weapons and equipment were checked for damage, frayed ropes were replaced and several minor leaks in the hull of the captured bireme were repaired. A foraging party was sent inland, and bundles of kindling were packed into the hold of the bireme. The pirates went about their duties in a mood of quiet determination, driven on by a shared hatred of Rome and a thirst for revenge. The successful attack on Senia had eased the tension between the rival crews, and at the end of each day the men chatted freely among themselves as they went ashore to chew on their cold rations. Even those captains who had been sceptical of Telemachus's plan at Petrapylae displayed a grudging admiration towards the young captain.

While the men toiled at the ships, Telemachus kept a watchful eye on the horizon. Although he felt certain that Canis would accept the pirates' challenge, he knew there was always a slim chance that the prefect might see through his deception. If that happened, his reputation would be ruined and his men would curse him for leading them on a pointless voyage into hostile waters. Virbius and some of the other senior mates had openly contested the decision to leave the Liburnian coast, arguing that they should have looted more ports and colonies rather than go into hiding. To add to his concerns, only a few days remained until the date of Nereus's execution. If Canis delayed his departure, for whatever reason, then Telemachus's efforts to rescue his brother would be doomed.

It was with a measure of relief, then, that he heard the lookout announce the arrival of *Olympias* on the fourth morning. Once Birria had given the correct recognition signal, Telemachus ordered his men to stand down and signalled for the other captains to come aboard *Poseidon's Trident* to confer. A wooden chest was brought up from the hold and a goatskin map of Ravenna spread out on top of it, with stones placed on the corners. The pirate captains and their lieutenants gathered round the map as Telemachus addressed them.

'Well, brothers,' he said once the last captain had clambered aboard. 'It looks like Canis has fallen for our trick. Birria and his men have sighted the Ravenna fleet.'

Criton stared at Birria. 'Are you sure it was them?'

The pirate captain nodded. 'We saw them yesterday morning, shortly after dawn. My lookout spotted the purple pennant flying from the mast of the flagship, *Neptune*.'

'Did they see you?'

'Aye. They spotted our ships against the rising sun and made straight for us. The others turned and fled, while I ordered my men to alter course and head for the open sea. The Romans went after the rest, just as we hoped they would.'

'And no one followed you?'

'I kept a good man on the lookout, but no attempt was made to pursue us. No doubt the Romans assumed that we had abandoned our comrades in their hour of need, and decided to give chase to the main force instead.'

'How many ships did Canis have with him?' asked Telemachus.

'Five biremes, plus the flagship. Every seaworthy tub at his disposal.'

'Then our ruse has worked. Ravenna is defenceless.' Criton thumped a fist against the palm of his other hand in excitement. 'We can finally stick it to those Roman scum!'

'It won't be that easy,' Telemachus said. 'According to that Roman optio we interrogated, we can expect a small detachment of marines to be guarding the base.'

'But we don't know that for certain, do we? Perhaps Ravenna has been left entirely undefended.'

Telemachus shook his head. 'Canis may be headstrong, but he is not a complete fool.'

'How many men are we talking about, roughly?' asked Gentius.

'No more than a century, the prisoner said.'

'Just as long as we know what we're up against. The last thing we need is to get there and find a nasty surprise.'

Birria snorted derisively. 'What are you worried about, Gentius? There's eighty of 'em at most, and more than four hundred of us. Those Romans won't stand a fucking chance.'

'Perhaps not,' Telemachus cut in. 'But they'll be well trained and equipped, and brave. If they're anything like the marines we fought at Senia, we can expect them to put up a tough fight.'

Criton nodded at him. 'When do you propose we attack?'

'Tonight,' Telemachus said, pointing a finger at the map. 'We'll set sail at dusk and approach the port in a neat line formation. I'll lead the way in the bireme we captured, with a skeleton crew to help me sail it. From a distance, and at night, the lookouts will mistake us for the Ravenna fleet. Once we've cleared the mole, we'll set the bireme alight and steer her towards the naval harbour. There are several old warships laid up there, apparently. They'll burn nicely. As soon as your lookouts see the blaze, that's the signal for the rest of you to pile into the base. With luck, the marines will be too busy dealing with the fire to realise what's happening. Birria, Gentius, Criton . . . you'll land at the quay along with *Poseidon's Trident*. The rest of you will deal with the warships moored in the harbour. Meanwhile, I'll take three of my men and rescue Nereus and the other prisoners. Calidus claims they're being held in a cell beneath the main headquarters block. If we move fast, we should be able to burn the warships, rescue the prisoners, destroy the base and escape over the horizon before sunrise.'

Gentius's wild eyebrows inched upwards. 'What if the lookouts see through our ruse?'

'Then we'll be sunk by the bolt-throwers,' Telemachus responded simply. 'But they won't have any reason to suspect us. Not from a distance, anyway. At night, under the cover of darkness, they won't be able to see anything except our sails. As far as they're concerned, we'll be Roman warships returning from a swift victory over the pirate fleet of Illyricum.'

'But once we draw closer, they'll realise that our ships aren't Roman. Won't they?'

'True. But by then, the lookouts and locals will be distracted by the blaze from the fire ship.'

'Perhaps we should reconnoitre the port first,' Gentius suggested. 'Form a clearer picture of the Romans' defences and strength.'

'We can't. There's no time. For all we know, Canis has already realised that we've deceived him and is doubling back across the sea to intercept us. We must act now. The sooner we attack Ravenna, the better our chances of escaping safely back to Petrapylae once we've sacked the base.'

Gentius shifted his feet. 'But we'll be sailing in blind. What if there are more Roman marines guarding the place? Or extra ships?'

Telemachus exhaled audibly and threw up his arms. 'Look, we've been over all of this before, Gentius. There's no other way. Either we do this and accept the risks, or we walk away and hand the initiative to Canis. I know which I'd prefer.'

Gentius pressed his lips together and fell silent for a moment. 'Very well. Tonight it is.'

'Good.' Telemachus took a deep breath as he glanced round. 'Any more questions, brothers? No? Then I suggest you return to your ships and brief your men. Geras, a word.'

The captains slowly dispersed to their vessels until only Telemachus and Geras were left at the side rail. Telemachus turned to his second in command and looked him hard in the eye.

'I want you to take command of *Trident* while I'm aboard the fire ship. Think you can handle her?'

Geras stared at his captain and friend. 'If it's all the same, I'd rather sail with you on the bireme.'

Telemachus shook his head. 'I need someone to take charge of *Trident* if anything happens to me. It has to be you. Is that clear?'

'As you wish,' Geras replied sullenly. 'Don't worry. I'll take good care of her, like.'

'I know you will.' Telemachus smiled. 'I'll also need a few of the men to help me steer that bireme into the port. Five should do it.'

'Aye, Captain. There won't be any shortage of volunteers wanting to go with you.' Geras paused. 'I'm just wondering when you're going to do something about that scheming bastard.' He tipped his head at Virbius as the latter went about his duties on the other side of *Trident*'s deck.

Telemachus frowned. 'What do you mean?'

Geras edged closer, lowering his voice. 'The word among the lads is that Virbius is planning a challenge to your leadership. Once this is over, he's going to put your captaincy to a vote.'

'You've heard this?'

Geras nodded. 'That treacherous snake has been going round the crew offering bribes in exchange for their support and threatening anyone who refuses to back him. He's planning to build up enough votes to rig the result and get rid of you. The bastard.' He snorted in disgust. 'Just give the order, and I'll have him weighed down with rocks and tossed overside. Nice and easy.'

'No,' Telemachus replied tersely. 'Not yet.'

'Why not? Come on, Captain. We all know that Virbius is a schemer.'

'We can't just get rid of him. Not without proof.'

'But if you don't stop him now, he's going to move against you. Gods, with the votes he's already got, he might even win. You can't let him get away with that.'

Telemachus grunted and looked away. Despite the animosity between himself and Virbius, the latter still enjoyed the support of many members of the crew. Men who would never forgive Telemachus for getting rid of one of *Trident*'s most experienced mates on the grounds of mere suspicion. Men whose support he badly needed. They were about to embark on a perilous mission, with no certainty of victory, and the last thing Telemachus wanted was an internal squabble among the crew at the precise moment when they must be united against their common enemy. And besides, he reasoned, Virbius was a skilled fighter. His expertise would be useful in the coming battle against the marines.

'Later,' he said at last. 'Now isn't the time. We've got to settle things with Rome first. Then I'll deal with Virbius.'

CHAPTER FORTY-ONE

Night had fallen and the light of a nearly full moon was shining as the bireme approached the shore. Telemachus stood in the bows of the warship, straining his eyes at the horizon. Ahead of them, no more than a mile away, stood the lighthouse marking the entrance to the port at Ravenna. A brazier burned on its roof, bathing the tall stone structure in a wash of orange light. Further along, Telemachus could see two more braziers burning at either end of the mole to guide ships into the harbour. The rest of the pirate fleet sailed less than a mile behind the bireme, maintaining a strict formation. Beneath the loom of the stars and moon, and at a distance, they would hopefully pass for the Ravenna fleet returning home after an easy victory over the Illyrian pirates.

Five men had volunteered to join Telemachus aboard the fire ship, enough to work the sail and steering. To maintain the deceit, they had changed out of their usual extravagant clothing, swapping their colourful tunics and motley assortment of weapons and equipment for the uniform and kit of Roman marines and sailors. Telemachus wore a brown tunic and leather belt, while Castor was dressed as a Roman officer, wearing an army cloak, leg greaves and a legionary helmet taken from one of the garrison at Senia. The other crews were also playing their part, lowering their black pennants and sailing their ships in a neat line rather than in the looser formations usually favoured by the pirates.

Telemachus marched aft and sought out Bassus. 'How much longer until we reach the harbour?'

The Thracian glanced up at the sail and squinted at the dark mass of the coastline. 'Half an hour or so, Captain. Maybe less, if this wind holds.'

'Let's hope it does,' Castor muttered. 'The less time we have to spend on this funeral pyre, the better.'

Telemachus glanced sidelong at the veteran and saw him staring anxiously at the forehatch. Half a dozen large bundles of kindling, flax and worn sailcloth had been piled in the hold, doused in oil and pitch to make sure the flames would spread rapidly. The timing of the attack was critical. As soon as the bireme had cleared the mole, the rest of the pirate fleet would rush forward under full sail. At the same time, Telemachus would light the fires in the hold and steer the bireme towards the ships moored in the naval harbour. The blaze would draw the Romans' attention away from the harbour entrance long enough for the fleet to steer into the naval base and land their forces on the wharf. Once the defenders were killed or taken prisoner, the pirates would be free to sack the base.

But even as he reflected on his plan, Telemachus was gripped by a twinge of doubt. What if the Romans saw through their ruse? At this very moment the enemy might be organising their defences, ready to repel the attackers as soon as they came within range of the bolt-throwers mounted at the entrance to the naval base. The pirate fleet would be sailing into a deadly trap. Many of their ships would be sunk or damaged before they could turn around and flee. The fragile alliance between the pirate captains of Illyricum would not survive such a crushing defeat. Canis would be free to strengthen his forces and hunt down the crews individually. And Nereus would be executed . . .

He shook his head clear, shoving aside his dark thoughts. There was no reason to doubt his plan. The marines would anticipate an easy victory over the pirates' less well-armed ships and would not be surprised at the reappearance of the Roman fleet so soon after they had departed Ravenna. Only when Telemachus and his men neared the naval harbour would their deceit become apparent, and by then it would be too late.

'Not long now,' he said quietly as he swung his gaze back to the lighthouse.

'We'd get there a lot faster if we took another reef out of the sail,' Castor muttered, glancing up at the mast.

'We can't.' Telemachus gestured to the sea behind them, the sails of the rest of the fleet barely discernible in the grey gloom. 'We'd pull too far ahead of the others.'

'But the sooner we get to the base, the sooner we can set fire to this thing and get off. And the less chance there is of the Romans seeing through our disguise.'

Telemachus considered, then shook his head. 'We're supposed to be a returning fleet. If we look like we're in a hurry, the lookouts might get suspicious. We can't take that risk.'

'We're taking a risk anyway. If them lookouts see through us, we'll never make it through the entrance.'

'They won't. Trust me.' Telemachus glanced at the

quartermaster. 'Look, I'm as desperate as you are to get off this tub and stick it to those Roman bastards, but we have to play our part.'

'We'd bloody better.' Castor nodded at the others. 'All the lads are itching for a fight, Captain.'

'We'll have our reckoning,' Telemachus reassured him. 'One way or another, our troubles with Rome end tonight.'

Castor grunted and spat on the deck. 'Just a pity that Canis ain't here to witness it. I would have liked to nail that aristocratic turd up by his balls.'

'We won't have to.' Telemachus flashed a smile at his comrade. 'Once the emperor finds out that his imperial base has been destroyed, he'll do the job for us.'

'Let's hope so.'

As they passed round the mole, the small pirate crew lined up along the side rail or stood beside the mast and gazed out at the harbour in front of them. Dozens of merchant ships were moored at the main quay, the tangled lines of their masts and spars dimly illuminated by torches and braziers flickering the length of the wide thoroughfare. Despite the recent raids along the Illyrian coastline, there appeared to be little disruption to the trade on which Rome's fortunes relied. Even at this late hour, teams of stevedores were hard at work unloading a steady stream of exotic goods and merchandise from the moored cargo vessels, much of it bound for the wealthy estates and towns of the interior.

At the far end of the main quay stood the entrance to the Ravenna base. Several military packets and light patrol craft were riding at anchor, while further away, half a dozen warships had been beached for repairs. Two larger triremes, unfit for service, were moored bow to stern at one end of the wharf. Beyond them stood an arrangement of warehouses, storage sheds and carpenters' workshops. On the far side of the parade ground Telemachus glimpsed the barracks blocks, along with a larger building that he realised must be the fleet headquarters. Somewhere beneath that building was the cell where Nereus and the other prisoners were being held, and he felt his pulse racing at the thought of finally seeing his brother once more.

A sudden noise drew his attention back to the harbour front. He looked over to where a small crowd of locals had gathered along the quayside to welcome back the returning heroes. Families shouted and waved at the men on deck, overcome with joy at seeing the fleet return so soon after it had departed. Several more stood in front of the gates to the naval base, punching the air in celebration. The pirates stared uncertainly at the cheering crowd, as if unsure what to do.

'What are you waiting for?' Telemachus snapped. 'Wave back, you fools! We're supposed to have won a big battle, so start acting like it!'

Castor and the others returned the greeting with feigned enthusiasm, waving and smiling nervously. Telemachus turned his attention back to the fortified gatehouse, but there was no sign of incendiaries being prepared, and it seemed the marines did not suspect a trick. As soon as the bireme had pulled clear of the breakwater, he turned to the steersman and pointed out the two warships moored along the naval quay.

'There! Make for those triremes.'

The steersman braced his legs and heaved on the huge wooden steering paddle, swinging the bireme round until her bows were lined up with the warships. In the wan glow of the torches, Telemachus could make out several tiny figures striding over from the parade ground to welcome home their victorious companions. Their excited shouts carried sharply across the night air, and Telemachus forced himself to wave back, in spite of the rapid thumping inside his chest. When the bireme was only a few hundred paces from the base, he turned and nodded at Bassus.

'Get those fires lit. Make it quick!'

'Aye, Captain.'

The Thracian produced a tinder box and padded over to the forehatch, his burly shape disappearing below deck. A short time later, he came jogging back up the narrow flight of stairs, a thin wisp of smoke trickling out of the hatch opening behind him. The smoke thickened into a swirling grey cloud as the fire below quickly took hold. The marines lining the quay did not appear to notice that anything was wrong, and as the bireme continued steering calmly towards the naval base, Telemachus called to the other pirates.

'Into the boat! Now! We're getting off this bastard!'

In a matter of moments the crew had hauled in the tender being towed behind the bireme. As smoke gushed out of the hatch, the men clambered over the rail and down the rope, dropping into the boat, until only Telemachus and the steersman remained on the deck. The latter looked a question at Telemachus, and the captain pointed at the rail, shouting to make himself heard above the crackle of the flames raging through the hold.

'You first. I'll finish up. Go!'

The steersman nodded and scrambled overside. Telemachus grabbed hold of the steering paddle, lashing it to the sternpost to make sure the bireme stayed on its present course. Behind him the blaze spread across the warship with stunning speed.

Gouts of flame licked out of the hatch opening, engulfing the foredeck and eating into the timbers. The heat from the fire was appalling, and he could feel it beating on his back as he fastened the paddle. When he had finished, he raced to the rail and lowered himself over the side, eyes stinging and throat burning from the acrid smoke. He could hardly breathe as he hurried down the hemp rope. In the next moment, he collapsed into the stern of the boat, coughing and choking, and at once the crew shoved off, rowing frantically away from the flame-wreathed vessel.

Telemachus caught his breath, wiped the tears from his smarting eyes and glanced round. The bireme was bearing down fast on the moored warships, aided by the breath of wind blowing in from the sea. By now the blaze had spread across most of the deck, shrouding the mast, spars and rigging in a fiery orange triangle. Panic quickly swept through the marines on the quay. Some ran off in the direction of the barracks to raise the alarm, while the rest snatched up axes and raced over to one of the triremes, hacking away at the mooring lines in a desperate attempt to get her clear from the path of the fire ship. But there was no time, and the marines scrambled clear moments before the bireme struck with a splintering crash of timbers. Her ram ploughed into the side of the larger warship, locking the two vessels together in a burst of flaming sparks. Almost immediately the fire took hold of the trireme, eating into the strake and side rail and smothering the decks in thick smoke.

'Yes!' Bassus cried excitedly, punching the air. 'Burn!'

As the flames spread across the trireme, a party of marines ran over from the direction of the warehouses, carrying water buckets and cloth sacks to dampen the inferno. Their efforts were no match for the intensity of the blaze, however, and the second trireme had already caught fire.

Just then a cry went up from the boat's crew, and Telemachus looked back at the harbour entrance to see *Poseidon's Trident* passing round the mole as she raced into the harbour. On the main wharf, several onlookers had turned away from the fires raging at the naval base and were shouting and crying out in alarm at the sight of the approaching pirate vessels. Most of them turned and fled down the thoroughfare. Some called out warnings to the marines, but their voices were lost to the roar of the flames, and the ships ploughed on unchallenged, dropping their sails and running out their sweep oars as they made directly for the naval base.

Telemachus pointed out *Trident* to the men crowding the small boat. 'There! Get us over there!'

The crew heaved at the oars as they rowed for their ship. *Trident*'s landing party had massed on the foredeck, and several of the men shouted at their comrades as they pointed out the small boat bobbing across the harbour. *Trident* slightly altered her course, bringing her alongside the boat, while the other vessels carried on towards their targets around the base. A rope ladder was hastily lowered and the pirates raced up the side of the ship. Telemachus scrambled up last, landing on the deck beside his companions. He scraped himself off the well-worn planking and caught his breath as Geras hurried over.

'Captain. You made it.' The first mate smiled with evident relief. 'Thank the gods.'

Telemachus grinned. 'That fire should give 'em something to think about. Now let's finish the job.' He pointed to a section of the wharf away from the raging fire. 'Take us over there. We'll land on the quay and cut the bastards down.'

'Aye, Captain.' Geras wheeled away and yelled at the men pulling on the sweep oars. 'You heard the captain! Faster, you lazy bastards! Or I'll have your hides for breakfast!'

As *Poseidon's Trident* bore down on the quayside, Telemachus hurriedly fastened the straps of his leather cuirass and took up his falcata and buckler, then joined the raiding party on the foredeck. To both sides he could see the ships captained by Perimedes, Scylla and some of the other pirate chiefs steering towards the vessels anchored in the harbour, while *Olympias*, *Lycus* and *Achilles*, the ship under Gentius's command, carried on towards the wharf. Ahead of them, some of the marines had finally become aware of the approaching pirate fleet and called a warning to their comrades. Those men battling the fires dropped their water buckets and snatched up their weapons, and they were swiftly followed by a large force of marines jogging over from the direction of the parade ground. Telemachus counted well over a hundred of them.

'Not good odds,' Castor muttered.

Geras frowned. 'Where did they come from? I thought there was only supposed to be a small detachment waiting for us?'

'That's what the prisoner said. Bastard must have been lying.'

The sight of the Romans sweeping forward from the parade ground chilled the blood in Telemachus's veins. He gritted his teeth and silently cursed himself for not anticipating the possibility that Canis might have left a larger force of men behind to guard Ravenna. Then the moment passed and he took a deep breath.

'We still outnumber the enemy three to one,' he replied

evenly, loudly enough for the other pirates to hear. 'We've faced worse than this and still won, boys!'

He tensed his muscles and felt the familiar dryness in his mouth at the prospect of battle, excitement mixing with the terrible fear of death or being crippled by some dreadful injury.

As *Trident* made her final approach, he turned to his men. 'Right, lads. You all know the drill. Go in hard and fast, and give the enemy no quarter. Once you've dealt with that miserable lot, you can help yourselves to plunder!'

The younger pirates erupted in a great roar of excitement. The more experienced hands knew better than to underestimate the massed ranks of Romans, and stared grimly ahead as *Trident* came up on the wharf. Then Geras shouted an order and the oars were hastily taken in with a dull grinding of timbers.

Telemachus steadied himself as *Trident* came to a juddering halt alongside the quayside, knocking several men off their feet. Recovering his balance, the pirate captain leaped over the bulwark, landing on the quayside, and pointed his falcata at the marines forming up ahead.

'Come on, boys! Get stuck in!'

CHAPTER FORTY-TWO

The pirates were still swarming over the side rail as the marines ran forward from the parade ground. Their commander shouted an order and those Romans clutching javelins hefted them up and drew back their arms. Telemachus instantly saw the threat and called out to his men. 'Raise shields!'

In the next breath, the marines released their weapons at almost point-blank range and a torrent of iron-tipped shafts flitted through the air. Most of the missiles found their targets, glancing off the curved rims of the pirates' shields or punching through the strips of leather-bound wood. Those men who were slow to react cried out as javelin shafts struck home. A few were cut down before they could reach the quay, impaled as they climbed ashore. Several others fell to the ground around Telemachus, clutching at the shafts protruding from their torsos and limbs, crying out for help. He spared them only a quick glance as he ran on.

There was time for the marines to loose a few more javelins before the men of *Poseidon's Trident* fell upon them, hacking and stabbing viciously. Telemachus pushed his way to the front of the melee and struck out at the man directly in front of him, a stocky optio with several deep scars lining his face. He was clearly an experienced soldier and he read his opponent's intentions easily, edging up his shield to deflect the blow. Telemachus's falcata glanced off the shield boss with a metallic ring, and before he could regain his balance, the Roman stabbed out at him, forcing him backwards as he parried the blow with a jarring clatter.

'My turn!' Telemachus growled.

He stabbed low, forcing the Roman to adjust his shield. As he did so, Telemachus clamped his fingers around its top edge, wrenching it down. The marine grunted in pain as the lower rim slammed down on his foot, crushing bone, and Telemachus followed up by thrusting out over the slight gap that had appeared above the Roman's shield. The blade caught the man in the throat and blood sprayed out of the deep wound, splashing down the front of his scale armour. He managed to let out a strained gurgle and then collapsed to the ground as another marine stepped forward to take his place.

This opponent was more cautious than his companion, keeping his shield raised as he aimed a measured thrust at Telemachus. The pirate threw his head back and the blade narrowly missed as it scraped over the top of his buckler. The marine's lips parted in a cruel grin as he readied to thrust again. Before he could stab out, a powerfully built pirate stepped forward and swung down with his boarding axe, roaring in triumph as he buried the blade in the Roman's spine. Telemachus just had time to nod his thanks before the pirate's cry was cut short as another marine ran him through the stomach with a spear tip, piercing his vitals.

Telemachus threw up his shield, crouching slightly as he glanced round. The early impetus of the assault had been lost, and although the two sides were closely matched in terms of numbers, the pirates' light armour and basic swordsmanship could not compete with the superior training and equipment of the Romans. Slowly the men of *Poseidon's Trident* were pushed back as the fighting skill of their opponents began to turn the tide in their favour. Around him Telemachus saw more pirates falling away, the quayside becoming slick with blood. The men of the Ravenna garrison were proving themselves to be stubborn opponents, and even in the midst of the struggle he felt a grudging admiration for them. Then he glanced over his shoulder and saw to his dismay that the pirates had been driven back almost to the edge of the wharf. Unless the rest of the fleet could land their raiding parties soon, he and his men were in danger of being overrun.

'No quarter!' he bellowed at his men, roaring his encouragement. 'Hold firm, boys!'

The pirates tore into the enemy with renewed determination. But despite their best efforts, more of *Trident*'s crew were cut down as the Romans retaliated with the grim desperation of men fighting for their lives. More than a dozen pirates had fallen and others lay clutching wounds. Amid the confusion of bodies and flickering sword points Telemachus saw young Longarus screaming for help, moments before he disappeared beneath a trample of Roman boots. Above the shouts and cries he heard the voice of the Romans' commanding officer urging his men on.

'Bastards are pushing us back,' Geras growled between snatched breaths. 'We can't hold 'em off for much longer, Captain.'

Just then a throaty cheer rose among the pirates and Telemachus glanced over at the quayside to see *Olympias* manoeuvring into the berth next to *Poseidon's Trident*. The crew vaulted across the gap to the wharf and fastened the mooring lines, then the gangplank came down, and with a mad roar Birria appeared at the front of a mass of pirates brandishing their weapons. They ran to join the fight, charging into the marines with a series of ferocious thrusts and hacking blows. The Roman officer bellowed at his men to hold their ground, but despite their best efforts they were slowly pushed back by the sheer weight of numbers opposing them. Soon Scylla's men had also landed on the quay, and under the relentless pressure the marines' resistance finally crumbled.

'That's it!' Telemachus shouted. 'We've got them now!'

Those marines further away realised that the fight was lost and backed away from the wharf. Their companions were quickly overwhelmed, with many slaughtered before they could turn and run. Others threw up their arms in surrender, but the pirates were in no mood for mercy. The Romans' pleas were ignored and they were brutally slaughtered where they stood. More pirates broke off to chase down the fleeing marines, killing them as they attempted to retreat across the parade ground. On the other side of the harbour, the remaining pirate crews had closed on the ships riding at anchor, and wisps of smoke trickled into the sky as they started fires in the holds of the Roman vessels.

'Thank the gods,' Geras said, sweat glistening on his brow. 'Took Birria long enough to catch up with us, though. Can't say I'm impressed with the timing of our brother captains.'

'No,' Telemachus responded curtly. This was not the time to indulge the petty rivalry that existed between the gangs. 'Virbius!'

The pirate strode over, breathing heavily. Telemachus fixed his eyes on him and pointed out the gatehouse.

'Get a few men over there and deal with the guards. I want those barrack blocks cleared out too. Once you've done that, you can start torching the base. Warehouses, storage sheds, workshops. Burn everything. Is that clear?'

'Aye, Captain.'

The ship's mate hurried off and yelled at a cluster of nearby pirates who were busy looting the corpses littering the wharf. They stuffed their spoils into their slings and followed Virbius over to the gatehouse. Further away, a section of marines was making a last defiant stand against Birria's men, but the arrival of the rest of the pirate ships had decided the issue and the remaining Romans were doomed. It was now simply a case of killing any survivors and ensuring the complete destruction of the base.

As the other men tramped off, Telemachus called Geras and Bassus over. 'You two,' he said. 'Follow me. We're going to free the prisoners.'

They set off at a quick trot across the parade ground, moving away from the skirmish as they headed for the fleet headquarters. Ahead of them a loose throng of guards, officials and off-duty sailors fled from the base through the main entrance, disappearing into the narrow dark streets of Ravenna. Telemachus shifted his attention to the fleet headquarters and quickly spotted the discreet studded door built into the side of the building, used to access the cells running beneath the ground. It was just as the Roman prisoner had described. Three guards stood outside, their spears held ready as they stared anxiously at their comrades fleeing for the gate.

As Telemachus looked on, one of the guards turned and

called out to his companions, 'Get down there and kill the prisoners!'

At once the two marines turned away and flung open the side door. Telemachus felt his throat constrict with dread as he saw them disappearing through the shadowy opening, and he broke into a sprint, roaring madly, 'Get them! Stop the bastards!'

He raced ahead of his comrades, chest pounding, driven on by a desperate urge to prevent the Romans from executing his brother. He raised his shield and barged the first man aside, cutting him down, then charged into the gloom, squinting in the flickering light provided by the torches fixed on brackets to the wall. In a few short breaths he was at the bottom of the stone stairs. A narrow tunnel stretched out before him, dimly illuminated by torchlight, with several cell doors on either side. The two marines stood outside the door at the far end, one of them sliding back the bolt while the other gripped his short sword as he prepared to kill the prisoners.

'No! No you fucking don't!' Telemachus yelled as he charged forward.

At the sound of his voice, the nearer of the two guards spun round, lowering his sword and shaping to attack. Telemachus raised his shield, tucking his chin against his chest as the Roman thrust at him. The sword tip glanced off the buckler with a clatter, and he carried on running. The Roman grunted as the buckler struck him in the midriff and knocked him to the ground. Before he could pick himself up, Telemachus fell upon him with a savage thrust through his eye, deep into his skull, killing him instantly. He pulled back his weapon with a slithering hiss just as Geras and Bassus raced past him and hurled themselves at the second guard.

The glimmering light from the torches threw shadows across the wall as they cut down the Roman in the confines of the tunnel. Geras had slammed him against the stone wall and punched his blade deep into the man's groin, twisting the weapon viciously as the marine squirmed and groaned, while Bassus roared as he hacked repeatedly at the guard with his broadaxe. He took another mighty swing at the man's skull, as if chopping wood, then looked up to meet Geras's amused gaze.

'What?' the Thracian snapped.

'I think he's dead, Bassus.'

'Come on,' Telemachus ordered, sheathing his sword. 'There's no time to lose. Hurry!'

He rushed forward, approaching the cell door, Bassus stepping aside to make way. From the other side of the door he could hear low voices, and he felt his heart thumping with longing as he worked the bolt free and pulled open the door.

A rank odour of shit, piss and sweat filled his nostrils as he entered the cell. There was a tiny window high up on the rear wall, covered with a grating that permitted only a thin shard of moonlight. In the near corner a slop bucket overflowing with human filth sat next to a pair of soiled straw mattresses. Several dark shapes were huddled together in the middle of the chamber, and at the sight of Telemachus, the nearest man edged away from the door, the chains chinking around his ankles and wrists.

'It's them fucking Romans,' the prisoner growled in Greek. 'They've come back for us. We're done for, boys.'

Telemachus glanced down at himself and suddenly remembered that he and Geras were still dressed in their Roman navy garments. He lowered his shield and smiled at the trembling figure in front of him. 'Try again.'

The man hesitated for a moment. Then he inched forward, peering up cautiously at Telemachus's forearm. 'Hang on. That mark. I recognise it.' He looked more closely, his eyes widening in their sockets. 'You're with *Poseidon's Trident*?'

The young captain nodded. 'I'm Telemachus, commander of *Trident*. These are my men, Geras and Bassus.'

The prisoner grinned. 'Name's Duras. How did you find us?'

'There's no time for that,' Telemachus responded as he sheathed his weapon. 'We'll explain everything later. Right now, we need to get moving. We're here to rescue you all.'

Duras breathed an audible sigh of relief and smiled, revealing several missing teeth. In the thin light of the cell, Telemachus could see that the man's body was covered in welts and bruises, his hair matted into clumps with blood. 'Thank the gods,' Duras croaked. 'D'you hear that, boys? We're saved!'

A few of the other prisoners whispered in excitement and relief. Others were too weak to speak, and it took all their strength to sit upright and lift their heads to look at their liberators. Telemachus glanced round at their drawn faces and frowned.

'Where's my brother? Nereus?'

Duras sniffed and lowered his eyes. 'They took him away.'

A feeling of cold dread twisted like a knife through Telemachus. He stared at the prisoner. 'When?'

'A few days ago.' Duras scratched his unkempt beard. 'Two of them guards came for him in the morning, just before dawn. Cruel, nasty pieces of work, they are. Nereus thought they were going to kill him, but they just laughed and said they had orders to take him on board the flagship. Said Canis wanted to take him out with the fleet when they set sail.'

'Why?' Telemachus demanded.

Duras looked at him. 'One of the guards said Canis had a special treat planned for you. He was going to crush your fleet in battle and then kill Nereus in front of you. The guards reckoned he was looking forward to seeing the look on your face as you watched Nereus die.'

'No . . . no!'

Telemachus balled his hands into tight, trembling fists. At that moment he felt a raging hatred for Canis, and he knew there was no death that the Roman prefect did not deserve, no torture that was too horrific for him. There was no way he could save his brother now, he realised despairingly. As soon as Canis learned of the destruction of the Ravenna base, he would surely put Nereus to death. His efforts had been for nothing.

'Captain,' Geras said softly after a moment. 'We have to get out of here. We have to leave Ravenna before Canis returns.'

'Yes.' Telemachus took a deep breath, pushing aside the black anger and grief swirling in his chest. He nodded at Duras. 'Can you walk?'

'I'll manage. But some of the others are in a bad way.'

'My men will help you.' Telemachus indicated the doorway. 'Our ships are waiting for us on the quay. We'll get you on board and sail out of here as soon as we've finished sacking the base.'

'What about the guards?' Duras asked.

'Taken care of,' Geras replied, cocking a thumb at the corridor.

Duras made a face. 'Pity. I would've liked to see those

cruel bastards suffer. The things they did to me and the other lads . . .'

Telemachus dropped to one knee beside Duras and worked the pins free from the manacles around his hands. Then he did the same for the shackles on his ankles while Geras and Bassus moved around the dank chamber releasing the other prisoners from their bonds.

Duras rubbed his swollen wrists and nodded faintly. 'Thanks.' He winced. 'Sorry about your brother. For what it's worth, he was a good lad. Tough. Never complained, never showed those Roman bastards any fear.'

Telemachus managed a sad smile. 'That sounds like the Nereus I know. Come on. Let's get out of this stinking pit.'

He offered his hand. Duras took it, grimacing as Telemachus heaved him to his feet. Then the pirate captain slipped an arm around his back and they walked slowly out of the cell, with the rest of the prisoners shuffling along a few paces behind. Several had been so badly beaten and starved that they were barely able to stand upright, and they made painfully slow progress as they retraced their steps down the tunnel.

An icy hatred closed around Telemachus's heart as they climbed the narrow flight of stairs leading to the dungeon entrance. He thought of Nereus, chained up in the hold of the Roman flagship, waiting to suffer a painful death. His anger hardened, and he swore revenge on Canis for what he had done, vowing to the gods that he would make the prefect suffer for the misery he had caused. Whatever it took.

CHAPTER FORTY-THREE

The first pale loom of dawn was fringing the horizon as the pirates emerged from the headquarters building. Outside, the destruction of the Ravenna base was already well under way. Fires had broken out in the store sheds as torch parties rushed from one building to the next, setting the base's supplies of cordage, spars and sailcloth alight. Another crew, under the command of Criton, had landed on the main wharf and looted the grain stores and commercial warehouses. Although the pirates were under strict orders to leave the local population unharmed, Telemachus had known that some of the men would disobey him, and the screams of womenfolk carried through the air as a handful of pirates pillaged the nearest homes, driven on by a combination of lust and greed.

Closer to the quay, more crews descended upon the beached warships, snatching up vats of steaming hot tar and tossing them over the hulls before they applied torches to them, the flames quickly consuming the pitch-soaked timbers. Soon roaring infernos and billowing smoke drove the raiders back and they went in search of fresh prey. Other parties carried across the loot from the base: the garrison pay chests and ample supplies of lead shot, javelin shafts and quivers of arrows.

The coming morning would reveal the full scale of the destruction. There would be nothing left of the naval base except ruined buildings and the blackened ribs of the warships. It would take months for Rome to repair the damage, at enormous cost to the imperial treasury. And then there was the incalculable damage to the Romans' arrogant pride. The shocking assault on Ravenna would live long in the memory of every Roman citizen.

Telemachus surveyed the scene with a feeling of satisfaction tinged with despair. The attack had gone as well as he had dared to hope. But any pleasure at the sight of the burning warships was tempered by the knowledge that his attempt to rescue his brother had ended in failure. Nereus was gone. In a few hours' time, he would most likely be put to death, and there was nothing Telemachus could do about it. An attack on the Roman fleet at sea was out of the question. Even if he could persuade the other captains to join him, Canis would almost certainly kill his brother before Telemachus could get to him. It was hopeless, he conceded bitterly.

A trio of deckhands stood beside the gangplank of *Poseidon's Trident*, arms folded as they enviously watched their comrades wreaking their destruction. Telemachus called out to the ship's carpenter.

'Get these men on board, Proculus,' he said, gesturing to the line of bedraggled prisoners. 'Take them below to the hold and see to it that they're fed and clothed. Fetch the medicine chest and treat their injuries as best you can.'

'Aye, Captain.'

As the first prisoners trudged up the gangway, Telemachus looked round and saw Virbius padding over, followed by a small party of *Trident*'s men. The pirate glanced quickly at the prisoners with an arched eyebrow. 'You found your brother, Captain?'

Telemachus shook his head, determined not to reveal his black mood. 'Canis has taken him. There's nothing we can do. What about the defences?'

'Fires are all set. Birria sent a few of his men over to the gatehouse to break up the catapults. It'll be a while before the Romans are able to get this place up and running again.'

'Did you take any prisoners?'

'A few of them Roman dogs barricaded themselves in one of the barrack blocks. I had the lads seal the exits and set fire to the building. They'll burn nice and slow, like.'

'Then our work here is almost done.' Telemachus nodded towards the devastated base. 'Round up the men and spread the word to the other captains. I want everyone formed up on the quayside within the hour.'

Virbius's expression soured. 'What for? Our lads ain't got round to looting the town yet, for fuck's sake.'

Telemachus pointed to the faintest glimmer on the horizon. 'Dawn's almost upon us. We must be out of here as swiftly as possible.'

'But Captain—'

'That's an order, Virbius.'

At the gangplank, Duras turned round and froze as he stared at the man Telemachus had been addressing.

'What?' Telemachus asked. 'What is it?'

'That name. Virbius. I've heard it before.'

Telemachus looked sidelong at Virbius. The pirate stared at Duras with a blank expression on his face, but Telemachus thought he saw a flicker of unease there. He turned back to the prisoner. 'When? Tell me.'

'About a month ago. When the Romans captured our ship.'

'You're sure?'

'I remember the day as if it was yesterday.' Duras winced painfully before he went on. 'Me and the boys were raiding off the Apulian coast. We'd had a successful voyage and were getting ready to set sail back to Illyricum when a Roman squadron showed up and trapped us in a bay. Most of our lads were cut down before they could surrender. A few of the crew tried to escape, but they were caught and killed, and the rest of us were put on a ship bound for Ravenna to be sold into slavery. One of the Romans started bragging during the journey. A right gobby bastard. He said the pirates weren't as much of a brotherhood as they claimed to be, and that a pirate called Virbius had even stitched up his own captain, telling them the whereabouts of his enslaved brother.'

Telemachus's gaze slid back to Virbius. 'Is this true?'

'Course it fucking ain't!' the mate exploded. 'Why in the name of the gods would I betray anyone to the Romans? He's mistaken, Captain. Or lying.'

'No.' Duras shook his head forcefully and pointed a trembling finger at Virbius. 'I know what I heard. Virbius . . . that's the name of the pirate who sold your brother out. I swear it.'

Virbius folded his arms across his broad chest and smiled thinly. 'It's your word against mine. You can't prove a thing.'

'Ask any of the other boys,' Duras said, addressing himself to Telemachus. 'They were on the ship with me. They'll tell you the same thing.'

Telemachus turned to Virbius and smiled cruelly. 'You

should have covered your tracks better. Then you might have got away with your plot to replace me as captain.'

A look of uncertainty flashed across Virbius's face. 'Plot, Captain? I don't know what you're talking about.'

'I think you do.' Telemachus took a step closer to the pirate. 'Duras's story confirms what I suspected. You see, I already know that someone handed over a scroll to the captain of a merchant ship, telling him to deliver it to Ravenna. A ship that we captured, as it happens. The *Delphinus*.'

Virbius's expression tightened. 'Who the fuck told you that?'

'That optio we captured,' Telemachus explained. 'Calidus. At first he claimed he didn't know the name of the ship in question. But he remembered it later on, after Sciron threatened to gouge his eyes out.'

'That don't mean a thing. Any one of us could've handed over that scroll.'

'But only one of us argued long and hard to spare the lives of the crew. You, Virbius.' Telemachus jabbed an accusing finger at him. 'Admit it. You're the one who handed over the scroll.'

There was a pause as every pair of eyes simultaneously looked towards Virbius. The mate glanced round at the faces of his fellow pirates as if gauging their reaction. Then he appeared to reach a decision and shrugged. 'All right. I did it. So bloody what?'

'Why?' Telemachus demanded.

'Why d'you think? You were the captain's favourite. It was obvious that Bulla would appoint you as his successor. I couldn't be having that. Some arrogant young twat taking from me what was mine by right.'

'So you hatched a plan to get rid of me. Is that it?'

'More or less. I knew about your brother after I overheard you chatting to some of the lads about him. Telling them that you'd do anything to get him back. All I needed to do was get a message to Ravenna and let the Romans do the rest. It would have worked, only that fool Bulla stopped you from handing yourself over to the enemy.'

Telemachus glowered at the mate. 'You betrayed me.'

'Bollocks!' Virbius spat, indignant with outrage. 'I ain't no traitor. I was doing what's right for the crew. Making sure they got the captain they deserved.'

'Meaning you.'

'This ain't about me, boy. You never deserved to be captain. Whatever I did, it was for the good of the ship.'

'Liar.' Telemachus stepped into the pirate's face, his right hand clasped around the ivory handle of his falcata. 'You're a traitor, Virbius. To your captain, and your crew.'

Virbius chuckled mirthlessly. 'And what are you going to do about it? Throw me in chains? Challenge me to a duel? With the support I've got from the other lads, you wouldn't dare.' His eyes glowed brightly. 'As a matter of fact, I think it's time for a change in leadership.'

He brought up his sword in a sudden blur of movement, aiming the point at Telemachus before the captain could wrench his weapon from its scabbard. Telemachus froze, the sword tip mere inches from his neck, as Virbius called out to two of his close comrades. The pirates, burly veterans, came rushing over to the quay, looking from the first mate to the captain.

'It's time, boys,' Virbius said, grinning at them. 'We're taking over the ship. Stick this worthless shit in the hold with the prisoners. We'll dump him overside as soon as we're clear of the port.'

Telemachus stared at him, veins simmering. Around him, several more of the pirates had hurried over to witness the drama unfolding in front of *Trident*. 'You can't do this. I'm your captain.'

'Not any more, you ain't. Me and these other lads are in charge of the crew now. As it should be. As for the rest of the men, some of them might still support you, but they'll soon fall into line once they see you being fed to the fishes. It's over, boy. No hard feelings.' Virbius smiled thinly and tipped his head at the veterans. 'Take him away.'

As the pair moved forward, there was a sudden gasp from Virbius. The first mate jolted, eyes bulging in shock and surprise. Telemachus lowered his gaze and saw the curved point of a sword protruding from the pirate's stomach. A dark red patch spread across his tunic as Virbius pawed dumbly at the glistening sword tip. Then the blade withdrew and he let out a grunt of pain before slumping to the ground.

Telemachus looked up and saw Geras standing over the dying pirate, blood dripping from his weapon as he looked round at the stunned crew, daring them to defy him. 'Who else wants to join this miserable wretch in the afterlife? Anyone?'

The two veterans either side of Telemachus hesitated for a beat as they stared in shock and horror at Virbius's bloodied body writhing on the deck. Bassus had also drawn his weapon and stood ready to attack. Then the pair stepped slowly back, raising their hands in surrender. Geras kept his sword pointed at them as he barked an order at the deckhands.

'Take these two traitors below. Put them in chains in the hold. If they protest or try to resist, kill them.'

The deckhands sprang into action, grabbing hold of the veterans and marching them up the gangplank and over to the aft hatch leading below deck. They were followed by Duras and the other prisoners, and the rest of the pirates, muttering among themselves as they stepped round the dying Virbius, who lay gasping for his last breaths.

Geras wiped his blade on the pirate's tunic and straightened up, staring down at the body with a contemptuous expression. 'Good riddance. I've been wanting to do that for a while.'

Telemachus nodded. 'I owe you.'

'What for? That twat was getting too big for his boots. About time someone cut him down to size. Besides, he was guilty of mutiny. Can't be having that now, can we?'

Telemachus smiled at his close friend, grateful for his loyalty in a world where every man seemed to be only looking out for himself. 'Thanks. For having my back.'

'Thank me later. With a drink. Or ten. After the night we've had, I could fucking use one.'

'Deal.'

Just then, one of the deckhands aboard *Poseidon's Trident* called out. 'Captain! Over here!'

'Shit,' Geras growled. 'What now?'

Without replying, Telemachus strode briskly up the gangplank and marched over to the side rail, stretching up on his toes as he squinted in the direction the pirate had indicated. At first he could see nothing except the harbour entrance and the open sea beyond. Then he stared again and saw it. The distinct outline of a large ship, black against the red of the gathering dawn. No more than a mile away from the mole and closing fast.

Castor and Geras had both hurried over to the rail and

caught sight of the vessel too. 'Merchantman?' the latter asked.

Telemachus bit his lip, then shook his head. 'Ain't likely. Any merchant captain worth his salt would have turned around as soon as they spotted the fires.'

'Then who is it?'

'Look, Captain!' cried the pirate to the right of Telemachus, thrusting out an arm. 'More sails approaching. Five of 'em!'

'Five?' Geras's face whitened in horror. 'No . . .'

'The Ravenna fleet,' Castor muttered. 'It's them. Has to be.'

The ships grew more distinct as they emerged from the gloom, and from the size of the leading vessel, Telemachus realised he was looking at a Roman trireme. *Neptune*. The flagship of the Ravenna fleet. Five smaller ships, biremes, were sailing in tight formation close behind, their rams churning up the calm sea as they came on. All six warships ran out their oars as they took in their sails and surged towards the harbour mole.

'How did they get back here so quickly?' Geras wondered.

'Canis must have realised we'd tricked him as soon as those ships turned and fled. He'll have ordered his crews to double back through the night instead of pursuing them.'

'Either way, the bastards have got us trapped. There's no way we can give them the slip now, Captain.'

Telemachus clenched his jaw as he watched the sails on the horizon. At their current speed, the warships would close on the harbour long before the pirate fleet could gather their forces and reach the open sea. Even if *Poseidon's Trident* and one or two of the faster sailers managed to somehow slip past the warships, the slower vessels would be easy prey, picked off by the enemy and captured before they could escape. But even as Telemachus cursed himself for being bested by Canis, another terrible thought prodded at him.

Geras looked sidelong at his captain. 'What about your brother? He's on the flagship, isn't he?'

'That's what Duras reckoned.'

'If he's still alive,' Castor said. 'And if he is, he won't be for much longer.'

'What are we going to do, Captain?' asked Geras.

Telemachus drew a breath, biting back on his frustration as he turned to Castor. 'Order the men back to the ships. I want everyone ready for action immediately. We'll give the Romans the fight of their lives.'

The quartermaster hesitated for the slightest moment before he turned and sprinted back down the gangway. Geras stared at his captain in astonishment. 'We're going to take on the warships, sir?'

'We can't escape,' Telemachus replied. 'There's no time. Fighting them is our only chance of getting out of here alive.'

'But they'll sink us, surely?'

'Not necessarily. If we take them on in the main harbour, our smaller ships will be able to outmanoeuvre their biremes. Which should give us the upper hand.'

'And your brother, Captain?'

Telemachus pointed out the trireme. 'We'll close on the flagship before any damage can be done to her. That'll give us the chance to take her out of the fight, overrun the crew and rescue Nereus before that dog Canis has a chance to kill him.'

Geras parted his lips in a wicked grin. 'Perhaps the gods will give us the chance to have our revenge on Canis after all.'

'If we live that long.'

As the men ran to their stations, Telemachus cupped his

hands and called across to *Olympias*. 'Pass the word! Every ship to form up on us! We'll attack the enemy in the main harbour!'

Birria and his men exchanged heated words, and for an anxious moment Telemachus feared that they would refuse to obey. Then Birria spun away from the rail and bellowed urgently at his men. The orders were swiftly relayed to those ships anchored in the naval harbour, while the landing parties ran back over to the quayside, scrambling up the gangplanks of their respective vessels. Once the last stragglers had returned to *Poseidon's Trident*, the gangway was taken in and the mooring lines were slipped. Then the deckhands took up the sweep oars and fended *Trident* away from the wharf, with *Olympias* and the other vessels following close behind. Their crews strained at the oars as they steered round the smouldering wreckage of the light craft and military packets and made for the main harbour.

As he looked beyond the bows, Telemachus saw that the Roman warships had drawn much closer now. The nimbler biremes had raced ahead of *Neptune* and were no more than a hundred paces from the mole. The flagship showed no signs of the damage she had sustained after running aground in the sandspit a few weeks ago, and Telemachus guessed that she must have been taken back for repairs at Ravenna shortly after. At this distance he could see the flagship's pennant fluttering like a purple tongue atop the masthead. He searched the tiny helmeted figures on the deck of the trireme, looking for any sign of Canis or Nereus, but it was still too gloomy to see properly.

He watched for a moment longer before he called out across the water to *Lycus*, the nearest vessel. 'I want the flagship taken in one piece! We need to capture it!'

As the hands on *Lycus*'s deck shouted the message across to the other pirate ships, Telemachus ordered Bassus to prepare slings and arrows. The Thracian moved off, shouting orders, and every spare hand on deck rushed to help carry up the supplies of lead shot, javelin shafts and bows they had seized from the naval base. As the rest of the pirates formed up on the foredeck, gripping their swords, axes and shields in preparation to face the enemy, the biremes cleared the breakwater ahead of *Neptune* and spread out as far as possible in the tight confines of the harbour, heading for the pirate vessels a short distance away.

Telemachus turned to the steersman and indicated the nearest bireme. 'Make for that ship, Calkas!'

'Aye, Captain.'

The bows swung round and *Poseidon's Trident* aimed head-on for the larger vessel. Across the harbour, the other pirate ships targeted the rest of the biremes. Telemachus knew he would have to tackle the smaller warships before he could turn his attention to *Neptune*. Even then, he might be too late to save his brother. The flagship might be sunk during the struggle. Or Canis might decide to execute Nereus before *Trident* could get close enough to board. The mental torment briefly threatened to overwhelm him, and he shifted his gaze back to the bireme directly ahead, willing *Trident* across the harbour. As they came within extreme missile range, he filled his lungs and addressed his men.

'This is going to be a hard fight, lads. Harder than we've ever had before. Fight like tigers, and don't give the Romans an inch. Remember Peiratispolis! Remember your fallen brothers!'

The men around him cheered wildly, stabbing their

weapons in the air and beating their shields as *Poseidon's Trident* bore down on the bireme. A mass of helmets and weapons were visible on the deck of the warship, glinting in the glow of the rising flames from the naval base. The two sides were closely matched in terms of ships and numbers, and Telemachus knew that the pirates would have to rely on their superior seamanship and fighting determination if they were going to triumph.

They were no more than a hundred paces away from the bireme when he heard a bellowed order from the deck of the other ship. A moment later, a shower of dark shafts arced through the pale sky and plunged down towards the massed ranks of pirates on the foredeck.

'Shields up!' Telemachus cried.

Most of the arrows were well aimed, thudding into raised shields, while others struck the timbers and the strake in front of *Trident's* bows. One arrow punched through the hand of a pirate who had braced himself against the side rail, pinning his palm to the rough surface. The man howled in pain and Geras ordered one of his comrades to prise him free. The bireme continued to hold her course as she headed directly for the pirates, and it was clear that her captain intended to ram *Trident* head-on. There was time for the Romans to release a few more missiles before Telemachus judged they were close enough. Then he called out to the steersman, 'Take her on the port side!'

Calkas made a slight adjustment to their course, pointing *Trident's* bows away from the bireme's prow. As she veered away, Geras roared at the oarsmen, and the sweeps were taken in moments before *Trident* surged down the length of the warship. The bireme was slower to respond, and some of her oars were smashed to pieces by the bows of the passing pirate vessel with a chorus of splintering cracks. Those pirates armed with bows or slings took the opportunity to release a savage volley at the marines and sailors on the deck of the bireme, killing or wounding at least a dozen. Their cries of agony split the air as *Trident* cleared the length of the bireme and came out beyond the Roman's stern.

'Got her!' Geras cried, punching the air. 'She's ours now, Captain.'

'Good work.' Telemachus nodded at the steersman. 'Now bring us around and let's finish the job.'

The deck shifted beneath him as Calkas heaved on the paddle, swinging *Trident* round as she prepared to ram the damaged bireme in the stern. The warship wallowed helplessly in the swell as the trierarch screamed orders at his sailors, urging them to use the remaining oars to turn the ship to face the enemy. But before Telemachus could give the order, another pirate ship lurched forward and raced down the side of the vessel. The pirates on board launched their grappling hooks and pulled the two vessels closer together, then leaped across to finish off the disoriented enemy in a shimmer of glinting sword points and spear tips.

'Greedy bastards,' Geras muttered. 'That was our ship.'

'Doesn't matter! One down, five more to go.'

Telemachus cast his gaze around the harbour, looking for *Neptune*. The two sides were locked in a desperate struggle, and neither had yet gained the upper hand. *Lycus*, the ship commanded by Criton, had been rammed by another bireme. The marines were pouring over the side of the stricken vessel, and hurling themselves on to the defenders. Another pirate ship had rammed its opponent close to the stern, and the bireme's deck was already flooding as the panicked sailors and marines jumped down into the water, where they were picked off by the archers and slingers lining the pirate ship's foredeck. Elsewhere, the remaining ships had closed on their Roman counterparts and the calm waters of the harbour had become a desperate battlefield.

Neptune had passed through the tangle of ships unharmed and was swinging her bows round to search for a pirate vessel to close with. Geras cried out, thrusting his arm across the rail, and Telemachus looked on in horror as Birria's ship bore down directly on the undefended side of the Roman flagship. Some of the marines were aware of the onrushing threat and shouted at the steersman, but the sluggish trireme was moving too slowly, and a few moments later a grinding crash filled the air as *Olympias* struck her in her side, shattering the hull. The impact knocked scores of the marines off their feet, and several men tumbled overside, screaming as they fell into the sea. As the water rushed into the breach, the first pirates launched their grappling hooks and leaped across, yelling madly.

Telemachus slapped a fist against his thigh. 'Stupid bastard! What the hell does he think he's doing?'

Geras shook his head bitterly. 'Not his fault, Captain. He doesn't know Nereus is on board.'

Telemachus cupped his spare hand to his mouth, pointing his drawn falcata at the flagship. 'Calkas! Take us over there! *Now!*'

The water churned beneath the oars of *Poseidon's Trident* as she swung round again until her bows were pointing directly at the other side of *Neptune*. Ahead of them, the marines had recovered and were putting up a determined resistance on the deck of the flagship, hurling javelins and shooting arrows at the pirates jumping across from *Olympias*. Telemachus watched the struggle, maddened with frustration. With the breach in her hull, it was only a matter of time before *Neptune* was lost to the sea. And unless *Trident* could close on the trireme in time, Nereus would go down with her, assuming he still lived.

Around them the battle between the two fleets continued to rage. One bireme commander had ordered his men to loose fire arrows, and the glittering missiles arced lazily through the grey sky before thudding down on the deck of the pirate ship she was attacking. The pirates frantically rushed across to extinguish the flames, distracting them long enough for the bireme to draw close and release her grappling lines, tethering the two ships together. Telemachus looked ahead again and saw that *Neptune* was less than a hundred paces away now, the sword points and helmets of the marines glinting on the deck as they clashed with Birria's men. A figure in a crested helmet and bright red cloak stood apart from the fighting, urging his men on, and Telemachus felt his heart harden as he recognised the man. Canis. The Roman prefect who had tormented him ever since he had turned pirate. Now, at last, he would have the opportunity for revenge.

Some of the marines turned away from the fight and looked on in horror as *Trident* rushed towards the beam of the Roman flagship. Telemachus grasped the rail with his free hand and shouted at his men as the gap between the two ships rapidly narrowed.

'Brace yourselves, boys!'

CHAPTER FORTY-FOUR

The pirates held fast to the side rails as *Poseidon's Trident* surged towards the trireme. *Trident* was too small to ram the flagship without damaging herself, and at the last instant Calkas hauled on the paddle, swinging the bows away so that the pirate vessel swept round and came alongside her target in a well-executed manoeuvre. The oars were hastily drawn in and there was a jarring shudder as *Trident*'s beam crashed up against the side of the Roman ship.

'Ready lines!' Telemachus roared. 'Release!'

At his command, those pirates wielding grappling lines swung them across to the warship and pulled them taut. They hurriedly cleated them and grabbed their weapons before rushing to join the rest of the boarders swarming up the ropes. Telemachus sheathed his own weapon, then grasped one of the lines in both hands and hauled himself up the side of the Roman flagship, clambering over the side rail and swinging down on to the deck. Landing with a thud, he tore his falcata from his scabbard and looked up.

At the far end of the deck, Birria and the remainder of his men had been pushed back towards the side rail as they fought desperately against the enemy. The oarsmen had abandoned their wooden benches, snatching up weapons and joining the fight. From across the deck Telemachus heard a shout as a section of marines broke away from the skirmish and rushed over to contain the new threat. Canis was obviously a shrewd commander and had foreseen that he must deal with Birria and his crew before he could turn his full attention to the pirates boarding from *Poseidon's Trident*.

'Go!' Telemachus called out to his men. 'Get stuck in! Quick, unless you want Birria's lot to take all the glory!'

The men of *Poseidon's Trident* charged forward, leaping over the collapsed rigging and shouting their challenges and battle cries as their curved blades and axes crashed down against Roman shields. Telemachus threw himself at a well-built marine wearing scale armour. The marine dropped his shoulder and thrust out with his short sword at the pirate captain. Telemachus met the blow with his buckler, then punched out with his falcata and caught the Roman on the chest. The blade did not pierce the armour, but the blow drove the marine back, and as he gasped for breath, Telemachus smashed his buckler into the man's face, knocking him to the deck. He followed up with a sharp downward thrust of his shield, slamming the rim against the marine's throat and crushing his windpipe.

Before the marines could close ranks, more pirates leaped down from *Trident* to the deck of the trireme and charged into the chaotic melee. The Romans fought hard to maintain their position, deflecting blows and aiming measured, precise stabs at the pirates. Amid the glimmering sword points and armour, Telemachus caught a fleeting glimpse of Canis's crested helmet as he shouted at his men, imploring them to stand firm. But despite their fighting discipline, the Romans were now heavily outnumbered, fatally trapped between the two pirate crews.

Telemachus sensed that the fight was turning in their favour, and he shouted encouragement at his men. 'We've got 'em now! Keep going, lads!'

The crews of *Poseidon's Trident* and *Olympias* threw themselves against their weakened opponents with renewed determination, cutting down more of the Romans. Nearly three hundred men now crowded the deck of the trireme. There was almost no space to move as the remaining marines were driven back towards the mast, while others retreated towards the stern. Above the cries and grunts of the fighting men, Telemachus heard the groan of timbers, and then he felt the deck shudder beneath him as water flooded into the hold, placing an intolerable strain on the ship. The deck shifted again, and several of the men on both sides lost their footing on the blood-streaked planking and slipped, tumbling to the floor in a dull clatter of weapons and equipment.

'We'll have to get off this ship soon, Captain!' Geras shouted. 'Before the bastard sinks and takes us with her!'

Telemachus gritted his teeth and nodded as he grasped the danger. With *Olympias* rammed into one side of *Neptune* and *Poseidon's Trident* tethered to her opposite side, both pirate vessels would be dragged down with the flagship once she succumbed to the water flooding her hold.

He surveyed the deck of the trireme, muscles glistening with sweat. Only a small cluster of marines continued to defy the pirates, their shields raised as they absorbed the torrent of blows raining down on them from the two crews. Telemachus pushed his way towards the front of the skirmish at the stern, searching for Canis amid the remaining Romans, but there was no sign of the prefect's crested helmet. He looked up as a marine launched himself forward and lunged at him. Telemachus threw his shield up and blocked the attack with a loud clang. Before the man could snatch his weapon back, the pirate to the left of him stabbed out with his spear, burying the tip in the side of the Roman's torso. The blow carried the man back, knocking two of his comrades to the ground.

The deck trembled again as the last marines retreated towards the mast. Some of them, realising that *Neptune* was doomed, hurriedly threw off their weapons and shields and jumped over the side, preferring to take their chances in the water. Most were lost as the weight of their armour pulled them down, while others died as scores of pirates rushed over to the rail and threw javelins down at the defenceless figures. Those still aboard tried to surrender but were cut down by the advancing pirates. With the death of many of their comrades, the will to fight on had gone, and the last Romans were swiftly hacked to pieces or run through with spear points.

Birria smiled with relief at Telemachus, his face and arms spattered with Roman blood. 'Took you long enough to reach us. Getting to be a bit of a habit, my friend. Coming to each other's rescue.'

Telemachus nodded. There was no time to berate the captain for his reckless decision to ram the trireme. 'Get your men across to your own ship and cast her loose. Quickly, before this one sinks.'

Birria nodded and called out, 'Back to *Olympias*, boys! No time for looting! Get a fucking move on!'

The men abandoned the bodies they had been searching and made their way back over the rail. Those who could walk helped their wounded companions to their feet and carried them across until the last man had abandoned *Neptune*. At the same time, Geras bellowed orders at *Trident*'s crew to return to their own vessel.

As the pirates clambered back across the narrow gap, Telemachus looked anxiously round the bloody carnage strewn across the deck. 'Where's Canis? And Nereus, my brother? Where are they?'

Birria frowned. 'I don't understand. Canis was here a few moments ago.'

Telemachus frantically scanned the broken bodies around the mast, looking for any sign of the Roman prefect amid the dead and dying. Then a strident voice called out from near the aft cargo hatch.

'Telemachus!'

The young captain whipped round and saw Canis emerging on to the deck from the narrow stairs leading down to his cabin. The prefect stopped in front of the opening, resplendent in his gleaming scale armour, polished helmet and ankle greaves. In front of him stood a hollow-cheeked figure, tall and dark-haired and dressed in a filthy torn tunic. Canis held a dagger to the man's neck, the tip pressed against his soft skin.

Telemachus took one look at the dishevelled figure and felt his throat choke with emotion. A face he hadn't seen in ten years, but one that he recognised all the same.

'Nereus . . .' He moved towards his brother, stepping over the body of a slain Roman at his feet.

Canis pressed the dagger tip harder against Nereus's neck, drawing a wince of pain from his captive. The Roman's cold blue eyes glared at Telemachus. 'That's close enough,' he said in Latin. 'Come any closer and I'll slice open his throat, I swear by Jupiter.'

Telemachus stopped a few paces away. A bitter rage fired

up in his guts as he took in the extent of his brother's injuries. Several scars and reddened welts were visible on his arms and face, and two of the fingers on his left hand had been severed, leaving gnarled stumps.

'What have you done to him?' he demanded.

'Nothing the wretch didn't deserve,' Canis replied haughtily. 'But he'll suffer even more unless you do exactly as I say.'

'Let him go, you bastard!'

The prefect chuckled. 'I don't think so. You see, I had planned on killing Nereus in front of you, after I'd crushed your fleet in battle. A fitting triumph, no? But after your little deception, he is worth far more to me alive than dead. Either you do as I say, or I'll kill him.'

'What do you want?' Telemachus asked warily.

'Safe passage off this ship. I'll need the ship's tender and two of my men at the oars. If any harm comes to me, or anyone attempts to follow us, Nereus dies.'

'Don't do it, brother!' Nereus pleaded. 'Don't let him get away with it!'

Geras drew alongside Telemachus and snorted at the Roman prefect. 'Do you really expect us to believe you'd kill him? You do that, me and the lads will gut you before you get very far.'

'I'm prepared to die, pirate. I've nothing to lose.'

'Bollocks to this.' Geras spat on the deck and took a step towards Canis, gripping the handle of his sword. Telemachus reached out and grabbed his friend by the arm, pulling him back.

'No! Hold fast! That's an order.'

'But Captain—'

'Quiet!' Telemachus swung his gaze back to the prefect. 'If I agree, how can I be sure you'll let him go?'

'You'll accompany me on the boat.' The prefect parted his lips in a thin smile. 'That way, I can be sure that none of your comrades will try any dirty tricks. Once we're a safe distance from Ravenna and your ships, Nereus will be released. No harm will come to you or your brother. I give you my word, as an officer of Rome.'

Geras turned to his captain and lowered his voice as he spoke in Greek. 'Are you really going to trust this lying shit? He'll kill you both as soon as he's out of sight.'

Telemachus pursed his lips. By now, most of the pirates had fled back to their ships, and only a handful of *Trident*'s men were left on board the trireme, some stealing valuables from the marines while others cut down those injured men still drawing breath. The timbers creaked in protest as *Neptune* slowly settled into the sea.

'Last chance,' Canis declared. 'Agree to my terms and help me get safely away from here, or watch Nereus die. Your choice.'

Telemachus stood gripped with indecision for a moment, torn between saving his brother and allowing his hated foe to escape. Then his shoulders sagged and he lowered his falcata.

'Very well, Roman. I agree to your demands.'

'Good.' Canis nodded at the pirates either side of Telemachus. 'Now have your men prepare the tender.'

Geras muttered a curse under his breath, but a look from his captain silenced him, and he summoned four men from *Trident*'s crew and gave them instructions. The men hauled on the pulley ropes, lifting the tender and dropping it over the side of the trireme, while two of the oarsmen who had surrendered to the pirates were ushered across to the side rail. As they climbed down into the boat and fetched up the oars, the last pirates jumped back across to *Poseidon's Trident*.

Geras turned to leave the flagship, looking with concern at Telemachus. 'Are you sure about this, Captain?' he asked.

'I don't have a choice,' Telemachus replied. 'It's this or Nereus dies. Now go.' He pointed at *Trident*. 'Get the ship clear before this one takes all of us down with her.'

'Aye, Captain.'

Geras leaped back across to the deck of *Poseidon's Trident* and bellowed a series of orders at the hands. Moments later, the boarding lines were taken in and *Trident* swung away, rowing clear of *Neptune* and giving herself room to manoeuvre away from the stricken trireme. At the same time, the men on *Olympias* pulled away from the other side of *Neptune*'s shattered hull.

Telemachus glanced over his shoulder to see the battle continuing to rage across the harbour. Three pirate vessels had been damaged or sunk, with the remaining ships pinned against the biremes. He turned back to face Canis, his anger hardening at the sight of his maimed brother.

'You'll pay for what you've done, Roman. Maybe not today. But one day, you'll suffer. I'll make sure of it.'

'I don't think so. The emperor won't stand for this brazen attack. You might have won a victory here, but we'll hunt you down eventually. You and the rest of your kind.' Canis smiled wickedly. 'Now drop your weapon and get into the tender.'

Telemachus threw aside his falcata and shield and approached the side rail. The flagship's timbers groaned noisily, and from the open cargo hatch he could hear the furious rush of seawater as it poured into the hold, accompanied by the rending collisions of the stores crashing about. The trireme was sitting dangerously low in the water, and he realised that it was only a matter of moments before she sank.

The deck timbers shuddered again and Canis lost his grip as his iron-nailed boots struggled for purchase on the slippery planking. He reached out to steady himself against the side rail, his right hand reflexively lowering the dagger and drawing it away from Nereus's throat. In a flash, Nereus slammed his head back, striking the Roman on the bridge of his nose. Canis gave out a nasal grunt as he stumbled backwards in pain, blood streaming from his nostrils, and Nereus scrambled away from the prefect before he could recover from the blow.

He made it a couple of paces before Canis caught up with him. The Roman wrenched his sword from his scabbard and struck Nereus in the back with the pommel. Nereus groaned as he fell forward, hitting his head against the wooden rail. In the same instant, Telemachus snatched up a short sword lying amid the tangle of bodies and shattered equipment and charged forward, launching at Canis with a defiant cry. Canis spun round and met the pirate captain's blow with a brittle clash of metal. He feinted, forcing Telemachus back out of stabbing range, then dropped to a slight crouch as he readied for the next attack.

'I should have killed you before. This time you die, you cur.' He spat out a globule of blood, his smooth features twisted into a snarl.

Telemachus shook his head. 'It's you who will die, Roman. Your life ends now.'

Canis stabbed out with surprising speed, roaring madly as he aimed down at the pirate captain's right leg. Telemachus reacted a fraction too late, and the sword point made a shallow cut in his thigh, slicing through flesh and tensed muscle. He gasped through the searing pain and instinctively struck back at his opponent, thrusting at his face, but Canis jerked up his sword and deflected the blow with the practised ease of a gladiator in the arena.

'Is that the best you've got?' The prefect smiled pitilessly. 'I've seen slaves fight with more skill than that.'

The taunt was obviously designed to enrage Telemachus and force him into making a rash attack. He kept calm and fought through the intense throbbing pain in his leg as Canis lunged forward again, attacking with a short flurry of blows and giving his opponent no time to retaliate with a strike of his own. Gradually Telemachus edged backwards, his arm muscles trembling from the repeated strain of parrying his enemy's blows. He risked a glance to his left and saw Nereus lying on the deck, barely conscious as blood seeped out of the wound to his scalp.

He gritted his teeth and forced himself to concentrate on Canis as the Roman came roaring forward again, blade outstretched. He read the move, throwing up his falcata to meet the blow before striking out again, thrusting at the prefect's sword arm. Canis neatly deflected the attack and Telemachus cursed as his weapon angled away from his opponent. He jerked backwards to avoid the Roman's quick thrust and tripped over the sprawled body of a pirate behind him, arms flailing as he fell. He landed on his back and lost his grip on his falcata, the weapon clattering to the deck out of reach. Canis stood over him, grinning in triumph.

'You're mine now, scum. I'm going to enjoy this.'

As the Roman raised his sword, shaping to plunge it

through his opponent's neck, Telemachus looked up helplessly, filled with bitterness and despair. He would die here, on this ship. He knew that. Canis had beaten him. The prefect would have his revenge and escape, and there was nothing he could do except wait for the dark embrace of death.

Suddenly the trireme lurched, the aft deck shifting down towards the surface of the water and throwing Canis off his feet. He fell away, landing with a pained grunt a few paces from Telemachus. The next moment, there was a tremendous crash as the mast snapped and the splintered timbers toppled, crashing to the deck. Canis had just enough time to look up and scream before the spar collapsed on top of him, crushing his legs and pinning him to the planking. He grunted weakly, pushing against it in a doomed attempt to wriggle free. Then the sea closed around the stern of the trireme and the aft deck was lost beneath the murky surface as water surged over the rails, flooding *Neptune* with broken equipment and lifeless bodies.

Nereus had roused himself and now clung to a section of the rail for dear life, while around him wounded pirates and marines tumbled screaming into the dark water. Telemachus hastened over to his brother, ignoring the cries for help from the men around him. 'This way, Nereus. Come on. The ship's sinking.'

Nereus looked at him in panic. 'I can't swim. I'll drown—'

Telemachus pointed at the strake. 'We'll head for the bows. It's our only hope. Quick!'

He grabbed Nereus and pulled him away from the side rail. The slope of the deck increased as the pirate captain and his brother picked their way forward. One badly wounded pirate had wrapped an arm around the foremast, but as the ship pitched, he lost his grip and slid down the planking, screaming as he plunged towards the gurgling water and debris near the stern. Telemachus spared the man no glance as he pushed forward. The water was washing across the deck now, rising up to his ankles, and it took every last scrap of his strength to help Nereus towards the bows. Behind him, Canis screamed for help, cursing as he tried in vain to shift the weight of the spar from his mangled legs.

Telemachus thrust out an arm and grabbed hold of the bow strake as he looked round for the tender. To his dismay, he saw that the oarsmen had already shoved off, making a desperate bid for safety. They were quickly shot down by a hail of missile fire from *Olympias*. The angle of *Neptune*'s deck steepened sharply, and Telemachus felt his arm muscles burning from the strain of clinging on to the bows.

'We're not going to make it!' Nereus cried.

'Wait! Look there!' Telemachus pointed across the open stretch of water between *Neptune* and *Poseidon's Trident*. The pirate vessel's skiff was darting through the gentle swell, steering past the flotsam, Bassus and Sciron straining at the oars. Geras stood up in the stern as the skiff drew alongside the raised bows of the half-submerged flagship.

'Get in! Hurry, Captain!'

Telemachus looked to his brother. 'You first. Over the side. Go!'

Nereus clambered up and dropped down into the skiff, rocking the tiny vessel from side to side. Telemachus waited until the motion of the craft had steadied, then followed his brother over the bows and lowered himself down, landing in the stern next to Geras. The first mate growled at the men to shove off, and as they rowed back towards *Trident*, Telemachus looked over his shoulder at the sinking Roman trireme. Canis's head was just about visible above the water as he shouted curses at the pirates. The deck lurched again, the timbers groaning, and the prefect gave one final gurgling scream before the water closed over him. Then the foredeck pitched up as *Neptune* slipped beneath the surface.

Telemachus stared at the darkened patch of water for a long moment, hardly able to believe that at last revenge was his. Then he snapped his gaze away and turned his attention back to the fight across the harbour.

Cries rose from the ranks of marines fighting aboard the pirate ships as they saw that the flagship had been sunk. With the loss of their commander and his ship, the thoughts of the remaining Romans turned to their own survival as they tried to scrap it out or take their chances in the water.

The last two biremes were swiftly captured, with the crews aboard both vessels cut down. Others leaped into the water and swam frantically for the quayside, subjected to a barrage of missile fire from the pirates lining the side rail. A third warship had tried to steer away from the pirate fleet in a doomed attempt to row out of the harbour. There was a sharp crack as Criton's men operated the catapult mounted on the stern of one of the captured biremes and a bolt arced through the air, dipping down and landing thirty feet short of the fleeing warship with a splash. The second bolt found its range and struck the vessel on its stern deck, shattering the timbers and impaling several of its sailors. The crew promptly surrendered. One of the pirate ships rowed over and sent a party of men aboard to claim the prize, and the surviving marines and sailors were thrown into the harbour.

A rope was lowered from *Poseidon's Trident* and the men in

the skiff clambered up it. Nereus collapsed to the deck, over-come with exhaustion, while Geras surveyed the harbour and eased out a sigh of relief.

'It's over, Captain,' he said. 'Thank the gods, it's really over.'

'Not just yet.' Telemachus pointed with his sword at the pirates floundering in the water from the sunken vessels. 'We'll send boats to pick them up,' he added. 'Any survivors are to be put on board the biremes we've captured. We'll take the ships back with us to Petrapylae as trophies. That should add to Rome's humiliation very nicely indeed.'

'I'd love to be in the imperial palace when news of this reaches Rome, Captain.' A grin played on Geras's lips. 'Those wretches will finally know what it is to face defeat at our hands.'

Telemachus nodded and gazed across the harbour in silent reflection as boats were lowered and rowed out towards the survivors of the sunken pirate ships. The shivering, soaking-wet figures were taken to one of the captured biremes whilst another boat crew hunted down any Romans still in the water, killing them as they thrashed about in desperation. Only a small number of marines had succeeded in reaching safety, hauled up onto the quay by their comrades. They could do nothing except look on in anger and despair as the pirates steered their prizes out of the harbour, leaving a scene of destruction behind them.

A mild breeze stirred as *Poseidon's Trident* emerged into the open sea. As the morning sun brightened, Telemachus gave the order to signal to the rest of the fleet to form up behind her. The weary crew summoned one last effort as Geras yelled at them to unfurl the sail. As *Trident* got under way, the other vessels also raised their sails, taking advantage of the faint breath of wind coming off the land, and soon the pirates had left Ravenna far behind them.

Telemachus moved away from the bows, took a spare waterskin from one of the mates and picked his way past the weary pirates. He found Nereus slumped aft, his back resting against the side rail as he touched a hand to the wound on his scalp. Telemachus dropped to one knee beside him and pressed the waterskin to his lips. Nereus took a long swig, then smiled weakly.

'Thanks,' he croaked. 'Brother.'

Telemachus managed a smile of his own. 'How's the head?'

'I've had worse. So have you, by the looks of it.' Nereus nodded at the scar on the young pirate captain's face.

'A few old wounds,' Telemachus said. 'Besides, it's nothing compared to what those Roman bastards did to you.'

'You can't begin to imagine,' Nereus responded bitterly. Then he shook his head. 'It doesn't matter. You came for me. That's all that counts.'

'Yes.' A brief pang of anger flared up as Telemachus glanced down at Nereus's missing fingers, and he felt his throat constrict with emotion. 'It's all right, brother. You're safe now.'

Despite their long separation, there was no awkward preamble between them. They simply reached out and held each other fiercely, the years of separation melting away. Telemachus felt his eyes moisten with tears as he choked back a swirl of grief and joy. They held on for a moment longer and then let go of each other as Nereus took in his younger brother's appearance. 'You've changed. You're not that skinny little runt who used to be such a nuisance round the house.'

'That's not the only thing that's changed.'

'So I've heard.' Nereus looked up at him with admiration in his eyes. 'The rumours Canis has been spreading are true, then? You're a pirate captain these days?'

Telemachus nodded. 'Are you surprised?'

'After the month I've had, nothing surprises me any more.' Nereus furrowed his brow. 'But I thought you hated the sea? You couldn't stand it when we were children, as I recall. You hated it when Father took us fishing.'

'I remember.' Telemachus smiled at the memory.

Nereus grinned at him. 'My brother, a feared pirate captain. How in the name of the gods did that happen?'

'It's a long story. I'll explain it later. Once you've had some rest.'

Nereus stared at him for a long moment. 'Thanks. For not giving up on me.'

Telemachus smiled. 'You didn't think I'd let the Romans hang you from a crossbeam, did you?'

'I'm a slave. You learn not to cling to hope.'

'Not any more. You're a free man. Now, you need to rest. We've got a long journey ahead of us.' Telemachus beckoned to Proculus, and the ship's carpenter hastened over. 'Take Nereus down to my private quarters. He can rest there. Bring him some food, and do what you can for his injuries.'

'What about you?' Proculus nodded at the shallow wound to Telemachus's thigh. In the madness of the sea battle he had quite forgotten about the throbbing, but now it came back with a painful intensity. 'You'll need to get that dressed.'

'Later,' Telemachus replied. 'Focus your attention on those who need it most, for now.'

'Aye, Captain.'

As Proculus helped Nereus below deck, Geras moved forward and approached his captain. 'How is he?'

'Tired, but alive. Which is all that matters.'

'Yes.' Geras was silent for a moment before he nodded approvingly at the clouds of smoke rising above Ravenna. 'Well, we did it. We bloody well did it.'

Telemachus smiled at his friend. 'Did you ever doubt me?'

'There were times when I thought it couldn't be done. But we've given the Romans a beating they'll never forget, that's for sure.'

'No,' Telemachus replied quietly. 'No, they won't.'

'What are your orders, Captain?'

Telemachus glanced back at the naval base, already fading from view on the horizon. He closed his eyes for a moment, overcome with a tiredness beyond anything he had ever known, after the longest night of his life.

'Take us back to Petrapylae. The other crews can return with us to our base and repair their ships. Then we'll feast and drink like never before.'

Geras grinned. 'Now you're talking . . .'

EPILOGUE

Five days later, the Illyrian pirates returned to the citadel at Petrapylae. At news of the great victory, traders set up wine stalls around the main square, keen to make a profit from their thirsty customers as the pirates gathered in the cobbled streets to celebrate.

Their ships had entered the bay earlier that morning, identifying themselves to the lookout on the headland before they rowed into the gentle waters of the anchorage. A heaving throng of locals gathered on the beach to welcome the returning fleet, cheering and waving as the vessels ground their bows on the shingle and their crews wearily disembarked. Only then did the pirates' families and loved ones grasp the scale of the losses they had suffered against the Roman navy.

Four ships had been lost in the battle. Over a hundred pirates had been killed and many more had sustained injuries during the fighting. The excited cheers of the crowd soon turned to wails as the pirates began unloading the wounded from the holds of the surviving vessels. Long lines of stretcher-bearers carried the most severe casualties ashore, followed by the walking wounded: a sombre procession of maimed pirates, blinking in the sunlight after days spent below deck in the shelter of the ships' holds. There were so many wounded to deal with that there was no space in the pirates' quarters, and Telemachus had to order the stables to be cleared out and used as a makeshift hospital.

The loss of so many men was compounded by the damage to the pirate fleet. Most of the ships had been beached to undergo repairs, including *Poseidon's Trident*, and some of the vessels were so battered that it would be months before they could put to sea once more. In the meantime, Telemachus had agreed that the crews could remain at Petrapylae until such time as their ships were ready to set sail.

At least the men could afford to celebrate, while they were ashore: although some of the loot they had seized from Ravenna had been lost in the sea battle, the garrison's pay chests had survived, and the crews could expect a handsome reward from their share of the booty. After disembarking, the victorious pirates had gathered in the square to celebrate. Many of them joined together as they sang lewd songs and toasted their captains. The rest simply shared jars of wine or quietly consoled one another as they grieved for their dead friends.

Although the pirates had suffered significant casualties in ships and men, the destruction of the naval base and the Ravenna fleet had achieved its principal goal: the Illyrian pirates were once again the prevailing sea power on the far side of the Adriaticum. With no Roman ships to patrol the seas, the crews would be free to raid the shipping once more without fear of reprisals. For a while, at least.

Moreover, the desperate victory had inspired a new camaraderie between the rival crews and they mingled freely with one another, with none of the ill feeling that had previously existed between them. Telemachus felt a warm satisfaction as he surveyed the drunken, happy faces of the men around the square.

At his side, Geras drained the contents of his wine cup and belched loudly. Then he wiped the wine dribbling down his chin and nodded at Telemachus. 'Another round, Captain?'

Telemachus looked down at his own cup, still half full. 'Maybe later.'

'Bollocks to that. Have another drink. You should be celebrating, after everything we've achieved. I insist.'

'And what have we achieved, exactly?'

Geras flashed a puzzled look at his captain. 'I'm not sure I follow. We've beaten the Romans. Their fleet is destroyed. They won't be troubling us again.'

'For now, perhaps. But this won't last for ever. Canis was right: the emperor will demand revenge when he learns about our attack on Ravenna. So will the rest of Rome, come to that.'

'So let them,' Geras replied with a dismissive wave of his hand. 'What can they do? They've got no ships left in the Adriaticum and they dare not risk redeploying the fleet from Misenum.'

'I agree. But they will build new ships to hunt us down eventually. And when they do, they won't make the same mistakes as before. We can expect a larger fleet. Which will mean more patrols and more convoys. More raids along our side of the sea.'

'Then we'll give 'em another kicking. Like we did at Ravenna.'

Telemachus shook his head. 'It won't be so easy next time.

The Romans will be prepared. They're good soldiers. We'll have a tough fight on our hands.'

'Aye, probably. But we can worry about that tomorrow.'

'That doesn't make the problem go away, Geras.'

'I disagree. Three more cups of this wine and I won't have a bloody care in the world. Just you watch.'

He stood up from the bench that had been set up outside one of the wine shops and rubbed his hands. 'Right. That's enough talk about Rome for today. I'm off to get pissed. And maybe sample some of the other pleasures to be had.'

'Enjoy.'

Geras grinned. 'It's cheap wine and tarts for me, Captain. If I can't enjoy that, then we really are in trouble.' He stumbled off towards the wine shop, cheerfully humming a tune to himself.

A short while later, Criton approached from a crowd of carousing pirates, his worn face crinkled into a drunken grin. He patted Telemachus on the shoulder and took up the free space on the bench next to him, gesturing to the crews across the square.

'The pirate gangs of Illyricum celebrating a great victory together. Quite the sight. I always believed in your cause, lad.'

'Really?' Telemachus arched an eyebrow at the veteran captain. 'That's not how I remember it. "It'll be a cold day in Hades before they agree to work together." Your words, Criton. Not mine.'

'All right,' Criton conceded. 'I was wrong. You've done well, Telemachus.'

'Thank you.'

'But I'm wondering what you plan to do next.'

Telemachus shrugged. 'What do you suggest?'

'Perhaps we should be thinking about a more permanent arrangement between our crews.'

'Extend our alliance, you mean?'

'Why not? We've achieved more in recent days than we've done in years sailing individually. And we'll need every man and ship we can lay our hands on, for the day when Rome tries to attack us once again.'

Telemachus stroked the knot of scar tissue on his chin. 'It's an interesting proposal. But what about the other captains? They're a fiercely independent mob. It was hard enough getting them to join forces this time.'

'There'd be a few dissenting voices,' Criton admitted. 'But I'm sure they could be persuaded to join us in this new venture. My word still carries some weight. Besides, most of them only care about getting rich, and if we sailed together, we could snap up more plunder than ever.' He paused and eyed Telemachus carefully. 'Of course, we'd need to elect a chief. A leader. Someone capable of uniting the crews.'

Telemachus looked at him for a beat. 'You're suggesting I lead these men?'

'Who else?' Criton shrugged. 'The gangs need a commander, and who better than the man who masterminded the destruction of the Ravenna fleet?'

'Assuming they would agree to it.'

'Oh, they would. Believe me, there's no better candidate. The pirates respect you. There are few captains who've had the balls to take on the Romans in a straight fight and win. You'd get more votes than any other captain.'

'It's tempting,' Telemachus said after a long pause. 'I'll think about it. But there's something I must do first.'

'Fine. Though don't take too long to make your mind up.

Strike while the opportunity is there, Telemachus. Something tells me you're going to be a thorn in the side of Rome for many years to come.'

The sun was already setting behind the mountains as Telemachus passed through the archway and entered the courtyard at the far end of the citadel. He walked stiffly as he headed for the stables built to one side of the yard, still feeling the effects of the wound he had sustained in his fight with Canis. Proculus had cleaned out the gash, closed it with sutures and applied a fresh dressing the evening after they had left Ravenna. Even so, his leg throbbed with a dull, constant pain whenever he moved. Then he heard the groans of injured men and felt a burning sense of shame that he had survived the fight against the Romans when so many others had perished or suffered crippling wounds.

He paced down the line of stables until he reached a tack room at the far end. The thin odour of sweat and horse manure hinted at the room's original use, with the only light creeping in through a small window high up on the far wall. Nereus was lying on a grimy palliasse below the window. At the sound of the approaching footsteps, he turned his head and looked up at Telemachus.

'You again?' he groaned. 'Haven't you got anything better to do than to keep checking on your older brother?'

'Bloody hell, if that's all the thanks I get, I'll turn around and leave.'

'Not unless you want a kick in the balls you won't.'

Telemachus smiled warmly. Nereus had been making steady progress in the days following his rescue. The welts on his back, arms and legs had been treated with unguents and bandaged, and some of the colour had already returned to his pallid complexion.

'How are you feeling today?'

'Better.' Nereus winced as he sat upright. 'No thanks to that ship's carpenter. The man's a bloody menace. If he comes at me again with any more stinking poultices, I'll knock his head off.'

'That's more like the Nereus I know.'

Nereus cocked his head at the stable entrance. 'I hear there's quite the celebration going on out there.'

'Something like that.'

'So why are you here instead of getting out of your skin on cheap wine? I know what I'd rather be doing.'

Telemachus took a breath and told Nereus about his conversation with Criton, and the latter's suggestion of a permanent alliance between the Illyrian pirates. Nereus listened in silence, and when his brother had finished, he scratched his bristly jaw and nodded thoughtfully.

'I see. And they want you to lead this new pirate fleet, is that it?'

'Yes.' Telemachus hesitated. 'The other captains would have to agree to Criton's proposal. But I haven't said yes to anything yet.'

'Why not?'

'I don't know.' Telemachus stared down at his feet. 'I thought perhaps I'd wait to see what your plans are.'

'I don't understand. What does my future have to do with anything?'

Telemachus lifted his gaze to Nereus and looked him in the eye. 'If you want to leave and start a new life, I'm ready to come with you. With the money I had saved up to buy your freedom, we'd have enough to start over somewhere together . . . somewhere Rome will never find us.'

'And do what, exactly?'

'Buy a fishing boat. Farm a plot of land. Sell trinkets. Does it matter?'

Nereus shook his head slowly. 'You can't. You're a leader now, Telemachus. You were destined to command these men. Even I can see that, and I've spent most of the time cooped up in the hold. Anyway, you'd be miserable if we retired somewhere. You're too ambitious to settle for the quiet life.'

'I don't care. I lost you once. I won't lose you again. Whatever you decide, I'm not going to leave you.'

'And where would we go?' Nereus managed a half-hearted smile. 'In case it's escaped your attention, we're not exactly inconspicuous. You're a notorious pirate captain and I'm a runaway slave. Wherever we try and hide, Rome would track us down.'

'We'd find somewhere,' Telemachus insisted. 'Somewhere far from here. If that's what you really want.'

'That's the thing. It isn't. In fact, I've already made up my mind.'

'What are you saying, Nereus?' Telemachus asked softly.

'This is the life for us now. For both of us. I'm not going anywhere.'

Telemachus stared hard at him. 'Are you sure?'

'What could be better than sailing and fighting alongside my brother? I might be a maimed ex-slave, but I reckon I could make myself useful. If you'll have me.'

Telemachus felt his heart lift, and he smiled warmly. 'I'm sure we can work something out.'

'You'd bloody better,' Nereus said. 'Now get back to your celebrations. It would be wise to let the men see you. I'm sure they'll want to raise their cups to the chosen commander of the pirate fleet.'

GLOSSARY

agora: the central assembly point or marketplace in cities in ancient Greece

bireme: a larger version of the liburnian (see below), measuring 30 metres in length and 5.5 metres across the beam

centurion: commanding officer of a century of men in a Roman legion

falcata: curved sword with a single-edged blade, originally from Hispania

garum: popular fish sauce, made from fermented fish guts mixed with brine, used as a condiment and occasionally as a medicine

liburnian: patrol galley, the most common type of ship in service in the imperial fleet

mulsum: a type of wine sweetened with honey

navarch: commander of a squadron of ships in the imperial Roman fleets; usually a naval officer promoted from the ranks, the navarch had command over ten ships

optio: second in command of a Roman century; reports to the centurion

prefect: commanding officer of an imperial fleet; under Emperor

Tiberius, the prefect had usually served as a tribune in the Roman legions

trierarch: commander of an individual ship in the Roman imperial fleet; responsible for the day-to-day running and sailing of the vessel, but in battle, command of the ship passed to the centurion in charge of the ship's marines

trireme: Roman warship, one of the larger types used in the imperial navy; a flagship in many of the provincial fleets

Discover more gripping *Sunday Times* bestsellers from Simon Scarrow and T. J. Andrews . . .

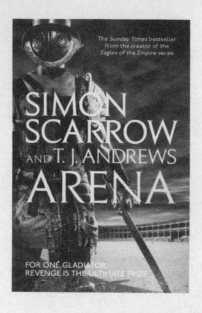

It is AD 41. The city of Rome is a dangerous place.

Optio Macro of the Second Legion, recently decorated for courage on the battlefield, can't wait to leave the teeming city behind. He's dismayed when he's compelled to stay in Rome to train Marcus Valerius Pavo, a young gladiatorial recruit.

Though fearless Pavo has fought for his life before, he's a novice in the arena. But he's a driven man, with a goal dearer than survival – to avenge his father's death at the hands of a champion gladiator. Will he live to face his nemesis?

HEADLINE

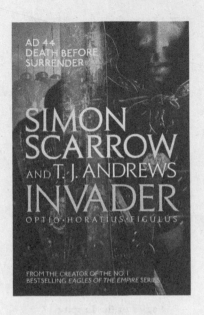

AD 44
DEATH BEFORE
SURRENDER

SIMON
SCARROW
AND T. J. ANDREWS
INVADER
OPTIO·HORATIUS·FIGULUS

FROM THE CREATOR OF THE NO.1
BESTSELLING *EAGLES OF THE EMPIRE* SERIES

Roman Britain, AD 44. The land is far from tamed. A puppet king is doing little to calm the hatred of the native tribes.

Fighting is in Optio Horatius Figulus' blood. His Celtic ancestry gives him the toughness essential for survival. That toughness will be tested to the very limit when he is sent on a mission deep in hostile territory. And Figulus knows that, even utterly crushed in battle, their warriors routed and the Druids driven from their hill forts, the tribesmen of Britannia will sooner die than surrender.

HEADLINE

Don't miss the latest action-packed novels in Simon Scarrow's *Eagles of the Empire* series . . .

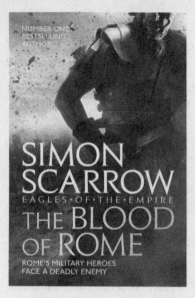

Eagles of the Empire 17

AD 55. As trouble brews on the eastern fringes of the Roman Empire, Prefect Cato and Centurion Macro prepare for war . . .

The wily Parthian Empire has invaded Roman-ruled Armenia, ousting King Rhadamistus. The King is ambitious and ruthless, but he is loyal to Rome. General Corbulo must restore him to power, while also readying the troops for war with Parthia. Corbulo welcomes new arrivals Cato and Macro, experienced soldiers who know how to knock into shape an undermanned unit of men ill-equipped for conflict.

But Rhadamistus's brutality towwards those who ousted him will spark an uprising which will test the bravery of the Roman army to the limit. While the enemy watches from over the border . . .

HEADLINE

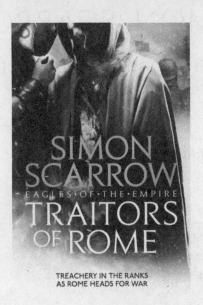

TREACHERY IN THE RANKS
AS ROME HEADS FOR WAR

Eagles of the Empire 18

AD 56. Battle-hardened veterans of the Roman army Tribune
Cato and Centurion Macro are garrisoned at the eastern border,
aware that their movements are constantly monitored by
spies from dangerous, mysterious Parthia. But the enemy
within could be the deadliest threat to the Legion . . .
and the Empire.

There's a traitor in the ranks. Rome shows no mercy to those
who betray their comrades, and the Empire. But first the guilty
man must be discovered. Cato and Macro are in a race against
time to expose the truth, while the powerful enemy over
the border waits to exploit any weaknesses in the Legion.
The traitor must die . . .

HEADLINE

SIMON SCARROW

WRITING WITH T. J. ANDREWS

Arena	£8.99
Invader	£8.99
Pirata	£7.99

THE *EAGLES OF THE EMPIRE* SERIES

Under the Eagle	£8.99
The Eagle's Conquest	£8.99
When the Eagle Hunts	£8.99
The Eagle and the Wolves	£8.99
The Eagle's Prey	£8.99
The Eagle's Prophecy	£8.99
The Eagle in the Sand	£8.99
Centurion	£8.99
The Gladiator	£8.99
The Legion	£8.99
Praetorian	£8.99
The Blood Crows	£8.99
Brothers in Blood	£8.99
Britannia	£8.99
Invictus	£8.99
Day of the Caesars	£8.99
The Blood of Rome	£7.99

THE *WELLINGTON AND NAPOLEON* QUARTET

Young Bloods	£8.99
The Generals	£8.99
Fire and Sword	£8.99
The Fields of Death	£8.99
Sword & Scimitar	£8.99
Hearts of Stone	£8.99

Simply call 01235 827 702 or visit our
website **www.headline.co.uk** to order

Prices and availability subject to change without notice.